TO ENTHRALL THE DEMON LORD

A Novel of Love and Magic

NADINE MUTAS

Nadine Mutas
PO Box 94
New Almaden, CA 95042
nadine@nadinemutas.com
www.nadinemutas.com

This is a work of fiction. Names, characters, places and incidents either are products of the author's imagination or are used fictitiously. Any resemblance to actual events or locales or persons, living or dead, is entirely coincidental.

Cover Design by Najla Qamber Designs
www.najlaqamberdesigns.com

Editing by Faith Freewoman, Demon for Details Manuscript Editing

ISBN-13: 978-1979451710
ISBN-10: 1979451710

Dedicated to every single reader who asked me about Maeve.
And to all survivors.

ACKNOWLEDGMENTS

My heartfelt thanks go to my husband, who made the timely completion of this story possible by jumping in and taking over *everything* else while I wrote, wrote, wrote. Your sacrifice, my love, is admirable, as Arawn would say. I love you more than I can express in words, and that is saying something, seeing as I'm an author and all.

More thanks to my great and understanding editor Faith, and to my cover designer Najla, who brought my vision of Arawn and Maeve's cover to life so incredibly beautifully.

Thank you to Jess Kolner and Chloe Elizabeth Brownhill for the suggestions for names for Juneau's side.

Many thanks go out to Riley Cole and Abbie Roads for providing such valuable insight into therapist-client relationships and the context of therapy for PTSD. Your info was super helpful, and any errors that snuck into the text are entirely mine.

And, I have to thank—with emphasis—all my readers who kept asking me about Maeve and when she would get her story, and especially the members of my reader group on Facebook, who are so amazing in their enthusiasm and love for my books and characters. I love hanging out with you ladies, and I so appreciate your support!

CHAPTER 1

Maeve's hand trembled as she picked up the pen. The first lines she scrawled looked as jittery as the fluttering in her chest, but she kept writing, and her hand steadied as she went. She couldn't stop. Had to get this down on paper before courage deserted her.

A last line drawn under her name at the end—done.

The pen clicked on the wooden desk, and her hand shook once more as she read the note she'd written to her sister, to her friends.

I know about the baby. I know you didn't want me to find out, but I'm glad I did. Merle, maybe you don't want to put me in this position, but it is where I need to be. This is my choice, my responsibility. I never wanted you in that position, never wanted you to have to make these tough decisions because of me. You've already done so much for me, risked so much, and I am so, so thankful. Which is why I can't allow you to risk anything else—anyone else—on my behalf.

I'm surrendering myself to Arawn, so he will stop using your magic. Your baby will be safe.

Please, don't come after me. By the time you read this, I'll be well on my way to his lair. It's long overdue, and it's what I should have done weeks ago.

Merle, I love you. You deserve to be a mom, and I'm so happy for you.

Rhun, I would have enjoyed getting to know you.

Lil, I love you, too. Please hug Baz and Hazel for me when they get back. I haven't known Alek long, but I'm so glad you found each other.

I'll keep you all in my heart. Maybe one day I'll get to see my niece.

— Maeve

The room resounded hollow with silence as she stared at the paper. The house was quiet, too. Alek and Lily were still asleep, had only gone to bed two hours ago, when the approach of morning turned the sky that special shade of indigo. Being *pranagraha* demons, Lily and her mate preferred to sleep during the day, since their kind was vulnerable to sunlight.

No one else was at home, Basil having gone off to Faerie to search for his lost adoptive sister Rose, his mother, Hazel, having gone right after him, and Merle and Rhun wouldn't come over this early. It was the perfect moment to leave—in part also due to the fact that now, with the morning sun gilding the frost on the grass, the demon sentinel keeping watch over the mansion for Arawn would be replaced by a shifter whose powers weren't bound during the day.

It shouldn't matter, considering what she was about to do, where she was going, and yet…the thought of approaching a —with her luck, *male*—demon to take her to Arawn's lair curdled her stomach with this cursed, instinctive fear she hadn't been able to shake in all these months. She was okay around Alek after a rocky start, and even around Rhun, though it took her the better part of summer to be able to breathe freely in Rhun's presence, that insidious panic clawing at her simply because he was a *bluotezzer* demon, same as the one who—

She blinked, shook herself. But a complete stranger? A male demon she didn't know?

She'd rather try her luck with a shifter. Might help keep the panic down. And, who knew? Maybe the sentinel on duty today would be a female. She didn't dare hope for that, but it would be the best option. Alek worked for the Demon Lord, and based on what he had said here and there, the enforcers keeping watch over Arawn's "asset"—i.e. her—were a mix of males and females. Physical strength wasn't quite as important a marker among otherworld creatures, what with magic being the true edge for most, and magic didn't differentiate between sexes. The Demon Lord's ranks thus featured males and females alike, as Arawn valued power above all else—and wasn't so short-sighted as to exclude great power based on gender.

Time to go before doubts had a chance to creep in after all.

She laid the note on her four-poster bed, on top of the neatly arranged blue comforter, and straightened one of the pillows again. A duffel bag packed with a week's supply of clothes, a few toiletries, her cell phone, and a framed picture, sat next to the door, waiting for her.

One last look at the room that had been her refuge for the past six months, had given her peace and comfort after she was freed from that place drenched in darkness and pain, and her heart hurt at the thought she'd never get to see this house again. Or the people who'd filled it with life and laughter for her, who'd never given up on her, even when she was little more than a broken shell hiding in her bed, staring at the wall for hours, for days.

Picking up the duffel bag, she went out the door, her breath hitching, her eyes burning.

A quiet voice inside her spoke up, a hopeful part of herself that not even blades dripping with her blood had been able to kill. Maybe she would get to see them all again. Maybe this was not the walk into darkness and more torture that she made it out to be. She didn't *know* what awaited her. Maybe the Demon Lord wouldn't—

A shudder whispered through her, and her stomach cramped. Insidiously, despite that part of her that clung to hope throughout a storm of nightmares, another voice grated across her nerves, slipped pervasively into the darkest corners of her mind, filled it with images of the worst that could happen to her—and it shook her to her foundations precisely *because* it had already happened.

You know what that feels like, the voice hissed. *You know you're powerless to stop it when it happens again. Don't pretend you don't know what you're walking into. You* know.

That voice...that voice... Spots of light danced in front of her, her breath so shallow she might as well have been choking. She barely made it to the bathroom down the hallway in time, heaved her breakfast into the toilet until her chest ached, her throat burned. Sniffling, she clutched the porcelain bowl for a moment before she got up, rinsed her mouth, gargled, and brushed her teeth with quick efficiency. Chucking the toothbrush and toothpaste back into her duffel bag, she crept out into the hallway again.

The fact she'd never hear that voice again in real life was too small a consolation. It was branded into her memory with the freshness of a bleeding cut, and she could still recall the sound of it after months, as if he'd just spoken, as if his breath still warmed her skin yet chilled her soul, making her tremble with impotent fear...

It wouldn't fade. It just wouldn't fade, no matter how hard she tried...because it had become the voice of every dark doubt inside her, whispered through her when she least expected it, froze her thoughts and dragged her back under, until she found herself emptying her stomach into the nearest bowl.

Rhun might have ripped him to shreds, but no one could slaughter the memory of his voice.

She quietly descended the large, curving, marble staircase leading down into the foyer. The morning sun shone through the huge window in the wall above the front door, glinted off the massive crystal chandelier dominating the room. She dropped her duffel bag at the entrance and headed to the kitchen, crossed to the French doors opening to the backyard, and walked all the way to the rear fence. To the spot where— according to Alek's inside knowledge as a former sentinel— Arawn's guards liked to keep watch over the property. Over her.

Nerves prickling, she stopped just a few feet from the fence. Cleared her throat. "I want to surrender myself to Arawn." Her heartbeat thudded so loud in her ears, it drowned out the early-morning birdsong. For the rest of the world it would seem like she was talking to air. And even though nothing indicated anyone's presence, she knew the sentinel was there, listening. "I'll be waiting at the front gate for you to take me to him."

And with that, she turned on her heel and marched back to the house, through the kitchen, the foyer, grabbed her duffel bag, and walked out the front door, making sure to close it quietly behind her. The last thing she needed was to wake up Alek or Lily now.

She came to a halt at the front gate, remaining within the perimeter of the magical wards protecting the property. Her pulse still raced as she dropped her bag on the gravel drive-way, crossed her arms, and waited. Minutes ticked by. The sun rose higher. Where was that sentinel? She threw a nervous glance at the house looming behind her. *Please let them keep sleeping...*

Would she have to go back to the yard and tell the darned sentinel *again*? She bit her lip and suppressed a frustrated groan. *I don't know if I have the guts to say it a second time.* The more time passed, the more her thoughts turned to the myriad ways why this was the most suicidal thing she'd ever done. Besides moving out of the protection of her witch community. Which had led to her being kidnapped and… Nope, not going there.

Merle's image flashed before her inner eye, and just like that, her spine locked, her shoulders straightened, and she lifted her chin. No, she had to do this. For Merle, for her unborn baby, for all the ways her sister had protected her until she bled—literally—and restructured her life around Maeve's needs. No more. Merle would have to suffer no more on Maeve's account.

A scuffle at the front gate snagged her attention. Breath stalled in her lungs, she waited.

"I mean it," she called out to the spot beyond the gate, where the tiniest flicker in the air hinted at a concealment spell of Arawn's making. "Take me to him now."

A second, a heartbeat, then—as if melting under heat like a desert mirage, the air shimmered, changed, and revealed the bulky form of the sentinel on duty. Maeve's stomach turned. Her fingers curled into her palms.

Of course. Of course it *had* to be a male.

She closed her eyes briefly, willed the anxiety scratching under her skin to quiet down. You can do this. *What's a little terror compared to the safety of Merle's baby?*

The sentinel cleared his throat, brows drawn together over light brown eyes in a rugged face, his skin a dark tan. "Just to get this straight" he said. "You want me to take you to the Demon Lord?"

"To complete the bargain my sister made with him. Yes."

"Are you sure? He hasn't…called it in."

"I know. But I am."

Because if she didn't, if she stayed in the protective bubble her sister had built for her with tears and blood and magic, if she kept living on stolen time, time *Merle* paid for by loaning out her powers to Arawn so he wouldn't come claim Maeve...her sister's baby would die the next time Merle had to uphold the balance of magic. As head of her family, as the oldest living witch of her line, Merle had to pay back to the Powers That Be for the magic she used, and with Arawn demanding she put her powers at his disposal, Merle had to pay back *a lot*. And the last time she did, she almost lost the baby.

Chest aching, Maeve picked up the duffel bag, opened the gate, and stepped through the wards onto the sidewalk, in front of this male she didn't know, whom she now had to trust to deliver her to the Demon Lord in one piece. *Breathe. He won't hurt you. He's not allowed to hurt you.* She had to rely on the probability that he wouldn't risk Arawn's wrath by touching her, had to repeat to herself, over and over, that she was safe from *this* male—because the Demon Lord wanted her for himself. Presumably *unspoiled.*

Not that she wasn't already the very definition of damaged goods. Heat flushed her neck, her cheeks. Her shoulders hunched forward, and she angled her head so the ginger strands of her hair would partially cover her face. That nasty scar running from one temple across her nose to the other side of her chin would still be visible, but...well.

The sentinel nodded to her and gestured down the street. "Car's parked around the corner."

Bag clutched tightly to her chest, she followed him, doing her best to ignore the fear snapping at her heels. Focused on the sound of his boots thudding on the sidewalk, the brilliant patterns of shadow and light on the ground from the sun shining through a dancing, lacy lattice of near-bare autumn trees.

At the car, he opened the passenger side door for her. She slipped in before her anxiety would root her to the spot. The slamming of the door made her jump, hug her bag even closer.

Too fast. She was breathing too fast.

It's just a car ride, damn it. Pull yourself together.

She stared straight ahead as the driver side door opened, and the car dipped a little when he got in. Another flinch when he shut the door. Even with her dull human senses, his male scent—condensed in the tight space of his car—pressed in on her.

He fastened his seatbelt, and she felt his eyes on her. "Buckle up."

"No." Choked out between her teeth. "Just drive."

To be in any way restrained in the presence of a man... A cold shiver rolled through her, iced her very bones. As ridiculous as it was, she couldn't even strap herself in while riding in a car with a guy.

An assessing glance from the sentinel, then he started the engine. "Name's Warrick, by the way."

A nod. That was all she was capable of.

Her heartbeat wasn't even thundering in her ears anymore. No, it had almost flattened out, the rhythm so rapid, so irregular, it could have been a hasty Morse code sent out during times of war. And what raged inside her *was* a battle after all. A struggle for control over her most basic functions, her body, her mind...control that had been wrenched from her during days of torture and humiliation, until the simplest tasks and situations would trigger an avalanche of panic, burying what was left of her.

The car's vibrations as it rolled along the street sank into her, and the next second a flash of memory short-circuited her brain. Another car, another time, another male... *Maeve panted, sitting in the front passenger seat, too weak to fight him even if he didn't hold her immobile with his telekinesis. He'd taken so much blood — too much — and she was dizzy, her head lolling from side to side with the movements of the car, her eyelids drooping despite the fear burning like corrosive acid in her veins. Up ahead a warehouse loomed in the darkness, a single lightbulb illuminating the wide garage door as it opened, ready to swallow her whole.*

She couldn't breathe. Chills rattled her, made her tremble. The world spun, spun, spun, everything lost color, became lighter, yet a weight pressed down on her chest, and she couldn't move, couldn't move, couldn't—

The car screeched to a halt. She rocked forward from the sudden stop, her duffel cushioning the impact as she hit the dashboard. She couldn't see, the world leached of all color, whited-out. The sound of a door opening, but it was dulled, as if filtered through cotton, far away. Fresh air streamed in, cool on her sweat-coated skin. Choking, she clutched her bag. Her legs tingled. Like a fish on land, she gasped for breath, that weight on her chest pressing in.

Gradually, it lifted. Bit by bit she could haul in air again, forcing her lungs to expand and breathe. Plastered to the dashboard, she focused on her surroundings. The controls of the radio. The scent of the leather upholstery. The sunshine as it glinted off the metal knob of the stick shift.

The empty driver's seat.

Feeling returned to her body, her limbs prickling like waking up after blood flow had been cut off. She blinked, looked around.

The car was parked next to the curb, the evergreen trees of a Pacific Northwest forest creating a backdrop of breathtaking beauty, misted by soft rain. The door on the driver's side hung open. A few feet in front of the vehicle, the sentinel—Warrick—stood with his back turned, hands on his hips, head lowered. His heavy breaths flexed the muscles in his broad back and shoulders.

She slid out of the car, her bag still clutched to her chest, walked around the open door, and cleared her throat.

Warrick turned, his features tense. "Are you all right?" His nostrils flared.

She gave a shaky nod, swallowed past a thick throat. "It's the scent, isn't it?"

For a shifter, with his sensitive nose, she must have been reeking of fear in that car.

He rubbed a hand over his face. "It's hard to...remain calm when we smell..."

It made perfect sense. The animal part of shifters, the aspect that wasn't human, wasn't controlled by millennia of civilized evolution, reacted to strong emotions based on instincts that warred with the human half. The smell of fear would send some animals fleeing, but in others—predators—it might incite a different impulse... She looked down, forced herself not to tremble.

"Tell me," Warrick rasped, "he died a bloody death."

She glanced back up at him.

"The one who made you this afraid."

Her fingers curled into the bag clutched to her chest. "He was ripped to shreds." Something deep inside her stirred in grim satisfaction, flexing talons in simmering darkness. She'd never get tired of saying that.

"Good." A muscle feathered in Warrick's jaw.

A moment passed while they looked at each other, and the tenuous bond that wove itself between them in those seconds made it possible for her to get back into the car, to breathe past the remnants of her panic and ride the rest of the way with him without another incident.

He parked the car close to a lake, and then led her down a dirt path toward the water. The surface glistened in the midmorning sunshine peeking through intermittent clouds, an eerie hush in the air. The lake...the sight of it jogged her memory, and she drew in a small, sharp breath as she realized—

"We'll have to go through the lake," she croaked.

Merle had said as much of course, when she recounted how she and Rhun had gone to Arawn to beg for his help in finding Maeve. But Merle told her about it during those first days spent in the MacKenna family's old Victorian after Maeve was rescued, and those days were hazy, Maeve's mind and body still numb from her prolonged torture. She'd forgotten this was the way to travel to Arawn's lair.

Warrick nodded, face turned toward the still lake. "I hope you can swim."

Swimming wasn't the problem. Her nails scratched over her duffel bag as she grabbed it tighter. She'd have to leave it behind. No way the contents would survive being dunked.

Heart aching, she set the bag on the ground. Maybe... maybe she could ask to have it retrieved later. If she was allowed to make any requests at all.

Warrick squatted at the edge of the rocky shore that fell sharply down into the lake. No gently sloping beach here. Only rough-cut stones and pebbles crunching under her shoes as she stepped up next to the sentinel, who had his hand in the water, making tiny circles with his fingers.

A moment later, a head broke through the surface, and a beautiful naiad swam closer, her dark hair dancing in the waves stirred by her movements. Skin the color of moonlight, she peered at Warrick with eyes holding the depths of the lake she called her home, then glanced at Maeve.

"I remember your sister," she purred. "She was an ember, but you...you're flame."

Maeve's heart stumbled.

"Come." The naiad waved an elegant hand. "Let my water cool your soul."

Warrick cleared his throat. "Just take us to the other side, please. We need to see Lord Arawn."

Regret flashed in the water nymph's eyes, but she inclined her head, swam back to make room. And Warrick jumped right in without so much as a flinch. He popped up again, shook his head, and, treading water, raised his brows at Maeve.

Alrighty, then. Deep breath, and she dove into the lake. The near-freezing water closed in all around her, shocked her heart into stopping for agonizing seconds, pierced her skin with a thousand fine needles. She hauled herself up, broke the surface and sucked in air. Her hair hung in her face, clung to her skin. She brushed it away with a quick move.

And froze at the wide eyes of the water nymph, fixed on her scar. The heat rolling up from her stomach through her throat and into her cheeks dispelled the chill of the icy lake. Always, always, that hated reminder of how much her life had changed. Even if she had good moments, even if she managed to forget the horror for a little while, inevitably the reaction of others to the visible proof of how she'd been damaged would shatter whatever brittle shield of normalcy she'd tried to erect.

A second nymph appeared, and after exchanging a nod with Warrick, she pulled him under. Maeve was still staring at where the lake had swallowed the sentinel when the first naiad swam up to her.

"Ready?"

As I'll ever be. "Let's go."

She glanced at the duffel bag sitting abandoned on the shore, and couldn't manage to draw in enough air before the nymph grabbed her and yanked her down into the depths of the lake. Deeper, deeper they went, until her ears ached with the pressure, until the breath she was holding burned in her lungs, until there was nothing but darkness closing in on her. Panic beat along her nerves, not just for fear of drowning, but because of the dense, unrelenting black surrounding her.

And then…the direction changed.

The nymph pulled her up again, the pressure eased, light filtered through the murky water, and within seconds she broke the surface, gasping for breath with aching lungs. The nymph who had pulled her through inclined her head and swam away, leaving Maeve treading water in…a different lake. A sandy shore framed this one instead of jagged rocks, and the trees surrounding the water loomed much closer.

She'd known about this magic way of reaching the heart of Arawn's dominion from Merle's tales, but to see it actually work, to realize she'd just crossed over what had to be miles in the span of mere seconds rattled her nonetheless. Warrick already stood on the small beach, wringing water from his T-shirt. Used to this style of travel, no doubt.

Shivering from the cold clinging to her skin through her soaked clothes, she trudged out of the lake as well, joined Warrick as he took a trodden path through the undergrowth. The air was colder here, her breath almost fogging in front of her, and she barely kept her teeth from clattering.

"Warrick." The female voice drifted out from between the trees shortly before a woman stepped onto the path. "Aren't you supposed to be on watch duty?"

"I was," Warrick drawled.

The woman's pale green eyes—striking against her brown skin—tracked to Maeve, who stood half behind Warrick. Taking a step to the side, the female angled her head, frowned as she gave her a once-over—and then those mesmerizing eyes widened.

"Is that…?"

"Yes." Warrick shifted on his feet.

"How…?"

"She's surrendering herself."

"And I do have a voice," Maeve said quietly. That voice was scratchy, hoarse, her vocal cords permanently damaged by her screaming marathon while shackled to a dirty bed for days. But it was steady. Firm.

The female blinked, and a small smile tugged at the corners of her mouth. "Yes. Yes, you do." She turned to Warrick. "I'll run ahead and let him know." She walked backward a few feet, still looking at Maeve. "And maybe I'll make some popcorn. This promises to be interesting." With a flash of a smile, she whirled around and jogged off.

"Wait!" Warrick shouted. "Where's he at?"

"In the Grove," came back the answer, the female almost out of sight. "Playing."

Maeve barely held back her flinch. She didn't even want to imagine what "play" meant for the Demon Lord. She trudged behind Warrick as he followed the woman's path, winding along a bubbling creek, between copses of trees that seemed to pulse with power—discernible even to Maeve's dull human senses. Witchborn as she was, she should have a keen awareness of everything magical, but since her powers were bound inside her at the age of eight, she had no access to her witch heritage, nothing but a weak, unreliable inkling in the presence of strong magic.

And this territory here, this land, the earth itself breathed such magic that even Maeve could perceive it. No way to tell if this was Arawn's influence—a sample of whatever strange, otherworldly power he commanded—or if it was a result of all the magical creatures he "collected" and kept close through favors and cunning. She'd spotted swarms of fairies flitting past, several kobolds peeking out from the under-growth, dryads—tree nymphs—watching her with forest-green eyes from their perch atop branches, and even the light itself seemed different, as if dancing, iridescent...*alive*.

Even though this was a forest, she couldn't shake the feeling of walking through a city instead, a bustling hub of otherworldly activity teeming with inhabitants. She couldn't *see* most of them, and yet their presence was so palpable it buzzed over her skin.

She'd once been to New York City, and the feeling...it had been so similar. Only now, instead of walking among a jungle of steel and glass and concrete, she was a tiny speck amid an enormous maze of wood and stone and shadow and light, woven with magic that raised the hair on her arms and neck, feeling a thousand pairs of eyes on her, tracking her every move.

Up ahead, a tighter grouping of trees loomed at the end of the path, set apart from the rest of the forest, like a building within the woods. The branches formed an intricate, interlocked pattern reminiscent of the elaborate grillwork found in windows and doors of faraway palaces, stretching down to the moss-covered ground, giving the impression of walls.

Scattered leaves fallen from the few trees shedding their autumn foliage rustled and crunched beneath their shoes as Maeve and Warrick approached the grove. A high double door of branches and vines opened on a silent wind before them, and they stepped into the...well, the best way to describe it was *cathedral of trees*.

"Grove" seemed indeed too small and humble a word for it. There was nothing humble about this building of living wood and green. Towering trees rose on all four sides, stretching up so high that Maeve had to crane her neck to make out the lofty, vaulted ceiling of twining branches above her. Moss covered those branches all over, some hanging down in gossamer threads and casting the light pouring in through the tracery in glowing green.

Its haunting beauty rivaled the cathedrals of old, the ancient mosques and temples decked out in carvings and glittering stones.

Power such as she'd only felt once before brushed her senses, snagged her attention away from the glory of this natural architecture, to the source of that force. Her heartbeat pounded in every cell of her body as she looked over the plush carpet of moss covering the floor toward a dais at the end of the vaulted hall, to the set of black chaise lounges facing each another, a table with some sort of board game in between, to the hulking form of the Demon Lord.

Sprawled on one of the chaise lounges, opposite another male who was about to make a move on the board game,

Arawn was…a challenge to her vocabulary. She'd seen him before, when he came to claim her after her rescue and Merle made that ill-fated deal with him, and then—as now—he pooled darkness around him even without a change in lighting. The very fabric of the world appeared dipped in ink around the contours of his shape, and instead of glinting off his onyx hair, the sunshine seemed to be absorbed by it, as if sucked away. As huge as this cathedral-like space was, his presence alone filled it.

Black dress pants molded to his long, muscled legs, and a burgundy button-down shirt hugged his massive frame, the sleeves rolled up to his elbows, exposing forearms corded with more muscles. There probably wasn't an inch of him that was soft, wasn't forged in brutal strength and unforgiving harshness, the epitome of hard masculinity. That thought alone should have catapulted her into dizzying panic.

She waited for it.

And waited.

But when he turned that face of dark bronze and bored arrogance toward her, when those eyes the color of shadowed woods swept up her body in a languid perusal with a whisper of sensuality underneath, she didn't cower in fear. She didn't wince. The part of her that recoiled in instinctive terror in the presence of males—the more powerful, the more she shrank away—now lay silent…and watched, in deference, as another, long-forgotten part of her stretched its talons in welcome…in appreciation.

There you are, it seemed to say. *I've been waiting for you.*

CHAPTER 2

F ew things had the capacity to surprise Arawn. One didn't live as long as he had, seeing everything this world had to offer, from the blunt reality of unnecessary, undeserved cruelty to the depths of grace in the face of darkness, without acquiring a sometimes-tiresome prescience regarding unfolding events, an acute understanding of the ways the minds and hearts of creatures big and small worked.

But he hadn't seen this coming.

There she was, the witch he'd been watching for the past six months—the duration a mere blip compared to the lifetimes he'd experienced, the coming and going of seasons and eras that honed his appreciation of *patience*—now standing before him, upending all his plans and carefully laid-out tactics.

And most curious of all? She didn't quail. Not a whiff of the acidic fear he'd smelled when he first went to claim her months ago, no sign of the terror that had frozen her that day. No, those delicate hands didn't shake, her posture not quite defiant but far from cowering. And when he locked gazes with her after a slow survey of her soaked appearance—had she indeed come through the bloody *lake?*—her eyes didn't shimmer with tears. They burned with an inner fire he hadn't seen since…

His magic stirred, as if in response to a silent greeting. How very, *very* interesting.

Maeve's eyes cut to the male seated on the chaise lounge opposite his, and she winced. A move so minuscule, he might have missed it, but the reaction following it was striking in its clarity. The sharp aroma of fear filled the air. If someone could tremble without actually moving, the witch in front of him managed it. Her already light skin lost even more color, the ginger freckles dotting her face now all the more apparent.

"Maeve MacKenna," Arawn said.

Her attention flicked back to him.

He rose from his seat, and she watched him with the alertness of a doe facing a noise in the woods, but her scent…calmed.

A movement on the chaise lounge next to him, and Maeve flinched as if ready to take a step back.

Deimos, he said mentally, without looking at his second in command.

I'm not even doing anything, the male replied along the pathway Arawn had opened for their telepathic conversation. Deimos shifted again on the seat, leaning back into a more relaxed position.

Maeve inhaled sharply, her hands curling to fists.

I never thought I would be less intimidating than you, Arawn said mentally. *Yet here we are.*

Deimos' chuckle echoed in his mind. *I'll…leave you to it, then.*

Check on Anselm's family and find out if there's anything else they need. Putting his hands in his pants pockets, he strolled down the dais, glancing from the youngest MacKenna witch to Warrick, who rose from where he'd bent the knee in deference to his lord.

Yes, sir, Deimos said.

His second made his way down the steps as well, trailing shadows in his wake, and when he passed Maeve going to the door, she scooted to the side, glancing furtively at the impeccably dressed male who moved with silken grace, his human shape betraying nothing of the nightmare of his true form. Yet those with finer senses—and a healthy instinct of self-preservation—always seemed to catch on to the lethal threat underneath the semblance of a charming appearance. Did Maeve belong to that group, or was her caution courtesy of a general fear of males?

"To what," he addressed the witch as the doors closed behind Deimos again, "do I owe the pleasure of your visit?"

He knew, of course. Lucía told him as much when she bounced in here a few minutes ago. She'd barely toned down her excitement, and was now leaning against one the wooden pillars holding up the vaulted roof of the Grove, arms crossed and eyes sparkling.

Maeve cleared her throat and swallowed, and the ripple of her throat muscles drew his focus to the elegant slope of her neck, to the water droplets clinging to her creamy skin. One of them ran down to the high neckline of her thick navy sweater. "I'm surrendering myself."

So hoarse. A result of her torture, obviously, and yet…the smoky quality of her voice seemed to echo the same aspect lighting her eyes just moments ago.

He sauntered toward her. "Did your sister send you here?"

Her answer didn't surprise him. "No. She doesn't know."

Given that he'd just returned from Merle MacKenna's home a little while ago, where he paused the deal with her after he found out the Elder witch was with child, it would have been highly unlikely that Merle would order her sister to fulfill the original bargain he made with her. And if Merle didn't know, if she hadn't sent Maeve to him…

"Why, then, are you here?" He prowled around her, still

several feet away, though close enough that she tensed. He waited for the scent of her panic to drench the air.

It didn't.

He smiled.

She followed his trek by half-pivoting with him, not giving him her back. "I'm...turning myself in so you'll stop using Merle's magic."

"And why," he purred, "now?"

She didn't respond.

Again, he knew exactly *why*. But that was not the point, was it?

"Why now," he continued, "after I have been using your sister's powers for half a year?"

Those eyes the color of fire and smoke narrowed. "Does it matter? I'm here. It's what you want, isn't it?"

"I want," he murmured, the mossy ground soft beneath his shoes, "many a thing. And knowing what *others* want is part of it." Another round circling the witch. "What happened to make you walk into the lion's den of your own accord?"

Her nostrils flared, and a muscle feathered along her jaw. That scar across her face stood out starkly when she ground her teeth. "It's time. I should never have let Merle make that bargain with you in the first place. You've harassed her long enough. You'll leave her alone now."

A movement in the corner of his eye made him glance at Warrick, who lingered a few feet away and looked decidedly uncomfortable, face pale as he gaped at Maeve. He'd get to the sentinel in a minute.

Focusing on the tiny witch again, he said silkily, "Perhaps you feel your sister is somehow more...vulnerable than before?"

Maeve stilled. Like Merle, she telegraphed her emotions clearly in her body language. Her breath flattened out. Her eyes widened just a bit. At this point, given his questions, she had to suspect he knew. And yet, she refused to reveal what she thought was her sister's secret, on the off-chance, maybe, that she suspected wrong and he wasn't privy to Merle's pregnancy. She refused, even in the face of a force like his, even knowing she'd have to bow to his demands.

Not that he would demand she betray her conscience.

"Your sacrifice is admirable." He stopped right in front of her. "And I accept."

Her lashes lowered over her amber-lit eyes, and for a second he stilled. *Copper.* Her eyelashes were copper-colored. He surveyed her from head to toe again, from her red hair dripping water on the ground to the soaked sweater that, though oversized, now clung to her body, revealing slender curves, to the loose jeans and the hopelessly wet sneakers that made annoying squeaky noises when she moved.

She angled her head, and when one of the strands of her hair slipped to the side, it revealed a tiny, fresh bruise on her temple. Something dark and furious shot through his veins, and he raised his hand to her face, wanting to brush away the rest of her hair to get a better look at the injury.

Maeve jerked back as if he'd slapped her. There it was, the acidic smell of her fear as it streamed from her pores. Her chest heaved with her quick breaths, and her right hand twitched as if to draw a weapon.

"Lucía," he said without taking his eyes off Maeve. "Please get our guest some ice for the *bruise* on her face." At the last part of the sentence he leveled his focus on Warrick.

The sentinel became impossibly paler.

While Lucía left the Grove, Arawn sauntered past Maeve toward the shifter, cold anger biting at his nerves. "And you...brought her here without notifying me first. You took her through the *lake*, when I would have come to pick her up myself, had you possessed the presence of mind to contact me first. And now she has an injury that looks like it is fresh from this morning, and I have to wonder just what exactly you did to her on the way here."

Warrick choked as Arawn grabbed the sentinel with invisible claws around his throat, lifted him three feet in the air. The shifter struggled, coughing and pawing at his lord's magical hold.

"My orders for you," Arawn continued, his tone all the more gentle for the rage inside him, "were to keep her safe. And yet—"

"Stop it!"

The hoarse voice made him turn, and he blinked at the trembling witch next to him. Only Maeve didn't seem to be shaking with fear this time. Her amber-gray eyes glinted again with an inner fire, her hands were clenched to fists, her ginger brows drawn together.

"Let him go," she said, her voice almost steady. Almost. "He didn't do anything. He was nice to me. I...didn't buckle my seat belt, and when he had to brake, I hit the dashboard. That was my fault, not his." Her eyes flicked to the still-struggling sentinel. "Let him go."

Well, now. That was the second time today that she managed to surprise him. Not many creatures dared to interrupt him, let alone *order* him to do anything. Especially not if they found themselves in the position Maeve was in. But as scared as she undoubtedly had to be, faced with uncertainty about her future, she stepped up to defend someone she barely knew— against a powerful being who held her fate in his hands.

Reckless. That's what it was. Imprudent. Brash.

And yet the corners of his mouth felt the foolish urge to twitch upward, and the magic keeping Warrick in an airborne chokehold lessened, receded. The sentinel slumped to the ground and coughed, clutching his throat.

"The next time," Arawn said to him, "when a situation changes from the baseline of your original mission, you get in touch with me to receive new orders before you act on your own. If you fail to do so, I will not be as lenient as today."

"Yes, my lord," Warrick croaked.

Arawn nodded toward the exit. "You are dismissed. Take the day off. I will assign you a new task tomorrow."

"Thank you, sire." And with a last anxious look at Maeve, the shifter hurried out of the Grove.

Leaving Arawn alone with Maeve in the green-filtered light streaming in through the foliage above.

Maeve, too, must have realized there were only the two of them left, because her spine locked and her breath became shallow as she did her best to study him without actually looking at him directly.

"I am not," he said quietly, "going to kill you, torture you, or touch you without your consent."

Her throat muscles worked as she swallowed hard, still not facing him.

"Look at me."

Copper lashes fluttering, she turned her eyes on him.

"While you are here," he continued, "no one else will harm you either. Is that clear?"

She gave a shaky nod, still holding his gaze.

"I do, however, have a vested interest in your powers, and based on the bargain your sister made, I lay claim to your magic and intend to use it." He inclined his head. "With your cooperation."

She lowered her eyes. "My powers are locked inside me. There's nothing I can do to access them. I can't...*cooperate*."

He allowed himself a small smile. It was the kind of smile that usually drained all color out of her sister's face, but contrary to Merle, Maeve didn't blanch at the sight. She *blushed*.

Interesting.

"We will work on unlocking your powers," he said. "Together. Your cooperation will consist of allowing me to look into the spell that binds your magic. Every spell can be broken. I simply need to study the spellwork in order to unravel it."

The door to the Grove opened again, and Lucía strode in, carrying an ice pack. She handed it to Maeve.

"Here. Press this on your temple."

"Thank you." Maeve applied the ice pack to her bruise.

"Maeve," Arawn said, "meet Lucía. She will...keep you company."

Maeve narrowed her eyes. "Like a prison guard?"

"Like a *body*guard," Lucía corrected, crossing her arms and giving her a half smile.

Maeve glanced at him. "I thought you said your lands are safe for me."

"I like to prepare for every contingency," he replied, his voice silken.

She raised her brows.

"Now," he said, putting his hands in his pockets again, "before we show you your new lodging, there is one more issue we need to deal with."

Maeve, he found, was incredibly skilled at moving without moving. This time, she gave every impression of taking a wary step back without actually retreating. *Fascinating.*

"The original bargain I made with your sister was a *carte blanche* favor, and when I came to collect it, my demand was for her to transfer magical custody of you to me."

"I remember," Maeve murmured.

"Even though you have come to me voluntarily now, Merle still retains magical custody over you. That is a problem."

She pressed her lips together.

"I would rather not," Arawn continued, "ask your sister to transfer custody to me now. She is sure to refuse and has displayed an irritating irrationality when it comes to you. And it is not enough for you to simply stay here of your own free will." He made a pause and added quietly, "To fulfill the bargain Merle made, you will have to sever the familial link to her and bind yourself to me."

Maeve made a small sound, her eyes rounding. "You can't ask that of me."

"Funny," he murmured. "Your sister said almost the exact same thing when I came to claim you."

"But," Maeve sputtered, "severing that link...it will mean I'm not..."

"...part of the MacKenna family anymore. Correct."

"We're *sisters*. I can't give that up."

"You will still be related to her genetically. Just not magically."

She jerkily shook her head. "No. I can't do that."

"If you do not sever the link, Merle can exercise the privilege and power she has over you as head of your family and compel you back by magic. Think of the lengths Merle has gone to in the past to keep me from claiming you, and then tell me she would not resort to *forcing* you back, if that is what it takes."

He wouldn't put it past Merle to be so desperate and irrational as to go for the nuclear option of exerting this kind of power over her sister, even though she had to be aware that it would very well feel like a violation to Maeve.

"I can't give up my *sister*." Her voice was but a whimper.

He was quiet for a moment, studying the quivering witch before him. Shrugging, he clucked his tongue. "Then go home." Signaling Lucía, he turned away. "Escort her back to the lake."

"What?" Maeve croaked.

He spared a glance at her over his shoulder. "We do not have a deal unless you sever the link."

"But—"

"That is the condition to fulfill the bargain. I will not accept the risk of your sister whisking you away at any given moment. As long as she retains magical custody of you, that scenario is a viable threat. And if you are not willing to sever the link, I will send you back and continue using Merle's magic."

He would do no such thing, of course. As long as Merle was pregnant, he'd leave her alone so as not to risk the unborn babe. But Maeve didn't know that.

And he'd be damned if he'd enlighten her.

A beat of silence.

"Don't," Maeve whispered.

He turned back to her, one eyebrow raised.

"Don't use her magic anymore." Her voice wavered. "I'll...do it. I'll sever the link."

"Good." He inclined his head, gathering his powers. "I will show you how. Your mental shields are practically nonexistent, so I will project the instructions for how to cut the connection right into your mind. Ready?"

A shaky nod, her chin quivering.

He sent the images and impressions, directing her how to reach deep inside her where that strong bond originated, its roots linked to her own magic. How to sharpen a mental talon, even without access to the simmering powers bound in her core, how to slice it across the thread linking her to all MacKennas, living and dead.

It was vital for her to do this herself. No one else could break that link. No one but her sister, as head of the family.

With his mind still reaching out to hers, he felt the exact moment she cut the bond. Like an earthquake in the microcosm that was Maeve, the severance rocked through her, shaking her down to her foundations. Crying out, she fell to her knees, her features twisted.

"Lucía," he murmured.

But his ward was already at Maeve's side, grabbing her shoulders and steadying her. Maeve didn't wince at the female touch—as he'd expected. It was one of the reasons he'd chosen Lucía as her companion. The other being that Lucía might look unassuming, but was a force to be reckoned with, able to handle some of his most deadly assignments.

A shame neither of her parents had accepted her into their folds. Or rather, lucky for him, for if they hadn't thrown her away back then, he'd have missed out on one of his best enforcers, not to mention some unexpected joy over the years, brought on by her shenanigans.

Maeve's breathing was calmer now, and she let Lucía help her stand up.

"Are you okay?" Lucía asked softly.

Maeve shook her head, her eyes glistening with unshed tears. "It *hurt.*"

She looked up at him then, and the reproach on her face, echoed by her thoughts—still visible to him—settled with heaviness in his gut. He retreated from her mind and slammed his own shields up once more.

It was necessary, he told himself. Repeated it a couple of times, until the tightness in his chest eased.

"What now?" Maeve rasped.

"Now," he said, "you need to bind yourself to me."

Her swallow was loud enough for him to hear. "How?"

"You need my blood."

"To drink?" Anxiety threaded through her voice.

With barely a thought, he formed a claw at his right index finger and slashed over his left wrist. Blood welled at the cut. "No. It needs to mix with yours."

A small, nervous sound broke from her throat as she apparently put together what that meant. He studied the scar across her face. According to his intel, that wasn't the only place she'd had a close encounter with a blade during her captivity. The sadistic demon who held her shackled for days enjoyed using a knife on her, and word was she still bore the proof of it on the rest of her body. Not to mention her mind.

To be faced with another situation in which she would have to endure a blade cutting into her skin…

Her eyes became glazed, her gaze turning inward, her breath too fast.

"Maeve," he said, and laid every ounce of his power into that one syllable, until the word rang in the vaulted space of the Grove like the sound of a gong.

Even Lucía shrank away from the sheer dominance in his voice. He rarely used it on her.

Maeve jerked, blinked, her instincts yielding to the compulsion of the magic underscoring his tone. She hauled in air and glanced around as if reorienting herself.

"Use the knife strapped to your right leg to make the cut." He cocked his head. "You choose where and how. But you better do it quickly, or else this here"—he raised his bleeding wrist—"will close, and I will have to cut myself again. You do not want to force me to do that."

Maeve bent down to retrieve the dagger from its hidden sheath on her shin, straightening again with a rosy blush on her cheeks. She peered at the blade, hesitating.

"This is different," he said gently. "It is you. Your hand wielding it."

Those reddish lashes fluttered again as she parted her lips. Lips he found himself far more interested in than the situation demanded. His focus slipped for a moment, and he realized with a start he'd missed the instant she slashed at her own wrist.

Her arm shook slightly as she held it out. "Here."

He raised his left arm, brought it close to hers as he called upon his powers. They rose, writhing and tangling, ever hungry and eager. Holding her gaze, he touched his wrist to hers, wound to wound, blood to blood. She jolted, and then a second time when he used his other hand to apply pressure on her wrist from the opposite side, pushing her arm against his. He breathed past the prickling of magic flowing through him at the touch, reined in his powers as they lunged for her.

"Do you bind yourself to me, Maeve Lonewitch?"

She gasped, and something broke in those eyes of smoke and flames at his mention of the new name that described her identity of a witch without family ties. "Yes," she whispered.

"In magic and blood?"

"Yes."

"Then I claim you as mine."

His magic struck, still only a fraction of the real power churning in his core, but enough to make Maeve stagger back. He kept his hold on her hand so the connection of their wounds wouldn't break yet, and wove his magic into hers. Roots to roots, vines along her branches, darkness to her fire. *Mine*, his powers whispered into every cell of her. *Mine*.

The bond snapped taut between them, a link that went beyond the fealty sworn to him by the creatures in his service, beyond the favors that bound people to his will. He felt her now. *Sensed* her like an extension of himself, sensed that simmering magic shackled inside her so much more clearly than before. So close, and yet so far from his grasp. For if he were to shatter those bonds and free what slumbered in her core…

He wouldn't go there. Yet.

Letting go of Maeve's hand, he signaled for Lucía to bandage her wrist.

Maeve's eyes met his for a searing moment, and he gave her a smile that colored her cheeks a lovely rose.

"Welcome to the family, Maeve of Arawn."

CHAPTER 3

Merle woke to warm darkness enveloping her. Slowly, her senses came back from the bleak oblivion she'd tumbled into, and she realized why she couldn't see—Rhun held her pressed to his chest, cradling her like the most fragile, most precious thing on earth. Because that's what she was to him, the feeling so clear, so strong through the mating bond linking them.

With a shuddering breath, she pushed back against him, and he loosened his embrace. Concern glinted in those eyes of pale blue-green, his dark brows drawn together, his expression pinched.

"I'm sorry," he murmured.

For a second she wondered what he meant. But then her eyes tracked to the note lying on the floor next to their chair, to the pained faces of Lily and Alek on the opposite couch, and her heart splintered anew.

Maeve. She was gone.

She left for Arawn's lair, surrendering herself to save Merle's baby. *It can't be, it can't be,* a part of her mind kept repeating, still unwilling to admit the irrefutable truth. And yet the proof of Maeve's sacrifice stared her right in the face, black on white in her sister's handwriting, and the sorrow of Maeve's decision clung to the paper like a whiff of perfume.

Her stomach knotted so tightly it felt like a cramp. *This is all my fault.* She made that ill-fated deal for an open favor with Arawn in the first place, not covering her bases enough to prevent the Demon Lord from demanding her sister as his price. And now…she should have called Maeve right away after Arawn paused the deal this morning. She should have told Maeve about the pregnancy, and that the baby was safe.

Closing her eyes, she shook her head. Damn it all to hell, but she'd wanted to tell Maeve face-to-face that she was expecting, she wanted it to be this beautiful moment between sisters, so she could be able to hug Maeve and cry with her. But if she'd realized Maeve already knew about the baby, that Maeve had one foot on the doorstep, ready to sacrifice herself, she'd have called her. And then Maeve wouldn't have felt the need to turn herself in. *She'd still be here.*

With a hand over her mouth, she covered her sob.

"Merle…" Lily tentatively said.

But she shook her head again. "I need…a minute."

There had to be a way. There simply had to be a way to get her back. Her mind started working feverishly as she untangled herself from Rhun's arms, combed through her hair with shaking fingers. How long had Maeve been gone? Maybe she wasn't even at Arawn's lair yet. Maybe she could…

With a soft gasp, she felt a piece clicking into place in her memory. Arawn wanted magical custody over Maeve…but Merle had to *give* it to him, didn't she? Maeve had gone to him without consulting Merle—and she hadn't agreed to a transfer of custody.

Merle was still head of the family. And Maeve was still a MacKenna, for all magical intents and purposes.

Could she…*compel* Maeve back? That was the right and power she held as the oldest living MacKenna, wasn't it? She could magically order Maeve to do something, and Maeve would have to comply. She'd never done it before, had never exerted her privilege as head of the family, but if it was the only way to pull Maeve back before she made the biggest mistake of her life…

She gathered her magic.

Rhun stirred next to her, and shock, then anger vibrated down the mating bond. He grabbed her shoulders, turned her to face him. "No."

"What?" Lily asked, sitting up straight.

"She's calling on her magic." His focus burned through Merle. "Whatever ill-advised idea you just had, little witch—don't."

"I can bring her back," Merle whispered.

Lily startled. "No," she echoed Rhun's sentiment, her eyes going wide.

Alek glanced between Rhun, Lily, and Merle. "Will someone please explain?"

"As head of the family, Merle can compel Maeve to come back," Lily said. "But it'll draw on her magic, and we don't know if it's enough to call for a payback to the Powers That Be…"

"Which would endanger our baby," Rhun gritted out, still gripping Merle's shoulders.

"We don't know that," Merle shot back.

It was only a little bit of magic, and she wouldn't even have to tap the power worked into the layers of the world to supplement her own…

Her powers swirled to the surface, ready to be wielded. She closed her eyes, and time slowed to a crawl. She barely heard Lily's protest, Rhun's muffled curse as she primed her magic—

Pain sliced through her. She cried out, sagged into Rhun's arms. What was hap—

Dark silence where a bond once thrived within her.

Aching, the spot was aching like a fresh cut, bleeding

magic in her core. She choked on a breath. Patted the severed link with mental fingers, wincing at the pain.

"No," she whispered. "No, no, no…"

Rhun's hands now cradled her face. "Merle. *Merle.* Look at me. What happened?"

"She's…she's gone."

He frowned, opened his mouth to say something, but closed it again.

"I can't feel her anymore." Her voice was scarcely more than a sob. "The link. It's severed."

Rhun's face fell, and Lily stifled a gasp.

There was only one explanation for why the familial link between witches broke—death. Maeve was…she was…

"That's not what happened." Rhun's features were grim, his voice determined. "That's not what happened, okay? She's not—" He broke off, clenched his jaw. "Why would he do that? Arawn wants her for her powers. She's worth more to him alive."

Silent tears now spilled from her burning eyes.

Rhun—his shape blurring—looked to Alek and Lily as if for help.

Alek cleared his throat. "Rhun's right. If there's one good quality about Arawn, it's that he's patient. He doesn't make rash decisions. He doesn't kill impulsively. He plays a long game, and keeping Maeve around as an asset yet to be used fits his MO."

Merle hiccuped. "Then why was the link severed? What other explanation is there?"

Lily leaned forward on the couch, her voice thoughtful. "Remember how my mom lost the link to me when I turned into a demon? She—and you—first thought it was because I died. You didn't know a witch could be turned into something else, and you couldn't have guessed the turning would sever the link. There *are* other explanations. We're just not aware of all of them yet."

"You think she was turned into something else?" Merle croaked.

Lily rubbed her temple. "No…well, it's a possibility, but I think it might be something else altogether. Arawn has a lot of strange powers we don't even know about."

"When Arawn came to claim Maeve," Rhun said, "didn't he say he wanted magical custody over her? And that you'd have to transfer it to him?"

Merle sniffed and nodded.

"What if he just did that? What if severing the link to you is part of the process?"

"It's…possible," Merle conceded, her chest a little less tight.

"Then we'll assume that as the most logical explanation," Lily said. "The other option doesn't make any sense."

"She's alive, little witch." Rhun caressed her cheek.

"That doesn't mean she's safe," she whispered back. "That…monster *owns* her now. And…all the things he could do to her…" Her voice broke.

"Merle," Alek said gently. "I'll do whatever I can to find out where exactly she is, and how she's doing." As one of Arawn's enforcers, he had the necessary connections.

She sniffed, wiped at her eyes. "Thank you."

The doorbell rang, startling all of them. Lily and Alek exchanged glances, then looked at Rhun and Merle.

Merle blinked, sat up. *Right.* They couldn't go out during the day because of their sensitivity to sunlight…

"I'll go," Rhun said with a long-suffering sigh. "Since I'm the only one not inconvenienced by a convenient sun allergy, or a bun in the oven."

"I'm not sick or disabled," Merle groused.

"No, but you're super-precious and growing a little witch volcano in your belly, which has all of my protective instincts running in overdrive, which means I'll coddle you until you strangle me." He winked at her as he walked out of the room.

And there it was. The familiar feeling of not knowing which she wanted more: kiss him or smack him.

When he returned a few minutes later, he was holding an envelope and frowning. "This was stuck to the front gate. It says 'Murray'."

He raised his brows at Merle and Lily, silently asking who should have it. Lily rose and took it from him.

"I'm still a Murray," she murmured and opened the envelope, pulled out the letter, and read it. Her eyes narrowed, her nostrils flaring. "It's from Juneau."

Merle's blood pressure soared just hearing the name. That conniving bitch of an Elder had driven the formerly united witch community apart by taking a hardliner stance when Lily was turned into a demon—through no fault of her own, at that. Juneau forced Merle and Hazel to fight her and her followers in order to protect Lily, and when Juneau declared Merle and Hazel traitors to witchkind and rallied half the Elders to agree, the other half walked out and joined with Hazel and Merle.

And now the community was divided, and each side had been eyeing the other for weeks without serious incident. But it felt like the calm before the storm. Merle and Hazel, and the other Elders on their side, had reached out several times to Juneau and her witches in hopes of mending the rift in the community. To no avail. Juneau and her followers didn't even deign to reply.

Until now.

Merle sat up straighter. "What does it say?"

"She wants to meet."

Merle blinked. That was...unexpected.

"Yeah," Lily said grimly. "I'm kind of flabbergasted, too."

Alek quickly typed something on his phone, one side of his mouth tipping up, and then he turned the device around so they all could see. "*It's a trap!*" an ugly-looking alien shouted in the short video clip.

Alek grinned at Lily. "You don't know how long I've been waiting for an appropriate situation to play that."

"I'm so thrilled the conflict in the witch community could feed your addiction to *Star Wars* references." Lily's flippant-sounding reply was undermined by the warmth of her smile as she looked at him.

"The brilliance of that reference notwithstanding," Rhun chimed in, "I tend to agree with the sentiment. It smells like a trap."

"I don't know," Lily said, chewing on her lower lip, her focus on the letter. "She says she wants the meeting in a neutral place with all participants bound by oath not to use magic or other weapons during the meeting. That sounds pretty reasonable."

Merle mulled it over. "I've got a bad feeling about this…"

Alek snickered, and Lily shot him a look and whispered, "Would you get your head out of the *Star Wars* universe now?"

Merle ignored them. "…but this might be our only chance to make peace before more blood is spilled." She caught Rhun's look, her heart twisting. "I don't want any more witches to die."

"Neither do I," he replied, his eyes softening. "But I don't trust Juneau to keep her word, and I wouldn't put it past her to turn this into an ambush."

She heaved a sigh. "We need to get in touch with the other Elders on our side. See what they think. And…ugh." She thumped her head against the backrest of the chair. "Hazel. She's still in Faerie looking for Basil and Rose. We can't have this meeting without her, but we can't let Juneau know we're stalling because Hazel's not here. Juneau and her ilk will see her absence as a weakness and pounce on us."

"By the way," Lily said into the heavy silence that followed, "we need to come up with names for both factions."

Merle frowned at her. "The what now?"

"Well, we don't have a snazzy name for our side. We just say 'our side.' And saying 'Juneau and her rabid acolytes' is quite a mouthful every time. We need something short and catchy."

Alek opened his mouth, but Merle signaled him to shut up.

"She's on a roll now," she whispered to him, eager to hear the fun stuff her best friend would come up with. "Let her finish her speech."

"Just think of *Harry Potter*," Lily went on, eyes gleaming. "The bad guys were the Death Eaters. The good guys the Order of the Phoenix, or the Order for short. And then there's *Star Wars*."

Alek perked up.

"There's the Empire on the one side," Lily continued, "and the Rebellion on the other."

"Don't forget the new one," Alek said. "They've got new names."

"Right." Lily snapped her fingers at him. "You've got the First Order for the baddies, and the Resistance for the heroes. See? Those are cool names! We need us some like that." And with that, she crossed her arms and gave them all a smug smile.

Despite the gravity of the overall situation, Merle couldn't help grinning. That's what best friends were for—making you laugh in troubled times.

"All right," she said to Lily. "I'm game. Let's come up with some snazzy names."

Rhun raised his hand. "Can't we just repurpose Death Eaters for Juneau and her devotees? It would certainly fit her brand."

"Nah." Merle crinkled her nose. "That might be an insult to the actual Death Eaters."

"How about Zealots?" Alek offered.

Lily nodded. "Ooooh, that's good."

"Draconians," Rhun threw in.

Merle turned to him. "I like that one better."

"Of course you do," Lily said. "He's your mate."

"Draconians does have a better ring to it," Alek grumbled.

A cocky smile snuck onto Rhun's face. "I *am* full of awesome."

Merle batted her eyelashes at him. "Well, then how about you grace us with an excellent suggestion for our side, oh exalted one?"

"I like that nickname." He pointed at her. "I want you to use it in bed tonight."

Lily groaned and covered her ears. "Stop! TMI."

Merle breathed past the heat of embarrassment rising to her neck and face and narrowed her eyes at Rhun. "You better toss in a *brilliant* idea for a name right now, or I'm going to strangle you."

"Aequitas," he countered.

"Bless you," Alek said.

Rhun leveled a glare at him. "It's Latin and stands for justice, equality, or fairness. Cicero saw it as a trifold concept of equity between the gods, the spirits of the underworld, and human beings. Since *our* side"—he winked at Merle—"seeks fairness in dealing with demons and doesn't want to label them all evil, but rather strives for a world in which beings aren't prejudged based on the species they were born to, while still keeping the human population safe from other-worldly threats, the name is fitting, don't you think?"

Lily gaped at him. "How...even...?"

"I've been alive for a century," Rhun said. "I did spend some of that time learning things."

"I love you so hard," Merle breathed.

Rhun grinned. "Does that mean you'll call me 'exalted one' tonight?"

CHAPTER 4

T he main part of Arawn's lair, it turned out, stretched out for what seemed like miles underground. Maeve followed Lucía and the new bane of her existence through tunnels upon tunnels and cavernous rooms and along galleries above yawning chasms, the bottom of which she couldn't make out in the dark. She suspected half of the trip through this subterranean sprawl was solely intended to intimidate her.

And it grated on her that he succeeded.

Merle had told her about her visits to Arawn's territory for the magic she worked for him, but from what Maeve gleaned of those tales, she could say with certainty that Merle and the others didn't have the slightest idea of how much power and influence and sheer number of forces Arawn truly had at his disposal. They still underestimated him—all but Alek, maybe. He didn't talk much about it, but he had to know.

One lengthy trip through his underground dominion was enough to give Maeve a more realistic notion as to the power and authority Arawn commanded. The range of his lands alone was impressive. More so, however, was the deference and submission with which his subjects greeted him. Beings would bow low, some of them even prostrating themselves before him, and none of them would meet his eyes. They spoke in soft tones, humble murmurs, the air itself hushing wherever he went.

And it drove home just how out of line she had been with the way she talked to him in the Grove, compared to the way his people treated him. She understood now why Warrick was so pale when she spoke to Arawn with an air of defiance. Because no one else here did. Ever.

She clenched her jaw. Well, she had no intention of groveling before him. She'd be respectful, but if he expected her to bend the knee and kiss his feet and whisper, "My lord," then he had another think coming. Certain parts of her...had not been broken during those dark days in the warehouse, so much as they'd been reinforced. Certain things...she would never do.

Not for him. Not for anyone.

The bare, earthen walls of the wide tunnel they were in changed as they went ahead, became roughcast and more civilized-looking. Fireflies still danced in the air, but they weren't the only illumination anymore. Crystals set in the walls glowed and bathed the hallway in soft, warm light, and here and there even beams of sunlight peeked through skylights that, at closer look, turned out to be vents that channeled the light through however many angled mirrors down from the real skylight in the surface.

Her eyes tracked to Arawn walking in front of her—Lucía was at her side—to the way his powerful frame moved with sinuous grace...far more grace than someone of his massive build should possess. It should have been a contradiction in and of itself, and yet...it fit. Like a tiger that, despite its bulging muscles and hulking form, still flowed with feline elegance.

And she couldn't wrench her eyes off him.

Off the firmness of his backside, the broad shoulders and

the corded forearms dusted with dark hair. Off the muscles flexing in his legs as he walked.

His magic was a steady beat of power inside her. Different from how the link to Merle had felt. *So* different. Darker, sensual, and...devastating. Because this constant reminder of his presence, his essence, made it so much harder to ignore the host of unbidden things she felt at the thought of him. Things she didn't believe she could experience anymore after...

In the months since, her body had been numb. No spark of interest in any male. The mere thought of intimacy terrified her. It continued that way for quite a while, and she almost resigned herself to never feeling desire again.

Until *he* showed up at the Murray mansion where she stayed. Oh, he was subtle, hiding mostly in the shadows, but every now and then...she saw him. Without a doubt because he *let* her see him. And of all the males to which her body could have the reaction she was yearning for, it had to be him. Like some cruel twist of fate.

She should be scared of him. Not...feel heat prickling in places she'd barely begun to reclaim with her own touch.

Closing her eyes briefly, she shook her head. She had to be more messed up than everybody thought.

Arawn stopped in front of a door and swung it open, gesturing inside. "Your room."

She had to walk right by him to get in there, so close that his body heat brushed her like a caress. Goosebumps rose on her arms...and tightened her nipples.

Gods, just kill me now. It would be a mercy.

This couldn't be happening. She couldn't react to him this way. Anyone but him.

Her cheeks and ears burned, and she crossed her arms in front of her chest as she assessed the room. Bigger than the one she'd occupied at the Murray mansion, and that was saying something. Like most of the rooms she'd seen so far in this underground lair, this one, too, had curving walls featuring tree roots that were decorative in their pattern, swirling in artful whorls that defied natural development. A huge bed with a frame carved from dark wood stood against the far wall, an armoire took up another one, and the wall to her right had a door leading to what she presumed was an en suite bathroom. Crystals glowed in the walls.

No windows.

The air rushed out of her. *A room with no windows.* Her heart raced. Dread curdled in her belly, like a fizzy tablet of fear had been dropped into her stomach and now quickly dissolved and poisoned her.

"Is there a problem?"

The deep bass of Arawn's voice barely reached her over the thumping of her own heart. She curled her hands to fists, hugged herself tighter, and managed to look away from those windowless walls threatening to close in around her.

Lucía was staring at her with a glint in her eyes Maeve knew all too well. She'd seen it countless times on Merle, on Lily, Hazel, Basil, Rhun, and every other damn person who was privy to her ordeal. Every time Maeve so much as trembled, they'd get that look.

Pity.

For what she'd been through. For how broken she was. For all the things she couldn't do anymore—like sleep in a room without windows—because it reminded her too much of that one in the warehouse, where the only light had been a lone bulb swinging above her bed, and it felt like she might as well have been buried six feet under for how removed it was from the world.

She was shaking now. Sweating. That fizzy tablet in her stomach foamed and wanted to spill over into the rest of her body.

"Would you like another room?" Arawn's voice was rough silk over her senses.

She opened her mouth to say yes. Closed it again. Swallowed. Fought the dizziness creeping up on her. She should just tell him.

But then he'd know exactly how fractured she really was. How crazy. He'd smile at her weakness, wouldn't he? Or worse...he'd pity her, too. She couldn't even look at him. Didn't want to know whether his face of harsh angles and rough beauty bore the same expression that greeted her on others whenever she stumbled while trying to navigate the wounds in her mind and body.

It's just a room, godsdammit.

Her blood heated, and she pressed her lips together, breathing in through her nose. She was sick and tired of pity, of being coddled and treated like a cracked vase that could shatter at the slightest vibration. Sick and tired of being controlled by her fear, and like hell would she let Arawn see her this weak.

Anger. Anger was good. It helped push back the panic beating under her skin. Helped her clear her throat and say, "No. This is just fine."

Lucía frowned and stirred as if to speak, but Arawn made a subtle gesture, and she held her tongue.

"Good," Arawn said. "Take today to rest and explore, if you wish, and tomorrow we will start looking into the spell binding your magic. If you need anything, ask Lucía and she will make sure you receive it. She will stay close to you."

"I'm free to...explore?" She raised a brow.

The smile sneaking onto his face was positively feline. "My secrets keep themselves. Wander around however you please, as long as Lucía is with you."

He turned to leave.

"There's one thing," Maeve said, her voice wavering over her thundering heartbeat.

Arawn halted, dark power whispering about his shoulders.

"I had a duffel bag. But I had to leave it at the lake when we came here. Is it possible to—"

"Look in the bathroom," he said, and walked out.

Maeve blinked, then padded over to the en suite room which indeed featured a fully modern bath. And her duffel bag sat on the counter.

"Gods, he can be so dramatic," Lucía sighed from the doorway.

Maeve turned to her. "How…?" She gestured at the duffel.

Lucía shrugged. "He's telepathic, you know. Probably sent someone out to check the lake and bring back any luggage."

"That's…almost thoughtful."

"He's not a monster," Lucía said quietly.

Maeve bit her tongue to hold back her reply. Instead she swallowed and said, "I'd like to take a shower and change."

"Say no more." Lucía smiled and held up her hands, backing away. "I'll be in the room right next to yours, to your left. Knock if you want to take a walk later. Oh, and if you're hungry, we'll grab something to eat."

The door clicked shut behind Lucía. Maeve waited a few seconds, then walked over to the door and locked it. She didn't have any illusions about it keeping out Arawn or Lucía if they wished to enter, but still…

She rushed to the duffel bag, zipped it open and rummaged through it until she found her cell phone. *Yes.* Her heart fell when she turned it on—no reception. *Of course.* Would have been too easy to be able to send a text or make a quick call. The display showed what the phone received before the signal was cut off—several missed calls and text messages, from Merle, Lily, and Anjali. Her best friend had also texted her back in response to the message Maeve sent her right before they stopped at the lake.

Maeve had said her goodbye to Anjali in that message, like she did to the others in the note she left at the Murrays, not knowing what awaited her once she went to Arawn's.

Maybe that was a bit fatalistic in retrospect, but she honestly couldn't have known the Demon Lord would treat her with anything akin to civility.

In any case, Anjali's response was a many-worded "don't you dare do that, Maeve MacKenna," just as Maeve expected. Which was why she sent a text instead of calling. Any protest and well-intentioned guilt-tripping would have only made her departure harder. But it wouldn't have kept her from going.

Well, even though she was still in one piece and surprisingly free to move, she had no means to contact Merle and the others to let them know. They had to be going crazy with worry about her well-being. Maybe she could ask Lucía for a way to get word to Merle. Unless she wasn't allowed contact with the outside world…

It couldn't hurt to ask. It was the least she could do to alleviate everybody's fear and concern.

She turned the shower on and quickly stripped out of her half-dried clothes. Didn't look in the mirror, didn't glance down her body. *Feeling* those scars when she scrubbed herself clean—always fast and efficiently, not lingering on this body that had given her so much pain—was difficult enough. She didn't need the additional visual reminder of an already indelible experience.

Not when she saw it reflected in the shock and pity on the faces of everyone she met.

CHAPTER 5

Dry leaves crunched under Arawn's paws as he ran, his tongue hanging out. The air had a bite to it here, a welcome chill to balance his heated body. Light rain pattered on his black fur, and the forest smelled of water-kissed earth and sighing plants.

A run was just what he needed to restore his thoughts to order and banish the memory of amber-gray eyes and red hair sticking to rosy skin. At least for a little while. So he could focus on other matters again.

Sire.

He didn't slow down at the mental voice of Deimos, kept running over the leaf-strewn forest floor. *Tell me.*

There is something you should look at, his second replied. *Right outside the northern border. Near the gnome colony.*

I will be there in a few minutes. He didn't question whether the issue was important enough for him to investigate personally. Deimos had decades of experience managing the day-to-day business and administrative tasks of keeping Arawn's growing empire running smoothly. If his second asked him to come, it would be something significant.

He ran to the next opening amid the trees, leapt off a boulder, and changed mid-jump from his wolf form to a large, black eagle. A few powerful beats of his wings later he soared above the forest sprawling over hills and mountain ridges, the rough, untamed beauty of the Cascades in his territory. Most of it was untouched by human taint, Arawn's magic being a powerful repellent to the people living nearby. Other parts of his dominion included human settlements, but this stretch was the pure wilderness of the Pacific Northwest, and, much like the fae sanctuaries, it was protected against human interference by strong magical wards. On maps it appeared as a national park that, for some reason, no one ever wanted to visit.

Nearing the northern border, he began his descent and spotted Deimos by the side of a creek. Arawn landed on the moss- and fern-covered ground a few feet from his second and shifted to his human form. A dryad peeled herself out of a nearby tree and brought him a pair of flowing black pants, one of many he liked to keep stored all over his territory for moments such as this. The tree nymph bowed low and retreated while he pulled on the pants, then turned to Deimos.

His second inclined his head in greeting. "Over there."

Arawn followed him, his nose twitching at the metallic scent drifting over on a breeze. *Blood.* Someone—or something—recently made a kill. A human kill. Unsanctioned as it was.

Granted, his territory ended here, and with it Arawn's jurisdiction, but few dared to spill human blood so close to his dominion. Killings tended to draw attention from human authorities, and having to deter their focus was aggravating. Cleaning up the mess even more so.

But Deimos wouldn't have called him here if this was a simple kill by rogue demons.

The smell of blood now hung heavy in the air, only dampened a little by the feather-light rain. He stepped onto the clearing behind Deimos and halted. The swaying was the first thing he noted. Stirred by the wind, the bodies swung slightly to and fro, suspended from the rope around their necks.

No. Not rope.

He prowled closer, stepping carefully so he wouldn't disturb evidence, and studied the scene more thoroughly.

The two dead humans were hung from the tree—by their own intestines. He tilted his head. *Interesting.* Wasn't the colon usually too soft to hold a body's weight? Another step closer. *Ah.* The intestines had been looped and braided several times to make them strong enough.

Both humans—a man and a woman in hiking gear—had bloody holes where their eyes should be, and their arms ended in sawed-off stumps instead of their hands. He glanced down to the ground below the bodies, where the severed hands of both victims were arranged with their palms up, cupping the gouged-out eyeballs.

Naturally, the bellies of the two bodies gaped open where the guts had been extracted. He peered into the wounds.

"Have any other organs been removed?" he asked Deimos.

"No."

"Feeding injuries?"

"None."

"What about blood loss antemortem?"

"Only due to the wounds, as far as we could tell. I had Sofia take a cursory look at the bodies." The lynx shifter worked as a coroner in a nearby human town, her senses sharp, and her experience handy when it came to analyzing sticky situations for Arawn. "According to her, cause of death seems to be the disembowelment and related blood loss. And it wasn't taken." He nodded at the dark stains beneath the

48

dead. Blood crusted the grass and moss, enough to account for the fatal loss.

"The killer did not feed," Arawn mused. Which ruled out the most common reason for killing humans. He stalked around the hanging bodies, drew in air and sampled the scents. "What do you smell?"

"Besides blood, gore, and feces?" Deimos curled his lip, shook his head. "No demon signature, not from what I can pick up. No shifter either."

Arawn closed his eyes, spread his senses, tasting the magic lingering in the air. "No fae."

"I was wondering if this might simply be the work of a human killer."

Certainly humans were more than capable of bloody slaughter like this. But... "I am not picking up another human scent."

Deimos sniffed and sighed. "Yeah. Me neither."

Underneath the different smells drenching the area, there *was* something, though... He couldn't quite pin it down. The faint trace wanted to jog a piece of his memory, but it was like tugging at a thread sticking out of a hopeless tangle of yarn. For someone who'd seen the dawn of time, had collected more memories than the largest human library could hold, trying to sort through this maze of knowledge and impressions could prove irritatingly difficult. Sometimes it took him weeks to unearth a single memory from the vaults of his mind.

He tucked the scent trace away, to be worked on in the background while he attended to other things. His focus landed on the arrangement of hands and eyes again.

"What do you make of this?" he asked Deimos.

"It's a statement."

"Obviously." But of what?

Deimos rubbed his neck. "I could come up with a dozen

clichés about what eyes and hands stand for, but unless we know more of the specific context of these killings..." He shrugged. "It could mean something. It might not mean anything."

Yes, given the myriad ways in which madness worked, this could simply be deranged, senseless violence. Or it could be a carefully crafted message.

Arawn studied the scene again, then the area. "I assume you did a sweep for any other tracks or traces."

"No signs of a vehicle, but we found hints that someone covered their tracks coming and going. Nothing beyond that, and even those few hints aren't enough to follow."

"If this was not for feeding," Arawn said, his voice echoing the deadly quiet he felt inside, "and yet it was dropped this close to my border..."

Deimos eyed him. "I haven't heard a peep from the demon clans or the shifter packs. They're all lying low, and word is no one has any desire to fuck with you, especially after Anselm."

As well they shouldn't. Some of them had become annoy-ingly uppity in recent times, making a display of power necessary. So when a clan of demons thought it wise to kill one of Arawn's enforcers without provocation, he reminded them why his people were considered untouchable among otherworld creatures. Echoes of the nightmares he unleashed upon them carried on whispers to the nooks and crannies of the community, and the subsequent hush of newfound respect for those who belonged to the Demon Lord was barely enough to calm Arawn's anger.

And if the usual suspects of discord in the area were still impressed by his recent show of force, it raised the question of who was insolent enough to provoke Arawn's ire with this kind of slaughter on his doorstep. If this was, indeed, meant as a threat or intimidation—the notion almost laughable—any opponent worth their salt would not have hidden their tracks. As an overture to war, it was pathetic.

That aside, killing humans as a way to get to him was... curious. Not to mention weak. They were the easiest to kill, no challenge whatsoever. A targeted assassination of Arawn's favor-bound creatures, on the other hand, would make for a stronger impression.

"Have Sofia do a full autopsy on the bodies," he ordered Deimos, "and dispose of the humans when she is done. Get the area cleaned up, and interview the gnome colony. Ask them what, if anything, they have seen, and make sure to follow any other creature's scent you find and interrogate them as well. I want to know who has been here recently and what they may have noticed. Pay special attention to the fairies, gnomes, and dryads."

In a living, breathing forest like this, someone was always around. It was highly unlikely the killer could have come and gone without at least one otherworld creature seeing them.

"Will do, sire."

"And keep your ear to the ground for any buzz in the otherworld community. Maybe no one telegraphed this move beforehand, but it is possible someone may claim it now." Although to boast about it in conversations, but not to the face of the Demon Lord would say a lot about the perpetrator's integrity. Or lack thereof.

He sneered at the bloody display in front of him. The least one could do was own up to one's kills, especially if they were meant as some sort of message.

He pulled off his pants, flung them at a nearby tree to be picked up by a dryad later, and changed into a giant black bear, his sense of smell strongest in this form. Nose on the ground, he tracked around the clearing, noting and archiving every single scent trace, to be sure.

That one elusive thread...

Stopping at a spot where the mysterious aroma was a bit more discernible, he drew in several tasting breaths.

"Got something?" Deimos asked.

I am not sure, he replied mentally. *I cannot place this one, but I have smelled it before.*

And he almost, *almost* remembered... But every time he thought he could grasp that particular memory, it slipped through his fingers like smoke.

I will keep pondering this scent, he told Deimos. *Reinforce border security and send out word to our people outside the territory to be on alert. Tell them to retreat to my lands in case of any more obvious threats.*

Many of Arawn's creatures lived within his dominion, but he'd long ago started spreading a wider net of resources, informants, and the favor-bound outside the boundaries of his territory proper.

Deimos gave him a nod, his cell phone already pressed to his ear.

Time for another run, this one along the border to check for any other scents. He started with a widening circle around the site of the murders, and went east when he didn't find anything else remarkable to pick up.

The long, curved claws of his bear paws dug into moss and earth and fallen branches, the light rain stroking his fur. Squirrels rustled in the trees above, birdsong a constant musical backdrop to his journey.

He was atop a cliff when he heard it. A whimper.

Sniffing the air, he followed the trace of the new scent on the breeze, down into a small forest valley. The magic of his border was a hum in the air. He crossed the invisible line to the other side, toward the bundle laid out on a moss-covered boulder.

He knew the species long before he got a look at the babe. An *algos* demon, feeding on pain. Wrapped in a torn and threadbare blanket, the youngling whimpered again, one of its legs deformed, its normally dark red skin paled to rose. Probably due to hunger and cold, having been out here who knew how long.

Surrendered to Arawn, like so many others.

He huffed, gripped the edges of the blanket with his teeth and carried the babe away.

Like so many others.

CHAPTER 6

"Plant your bottom here," Lucía said and patted the spot next to her on the log.

Maeve sat down carefully, positively surprised at how cushiony the seat was. The ever-present moss covered the fallen tree trunk much like it did most everything else here in the wet climate of northwest Oregon. Although Maeve couldn't say with any certainty whether she *was* still in Oregon…maybe Arawn's lair was actually in Washington? Who knew how far she'd traveled when she went through the lake…

She shook her head and bit into the wrap, part of the dinner she and Lucía bought from the brownie kitchens belowground, her attention on the gorgeous sight of the tumbling waterfall a few yards away. Fairies flitted to and fro, leaving colorful glitter in their wake.

Maeve blinked, tilted her head. *Colorful glitter?* She'd never seen fairies produce that before. Was that a special thing they did in Arawn's territory? Some sort of influence of his magic?

"Whatcha thinking?" Lucía asked around chewing.

Maeve had already resigned herself to the inescapable

truth that Lucía was a talker. The exact opposite of her intro-vert self. While they'd been out strolling around Arawn's above-ground dominion, since Maeve didn't want to spend more time than necessary enclosed by earth and stone on all sides, Lucía would stop time and again and just chat with... everybody. From human-looking otherworld creatures— Maeve couldn't tell whether they were shifters or demons, lacking that magical sense due to her powers being bound— to the smaller beings able of speech. *Any* smaller being.

If it could talk, Lucía would talk to it.

Well, even if it couldn't speak, Lucía would chatter at it, as she'd done with a friendly fox that ambled close and allowed her to pet it.

How someone was capable of spending all these words in one day and still have more to say, Maeve couldn't fathom. She'd always been the most reserved of her family and friends—well, no, that wasn't entirely true, was it? Up until she was eight years old, she was a bubbly little girl who talked as much as she breathed, according to others. Maeve barely remembered that time. Same as she couldn't remember the day it changed, and with it the makeup of her family.

She only had bits and pieces of memories of her mom and her oldest sister Moira, who both died that day...

"Oh, no, is the wrap that bad?" Lucía gaped at her, pale green eyes wide. "Wait, mine tastes really good. Do you want to switch? We can switch. The avocados in this one are superb."

"No, it's okay. I was just...remembering something."

"Hmhm. Now, don't let the brownies hear that your wrap is just 'okay.' They'll be livid, and the next thing you get from them will be food poisoning." She curled her lip and stared off into the distance. "Been there, done that."

Maeve ate another bite. "Doesn't it bother you," she asked after chewing, "to be stuck with babysitting me?"

Lucía snorted. "You know, there's always two ways

you can look at something. To you, this may seem like babysitting—which, I gotta say, is so not true, because I've done *actual* babysitting, and let me tell you, you are a vacation compared to those brats I had the pleasure of running after—but anyway, to me, this is on par with my most important assignments. If you haven't yet figured it out—you're Arawn's new crown jewel. He wouldn't just trust anyone with guarding you. So, no, it doesn't bother me at all." She shrugged, her leather jacket creaking with the movement. "Also, you're adorable."

Heat washed up to Maeve's face. Purely in reaction to being called adorable, of course, not because of anything else Lucía said. She cleared her throat, and her next question slipped out before she could smack herself upside the head. "So, are you and Arawn...?"

Lucía frowned in the process of taking a sip of her rose-flavored water—a specialty from the brownie kitchens, she'd proclaimed, and cheerfully bulldozed Maeve into having one, too—then she froze, her eyes rounding, and spit her water out in a coughing fit. "Holy hellfire, *no!*"

O-kay. That was quite an answer.

Lucía kept coughing and brushed off the splattered liquid on her front. "That would be like banging my uncle, and —ew. No."

"You're Arawn's niece?"

"No, not even close. Well, not in terms of blood relation or anything. No one's related to him like that." She tilted her head with a bemused look. "At least not that I know of. I have never even heard of another being like Arawn..."

"What are you to him, then?"

"Me?" She snapped back to attention and turned to Maeve again. "Oh, right. I wouldn't go so far as calling him my adoptive father, because he didn't *actually* raise me himself, but he kind of took me in and kept me closer than the other kids, so I guess technically I'd be his ward? Protégée?" She waved a hand. "Particulars."

Maeve drew back a little. "Other kids?"

Lucía's eyes sparkled like sunshine on a lake in the slanted afternoon light. "Hm. Right. You wouldn't know." She took another sip of her water. "Since you were raised in the witch community, I'm sure you've heard the tales of Arawn coming to take away babies and kids, right?"

Maeve gulped, her stomach too sour to eat more of her wrap. "I remember, yes."

"Well, those are *kind of* rooted in truth."

"What?" Her voice was embarrassingly squeaky.

"Now, he doesn't *eat* them, contrary to what some would have you believe." She rolled her eyes. "And he doesn't steal them either. Most of them are surrendered these days." Her tone became quieter. "Or tossed away like garbage."

Her chest tightened. "Were you?"

"Pretty much. It's what happens when you're a half-breed in our world." Lucía's soft features hardened. "Neither side of your family wants you."

"I'm sorry."

Lucía cut a glance at Maeve, a smile gentling her expression. "Yeah, well, I always say they wouldn't have been able to handle my awesomeness anyway."

"Why are…half-breeds despised like that?"

A snort. "Obsession with blood purity isn't just a thing among humans. Otherworld creatures are just as stupid about it. Shifters only mate with shifters, some even only with those who change into the same animal, and don't even get me started on demons. Oh, and when you happen to have some *human* in you, you might as well crawl into the sewer to die." She shook her head.

"Used to be," Lucía went on, "those kids were killed right after birth. Or just kicked out into the elements. Now, some give them to Arawn. As a sacrifice? I don't know. It's not widely known that he doesn't eat them, so maybe these morons think they're truly appeasing the Demon Lord by offering him a snack or something."

Maeve shuddered at the thought. "And he just raises them?"

"Not himself. He's got a system of foster families. The kids grow up to work for him, mostly. Some might say he raises them to be in his service. I'd say he gives them a home, a life, and a purpose. I wouldn't be alive if it weren't for him." She took another bite of her almost-finished wrap. "Like I said, there's always two ways to look at something."

Maeve considered that for a moment, then filed it away to revisit later. "You mentioned you're a half-breed…" She trailed off, glancing at Lucía, unsure if it was even polite to ask an otherworld creature what exactly they were.

"Yup. Demon-shifter hybrid." She finished her meal, dusted off her hands and grinned at Maeve. "Wanna see my animal?"

"Um. Sure. If it's not too—"

"Pfft." Lucía waved that away. "One thing you gotta learn about shifters. We're super eager to show off our second skin. We're kinda vain that way."

The other woman shrugged out of her jacket and pulled off her T-shirt, completely unabashed. Maeve startled and jerked her head in the other direction, staring intently at the spiraling, uncurling ferns. The sound of more clothes rustling, boots thudding on the forest floor, followed by a shift in the air. The hair on Maeve's arms and neck rose, goosebumps cascading over her skin.

And then…the sleek beauty of sandy fur, of massive strength poured into a supple body of feline perfection.

Even with the forewarning and knowledge that this was Lucía, Maeve winced and drew back, her heart thundering with visceral fear at the sight of the kind of predator any sensible person should run from. Or not, given that a mountain lion could easily chase them down. Swallowing hard, Maeve dug her fingers in the moss on the log and forced herself to remain in place.

Her eyes the same pale green in this form, Lucía cocked her head in a distinctly feline way, and Maeve could have sworn her expression bordered on smug. She padded closer, close enough to touch if Maeve were to reach out and run her fingers through that soft-looking fur.

A rumbling sound filled the air. Maeve blinked.

"I didn't know cougars could purr," she said.

Lucía uttered a hoarse squeak, followed by what could only be described as puma chatter. Even in this form, the woman was talkative.

"You're very pretty," Maeve murmured.

That purr took on a decidedly cocky note. Lucía rubbed her cheek against Maeve's shin, first one, then the other, before she sauntered over to a tree and scratched it, stretching herself and arching her spine. Muscles rippled under her beige-brown fur, a whisper of lethal elegance. A second later, the air shimmered around her like a desert mirage, and Maeve quickly looked away as Lucía changed back.

Her puma's purr still in her throat, she dressed and sat down next to Maeve again. "Hm, that stretch was good. I gotta go for a run later and work out some more kinks." She rolled her shoulders.

"Do you hunt in this shape?"

A grin that showed partial fangs. "Sure do."

Maeve raised her brows. "So what is your demon side?" She bit her lip. "Sorry if that's not polite to ask. You don't have to tell me…"

"Nah, I'd rather show you." She bumped her shoulder against Maeve's. "But we gotta wait till the sun goes down."

Right. Demon powers were bound to the night, lay dormant during the day. Not that it had stopped—

"Night's over," he rasped, breath fanning against her sweat-slick skin, *"but the fun's not."*

The light of the lone bulb glinted off the blade.

"Lucky for you, I'm not tired yet."

Her hands jerked against the shackles, the metal biting into her wrists, rubbing over the raw wounds from her struggles.

She wouldn't scream, not this time. That only egged him on. She wouldn't scream, wouldn't scream—

The knife sliced into her thigh.

And her scream filled the warehouse.

"Maeve!"

Shadows and light, mist and memory, her brain caught up in horrors she couldn't shake.

Someone shook her.

Hands on her shoulders. Different. Finer, not as rough. A face came into focus. Warm brown skin, elegant dark brows drawn together over luminous light green eyes, mouth pinched in a tight line.

Maeve hauled in a breath that hurt in her entire chest, her heartbeat an erratic drum rhythm in her head, in the tingling in her limbs. Something salty coated her lips. *Tears.*

"Hey." Lucía squeezed her shoulders. "Hey. You back? Look at me."

"I'm...fine." Her throat felt like a cheese grater had done a number on it.

"No, you're not." Lucía's voice was gentle despite her words. "I know you're not. And you don't have to act like you are. I underst—"

"I want to go back. To my room." She needed to take a shower.

Maeve made a small move, and Lucía immediately let her hands fall from her shoulders, withdrew a bit to allow Maeve to stand up. Not looking at the other woman, Maeve turned toward the path leading back to the underground lair.

For the first time that day, Lucía followed her in silence.

CHAPTER 7

Having spent an inordinate amount of time in the bathroom—until the water pattering down on her bowed back ran cold and she shivered from something other than the terror of her memories—Maeve dried off and dressed quickly in the matching long sleeve shirt and ankle-length pajama pants.

She used to sleep in the nude before, but after the warehouse...she couldn't stomach it anymore. The feeling of sheets on her naked body could set off some of her worst panic attacks.

She crawled onto the bed and eyed the crystals in the walls. How was she supposed to turn them off? Did she want them off?

She swallowed past a thick throat. The bulb in the warehouse...sometimes it was on, sometimes not. Both light and darkness held horror, and there was no safe way she could go to sleep here. Maybe she should just ask Arawn—

No. She shook her head as if to clear it.

Pathetic, to be so limited by one's fear. She could do this. Her fingers curled into her palms.

"It's all in my head," she whispered to herself, lay down on the silky-soft pillow, and closed her eyes.

The fresh scent of the laundry detergent used for the bedsheets tickled her nose, mixed with the dark aroma of the earth and the lingering humidity from her shower. *This is different*, she reminded herself. *A different room. A different place. I'm safe here.*

She kept repeating it like a mantra against the shadows of her past until she slipped into sleep's arms…into a nightmare that shattered the tenuous calm in her mind, sliced her open with glinting blades, fangs piercing her skin, a voice that soured her blood, iced her bones.

His hands on her, his fingers digging in, taking what he had no right to. Powerless, she thrashed, thrashed, struggled and screamed against those hands—

Wake up!

The voice came from far away, drifting through mist. Not *his* voice.

And yet the heat of him still branded her skin, and she couldn't breathe, gasped for air—

"Maeve!"

Her eyes flew open, her pulse jackhammering. The light blinded her, the world spinning.

A shape in front of her. *Above* her…

Fire licked out from her core.

The blaze erupted in an explosion of sparks and flames and scorching heat, and in the second before it engulfed the person leaning over her, Maeve saw her face.

Lucía.

The force of the firewall rolling out from Maeve hurled the other woman off the bed. The storm of flames and heat built, until the swirling dance of sparks and waves of fire eclipsed everything else.

"No," Maeve whimpered, crawling over the burning bed, her clothes turned to ash—her body untouched.

She couldn't see Lucía through the blaze, couldn't see anything but destruction in shades of orange-red. *No, please.*

Tendrils of darkness shot into the room, chill and smooth, dousing the flames. The fire died down, extinguished on a hush. Sudden gloom spread like ink thrown into water, and even the crystals in the walls lost their light. Power drenched the air, familiar through the beacon of it inside Maeve, and when her eyes adjusted to the dimness, the contours of a man's shape loomed against the low light of the hall.

"Maeve," Arawn said, and stepped into the room still dipped in shadows.

His power brushed her mind, a gentle mental touch, not intruding, more like a cursory pat-down to check for injuries. He withdrew his psychic presence, apparently satisfied that she was in one piece.

Unlike someone else in the room. *Oh, gods…Lucía…*

Maeve smothered a sob, scooted off the other side of the charred bed and hid behind it, too self-conscious about her bare, scarred body even in the darkness. "Lucía. The fire…she…"

"…should have handled it," Arawn grumbled.

What?

"After all," Arawn went on, lighting up the crystals in the walls with a lazy wave of his hand, his face half turned away, "she was trained for this. Wasn't she?"

The question held a pointed edge, and seemed directed at the opposite wall—no, at the crumpled female shape on the floor in front of it. The shape stirred, and Lucía groaned as she sat up. She was naked, too, her clothes incinerated like Maeve's, but she kept her private body parts hidden by her drawn-up legs in front of her.

Maeve's jaw dropped as she studied her, the unburned skin, the unsinged hair. "How…?"

"I didn't see that coming," Lucía rasped.

"You should have." The soft light of the crystals bathed Arawn's harsh features in a gentle glow.

Maeve swallowed, gaze trained on the other woman. "Your demon power...it's..."

"Fire," Lucía confirmed. One side of her mouth tipped up in a wry half smile. "I really wanted to show you, but look how utterly I failed. If I'd known you'd explode like that, I'd have been able to contain it. It just happened too fast."

Arawn tsked. "Lousy excuse. You are getting out of shape."

"Fine." Lucía rolled her eyes and blew a lock of her midnight hair out of her face. "I may have let my training slide a bit. I was just surprised, is all."

Arawn shot her a dark look, the muscles in his shoulders flexing underneath his tailored shirt as he slid his hands in the pockets of his black pants. He jerked his head toward the door, and with a sigh, Lucía shifted into her cougar and padded out of the room.

Maeve shivered on the bare floor behind the bed and hugged herself. "You knew this was going to happen," she whispered to Arawn, having read the subtleties in his demeanor.

"Eventually," he replied without looking at her, instead examining the devastation of the room—burned furniture, smoking piles of ash, blackened walls and ceiling, the decorative branches charred. "I did not think it would occur so soon."

She realized with a start that he kept his eyes averted on purpose, a shred of decency which would have surprised her a day ago. But she'd since had a few perplexing glimpses into aspects of his character that contradicted his reputation.

"I didn't mean to...do that." She hugged herself tighter, a part of her still marveling at the fact she was unscathed while the rest of her drowned in embarrassment.

"No." Arawn prodded a heap of ash with his shoe. "You were defending yourself."

She blinked. Thought back to the sequence of events, what had triggered the outburst. Eyes filling with tears, she shook her head, her voice thick. "But that's never happened before. Not even when…" *I would have needed it most.*

Arawn stared down at the blackened floor, his expression thoughtful.

Lucía sauntered back into the room, now in human form —dressed—and carrying a bunch of folded clothes and a pair of shoes.

"Here," she said and handed Maeve the new clothes. "Your wardrobe's turned to ash, I'm afraid, but I think some of my stuff should fit you, at least for the time being. It's all fresh out of the laundry. We can go shopping tomorrow—"

"We will have something delivered," Arawn cut in, his tone brooking no argument.

Lucía slanted a glance at him, but he'd already turned toward the door.

"Get dressed. Meet me outside." He strolled out.

"I'll wait for you in the hall," Lucía murmured to Maeve, and followed Arawn out of the room, closing the busted-down door as completely as possible. Lucía must have rammed it open when she tried to get in.

Did she hear Maeve screaming during the nightmare?

She'd been doing better at the Murrays, hadn't had an incident this bad in weeks. Well, she'd never had one *this* bad, anyway… Burning down a room? Inconceivable. She never had access to her powers after her grandmother bound them inside her, not even subconsciously. If she did, that fucker of a demon would have died a fiery death before he ever got her to the warehouse.

No, her magic—the special, *special* magic that was the reason the demon abducted her—had never done *shit* for her.

She could have died in that hellhole, and her powers would have continued to slumber, locked away beyond her reach.

Bitterness coated her tongue and curdled her stomach as she quickly pulled on the loose yoga pants, T-shirt, socks, and sneakers. The clothes were a bit too big for her—she and Lucía might be the same height, but the demon-shifter packed more muscle, despite looking delicate—but it would do.

Her attention snagged on one of the heaps of ash in the room, and her heart sank. Her duffel bag had been cremated, including its contents. She hadn't fully unpacked yet, and when she went to take a closer look at the pile, she could make out the melted remains of her cell phone.

So much for maybe trying to call Merle tomorrow. She'd forgotten the phone in the room when she went out with Lucía earlier in the day, and only remembered when they'd already wandered so far it seemed impractical to turn around to retrieve it. She hadn't even gotten the chance to check whether she could get a signal above ground.

Dammit.

Something else poked out of the ash pile, and it stopped her cold when she understood what it was. She sank down next to the heap, pulled with shaking fingers until she held what remained of the picture frame she'd brought. The metal frame had survived, but the glass had shattered, the back had burned, and the photo...was incinerated as well.

Nothing left of the picture showing her family before death and destruction ripped them apart. She used a finger to trace the vanished lines and shapes as she remembered them. The open, warm smile of her mom, her dad's more reserved joy, Moira with a glint in her eye contrary to her serious attitude as the oldest sister, spunky Merle, her strong, dignified grandma, and little Maeve, beaming, in the middle. Only three of them still lived—Merle, Maeve, and their dad—the MacKenna family decimated and broken. And now...only Merle was officially a MacKenna by blood.

No. There's one more.

Maeve smiled through tears at the thought of the spark of hope Merle was carrying, the future of their family.

Her chest tight with both joy and grief, she let the ruined picture frame fall onto the ashes and walked out to join Lucía.

⚜

"You shouldn't have given her a room down here, without windows," Lucía said as soon as the door closed behind her.

Arawn leaned against the wall, arms crossed. His ward certainly never missed an opportunity to call him out.

"It was obvious she was uncomfortable when she walked in," Lucía pushed on, hands on her hips. "Which, considering where that scum of a demon held her, makes sense, and you know it. Why put her down here in the first place?"

His mouth twitched the tiniest bit. "You two seem to have bonded well today."

"You saw how she reacted when she entered that room."

He sighed. Of course she didn't take the bait. *Feline obstinacy.*

"Why didn't you—"

"What I saw," he interrupted her tirade, "was someone on the brink of implosion, not because of too much pressure, but rather due to lack thereof. Someone who had, by fault of good intentions, been treated like the burned corners of a parchment which might disintegrate at the slightest draft. Someone in need of *some* pressure, so she can discover for herself what she is capable of enduring, instead of others deciding it for her."

Lucía stared at him with her most thunderstruck expression. She blinked several times before she apparently regained her ability to speak. He tried not to feel smug about

robbing her of speech for a good half minute—a new record?
—and barely held back his smirk.

"Sometimes," she said, "I forget what a sly jerk you are."

He could count the number of people who could get away
with calling him that on one hand without even using all his
fingers. Lucía was one of the lucky few, and she knew it.

"So *you* decided for her by putting her down here," she
poked further.

"No, I gave her a choice. The chance to take another room,
or to try to make it work with this one."

"Well, it obviously *didn't* work."

"Which is another matter."

She huffed, mirrored his pose with folded arms, shoulder
to the wall. "And now?"

"Now," he said, angling his head toward the room, having
picked up on Maeve's movement inside, "you can take off for
the rest of the night. I will handle it from here."

She narrowed her eyes and lifted her chin, looking down
her nose at him the way she'd been doing since she was three
years old and too innocent and adorable to realize she was
glaring at the Demon Lord himself, fully capable of killing her
with a thought. Some days, her still-irreverent and haughty
glare was his greatest source of amusement.

"Mmm-hmm," she eventually hummed in that puzzling
way which seemingly encompassed a whole essay of judgment in two syllables, and stalked off to her room.

He rubbed the bridge of his nose with his fingers, one arm
still crossed over his chest.

Maeve exited her room a moment later, Lucía's clothes a
tad too large for her, making her look even more delicate than
usual. Pieces of ash still clung to her unbound hair, the
tumble of red strands a visual reminder of the fire inside her
core. A streak of soot decorated her cheek, and he fought the
urge to wipe it away.

She wouldn't meet his gaze, arms folded, posture defensive, pulse a fast tick in her neck.

He did not want to lick that spot.

Did. Not.

"For obvious reasons," he said, watching her come to attention without actually moving—she was *good* at that—her nostrils flaring a bit, "you cannot use this room any longer."

She swallowed, copper lashes fluttering. An open book, that's what she was, her thoughts and emotions spelled out in detail, even without him accessing her mind. She was waiting for him to say it, to ask her if she now wanted a room with windows, forcing her to admit to her weakness in front of him, to declare defeat in the face of her nightmares.

And she would hate having to agree with him. She was starting to quiver, her mouth pinched, her amber-gray eyes— reminiscent of the fire and smoke she called upon—glazing with a sheen of unspilled tears. The subtleties of psychology… It was one thing for her trauma to have shown itself so clearly in her outburst, but it would be worse for her to actually say it.

Pride was such a brittle thing, wasn't it? Right now hers was already shredded. He wouldn't rip it further, not for this.

He inclined his head. "I would offer you another room down here so you can be close to Lucía's quarters. Unfortunately, all the others are currently occupied or not adequate for your needs. I will have to relocate you to a different area, where I can make the necessary adjustments in light of your emerging powers." He paused, studying her closely. "Those quarters are above ground."

Her head jerked the tiniest bit, and she glanced at him. So quickly, the contact there and gone, her eyes lowered again the next second. His fingers twitched with the impulse to lift her chin, make her look at him once more, longer.

"Follow me," he ordered and walked ahead, his gait brisk.

Her scent was tickling his nose, unbidden and quite distracting. *Fire and wind, licked by sweetness.*

The patter of her soft-soled sneakers trailed behind him as he led her through the underground halls and up a winding staircase ending in a massive oak which he still remembered as a seedling. From there he guided her farther into the forest, fireflies swirling around them, and halted in front of the short wooden hanging bridge that connected this slope to a cabin propped on sturdy pillars, wedged between two large firs.

It wasn't a true tree house, its other side half attached to the rising forest floor behind it, and the drop to the ground from the front veranda was barely six feet. A string of fairy lights hung above the bridge, illuminating the wooden planks, and crystals cast a soft glow in the interior, visible through the huge windows taking up most of the walls.

Maeve paused next to him, her breath fogging in the chill of the night, her eyes on the small domicile. He gestured for her go ahead, and after a second of hesitation, she grabbed the rope railing of the bridge and carefully made her way to the veranda. He followed, the bridge swinging with his steps, and watched while she walked into the one-room cabin.

Big enough to accommodate a king-size bed, a couch and table, as well as a tiny kitchenette, the house also featured a private bathroom with functioning facilities. He might like the outdoors, and have lived through the age before plumbing, but he still appreciated modern amenities where applicable.

Maeve turned in a circle and studied the open windows. They were truly open. As in, literally, no glass. Would she ask...?

"Who worked this magic?" She'd raised her hand to one of the windows, her face holding a quiet sense of wonder as her fingers passed the invisible barrier that kept the warmth inside the cabin.

"Your sister."

Her expression shattered into sorrow, quick and piercing. She withdrew her hand, lowered her eyes.

"The cabin is also heavily warded," he said, "and nothing —or no one—from the outside can reach through those windows or the door. Unless you wish it."

A slanted glance at him. "Even you?"

He raised a brow. "If you tell me to stay out of this cabin, I won't set foot in it. This is your space." Turning to the door, he added, "I do, however, expect you to come out when I request it, and I have no qualms about *compelling* you out, should you cloister yourself in here."

When she sent him a withering look—a spark of hidden temper showing—he paused and prowled back to her, so close that she inched to the side. And yet her scent remained free of fear, even as he loomed over her.

"You are mine now," he said in a low voice that seemed to cause a tremor in her, "and one thing I will not allow is for you to revert to a living vegetable, never leaving your room." He mapped her face as he spoke, noted the tiniest twitch of each muscle in reaction to his declaration. "Fire needs air to breathe. And yours has been choked long enough."

Those copper lashes quivered again, and her lips parted on a soft inhale. For a searing, short-lived moment, she met his gaze full-on...and his magic blazed inside him, as if in answer to hers. Something primal lurked in those eyes, age-old and feral, so similar to his own nature.

That quickly, the moment was over, the connection broken, and Maeve shifted away with the grace of a doe. "There's a lot of wood here," she said, her voice soft, "and I'm surrounded by trees. What if it happens again? Aren't you worried I'll start a wildfire?"

"*Worried* is not the word I would use. Eager may be more apt. Make no mistake—I *want* to see that wildfire of yours."

A delicate blush painted her cheeks.

"In any case, though," he continued, "it will be contained.

71

The wards are also meant to keep an explosion like this from spreading to the forest, and for tonight, I will stay close and cast additional protections. Tomorrow, we will start working on the spell that binds your powers."

She gave a jerky nod, frowned. "It's coming undone, isn't it?"

He inclined his head at her conclusion. "That seems to be the case, yes."

"Why now? It's held all these years."

There was no reason not to let her share in his own conclusions, since they affected her. "Your grandmother was the one who worked the spell, and I suspect there is a flaw in the magic she wrought that she could not have foreseen. If the spell she cast was bound to the MacKenna line, drawing on the family as a bond to keep the spell active even after her passing, it makes sense that it would disintegrate now."

A soft sound of dismay. "Because I'm not a MacKenna anymore."

"Severing the link may have loosened some of the shackles of the spell, causing tendrils of your powers to rise to the surface. Whether it is enough to make the entire spellwork unravel remains to be seen."

Her features slackened. "You call that explosion *tendrils*? What the hell will it look like when all of it bursts out?"

One side of his mouth lifted in a wry smile. "Perfection."

CHAPTER 8

Light and the chatter of birds pulled Maeve from her slumber.

She squinted at the sun streaming in through the huge, open windows, gilding the interior of the cabin. Fresh forest air filled the room, though the warmth remained inside, thanks to the spell on the windows.

Maeve closed her eyes again for a moment to simply enjoy the peace of the morning before reality could steamroll her. The cabin still stood. No more nightmares. No more fire. The bed was soft and welcoming, her body loose and rested, and she floated on the vanishing mist of a dream, impressions and feelings lingering.

She made a contented noise in the back of her throat and tried to remember the dream. The sensations remained so intense, her every cell felt branded with them—even though she couldn't recall a single detail. Just this overall drifting feeling…pleasant yet powerful. Weaving itself into every thought, every breath, an underlying rhythm she found herself chasing after.

She loved it when this happened, when the fragmented

memory of an elusive dream would whisper at her throughout the day, would color everything and change the way she walked, talked, thought, because the *feeling* wouldn't let her go, and she'd find herself pausing mid-sentence, a piece of memory suddenly returned, tumbling her further into reminiscence.

With a yawn, she eventually rolled out of bed. She showered again last night before going to sleep because ash still coated her skin, and she didn't want to dirty the sheets. And she'd thoroughly beaten the pajama set to remove any remnants of soot before slipping into bed.

She opened the door to the veranda, and stopped short, studying the tray of covered food and the pile of clothes in front of her feet.

A piece of paper was tucked under the thermos that—by the faint trace of its scent—contained coffee. She picked up the thermos and the note, opening the latter.

I will meet you here at twelve. Be ready.

— A

She jerked as a detail of the elusive dream flashed before her inner eye, flooded her with a sensual memory that short-circuited her brain.

Her fingers running over dark bronze skin. Heat and friction, murmured teasing. Lips on her shoulder, trailing down to her breasts. She shivered and burned—for all the right reasons. Shadowy green eyes intent in a face of harsh angles, solely focused on her. "I want to see that wildfire of yours."

The thermos slipped from her hand. Hit the floor with a metallic clank, bounced and landed with another thud on her foot.

"Ouch!"

She jumped back with a wince, bit her lip and fell on her butt, holding her foot to alleviate the pain. The hurt, however, wasn't sharp enough to eclipse the surge of tangled emotions at the realization that—

"Oh. My. Gods."

She buried her face in her hands. Shook her head. Didn't help. She still remembered.

I had an erotic dream about Arawn.

Heat shot into her neck, her cheeks, her ears, and she half expected the cabin to catch fire after all. Would serve her right.

This was not possible. She couldn't—why would she—?

"What is *wrong* with me?"

With a groan, she thumped her forehead against the hardwood floor. More images from the dream floated up, turned her blood to liquid fire, heat blooming between her legs. She couldn't shake the *desire* hammering under her skin, the pleasure at his imagined touch.

Her heart went quiet as a realization swept through her. In that dream, while being intimate in a situation that was a minefield of potential triggers, she was...completely free of fear.

Slowly, she sat up, staring unseeing out at the veranda and the forest beyond, her mind numb with surprise. After the warehouse, the only dreams she had involving sexual action were the nightmares that woke her up soaked in a cold sweat and sent her running to the bathroom to puke her guts out. As twisted as it was, her mind apparently conflated sex—the good kind—with the terror and pain she experienced shackled to that bed, unable to differentiate between the two.

She'd expected the first dream of *consensual* sex to be fraught with the same kind of fear and hesitation she struggled with in her waking life whenever her thoughts turned to intimacy. But in this dream...there was only lust, and pleasure. Nothing but sensual hunger and open enjoyment, and the ability to let herself fall—knowing he'd catch her.

Something tracked down her cheeks. When she touched it, her finger came away wet. She hauled in a shaky breath, her chest *aching*. For what she'd lost, for what had been ripped from her. That kind of trust and easiness, the ability to sink into intimacy, untainted by fear and the dark specter of her trauma. Would she ever get it back?

This dream was cruel. A taste of what she might never reclaim, mocking her with how easy it seemed. She craved it so much, her entire body shook, her heart clenching in pain.

I want this.

But not with Arawn. Never him.

She rose to her feet, balled her hands to fists. He was all sorts of wrong for her. She could never…the very idea was ridiculous.

Liar, a tiny voice inside her piped up, and pointed to the fresh memory of her dream, of skin on skin, and dark power stroking her senses with a mental caress, of rough fingers running up her thighs and—

"Oh, would you stop!"

She made a frustrated sound and scrubbed her face.

No, even if she was ready to reclaim her sexuality, she should do so with a man who was patient, loving, understanding, kind, gentle, and *safe.* Arawn couldn't be more opposite. The surprising glimpses she caught of a different side of him notwithstanding, he lived and breathed ruthless power, oozing authority and dominance, and an underlying aura of danger. She should *definitely* not be thinking about inviting him to her bed.

All that aside, he also seemed to be either extremely long-lived or even immortal. No one really knew, and rumors were all she had to go on here, but one thing was crystal clear—to him, human-length lives like hers had to be little more than a blip on the radar, so ephemeral as to be hardly worthy of attention. Being intimate with her would only be a fleeting pastime for him, a passing fancy maybe. But for Maeve…it would mean a hell of a lot more.

She couldn't do casual sex. Lily had always been good at that, and Maeve had secretly admired her ability to enjoy brief, strings-free intimacy. For Maeve, though, opening her body to someone required not just desire, but strong affection and deep trust, which took time to build. And that hadn't changed, was now even more paramount in light of what she'd been through.

No way could she jump into a casual sexual relationship now, and especially not for the first intimate contact after her torture. But being with Arawn could never be more than that, and she refused to be an immortal's short-lived plaything.

So, yeah, that stupid sex dream could just suck it up and stop haunting her already.

Huffing out a breath, she picked up the thermos and the note again, and paused. There was something else written on it she didn't notice before.

PS: Lucía will keep you company tonight. For today you will have another guard, who will stay out of sight unless you wish otherwise. His name is Kelior, and he is within shouting distance if you need anything.

Her stomach cramped. A male guard. Her anxiety spiked at the mere thought of an unknown man in her vicinity.

Closing her eyes, she took a deep breath, tried to calm her nerves. If Arawn picked the guy to guard her, he'd be safe. No need to get all scared.

Still, she couldn't help scanning the surrounding trees for any sign of the male's presence while she scooped up the clothes, plopped them on the bed, and carried the tray of food to the table. Sitting down in the breakfast nook, she uncovered the plates—and froze.

All the things she liked for breakfast, including hash browns with applesauce, cooked rolled oats with honey and blueberries, and cut pieces of honeydew melon. Her heartbeat pounded in her ears.

Arawn sure had learned about her through the eyes of his sentinels guarding her the past half year. What else did he know about her that she wouldn't have guessed? How much had he seen of her, and how much figured out?

Well, he definitely knows how to play your body like a harp, that tiny, annoying voice inside her spoke up again.

"That was a *dream*!" she shouted and thumped her head against the table.

CHAPTER 9

"I still say it's a trap," Rhun grumbled from the driver's seat.

Merle sighed and rubbed her forehead. "I know. I'm wary, too, okay? But this is still our best chance for peace."

Pale blue-green eyes met hers, the intensity in them jolting. "You could have at least pressed her for a meeting time at night. If something goes wrong in there, I can't help you with my demon powers." He paused. "Although I will enjoy ripping Juneau to shreds with my bare hands if I get a chance today."

He had a point there. Lily and Alek had to stay home altogether since they couldn't even risk the exposure to sunlight. And considering that Merle wouldn't be able to use her magic if push came to shove…

But— "You're acting like I'm not joining up with half a dozen other Elder witches, who each pack enough of a punch to splinter your spine with less than a thought. If something goes wrong, we'll have enough firepower on our side to get out of there."

"You're short on numbers, though." A somber statement,

his concentration steady on the road. "With Hazel still gone, and you unable to tap your magic, Juneau has two more witches ready to fight."

She grabbed his hand over the console, squeezed. "Nothing will happen to me. Or our baby. We'll just see what Juneau has to say, and—the gods willing—we can end this damn conflict and unite the witch community again."

His mouth pinched into a tight line. "Those gods don't have a very good track record for working in our favor, little witch."

She didn't reply, only squeezed his hand again, stewing in her own thoughts until they reached the pre-meeting place where she would join up with the others from Aequitas. They'd walk to the spot of the proper meeting together, having decided that to arrive as one was the safest bet.

Last night Merle convened a quick meeting with the other Elders on her side to discuss their response to Juneau's call for a talk. Turned out the other heads-of-family had received the same letter as the Murrays—and Merle had, indeed, found one at her own home as well.

Hazel's continued absence was a hot topic, and even though it would be highly inconvenient to attend the meeting with the Draconians—the names had been accepted as fitting by the rest of the Elders—without Hazel, everybody agreed that postponing the meeting for an indefinite amount of time might be too risky. They had no idea when Hazel would be back. If it took a week or more, would Juneau change her mind in the meantime?

Better to meet now and grab this chance at peace, even if it meant Juneau would realize they were one witch short.

Rhun parked the car in the lot of a small business park, and Merle walked ahead to the group of the witches already present, standing next to the distinctive bright red truck belonging to Patricia, the head of the Jones family. They waited a few minutes for the last one, Kristen Frost, to arrive, and then made their way down a few blocks to the small city park where the meeting with Juneau was supposed to take place.

They'd all agreed on a public venue in the bustle of the city. Less likely for any of them to resort to violence with so many humans around. If there was one thing Aequitas and Draconians *both* still cared about, it was safeguarding the human population.

Additionally, wards would keep the peace of the meeting, and all participants were to swear an oath not to harm each other for this conference.

"How are you feeling?" Elaine, head of the Donovan family, asked as they walked together.

The other Elder was privy to Merle's pregnancy, being one of the witches Merle trusted completely. Elaine was the one who walked out of the final Elder meeting convened before the community broke apart, after Juneau declared both Hazel and Merle traitors to witchkind for their refusal to hand over Lily after she was turned into a demon. Elaine had also called Juneau a warmongering bitch on her way out, making no bones about the fact that she couldn't stand the attitude and tactics of the head of the Laroche family. Half the Elders followed Elaine's lead, and thus the two factions came into being.

"Pretty good, actually," Merle replied. "The nausea's not too bad."

Elaine nodded, her chin-length brown hair bobbing with the motion. "Let me know if it gets worse, and I can have Becky help you out a little."

Becky Donovan, third daughter of Elaine, was one of the most talented healer witches in the community, her gentle nature never failing to calm anyone, often just by being in the same room.

"Thanks." Merle gave the older woman a smile, her heart stinging a bit despite the friendly offer.

Usually this kind of caring for a pregnant witch's needs was done by the head of the family, or other, older female relatives.

Merle didn't have anyone like that anymore. She was the oldest witch in her family—with no mother, older sister, or grandmother left to care for her needs. It was a selfish hurt, but it hurt nonetheless.

They neared the arranged meeting place, a cluster of picnic tables and benches under the cover of looming firs in the small city park. Such an innocuous backdrop for what promised to be tense negotiations between warring fronts. The Draconians were all present already, waiting in a half circle for the others to approach. Merle nodded at Rhun, and her darling demon fell back to take position under a nearby tree, watching the meeting from there.

A few humans mingled in the park, but kept conspicuously clear of the meeting area—likely held at bay by repellent wards so they couldn't overhear what wasn't meant for their ears.

Juneau's white hair gleamed in the sun as she raised her chin, watched the Aequitas draw closer. Around Merle, the rising power of the Elders on her side filled the air, the witches preparing for defense. Should one of the Draconians make a move, they'd be ready.

"Welcome," Juneau called out. "Before we start, let us swear to keep the peace for this meeting."

Nodding all around.

"We vow," Juneau continued, "not to use magic or other weapons to harm another witch for the duration of this meeting. By staying within the lines of these wards"—she indicated the shimmering perimeter—"we all agree to be bound by this promise."

Again, all witches present nodded their consent, some saying, "Aye."

"Good," Elaine spoke up. "Let's get started then."

Juneau sent her a cold glance. "I called this meeting in a heartfelt effort to reunite what should never have been broken. Our community depends on the strength of our union to survive. We cannot afford to remain splintered in the face of our enemies."

Merle's heart beat faster with foolish hope. Maybe, just *maybe*, Juneau had come to her senses and let go of her irrational bigotry...

"We agree," Hanna chimed in. The head of the Roth family stood next to Merle, arms crossed, tight brown curls pulled back into a thick ponytail. "It's time we settled this. Amicably."

Murmured assent in the ranks of both parties.

Juneau smiled, though her expression lacked any warmth. "I am happy to see reason returned to those of you who broke away."

Merle gritted her teeth to bite back her tart retort to that underhanded accusation. As if the witches of the Aequitas were errant children who ran away from home on a misguided impulse. Elaine seemed about ready to lunge at Juneau for that comment alone, judging from the way Kristen, head of the Frost family, had to soothingly hold her back with a hand on her arm.

"I think it only reasonable then," Juneau went on, "that you will meet our conditions for mending the rift within our midst."

Merle's spine locked. *"Conditions?"*

The glint in Juneau's deep green eyes was merciless. "There are laws to be upheld, dear. You will surrender Lily Murray for the assault on my granddaughter Selene, as is right for the initial transgression she committed. Further, you will also hand over Basil Murray for the murder of Elder Catarina Gutierrez, as well as the demon mate of Lily, for the murder of Elder Birgit Meyer."

Merle's blood froze.

"Since it is not clear," Juneau kept talking over Merle's shock, "whether it was Merle MacKenna or Hazel Murray who killed Elder Eva Baldwin, we shall conduct an interrogation to find out which of you cast the killing spell, and bring the one responsible to justice."

Gehenna. She was talking about the Battle of Gehenna, that violent, bloody altercation they had weeks ago, named after the demon bar near where it took place. Juneau, with the backup of four other Elder witches, jumped Merle, Hazel, Basil, and Rhun as they were following the trace of Lily's kidnapping at the hands of the demons who had turned her.

"We were defending ourselves," Merle gritted out, barely able to speak past the thundering of her heart, the outraged shaking in her limbs. "How dare you throw that back at us when you were the one who drew first blood?"

The coldness in Juneau's gaze could have iced over the air. "I did no such thing."

Merle let out a dry laugh. "Oh, really? May I remind you that you *viciously attacked my husband Rhun in front of me?*"

After which all hell had broken loose, both Basil and Hazel firing back at Juneau while Merle tended to Rhun, Alek joining the fight later, the snowball of aggression rolling up into an avalanche of violence with lethal consequences for Juneau's side. The three witches died as a direct result of Juneau's initial strike against Rhun.

"He is a demon," Juneau hissed, "and we are not obliged to protect him, not even through that supposed loophole you used. Marriage to an Elder witch might ward humans against aggression by other witches, but that law does not apply to demons."

"That is a lie." Merle took a step forward. "I read the law. It doesn't exclude demons."

"It does not mention them," Juneau shot back, "because it is implicit that they are the enemy, and therefore do not fall under our protection."

Merle balled her hands to fists. "That is *your* interpretation."

"It is the underlying logic of *all* our laws." Juneau's features hardened. "And speaking of which... The fact that you should be brought to justice if it was your spell that killed Eva notwithstanding, if you want peace for our community, you will annul your marriage to that demon and break the mating bond, as will the young *chaya darshini* of the Gupta family."

Shobha Gupta came to attention. Her gray-streaked dark hair pulled into a chignon, she angled her head, her shrewd eyes narrowing. "I beg your pardon?"

Juneau faced the other Elder. "Your granddaughter's aberrant relationship with a demon should never have been permitted. It is against our nature, against everything we ever stood for as a community. We cannot condone fraternization between witches and demons any longer. Our community will remain divided unless we eliminate this dangerous sickness before it spreads even further."

"That *aberrant relationship*," Shobha said with lethal quiet, "saved my Anjali's life. I might have agreed with you not too long ago, but it was before I saw with my own eyes how someone I considered my enemy all my life makes my granddaughter happier than she has ever been. I will not order her to leave him. He is part of our family."

It might have taken Shobha months to grudgingly accept Thorne into her folds, from what Merle had heard, but once she took someone in, she did so for life. The Guptas were notorious for their family loyalty.

"And I will *never* give up Rhun," Merle said, shaking so hard her teeth clattered.

A muscle ticked in Juneau's jaw. "Then there is no ground for peace."

Heavy silence fell after those words. The air stood still, thick with gathering magic.

Merle took a slow step back, her eyes fixed on Juneau, her stomach a tight knot. "You swore not to harm us here."

The other Elders of the Aequitas closed ranks around her, muscles tensed.

Juneau's smile was serpentine. "I swore not to harm another witch."

Merle's heart stopped cold. Her breath stuck in her lungs, she whirled around, toward the spot several yards away where Rhun stood—*had been standing*.

He convulsed on the ground, spittle frothing around his mouth, face pale. Three witches rushed toward him from their hiding places in the park—which was wiped clear of humans now, an eerie quiet settling.

Merle's stomach lurched. *"Rhun!"*

She ran toward him, only to collide with an invisible wall right at the line of the wards. A barrier. That bitch had snuck a magical barrier into the perimeter of the meeting.

She pivoted to Juneau again, wanted to hurl her power at her, consequences be damned...and found her magic bound by the oath she took. She couldn't harm Juneau. Not in here. And she couldn't go outside the circle either.

The other Elders of the Aequitas strained against the peace vow as well, exertion hardening their faces.

"Stop this!" Merle yelled. "Let him go!"

At least it looked like the Draconians were indeed bound by the same oath—they had yet to attack the Aequitas.

"You cannot fight us here," Juneau said, much too calm for the uproar around her. "And I don't want you to. I want you to consider the consequences of your refusal to uphold our laws. We will leave here, and so will you, and you will take some time to rethink your irrational behavior. When you have come to your senses, we will be ready to accept your surrender to justice."

She nodded at the three witches holding Rhun. IIe had

gone limp, his skin coated with sweat, and they had tied him up with what looked like magical shackles.

"Meanwhile," Juneau added, "we will take that obnoxious demon husband of yours. As an incentive, as a warning." She tilted her head, raised her brows. "Agree to our terms promptly, and we might let him go. You will still need to divorce him, of course. But the longer you take to surrender to our laws, the more he will suffer."

Merle didn't weep as they dragged Rhun away. She didn't sob, didn't crumple at the raging pain inside her. No. Her blood burning in her veins with the power of her line, she turned to Juneau, spit in her face and yelled, "*I will rain hellfire on you!*"

CHAPTER 10

By the time noon came around, Maeve had managed to convince herself that dreams were but shadows and lies, and she was going to be composed and rational and not be bothered by the illusions of some deranged part of her mind.

And it all went to hell the second Arawn strolled up to her cabin.

The sunlight filtering through the canopy stroked over his face, his neck, over the bit of skin exposed by the open top button of his dark green shirt. He had the sleeves rolled up to his elbows again, baring forearms twice the size of hers, a perfect example of muscle definition and brute beauty. He moved with lethal grace, every inch the predator, each step steeped in the sure knowledge he owned everything around him.

Leashed power in the tension of his muscles, in the slow, controlled thrusts that brought her to the precipice, held *her there, teetering on the edge, shivering under the searing focus that stripped her bare, soaked up every part of her, each tiny reaction, as if he were starving for grace and she his salvation...*

Her heart pounded so loud she didn't even hear his greeting.

"Hi," she squeaked.

Squeaked.

Her face burned, the sweater she wore suddenly much too hot, in spite of the chill in the winter air.

Arawn halted on the veranda, a few feet away, a curious glint in his eyes. He studied her, head to toe and back up again, undoubtedly noting every tiny tell.

He cocked a brow. "More bad dreams?"

Oh, gods, just kill me now… If her face got any hotter, she'd combust. Again.

She simply shrugged. Didn't trust herself to speak just yet.

"You did not incinerate the cabin," Arawn said, glancing inside. "I take that as an improvement."

"Um-hm."

Again, a probing look from him, those eyes of forest shadows far too discerning. "Ready for our session?"

I'm still reeling from a wholly different session we had, so…no?

"Sure," she rasped.

"Follow me." His voice was a rumble in the quiet of the woods.

She knew what the vibration of that voice felt like against her skin, against the sensitive spot at the apex of her thighs…

No, I don't! That was a dream, dammit.

She bit back a frustrated sound, so *irritated* with that stupid brain of hers. How hard could it be to keep reality and fantasy separate?

Fuming, she trailed behind him as he led her away from the cabin to a clearing with a waterfall tumbling into a small lake from a fern-covered ridge. A fox lay in the grass, her two half-grown pups tussling around her. When she noticed Arawn, the wild canine rose and trotted toward him. Her young followed her, tongues hanging out.

The mother fox tapped her muzzle against Arawn's

outstretched hand and wandered on into the underbrush. The two pups jumped up Arawn's legs until he patted their heads, then snapped his fingers at them to run after their mom. They dashed off.

"In a movie," Maeve muttered, "this would qualify you as a fairy-tale princess."

She gasped, clapped both hands over her mouth. She did *not* just say that. To Arawn.

Breath paralyzed, she slowly turned her head to peek at him. Unforgiving hardness in his features, the tense line of his broad shoulders. Darkness misted his form, power pouring off him like steam.

"It would not," he said, his tone dangerously calm. "I have a terrible singing voice."

Her heart stumbled. Was he—? Was that—? Did Arawn just make a *joke*?

A spark in those dark green eyes as he sauntered past her, hands in his pockets. "You can take a seat on that boulder if you wish. I will start looking into your mind for the threads of the spell binding your magic."

It took her a moment. Then the impact of his statement hit her. *Looking into your mind…* "No!" she squealed.

He shrugged. "Suit yourself if you would rather keep standing."

"No, not that." Her heart pumped blood so fast she got dizzy. "Don't look into my mind."

The things he'd see in there… *Her fingers digging into his shoulders as she pushed against him, slinging her legs around his hips, relishing the abrasion as his stubbled jaw rasped over her throat…*

He turned to her, one brow raised. "It is necessary in order to study the spellwork. Part of it is rooted in your mind."

She shook her head wildly. "No. You can't look in there."

"You agreed to cooperate," he said, strolling toward her. "I could do this without your consent, but I would rather you give me permission."

"And if I don't?"

For a moment, he just stared at her, magic whispering about his massive form, echoing inside her. Her breath flattened out.

"It seems you are unaware," he murmured, "of what is at stake."

Maintaining eye contact with him was too intense. She lowered her gaze, lest the connection singe her from the inside out.

"It is imperative," he went on, prowling ever closer, "that I take a look at the spell keeping your magic contained, especially now it has begun to unravel. Those powers inside you...they are not witchborn."

She jerked her head up. "What?"

"A long time ago, something took refuge in the magic of your bloodline." He circled her. "Something feral, primal, too fierce and powerful to roam the earth unchecked."

Another round, and she pivoted with him.

"The Powers That Be"—his tone dripped disdain—"decided the ancient beasts were a threat to humankind, their precious pets. They soon found they could not kill the beasts, for they are integral to the balance of magic in this world, their own immense powers woven inextricably into the fabric of all we know. So the gods forced them to sleep."

Her heart beat a frantic tattoo against her ribs.

"Power draws power, and most of the ancients sought out places rife with magic to retreat to for their slumber. A volcano. A rift at the bottom of the ocean. A mighty river. Some of them, however, were drawn by the strongest sources of magic at the time, pooled in the bloodlines of witches. One of the beasts fused its essence with the magic of what would become the MacKenna family, and it has lain dormant in your line ever since." He paused right in front of her. "Until you."

She might have made an undignified squeaky sound again.

"Generation upon generation, this essence has been passed down, growing stronger yet again with the accumulation of power in your family, until it reached a saturation point where it would reincarnate in full force."

"In me," she whispered.

He nodded. "In you."

"And you know this how?" Her voice was reed-thin, too many revelations pummeling her brain.

A sly smile. "I was there when the beasts were forced to sleep. I have had a long time and many resources to devote to finding out what exactly happened to them, and where they are." He cocked his head, the movement pure predator. "For a while now, the winds have been shifting. Magic is changing, and those who once were without power are finding themselves returning to old strength." A gleam of hunger in his eyes. "The beasts are awakening."

Maeve swallowed hard, too thunderstruck to speak for a few seconds. "What does this mean for me?"

"There are some...uncertainties. I have yet to see the reincarnation of an ancient beast awaken in a mortal body. The power inside your core is immense. If it were to break free all at once, either because the spell unravels completely in one go, or because I break it down by force...the beast would survive it. But you might not."

Her fingers had gone cold, numb, her chest tingling with chills.

"Our best bet, if you are to live, is for me to study the spellwork and the power it keeps contained, so I can dismantle the spell in a controlled fashion and...*guide* the beast out, if you will. There is a chance its essence has fused with yours to the point that the two of you could coexist with a little assistance."

She crossed her arms. "W-what kind of beast are we talking about here?"

The hint of a smile on his face, an age-old whisper of appreciation in his tone. "Humans spun tales about them, having seen the last of the beasts in the earliest times of burgeoning civilizations. They are still known in the modern world, though they are nothing but fables now. Can you think of one of them? Can you guess at what prowls underneath your skin?"

Fire and smoke, talons stretching in the dark... Still, she couldn't say it, the idea too absurd. So she just shook her head.

And Arawn's smirk clearly said he knew it for the lie it was. "Just as well. We will see it soon enough, I suppose."

"So the gist of it," she said, brushing a lock of hair behind her ear—then froze and pulled it back in front of her face again, even though Arawn must have had ample opportunity to study her scar by now. "The gist of it," she repeated, clearing her throat, "is that you're trying to save my life by looking at the spell?"

Eyes piercing with perceptiveness examined her every move, having surely noted her little gesture of shame. "Yes. For this reason, you might want to play nice and let me enter your mind. Seeing as it is crucial to your survival."

Well, crap. Let him look into her mind and see all the embarrassing details of her stupid sex dream...or take a ticket to a most certain death?

"Maeve?"

"I'm still thinking!"

۞

"WHAT," ARAWN SAID, TRYING NOT TO SNAP AT MAEVE, "IS there to think about?"

A blush darkened her cheeks, and she delicately angled

93

her head away, as if wanting to hide from his scrutiny. "Maybe," she rasped in that husky voice of hers that he had found himself looking forward to hearing all morning, "there are some things I'd rather you don't see."

Understanding dawned on him as his attention snagged on the jagged scar crossing her face, only half concealed by the shining red strands of her hair. The stiff way she held herself, her shoulders slightly curved forward, arms folded in front of her chest... Anxiety vibrated around her, nearly visible in the air.

He had long ago learned details of her ordeal, or at least as much as leaked out of the tight bubble of protection her family and friends drew around her after her rescue. He could very well imagine the rest, even if he didn't much like it. He had seen enough over the millennia to have acquired an acute understanding of the many ways sadists enjoyed their "games." And he had no desire to peruse that painful part of her memories.

Seeing those might prove quite dangerous, since none of those responsible were left to torture to a slow, agonizing death, no one left alive on whom to vent his rage. His blood would boil, and he would not know whom to kill to cool it.

"I will not touch your memories," he said to Maeve, keeping his voice soft despite the churning of his powers. "I will not go rifling through your thoughts, and I will not look at what is not connected to the spell. Whatever you wish to keep in the shadows will remain there." He paused. "I cannot help, however, glimpsing what you might throw at me."

Her ginger brows drew together. "Throw at you?"

"You have a certain amount of power here. Whatever you bring to the forefront of your mind will be visible to me, even if I am trying not to look." He shrugged. "Now, if you wanted to conceal a memory from me, all you would have to do is think *hard* about singing fairytale princesses."

The corners of her mouth twitched, and his magic quieted,

his focus zeroing in on that fragile almost-smile. It occurred to him he'd never seen her laugh. All the times he'd gone to watch her himself while she stayed at the Murrays', she'd always been serious, withdrawn.

For a simmering second, the desire to coax a full smile out of her hijacked his senses.

"Okay," she muttered. "I think I can manage that." She gave him a determined nod, though it looked like she did it to convince herself more than him.

She walked over to the boulder he mentioned and took a seat, crossing and uncrossing her legs a couple of times, fidgeting with the seam of her sweater. Clearing her throat, she scratched at her chin.

"Think of Snow White," she murmured, almost inaudibly. "Think of Snow White."

He prowled closer. "Ready?"

She shrugged, avoiding his gaze. "Um-hm."

"All right, then."

And he dove in.

Fire-edged darkness and sparks on ash, threads of emotion glowing like embers, whispers of magic... He moved to follow those traces of power—past the image of a dancing cartoon princess that made amusement curl inside him—when it slammed into him.

The chain of thoughts, memories, impressions rolled over and through him like a tidal wave of sensation.

"I want to see that wildfire of yours." Spoken from between her legs, his lips feathering over the dark red triangle glistening with her arousal.

Pleasure arced through her at the vibration and intent of his words, his touch, her mind shattering at the first stroke of his tongue. Her hands grabbed the sheets, her back bowed off the bed. Pulses of lust, zinging out from the throbbing center between her thighs, laid open before him. And he feasted.

Her orgasm rocked through her, an explosion of bliss. Her sight still hazy from the storm of pleasure that ravaged her, she gasped as he flipped her onto her stomach, nipping her butt as he crawled over her. His weight bearing down on her in the most erotic pressure, he parted her legs with his knees.

Ready, so ready for him, she arched her back, pushed her hips toward him.

"Will you burn for me?" His teeth on her neck, his heat all around her.

"Make me," she whispered.

Arawn blinked as a force kicked him out, the backdrop of fire-framed darkness falling away to reveal the reality of bright sunlight on the deathly pale face of the witch in front of him.

Maeve sat so still she didn't seem to breathe, her amber-gray eyes wide and horror-stricken. His own breathing unsteady, his body hardened to the point of pain, he stared at her. Raised a brow.

She made a high-pitched sound, shook her head and buried her face in her hands. Muttered something that might have contained the words "hole" and "swallow," and it took him annoyingly long to parse together the meaning of that as her wishing for a hole to open up and swallow her…and not the other things his mind had suggested.

He cleared his throat. "That was…unexpectedly vivid."

She waved her hands, jumped up, and stormed off toward the path in the woods, her face the brightest shade of red he'd seen on her yet. It almost matched her hair.

He remained where he was, hands in his pockets. "Where," he said calmly, "do you think you are going?"

"To cloister myself in my cabin," she hissed over her shoulder.

"We are not done here."

With a flicker of his thoughts, he sent out a pulse of his power, tugged at the bond between them to bring her to a halt. Gently. Like the civilized brute he was.

"As…entertaining and illuminating as this glimpse was," he said, sauntering over to her, "I have yet to study the spellwork."

She still had her back to him, her hands clenched to fists at her side. "You are *not* looking into my mind again."

"Why not?" He fought a losing battle not to smile. "Is there more?"

He could have sworn sparks erupted around her, and she shot a look at him over her shoulder that was nothing short of murderous. His magic purred in appreciation.

"So there is," he drawled.

She rounded on him, her eyes a storm of fire in smoke. "You were *not* supposed to see that. You promised you wouldn't look."

"It is incredibly difficult not to look when you are bombarding me with it."

"I was *not*."

"It would have had less impact," he said, enjoying this far too much, "if you hit me with a shovel."

Her nostrils flared. Was that smoke rising from them?

He shrugged. "Or run me over with a freight train."

"You are insufferable." Gritted out through clenched teeth.

"So I have been told." He clucked his tongue. "I still need to look at the spell."

"No." She crossed her arms.

"You would rather die?"

She turned around and tried to walk off again. To no avail. He still held her.

"Right now," she grumbled, "that seems like the better option, yes."

So obstinate. She could give Lucía a run for her money. And at the moment he was too enthralled by the surprising discovery of her explicit dream about him to press the issue.

"You are correct," he said, pitching his voice to silken seduction that would caress her senses. "We should reschedule for tomorrow. You do seem in need of some time to cool off...*Wildfire.*"

He let her go at that moment, and she stumbled forward a few steps on the path. Catching herself, she stalked off into the forest, and a snarl broke from her throat that carried an age-old, feral echo.

The grin taking over his face was so rare a thing, he barely remembered what he looked like with one of those wickedly amused smiles. Delight an effervescent dance in his blood, he stared after her.

Timid and reserved Maeve harbored lurid fantasies about him. What an *intriguing* turn of events.

And it changes things.

Because up until now, he'd ignored that deepening beat of interest for her, its pulse growing stronger the more he saw her. He'd restrained the whisper of hunger hushing his thoughts in her presence.

But now... Now he knew she wanted him. And that sneak peek into her desire only whetted the appetite he'd been trying to curb.

He would curb it no more.

CHAPTER 11

Merle stared after the retreating witches, her focus on Juneau burning with a lethal force that ignited her blood. Her instincts screamed at her to run after the bitch, to melt Juneau's inner organs in a firestorm of rage, and if the wards didn't stop her, she would have already lunged at the Elder witch.

But cunning as the head of the Laroche family was, she'd calibrated the protective spells around the meeting place to allow her own people to leave…while the Aequitas remained trapped inside. The wards would fall in a few minutes, Juneau had said, once she and her acolytes had a head start.

Yeah, that spiteful piece of trash knew all too well that Merle wouldn't have let her leave.

"Merle?" Elaine asked form beside her, voice gentle.

"I will get him back," she said through gritted teeth. Turning to the other Elders, she added, "*We* will get him back."

Kristen, head of the Frost family, shifted her weight and cleared her throat. "Maybe we should discuss this."

"There is nothing to discuss." A dull pain throbbed behind

Merle's temples. "By the gods, I will go get him all by myself if need be, but I'd rather have you all backing me. I'd do the same if it was one of your family in Juneau's clutches. And it could be. This is bigger than just me."

"Merle is right," Shobha said, her sari swishing around her feet as she walked closer. "This is not simply about Merle and Juneau. It could just as easily have been Thorne she took," she added, mentioning the young shadow demon who was mated to her granddaughter Anjali. "There is hatred behind Juneau's actions, a dangerous sort of fanaticism, and it can and will spread to anyone else who stands in her way."

Hanna nodded. "She would have come after Sarai, too. If not for Alek and Lily's help..." The head of the Roth family swallowed hard, the pain of recent events darkening her expression.

Like Lily, Sarai—the heir to the Roth line—had been turned into a *pranagraha* demon during a nefarious scheme by some "seriously underfucked demon bastards," as Lily so succinctly put it. Sarai was forced into a mating with a cruel son of a bitch *pranagraha*, her prospects bleak—once mated, *pranagrahas* had to stay together for life, and if one partner died, so did the other.

The potion to reverse the transformation couldn't be brewed until Alek procured the rare missing ingredient from Arawn...in exchange for a lifetime of service to the Demon Lord. Lily, for whom the potion was actually intended, decided to stay demon so she could mate with Alek, giving Sarai the one and only chance at turning back into a witch.

The transformation also severed the mating bond to the demon who had abused her, killing him in the process. An event Sarai celebrated with flowing champagne and a roaring party.

"We owe Lily and Alek," Hanna said, her brown eyes hard. "I will never agree to surrender either of them to

Juneau. And we will stand with you, Merle, to get Rhun back."

Merle gave the older witch a grim, thankful nod.

"Are we all agreed, then," Elaine asked, "that Juneau's conditions for peace are unacceptable?"

A chorus of assent.

"So we fight," the head of the Donovan family said. "And that includes fighting for the freedom of Merle's husband." A pointed look at Kristen. "We just need to be smart about it."

The magic of the wards began to crack.

"I'll cast a locator spell to find out where she's keeping him," Merle said, and exchanged a glance with Elaine.

The other witch nodded, aware that Merle wouldn't actually be the one to do it, since she wasn't allowed to draw on her magic. "I'll come with you so we can talk details."

More cracks in the wards.

"We'll be in touch once we know where he's being held." Merle looked at each of the Elders in turn. "Until then, we all need to be on our guard and warn our families. I'm not convinced Juneau won't stoop to a surprise strike at our most vulnerable."

Sinister faces all around, the gravity of the situation settling about them like a coating of ash.

The wards dissolved on a whisper in the air. Merle nodded at Elaine, and they hurried back to the parking lot.

"I'll have to ride with you," Merle said, her breath coming short from the brisk pace. Her heart stung, but this pain had nothing to do with physical exertion. "Rhun has my car keys."

Elaine shot her a sympathetic glance.

Merle's cell phone rang just as they drove off.

"Lil," Merle said when she accepted the call. "That bitch has Rhun."

Her best friend let off a streak of curses that would have

impressed a seventeenth-century sailor, and demanded the full story. So Merle told her. How she managed not to cry, she didn't know. Perhaps because her rage was so overwhelming it eclipsed everything else. And maybe because tears wouldn't bring Rhun back. Focused wrath would.

"You're coming to the mansion," Lily ordered. "I still can't go outside, and I want to be there for the locator spell. And all the sneaky war planning."

"Of course," Merle said, feigning offense. "You know I wouldn't plan a prison break without you."

"Damn straight."

They had to make a quick stop at the Victorian to pick up supplies for the spell, and arrived at the Murrays' a few minutes later. Elaine parked in the circular driveway in front of the stately mansion, and Lily and Alek greeted them in the foyer—though the two *pranagraha* demons took care to remain out of the direct sunlight shining through the huge window above the door.

"We prepared the sitting room," Lily said, leading them into one of the numerous salons of the mansion, whose original purpose seemed to have been an ostentatious display of expensive furniture. The Murray family came from old money, the house a testament to priorities of a bygone era.

Nowadays, especially since the death of Hazel's older sister, Isabel—incidentally, the witch who instigated Maeve's kidnapping with the aim of letting the demon steal Maeve's powers for Isabel—the rooms of the mansion slowly underwent a change from prestigious declaration to charming gallimaufry. Hazel's many-faceted hobbies had started filling up a lot of the less-used salons, and the sitting room currently resembled a quilting workshop.

Lily had cleared one low table and set a detailed map of Portland on it. Merle took the candles out of her bag, placing one on each cardinal point—east, south, west, and north. Next she pulled out Rhun's brush from the bathroom at home, plucked a few strands of hair from it, and attached them to the pendulum she'd fetched.

"Elaine?" She held out the salt.

"I've got it from here."

The Elder witch took the salt, pouring it in a circle around the table as a ward against intrusive spirits which might impair the spell.

"If you would light the sage?" Elaine asked.

With a nod, Merle pulled out the dried herbs, lit them, and waved the heavy smoke in the room to dispel negative energy, another precaution to ensure the spell wouldn't be corrupted.

"This is fascinating," Alek murmured from his spot against the wall, arms crossed. "I've never seen witches work before." He cleared his throat. "Well, not from a friendly vantage point, I mean. Usually I had to duck and run, so…"

"Shush, *prana*-groupie." Lily patted his shoulder.

Magic rose in the air, crackling like electricity. Elaine swung the pendulum over the map as she murmured the words of the spell.

"That which is lost shall be found.
Those who are hidden shall be seen.
From the traces in the ground,
Their location I will glean."

Merle's heart pounded up into her throat as she watched the pendulum swing, swing, swing while the power in the room grew to a crescendo. Lily and Alek winced, the magic no doubt abrasive to their demon senses.

With a hush, the power flattened out, the light of the candles extinguished on a whisper of magic. The pendulum flew out of Elaine's hand as if yanked away, its pointy tip embedding in the opposite wall.

Silence.

"Does that mean we need to go that way?" Alek asked, brows raised and eyes on the pendulum.

"No," Merle choked out. She could barely breathe past the pressure on her chest.

"It means," Lily chimed in, her voice soft, "the spell failed."

Alek pushed off the wall. "What? But doesn't that only happen when—"

"He's still alive." Merle rubbed a hand over her breast-bone, where she felt the mating bond. Weaker, and with an echo of pain, but intact.

"Then how...?"

"Juneau is likely blocking him," Elaine said, the corners of her mouth turning down.

Alek looked at Lily. "Like Isabel blocked the demon who kidnapped Maeve?"

She'd undoubtedly told him most of the tale of how Merle and Rhun met half a year ago, under circumstances that were anything but romantic. The fact that Isabel had indeed blocked the psychic signature of the demon so Rhun couldn't find him was the reason Merle had to make the ill-fated bargain with Arawn in the first place—the Demon Lord was the only one who could break the blocking spell.

"Yeah," Merle said, her heart heavy, her arms starting to shake with the drop of her adrenaline. "And like hell will I make the same mistake twice." She met Lily's eyes, then Alek's. "I will not ask him," she added, steel in her voice. "Not again."

She'd lost her sister the night she went to Arawn for help.

"I don't think you have to." Elaine cleaned up the salt circle with a dustpan and brush. "When you were looking for that demon, you had no idea where to start or whom to ask. This is different. Juneau is likely holding him in the home of one of her witches, and even if she is not, there should be several witches among the Draconians who would know where she's keeping him. Juneau didn't drag him there herself. So." She straightened, threw the salt in the trash, shrugged. "All we need to do is catch a witch who can tell us where he is."

"Oh, great," Merle grumbled. "Let me just get my old witch trap out of the basement, and we're all set."

"Look at the bright side." Lily walked over to her, slung an arm around her shoulders. "When we do catch one, you get to *torture* the information out of her."

"That's more of an *if*," Merle muttered. She was shaking hard now, had to sink down on one of the couches, with Lily propping her up.

Maeve had left, and now Rhun was gone too, and she was so damn powerless—literally. She couldn't even use her magic to get either of them back. *The gods must hate me.*

And catching a witch... It was going to be impossibly difficult. Witches were hard to ambush in general, as they rarely went out alone, and had their guard up most of the time. In light of the tense situation in the community, Juneau's witches would be even more alert, harder to catch unawares. It might take days to trap one.

And all the while Rhun would suffer.

"He's hurting," she whispered.

"Hey," Lily said gently, squeezing her shoulder. "You know how tough he is. Remember how he was all charm and swagger when you found him chained up in our basement? Juneau and Isabel couldn't even crack him a little. And if anyone is able to endure pain, it's him. He spent *two decades* in the Shadows, and he came out all right." She shrugged. "Well, mostly all right. He does have that OCD thing going, but I'm not sure he didn't have that even before doing time."

Merle's mood took a turn for the worse at the thought of the dark, torturous prison dimension where her grandmother bound Rhun as a punishment for a crime he didn't even commit. Yes, he'd survived those twenty unending years of drowning in agony…but that was all the more reason she needed to get him out, and soon.

Rhun had seen enough pain to last him for the rest of his life.

CHAPTER 12

S uch. An. Infuriating. Male.

Maeve stomped down the forest path toward her cabin, surrounded by woods way too cheery and lighthearted to suit her own mood.

She should have known Arawn was going to be a jerk about this. That annoying smile of his...she wanted to wipe it off his face with a shovel. Fire licked along her veins, wanting out. Deep inside, that presence she first felt when she walked into the Grove and saw him shifted and hissed—though it seemed far from enraged.

Maeve frowned. In fact, that rattling, flame-encased darkness appeared to be...amused? As if readying for play. A very primal, feral sort of play.

Blinking, she shook her head. She was losing it. Barely two days in his dominion, and her sanity was unraveling like a loose ball of yarn. She was in dire need of some downtime, a few peaceful hours spent in the cabin with a good book and nothing but silence all around her.

To her surprise, her new lodging came equipped with a shelf full of books, all from her favorite genre. Since Arawn didn't seem like the romance-reading type, it was likely courtesy of his acute observations of her tastes, the books a thoughtful amenity. She'd already finished a historical this morning, would start on the paranormals next.

Maybe that would banish the image of—

Her foot caught on a root, she stumbled, crashed, tumbled down the deep slope on the side of the path, branches snapping at her, roots and stones scratching at her clothes, her skin...until her fall stopped abruptly. Steel bands of muscle held her, a stranger's heat brushing over her body.

A flash of light red, blue eyes in a face of gold-kissed white, the features elegantly masculine. "I've got you."

Shifting time and space amid an inexorable wave of horror.

"I've got you." His arms wrapped around her from behind, hauled her back from the window in the main room of the warehouse. "You can't escape me, pretty little Maeve."

She sobbed, rammed her elbow back trying to hit his stomach, but he held her fast, and she didn't have enough room. Her bare feet dragged across the rough concrete floor as he hauled her back into the adjacent room. Back into her windowless hell.

"It seems," he said, his breath acrid on her skin, "that you're not good enough to be left unchained. This is on you. You leave me no choice but to use the shackles."

The mattress springs shrieked as he threw her on the bed, the sound firing off a thousand warning bells in her bruised and battered mind, connecting it to—

She heaved, though nothing came up, her stomach empty.

He yanked her arms up while she was still shaky from the dry heaves, and locked the manacles around her wrists. She tried to kick him. His hand closed around her ankle, twisting until it cracked.

Her scream shredded her throat.

"Pretty little Maeve," he mused, his blue eyes glinting with a cold fire. "Maybe I need to do something about that beauty of yours. Mark you so you know who you belong to."

The light glinted off the blade as he brought it to her face.

Fire. Flames rolling out from her core with a roar of primal wrath, her conscious mind frozen in terror.

The next second, the blaze died down, as if a burner had been turned off. She sat backed up against a tree, breathing so fast she saw lights swirling in front of her, and an unknown male crouching several feet away, his hand outstretched. He made a soothing gesture, as if petting down a wild thing, and the last of the embers in her blood extinguished.

"I'm sorry," the male said gently, a tremor underneath his words. "I shouldn't have touched you. You were falling and I... I'm sorry."

Cold sweat slicked her skin, and she shook, shook so hard the bark scratched her back. Her stomach turned, and she whirled around to the side and vomited in the nearest bush.

Leaves rustling beside her. She didn't look up, couldn't, her body caught in the vise grip of her nausea.

Dark warmth whispering over her nape, fingers gathering her hair up and away from her face.

"Kelior," Arawn said, his voice quiet as he held Maeve's hair without ever touching her skin. "Leave."

"Yes, sire." A murmur of regret, and then the soft sound of the other male's retreat.

She heaved, again and again, until nothing came anymore, her gut cramped and hurting. And all the while Arawn's presence was a hum of patient darkness beside her.

Trembling, she hung her head, sniffling, her fingers digging into the earth and moss. *Brittle.* She felt so brittle, as frangible as the cracked vase everyone assumed she was. And wasn't it true? Wasn't she broken beyond repair?

A sharp tug on her scalp.

Her spine locked. Slowly, she raised her head, turned it, swept her eyes up the muscled length of Arawn's legs, over his groin—she swallowed—to his torso, to that face of harsh angles and brutal beauty. Which currently sported a sensual smirk.

"I do like seeing you in this position, Wildfire."

Another, longer tug on her hair, making her heart race and wholly inappropriate tingles shoot down her spine...and right between her legs.

She scrambled to her feet so fast she staggered. He let go of her hair, let her back up, but that smirk remained on his face, along with the spark of hunger in his eyes.

Heat washed over her, and she ground her teeth and curled her hands to fists, anger a sizzle in her blood. "You're shameless."

"Hm." He surveyed her, his perusal far too *interested*. "You only singed your clothes a little this time. Pity."

She refused to glance down at herself. Re-fused. Instead, she muttered an insult under her breath and stormed off, lest she make a rude gesture at the Demon Lord. Even if it served him right.

By the time she reached the cabin, she realized her limbs no longer trembled, and the feeling of shattering at the slightest touch was gone, chased away by steely fire and flexing talons in her core...in response to a certain Demon Lord's teasing.

That fire lasted her throughout the rest of the day, through dinner with Lucía and the chill kiss of the evening, her mind settling back into timid quiet only when she was about to crawl into bed. Specters of her past crept up her spine like icy shadows, made her shiver despite the warmth in the cabin.

A thump on her door. Her pulse spiked, those icy fingers of dread closing around her heart. She inched toward the door, peeked out through the open window pane. A small dark...thing lay in front of the door.

Opening it, she bent down, inspected what turned out to be an animal. The bat shook its tiny head, flapped its wings, and flew off again. Leaving a note.

Wary, she picked it up, read it—and crumpled it to a ball.

"Jerk!" she shouted into the night, and slammed the door shut.

Snarling, she stalked to the bed, slipped in. When she fell asleep later, it was to glowing embers of her simmering anger, spiced with sparks of amusement she would never admit to.

No matter how much a tiny part of her laughed at his nerve of wishing her, "Sweet *dreams*."

CHAPTER 13

Arawn knocked on the wooden door off a side tunnel in the innermost part of his underground dominion, making sure to keep the sound low. A few seconds later, the door swung open to reveal a woman with tawny skin and untamable brown curls, her eyes just a shade lighter than her hair.

"My lord," she said, inclining her head.

Stepping back, she opened the door further and bid him inside.

"Simone," he greeted her and entered the room.

His hands in the pockets of his pants, he glanced around the warmly decorated interior. The door to the bedroom stood ajar.

"Do you have everything you need?" he asked.

"Yes, sire."

"How is he?"

A beat of silence, the face of the female *bluotezzer* demon drawn with pain. "I'm afraid he won't make it."

His power coiled in the pit of his stomach. "What does he need?"

Simone shook her head. "It's not—" A sigh of defeat. "He

was so malnourished when he came here... I think he lay there too long before you found him, and from the looks of it, he's been neglected even longer." She pressed her lips together, her eyes shimmering. "I've been feeding him, but he's just getting weaker."

"Let me see him."

With a curt nod, she went into the bedroom, came back with the swaddled *algos* demon in her arms. His eyes closed, the babe was barely breathing, his skin even paler than when Arawn picked him up yesterday.

"Has the healer seen him?"

"Yes, my lord." Simone's voice was but a whisper. "She says there's nothing she can do. His body is just shutting down."

He touched the babe's cheek with a finger, listened to his faint heartbeat. His magic, that curling darkness inside him, wasn't of the healing kind...but there *was* something else he could try. It might be enough to save the child.

Forming a claw at the tip of his right index finger, he pierced the pad of his left thumb, brought that finger to the babe's mouth. The infant's lips parted only after he prodded him, but he wouldn't even suckle on his finger. Arawn had to squeeze a drop of his blood into his mouth.

Slowly, the babe smacked his lips, drew the tiny amount of liquid in.

Arawn stared. And waited.

Simone didn't say a word, her eyes flicking between him and the infant, her hold on the babe full of unconditional care. She was one of the few trusted foster mothers in his service who lived and breathed for this purpose, the desire to nurse and raise the young a part of her, blood and bone.

He once offered her a different job, thinking it might be hard on her after all those decades.

She'd huffed in his face, told him she wouldn't give up her babies for all the money in the world.

He stroked his finger over the infant's cheek again, noting the skin gaining warmth. The color deepened infinitesimally.

His blood didn't have healing qualities per se, but it carried such potent energy and power that it could very well catalyze a body's self-healing ability. And it might just be enough.

"Do you need anything else?" he asked of the tiny *bluotezzer* female, whose heart was still so big after all these years, soft and strong enough to take in even the hopeless cases. He knew how many babes she'd been forced to let go because they didn't make it, when not even his blood was enough.

He knew every single one.

"I'm fine," she replied, her focus on the sleeping *algos* demon. "I'll be with him, either way."

And the babe would know warmth, would know love, even if these were to be his last hours.

Arawn nodded at Simone, turned away—and the infant uttered a sound. Not a whimper. Not a cry.

A quiet burp.

Arawn pivoted slowly, studied the darkening skin of the babe, now a shade much closer to the red it should be. Simone met his gaze for a second, and a small smile lit her face, her eyes.

"Thank you," she said.

He nodded again, his throat uncomfortably thick. "I will return tomorrow."

He made his way back out of the heartland of his underground domain and ascended to the surface, into the forest misted with rain. The sun hid behind a layer of clouds, the air a humid kiss on his skin, but the foliage kept most of the drizzle from reaching the ground. A light winter shower in the Pacific Northwest.

Even so, rain made it harder to follow trails, as it washed away most scents. So when he came to Maeve's cabin, found it empty, and neither Kelior nor Maeve around, he ditched his clothes and changed into his bear. His nose now more sensitive than in his human form—though nothing else of him was *human*, to be precise—he had no trouble tracing the wildfire scent of Maeve to the stone bench on a knoll overlooking the crystalline blue of Moon Pond.

Kelior lingered nearby, out of sight, but departed at a signal from Arawn. The fae male had apologized profusely to him after setting off Maeve the day before. Arawn had already given him precise instructions not to go near her unless asked, but the protective instinct of the male when he saw Maeve tumble overrode Arawn's instructions.

The fact that Kelior's intervention saved her from possibly breaking a few bones was the only reason Arawn hadn't broken any of his.

Well, that and the fae's elemental affinity for fire, which made him the best daytime guard for Maeve.

Still in bear form, Arawn approached the stone bench where Maeve sat, her face turned toward the serene beauty of Moon Pond. In the light of day, the name made no sense, the water a deep blue that had nothing to do with the celestial body. At night, however, it revealed a splendor that more than explained the reason behind its naming.

He should bring Maeve here again sometime, after sunset.

She didn't notice his presence until he stood a few feet behind her, and he might have been a bit too sneaky, having moved too quietly. When she did realize she wasn't alone anymore, she stiffened, turned to look over her shoulder by minute degrees, until her eyes landed on him—widened.

He had to give her credit. She didn't scream. Most humans would when suddenly faced with a giant grizzly.

Maeve, however, just swallowed hard, the muscles in her throat working underneath that creamy skin. Those copper lashes fluttered yet again over eyes of smoky amber as she beheld him with a calm that appeared to be an integral part of her, despite the bursts of fire every now and then.

"Your eyes," she said in her husky voice, "in this form are different."

If he were in his human shape, he would have smiled. So perceptive, she wasn't fooled by his masks, probably knew it was him due to the beacon of his power inside her. It called to his own, the bond between them a constant pulse.

He prowled up to her, sat down next to the bench, the area dry thanks to the dense canopy of the tree overhead. Maeve's gaze on him was a brand on his senses, her attention a palpable thing, like a fluttering bird gracing you with its presence…as long as you didn't move.

He didn't move.

Keeping his eyes on the pond in front of him, he let her look her fill. When the fire kiss of her focus would have wandered away from him, he changed his shape.

Maeve jerked, gasped. "Merle told me about this one," she murmured.

He flicked his left wolf ear in a lazy gesture of dismissal.

"How many shapes do you have?"

So he showed her, shifting from one animal to the next, then back to those forms that elicited the most delighted reactions in her. The wolf and the panther seemed to be her favorites. The snake made her yelp.

When he finally changed back to his human shape, he didn't bother to withdraw into the undergrowth for modesty's sake. Her attention was still fully on him as he shifted, since she probably expected him to show her yet another animal form, and for a glorious two seconds, her eyes were glued to his naked body.

Then she startled, choked off a high-pitched sound, and turned her reddening face away. "You did that on purpose."

"I thought I should correct a few assumptions from your dream."

She massaged her temples, muttered to herself, "It just keeps getting worse."

"If you need a closer look at my backside for better detailing—"

"Stooooop," she groaned, her face buried in her hands.

"You did get the chest hair right."

"Would you *please* put on some clothes?"

He sighed. "You bruise my ego, Wildfire."

Half hidden behind her hands, the corners of her mouth twitched up.

His chest feeling light with some amusement of his own, he called forth a dryad from a fir a few yards away, and the tree nymph brought him a pair of loose black pants, retreating again with her head bowed.

Maeve was studiously staring at the pond as he got dressed, and when he stepped in front of her, she frowned. Her eyes flicked to his bare torso, drank in the display of muscles and skin before she blinked and glanced away again, her cheeks darkening once more.

"Are all your shirts in the laundry?"

Such bite to her this morning. He liked that. Much better than the overwhelming despair and broken sadness that still haunted her at times.

"You seem tense," he said, keeping his voice at a sensually low level. "Did you not sleep well?"

She narrowed her eyes at him, pressed her lips together. He wanted to lick them open.

"I wouldn't have expected the Demon Lord to be so childish about this."

"Trust me," he purred, "my feelings concerning your fantasy about me are very much adult."

She shifted on the bench, cleared her throat and glanced away again. Human as his form might be, his senses were still sharper than those of a man, his nose picking up the faint note of her interest. His power hummed under his skin, wanting to tangle with her fire.

"I've been meaning to ask," she said, her back straight, her posture prim. "Did you let Merle know I'm okay?"

"Should I?"

With an irritated huff, she rolled her eyes. "Yes?"

"And what, exactly, would you like me to tell her?"

"I don't know," she grumbled, raising her hands and letting them fall back into her lap. "Just let her know you... haven't eaten me yet."

"Much to my chagrin," he murmured.

She froze, color flushing her cheeks once more.

"I need to look at the spell," he said, watching how the wind blew a strand of her hair across her face until it got tangled on her lashes. Those *lashes*.

She pushed the hair off her face, only to pull some of it back again the next second in yet another futile attempt to hide her scar. "No."

"I will not see more of your...charming dreams if you refrain from hurling them at me."

She spoke through her teeth. "I did *not*—"

"Although I feel like I should have the right to look, seeing as they feature me in a leading role."

"One. It was *one* dream." A slanted glare up at him. "And I don't want you in my mind again."

"Even at the expense of your life?"

She folded her arms, raised her chin.

"Now who is being childish?" He mirrored her pose, cocked a brow.

He could have simply waltzed into her mind at any given moment, her shields so flimsy he wouldn't even have to break them down. Yet he waited for her consent.

Sighing, she closed her eyes. Uttered a sound of frustration. Glowered at him. "Fine."

"Good," he said, and entered her mind on a whisper of thought.

Embers in the night, velvet darkness glittering with sparks. Of anger, of amusement...of *lust*. He itched to touch his mental fingers to those sparks, caress them into a blaze. *Another time*, he promised. To himself, and to the woman who harbored such fiery potential, if only she'd let it free from the tight leash she kept it on.

He followed the traces of her magic before she could sidetrack him with another unruly thought. Not that he'd mind being run over again by the freight train of her fantasy. If she were to offer... But this exercise was not about his pleasure, or sampling hers.

Studying the spellwork *was* a necessity. Twice now in as many days, her powers exploded out of her and onto others, both times in situations of high stress and panic attacks due to her lingering trauma. The risk that her magic might hurt her with the next eruption was only growing. He needed to study the spell and figure out how to dismantle it safely, and to coax her beast out in a way that wouldn't obliterate all that was Maeve in the process.

He went deeper, descending into the stygian blackness of her innermost core, the soft threads of her magic his only guide. Rowan MacKenna had taken great care to incarcerate these ancient powers so they didn't even surface in Maeve's darkest hours, the witch's spell a mighty bulwark against a force from the dawn of time. The late Elder witch likely had no real idea of what she was up against, the knowledge of the true existence of the Old Ones long forgotten, but one thing she grasped—how destructive these powers could be, how much of a threat they posed, not just to the people around Maeve, but to Maeve as well.

She made damn sure to weave a spell of tangled intricacies and adamantine strength, and as Arawn beheld the first layers of Rowan's work, he paused in admiration.

And sighed.

This was going to take some time.

Minutes stretched to what felt like hours as he studied the spell without touching it yet. As with one of those towers of blocks children played with, moving one piece at the wrong point could bring the entire structure crashing down. Which could prove fatal.

So he examined and scrutinized and analyzed the interlocking magic, until one part of his consciousness noticed the decline in Maeve's energy. His other senses, the ones he kept alert to the outside world, picked up on the way Maeve's posture slumped, her breathing becoming too shallow.

She needed to eat and drink, and rest. He'd been studying the spellwork for far too long, and all the while she sat there patiently, not a word of complaint or deliberate signal of distress. When in reality she was drained.

He saw as much in the slow, erratic pattern of her thoughts as he ascended from the depths of her core, despite trying not to look. Like he told her, it was hard to keep his mental attention averted from what bombarded him without his active involvement.

And it was likely because of her exhaustion that she let so much slip, let him see—though inadvertently—what normally must have been tightly guarded thoughts. Each of them a blow to a part of him that ached, that bled, that raged on her behalf.

Broken. Weak. Disfigured.

You think anyone would want this, want you? You're not attractive. Not anymore. I made sure of that. Made sure you're too ugly for any other male to desire.

Broken beyond repair. Damaged goods. You can't even touch a man without puking your guts out.

And you dare think a male of power like the Demon Lord would look at you and feel anything but revulsion? You think his teasing is real?

He pities you, like everyone else. Any attention he tosses your way means less to him than breadcrumbs off his table, and whatever interest he shows is a pity fuck in the making.

I broke *you. You like to bask in the knowledge that I'm dead, that I'm gone, but I took the best parts of you —*

Arawn drew back, out of her mind, before his power leveled the woods.

CHAPTER 14

From the start, Maeve was never really scared of Arawn. Intimidated, yes. Scared? No, even when it would have been reasonable.

But she could learn to fear him given the look on his face right now.

He glared at her with such a fierce, wild glint in his eyes, such shadows swirling in their depths, that a quiver started in her core, the tremors spreading outward until she shook even though she was sitting down. He was a contained storm of rage, every fast, heavy breath loosening the leash on the primal power pulsing under his skin, visible to her growing sense of magic.

In the primitive gecko part of her brain, she knew that if he snapped, he could lay waste to miles around him.

What had he seen in her mind to enrage him so?

She was so exhausted her body felt twenty pounds heavier, so hungry she was past *feeling* hungry and now in that state where dizziness crept in. Her thoughts sluggish, she had no idea what he might have glimpsed. Had she pestered him with the details of her shame? Had he seen how weak she'd been, how pathetic? How she'd begged and debased herself? Had he finally learned just how broken she was, how tainted?

See? that nauseating voice inside her hissed. *He finds you repulsive. He's disgusted by you, and —*

"He did not," Arawn snarled, his expression murderous.

She glanced up at him, cowered back a little.

"He did *not* take the best parts of you." He glowered down at her, the rain quieting all around, as if the sky itself held its breath. "No one can. You are not some bloody *treasure chest* that can be looted." He spat those words, dark power flaring out from him, making her breath hitch.

Her pulse pounded in her head, and she rose to her feet, swayed. Arawn's hand shot out as if to steady her, but he curled his fingers into his palm at the last second, pulled back. His magic hovered, bearing down like the pressure before a thunderstorm.

Nerves frayed from her exhaustion, she had no shields anymore, every painful wound laid bare, bleeding. "Then why am I missing those parts?" she rasped. "Why am I mourning who I used to be? He killed pieces of me. And I'll never get them back."

"That is not true." A muscle feathered in Arawn's jaw. "Have you never talked with anyone about this?"

She blinked, frowned. "Merle…" Pressing her lips together, she glanced to the side.

Her sister had signaled she was open to listen if Maeve wanted to tell her, if she wanted to unload in order to process…everything. And for a second there, she'd considered it, sensing that the tangle of shame and anger inside her would only fester if she locked it up.

But as she sat down with Merle, she noticed the tension in her sister's shoulders, the pain flickering behind her eyes she was trying to hide yet couldn't quite conceal. Merle was already hurting on her behalf, her soul already scarred by what she saw in that room in the warehouse when she and

Rhun freed Maeve. If she were to learn of the full scope of Maeve's ordeal, of how hard she truly struggled... Merle's heart would splinter all the more.

No, Maeve couldn't tell her. Not just the details of her torture, but also the depth of her emotional impairment. If Merle—and the others—knew how fractured her thoughts were, they would treat her even more solicitously, like a failing figurine of spun glass, threatening to shatter at any moment. They already tiptoed around her with wary glances. And the damn pity in their eyes, as if she was terminally ill, as if they had to keep her environment free of any contaminants or else her body and mind would break down and die.

Imagine if they knew the strength of the demons she fought every day, inside her heart and soul.

She'd felt the same way about talking to her best friend Anjali, or to Lily or Basil. Hell, Lily was so damn strong, she never would have been abducted in the first place. She'd have kicked the demon's balls so hard he choked on them, as Lily would undoubtedly phrase it. The thought of baring her shame to Lily made Maeve withdraw even further into herself.

"Not your sister," Arawn cut into her thoughts. "Not your friends. I mean someone with knowledge of the mind."

She swallowed past a knot of guilt and embarrassment. "A shrink?"

He nodded, his forest-green eyes mapping her face.

"I...tried. It didn't work." She shook her head with a soft scoff. "How are you supposed to open up and tell someone about it when that person doesn't even know demons and witches exist? Doesn't know what it means when you talk about powers and mind control and a *bluotezzer* drinking from—" She broke off, closed her eyes.

The therapist she'd seen meant well, and Maeve had yearned to tell *someone*, someone who might be able to help in ways her friends couldn't, but the human woman was oblivious to otherworld creatures and their powers. Maeve faltered when she tried to talk about her torture because she had to withhold so many details that what she *could* tell the therapist hardly made sense.

She shook her head, sorrow dragging down her shoulders, her heart so incredibly heavy.

"Eat." A gruff command.

Opening her eyes, she found a sandwich right under her nose.

"I don't want to know where you pulled that from," she muttered while accepting it.

The quiet sound from him could have been a choked chuckle, but when she looked up, his face was a mask of relentless hardness. He was still so *angry*. Until now, she'd only seen him in complete, smooth control masked by predatory languor, and never this close to the tension of a tightly curled cobra ready to strike.

"Here," he said with a rumble reminiscent of one of the large cats he could turn into, and handed her a flask of water.

"Okay, seriously, where are you hiding this stuff?"

She angled her head and looked him up and down, yet another excuse to drink in the brute beauty of his massive body, all those clearly defined muscles bunching under strokable bronze skin, the dusting of hair on his chest, trailing over his stomach to—

"Would you like to pat me down?" A gleam of dark hunger in his eyes.

She startled, stiffened, and glanced away, ignoring the slow-building heat in decidedly feminine parts of her body. She ate the sandwich instead, almost groaned at the taste, realizing just how starved she was. He nudged her to take the flask, drink until it was empty. Some energy returned to her, yet her limbs were still as tired as if she'd run a marathon.

Why on earth? She'd only been sitting here...

"You need rest," Arawn said. "Return to your cabin. We will resume tomorrow."

She fell into step beside him as he took the path back. "What about the spell? What did you find?"

"Your grandmother was a brilliant witch." The leaves rustled softly as he walked next to her, a looming shadow of coiled power. "The spell is highly complex. It will take time to dismantle it. I have barely studied the first layer."

"What?" she squeaked. All this time she'd been sitting there, and he hadn't even started taking the spell apart?

"From what I could tell, it seems that at least the spellwork is not in danger of crumbling anytime soon." A dark glance at her. "It will happen, however, and we should not wait until then."

"Okay, then why don't we continue right now?"

Not that she was eager to have him in her mind again... even if the feeling was nothing like when the demon—

A sharp tug on that bond inside her made her stop and catch her breath. She turned to him, her eye twitching...in annoyance, in disbelief.

Arawn studied her body with sensual focus, his attention lingering on those parts that grew irritatingly hot and tingly under his regard.

"I sure would like to spend more time in you," he murmured at a pitch that was a complement to the caress of his eyes, "but these spellwork study sessions drain you of energy. Another one too soon will leave you in a limp heap." One corner of his mouth lifted, making her stomach flutter. "And, no, this is not how I want to render you limp."

The fluttering in her stomach grew into a flip, then shot out waves of prickling excitement over her nerve endings.

He resumed walking, and she followed on legs that were inexplicably wobbly.

When they arrived at her cabin, he accompanied her inside, his presence filling the room despite the open windows. It was as if he displaced the air with his power, and standing in an enclosed space with him was akin to being enveloped in his energy without even touching him.

He nodded at the covered plates on the table. "Eat some more. Then rest. Lucía will come by later if you wish for company."

A lingering look of swirling shadows as he turned to the door.

"I would really like to touch you." The words were out of her mouth before she knew what was happening.

Blame it on her exhaustion, on those abraded, whittled-down shields of hers. Apparently the filter in her brain had vanished, leaving all sorts of unruly thoughts and irrational desires to flow freely out her mouth.

Desires like the one which had been smoldering in her blood for quite some time now, its embers kindling and flaring, while this impossible, intimidating male who was *all wrong* for her kept such aggravating distance she'd reached the point where she wanted to rub against him and find out just how hard he—

Arawn came to attention. He paused, the muscles in his broad back locked, and ever so slowly, he turned to her. Everything about him hushed, reminiscent of the way a feline predator would go still before it pounced.

"If I get to touch you, too." A calculating spark in those eyes of forest green.

For a second, she hesitated, a million reasons why she shouldn't clashing inside her, but—her desire to feel him won out. "Okay."

Dark power curled about his shoulders, his arms and hands, then drew back again, as if brought to heel. He prowled closer, his focus an unrelenting burn on her, until his heat brushed her skin, only a few inches between them.

Heart beating too fast for her to catch a breath, she raised her hand toward his face, paused. He was so much taller, she would have to go on tiptoe to reach him...

Arawn inclined his head, allowed her easier access. His gaze rested steady on her face, though she didn't dare meet his eyes. The intensity in that contact might rob her of her courage to claim the other touch he'd agreed to.

Slowly, tentatively, she grazed his cheek with her fingertips, marveling at her new streak of bravado—she was touching Arawn's face, the *Demon Lord's* face, and he *let* her, allowed her this close, granted her something that very likely few others were entitled to. She had yet to see him interact physically with...anyone, really.

She stroked along his jaw, the stubble rasping over her fingertips, then brushed the very edge of his lips, not quite daring to fully touch them. Her hand slid lower, and with a pounding heart, she watched his expression as she stroked down his throat. A vulnerable part of the body, even for a creature of Arawn's power, and the fact that he didn't budge an inch, calmly let her explore him, it did something to her.

She gasped and withdrew her hand, her fingers tingling from the warmth of his skin. Swallowing, she clenched her hand to a fist as if trying to hold on to the elusive sensation.

"My turn." The deep bass of his voice resonated through her.

And at that, Maeve stilled.

Dear gods. She'd been so focused on wanting to feel him, she hadn't specified what kind of touch she was willing to allow. What if he touched her intimately? Despite the freedom of her fantasy about him, despite the *want* pulsing in her core, it was one thing to imagine physical contact in the safety of her mind, but to face the real possibility of it? What if, based on what he'd glimpsed of her dream, he thought he could—

Her burgeoning panic fizzled out as he lifted his hand to her face, mirroring the way she'd touched him.

Stomach sinking, she closed her eyes, tingling heat

flushing her face, her ears. Of course he'd want to trace that jagged line of the scar marring her face. The first thing anyone noticed about her. The one feature guaranteed to snag people's attention—and hold it. Even when they tried to ignore it, their eyes would skip back to that scar every couple of seconds, and the longer they had to pretend not to want to stare, the more uncomfortable they'd get. Until they'd find an excuse to wiggle out of the conversation, if only to spare themselves the awkwardness…

A feather-light touch of Arawn's fingertips on her lashes.

She gasped, her breath stuck in her throat. He was touching her *eyelashes*. With a tenderness she would never have imagined him capable of, he grazed them, one eye after the other, the touch soft and almost…reverent. His fingers withdrew, only to be replaced by the warmth of his breath the next second as he leaned in—and gently, lightly, kissed her eyes, his lips deliberately brushing over her lashes, as if seeking that tactile stimulation.

After a moment of aching heartbeats he drew back, leaving her shaken to her core.

"Take some time to recover," he murmured, and she wasn't at all sure he meant from the exhaustion of the spellwork study session.

CHAPTER 15

The statement, this time, was even more blatant.

Arawn stared at the butchery in front of him, the human limbs strewn on the ground, arranged so it denied any natural feeding pattern. As Deimos—who had examined the scene first—confirmed, the visible wounds were not consistent with those made by predators killing for a meal, whether of the natural or otherworldly kind. As with the first one found two days ago, this slaughter spoke of either senseless violence, or a *very* deliberate provocation.

He crouched down, studied one of the piles of internal organs topped by the human male's head. The man's face was frozen in an expression of horror, unmistakable even though his eyes were missing, his tongue cut out of his gaping mouth. The other two human heads—another male and one female, propped on top of their respective heaps of organs—displayed the same kind of mutilation. The eyes and tongues were all laid out before the heaps of organs, along with the brains from the opened skulls.

Though humans were more than capable of sociopathic brutality of this caliber, something about this particular butchery whispered of the sort of detached yet feral cruelty most commonly found in long-lived otherworld species, especially demons or fae. Shifters were rarely this precise in their slaughter—when they snapped, they rampaged. They didn't arrange their kills in a calculated pattern like this.

They would also have eaten all the organs.

Someone with more sense than a shifter running amok was making a game of killing humans—and dumping the bloody remains in a way that could not be interpreted as anything but a provocation.

Because this time…the scene was laid out *within* Arawn's territory.

His blood burning with cold fury at the slight, at the *insolence*, he rose and turned to Deimos, who was glowering at the bloody arrangement while leaning against a tree. His second clearly shared his mood, no doubt taking this as an insult to his ability to keep Arawn's dominion safe.

"What have you heard in the grapevine?" Arawn asked him.

Black lashes lowered over eyes of piercing blue, rose again as Deimos looked at him. "No one we know did this." He pushed off the tree, approached the slaughter with careful steps that spoke of leashed power. "I talked to the demons, the shifters…nothing. There's unrest growing in Faerie since the royal court was murdered, but no reports of fae fleeing the realm yet. No rumors of a fae gone off the deep end and leaving corpses in their wake."

"This smells of old magic," he murmured.

Deimos' expression sharpened. "The scent you picked up?"

Arawn nodded, drawing in that elusive trace yet again. "I have a theory."

"Care to share?"

"Do you recall," he said, the grass beneath his bare feet soft and wet from the recent rain, "the conversation we had all those years ago?"

The other male became still in that way so intrinsic to all predators. "I have not found a single trace. No whispers. If this is one of them…"

There was no amusement behind his smile. "They are bound to be sneaky, Deimos."

A long look from his second, then a scoff. "If they are anything like you, yeah."

This time, real humor caused him to smile. Deimos was among the select few entitled to speak to him this way, had earned that right through unflinching loyalty over hundreds of years.

"I cannot be sure yet," Arawn said after a moment, "whether my theory is correct. At this point, it could still be the work of a mind gone mad."

For if the perpetrator was a regular otherworld creature, then dropping heaps of blood and gore not just close to Arawn's border, but *in* his territory, indicated some form of insanity.

"In which case, though," Deimos added, "there should be more clues to their identity, more tracks and evidence to follow. This"—he gestured at the scene—"is almost pristine in terms of arrangement. Whoever did this took great care to conceal who they are."

"Because they are playing a game." Arawn tilted his head, pondered the blood-drenched display. "It is not an open declaration of war. Not a surgical strike to my dominion." For that, the perpetrator would have had to hit something entirely different than a few random humans. Which made this all the more puzzling.

"But it *is* a provocation." Deimos narrowed his cerulean eyes.

"Yes."

Because, looking at the two incidents, whoever did this was moving *into* Arawn's territory, a deliberate poke.

He didn't like being poked.

୧୬୬

"All right. Here goes."

Maeve took a deep breath and stepped out of her cabin, onto the hanging bridge. The wood creaked beneath her shoes, the bridge swaying slightly as she crossed over to the slope. The late afternoon sun peeked out through intermittent clouds that had released drizzles of rain earlier, leaving the ground still wet, the air heavy with moisture.

On the slope in front of the bridge, she halted, cleared her throat. "Kelior?"

A few seconds ticked by, so she followed up with, "Hello?"

The soft sounds of footsteps on cushioned forest ground, and then the male she almost charbroiled yesterday emerged from the brush. Shoulder-length red hair framed a face of finely sculpted masculine beauty, his skin white with a golden shimmer.

"Maeve," he said, bowing his head in greeting. "Is there something you need?"

"Yes." She wet her lips. "I want to apologize."

Red brows drew together over his light blue eyes. "For what?"

"For freaking out yesterday." She fidgeted with the seam of her sweater. "It wasn't your fault, you know. And I just want to let you know it's nothing personal. I just...have some issues."

He shook his head. "No apology needed. I overstepped my bounds. I shouldn't have—"

"You stepped in to help me." She swallowed. "I appreciate that."

If he hadn't caught her, she'd have gotten a lot more than those few bruises and scratches—which had perplexingly healed overnight. *And if I wasn't so messed up, I could have simply thanked you instead of trying to burn you to a crisp...*

He bowed, this time from the waist. "I bear you no ill will."

"Neither do I." A sigh of relief. "Want to take a walk?"

His eyes flickered with surprise, but he caught himself quickly. "It would be my pleasure."

She nodded, and together they strolled down one of the many meandering paths near her cabin. Anxiety still a buzz in her blood, she made herself breathe slowly, steadily, while walking next to this male who was as yet unfamiliar to her, a fact that made her pulse flutter as fast as the wings of a bird trapped in a cage.

Which was exactly why she forced herself to do this. *I don't want to be snared by fear anymore.*

"How did you control my fire?" she asked. "You're not a demon, are you?" Given he was her daytime guard and able to use his magic when the sun was up, he had to be of a different species.

"No, I'm not." The light caught in his red strands as he angled his head, and the motion revealed the pointed ends of his ears that had been hidden by his hair.

"Fae?"

He nodded. "Fire fae. I can't create it," he said with a self-conscious smile when she opened her mouth to ask that exact question, "but I can control any flames I encounter."

Intrigued, she regarded him, his medieval-looking hunter's attire, the daggers strapped to his sides, the sword on his belt. "I've never met a fae before."

Well, that wasn't *quite* true. Basil Murray, one of her best friends with all the makings of a big brother, if not by blood then by bonds of affection, recently turned out to be half fae, half demon. He wasn't related to the Murrays after all, but rather taken in as a baby and raised as Hazel's son and Lily's twin brother. The complex story of how he was swapped for Lily's real twin sister, Rose, by a fae who bound Hazel to secrecy about it all was the stuff of an adventure novel.

Basil had recently run off to Faerie to find Rose and bring her back, and Hazel followed him not much later, with Basil's father, the demon Tallak. Maeve's head still spun from putting and keeping all those pieces together, and a part of her hungered for news of how Basil and Hazel were doing... whether they were back yet. Unharmed.

"There aren't that many fae outside of Faerie," she said to the male walking next to her. "Meeting one is very rare."

"Yes, we do prefer to stay safely ensconced within our borders."

She peered at him out of the corner of her eye.

"Go on," he said with a sly smile. "Ask me."

Well... "Then why do you live here, in Arawn's dominion?"

"I had to flee Faerie and ask the Demon Lord for asylum. There was a price on my head, and entering Arawn's service was the only way I could obtain the necessary protection to avoid the bounty hunters sent after me. I bargained for my life in exchange for sixty years of working for Arawn."

She gasped. "*Sixty* years?"

"It might seem long to a mortal. For fae, that's a tiny fraction of our life span. And it's not too high a price to pay to evade the court's wrath."

"The fae court?"

He nodded, shrugged. "I made the mistake of seducing the mate of a highborn noble, and drew the male's unending ire."

"He wanted you dead simply for sleeping with his wife?"

A humorless chuckle. "Fae males are notoriously possessive and territorial, and they defend their honor relentlessly. So, yes, cuckolding him was sufficient reason for him to unleash bounty hunters on me." He sighed, his eyes turning flat. "So even when my service with Arawn ends, I won't be able to return to my homeland. He'll never stop hounding me, and he'll *know* it as soon as I step foot across the border."

"But," she said with a frown, "the entire royal court was murdered about a week ago."

Kelior stopped dead in his tracks, his body tense. "What?"

"You…haven't heard?"

"No," he choked out through clenched teeth. "How do you know?"

She pushed a stray lock of her hair off her face where it tickled her nose, only to pull it back again right away, familiar embarrassment heating her cheeks. "The…demon who did it showed up on the Murrays' doorstep. He pretended to be the fae who'd exchanged Basil for Hazel's real daughter right after birth, and claimed to have come for him now. But Hazel was suspicious and hit him with a truth spell, forced him to come clean about his real identity, and the fact that Basil is his son from an illicit relationship with a fae. Apparently, the fae court imprisoned him twenty-six years ago and he only recently managed to escape." A pause. "He killed all the royals in revenge for his lover and child. He believed both of them had been murdered, until he learned Basil was still alive."

Kelior blew out a breath that was half a laugh. "They're all dead?"

She nodded. "Hazel's truth spell was incredibly powerful. The demon couldn't have lied about it."

Hope lit Kelior's light blue eyes for a moment before a shadow passed over his features. "Well, I still can't return home. Not yet. I have another thirty years on my contract."

"Oh," Maeve whispered, feeling the sting of disappointment on his behalf.

She was about to suggest he ask Arawn for a reduction of his term of service when Kelior froze. Signaling her to be quiet, he drew his sword, angled his head as if listening. She strained to hear whatever it was that had alerted him, but her ears picked up nothing but the usual forest sounds.

With a gesture for her to stay back, he rushed into the undergrowth, vanished in the maze of the woods.

Heart pounding, she waited. Listened.

There. Faint sounds…of a struggle. Rustling, snarling, hissing. Silence.

She peeked between the trees, made out the form of Kelior a few yards away, bent over something on the ground, hidden by ferns. His posture wasn't tense anymore, and he sheathed his sword, so she gave in to her curiosity and inched closer.

When he noticed her approach, he didn't order her to stay back, simply grimaced and said, "I'm not sure you want to see this. Maybe you should…"

But she'd already glimpsed it, was there before she could make the conscious decision to do so.

A choked sob built in her throat. Her hand shook as she raised it to cover her mouth. "Is it…?"

"Not yet." He clenched his jaw. "It might be a mercy to end it, though."

The bobcat's paws twitched, a heavy breath rattling in its chest. There was so much damage…

"What did this?" Her voice was a broken whisper.

"My best guess…some sort of acid, or maybe kerosene and fire"—a pause, a hard swallow—"judging by how much fur and skin is burned."

"Who would—" She blinked against the blur of tears.

"Some…humans are known to torture animals thus." He unsheathed a dagger. "I suppose it was attacked outside Arawn's lands, near a settlement, and it managed to get away before they killed it, then dragged itself this far."

The tears spilled over now, warm and salty on her lips, dripping onto the bobcat's fur as she leaned over the suffering animal. "Can we… Is there anything we can do? Maybe we can get it to a healer?"

She reached out to the limp cat with hesitant fingers, her chest *aching* with the need to help.

A hiss, a flash of claws and teeth, sharp pain shooting up her arm. Droplets of her blood settled on her clothes and on the snarling bobcat as it sank back to the ground, quivering from the last-ditch effort to defend itself. Kelior lunged forward, his dagger at the ready, but she held him back with her good arm, pressing the other to her front.

"Don't!" She sniffled, more hot tears tracking down her face. She wiped them off, her hand wet from her tears, her blood.

"It'll be cruel to let it suffer longer," Kelior replied.

She pressed her lips together. Reaching out once more to the bobcat, she managed to lay her hand on its flank this time, on the part not burned. The feline whimpered, its paws flexing, but it held still.

"I'm sorry," Maeve whispered.

She withdrew her hand, closed her eyes, and nodded at Kelior.

But the fae didn't kill it.

"Look," he said instead, a strange note to his voice.

So she did. Opening her eyes, she frowned at the cat… whose wounds were healing. Fresh pink skin where minutes before its flesh was charred and twisted, new fur growing where it had burned off.

"Are you doing this?" she rasped, gaping at Kelior.

He shook his head, eyes wide. "Are you?"

"No." She swallowed hard. "I wouldn't know how, even if had access to my witch powers. I never learned how to heal."

Never learned how to wield her magic *at all*, since it was locked inside her when she was eight.

"Well, *someone* has to be doing this," Kelior muttered, "because this cat was dying, and now it's…"

"Purring." She blinked, her thoughts frozen in sheer disbelief.

Its lighter wounds were now almost completely covered by spotted fur again, the worse ones still healing, with new skin, the bobcat rose on wobbly legs. Maeve gaped as it moved, its feline grace returning to limbs that were all but limp with impending death just moments ago.

A long, unreadable look out of fathomless yellow eyes, and then the cat bounded—*bounded*—away into the growing shadows of the evening woods.

"What just happened?" Maeve asked, her voice expressionless.

"I have no idea," Kelior said just as flatly. "But if I were Death, I'd be thoroughly vexed right now."

CHAPTER 16

Merle disconnected the call and pocketed her cell phone again, walking out of the room she currently occupied at the Murray mansion, down the hall to the staircase. After the escalation at the meeting with the Draconians, she and the others agreed it was better for her to stick close to the Aequitas, since—without Rhun—she was the only one living at the Victorian. The Murray mansion offered more than enough room for her to bunk down, and she'd be with Lily and Alek, who were still camped out here, too.

And now Hazel was back from Faerie, Merle had the additional protection of a powerful Elder witch living with her.

This afternoon's return of Hazel, Basil, and Tallak—Basil's demon father, something she still couldn't wrap her mind around—this afternoon was a welcome surprise, all the more joyous in light of Basil's mating to his newfound love, the fae Isa, as well as the fact they found Rose alive and were able to bring her home.

So now the Murray mansion was filled once more with love, laughter, the occasional snide remark, all in good humor, and above all, *hope*. After losing both Maeve and Rhun in such a short time—she couldn't stop to think about that, or else she'd break down—Merle sorely needed the company, the comfort, and the support of her friends who were like chosen family to her. If she didn't smile or joke with them at least a little, she'd crumple to dust under the pressure of needing to find Rhun, of needing to make sure he didn't hurt anymore.

Hazel's presence in particular was reassuring, the other Elder witch's magic as warm and nurturing as it was powerful. Having Hazel back gave Merle more confidence that they could soon free her mate.

Which brought her back to…

She entered the kitchen, joined Hazel and Lily where they sat in the breakfast nook, looking out at the moonlit garden. Rose lay on her back on the grass, where she'd been for over an hour already. Even though she was Lily's identical twin, and should resemble her in appearance, the difference—born of years of neglect and starvation, both physically as well as magically—was striking. It hurt Merle to even look at Rose, the other witch's cheeks too hollow, arms and legs too thin, her aura subdued, her powers stifled.

Hazel would feed her back to strength, in more ways than one, but until then, Rose was a wraith, the shadow of a husk of what she should be.

Merle swallowed, forced her attention away from the young woman who seemed to have suffered an even worse ordeal than Maeve. "Where's Basil?" she asked instead.

Lily smirked, humor lighting her indigo eyes. "He's…busy."

Merle realized Isa was nowhere to be found either and grinned. "Riiiight."

Good for him. Her heart jumped with joy for Baz, her chest a little less tight just knowing he'd found happiness and love. They needed more of that in these difficult times.

"What about Tallak? Where's he off to?"

"Brooding, for all I care." Hazel folded her arms, her usually warm brown eyes chilled at the mention of the *hæmingr* demon.

To say she and Basil's biological father had gotten off to a rocky start was quite the understatement. One would think they'd have a lot in common, seeing as they both loved Baz as their child, but putting these two together in one room—or simply in the same general metro area—was akin to throwing a cat and a dog in the same crate. Highly entertaining, as Rhun would say, but also a bloody mess of fur and claws and teeth that could only end badly.

"So," Merle said, changing the subject before Hazel's hackles rose too much, "I just got off the phone with Shobha Gupta. It seems we've got a good chance at snatching a witch after all." She drummed her fingers on the table, biting her lip.

"Merle," Lily sighed, tilting her head, "don't *make* me pull it out of you, because I *will*."

Grinning at her best friend since kindergarten, she explained, "Anjali's mate is a shadow demon."

Lily narrowed her eyes, but Hazel caught on.

She raised her dark brows. "They're going to use his skills to sneak up on one of Juneau's witches."

"Yes." Merle smiled. "It's perfect. Thorne can get close to them without anyone noticing, and he can even pull someone into his shadow cloaking to conceal them as well. With the right tools and some assistance, he can not only trap a witch, he can bring her to us unseen."

Lily straightened. "That's brilliant."

Merle nodded. "The Guptas will send a witch with him to help render the Draconians' witch unconscious and all, and they'll let us know as soon as they have snatched someone."

"I can't tell you how much I love it that we've all gone Dark Side," Lily said with a smug smile. "Using demon powers alongside witch magic." She shook her head, still grinning. "How devious."

"And not too long ago," Alek said, strolling into the kitchen, "that idea would have made you go into cardiac arrest."

Lily angled her head back to accept Alek's kiss as he leaned over from behind her chair. "Well, I *am* capable of change. I stopped fighting my demons." An unrepentant grin. "Now I snuggle with them instead."

"Oh, please." Merle rolled her eyes, pointed her finger at Lily. "I was the first of us to snuggle with a demon."

"Funny how more and more of you witches seem to end up with one," Alek mused.

Hazel startled after a moment, glanced around. "What are you all looking at me for?"

"Nothing," everybody said, a tad too quickly.

Alek cleared his throat, his expression turning somber as he looked at Merle. "I have a summons for you."

Merle froze. "What? From Arawn?"

Jaw clenched, Alek nodded.

"What does he want? Is it Maeve? Did you hear anything from her?"

He combed a hand through his hair. "I haven't been able to find out how she's doing. Where she even is. But Arawn wants to see you. Tonight. He didn't say why, just that you're supposed to come with me."

Heart threatening to beat out of her ribcage, Merle rose.

"Wait." Lily laid a hand on her arm. "You're not walking in there just like that, are you?"

"He's promised safe passage in and out," Alek said grudgingly.

Merle hesitated for a moment, then nodded at the *prana-graha* demon. "Let's go."

They went out to Alek's pickup, drove off under cover of new camouflage spells courtesy of Hazel, meant to confuse anyone staking out the house, so they wouldn't be able to focus on a vehicle leaving the mansion. The spell was strong enough to cling to a car driving off the property, then continue for a few miles before vanishing. Made it near impossible to ambush anyone close to the house.

When Alek didn't take the route to the infamous lake that so far was the only means to reach Arawn's lair, Merle frowned at him.

"I thought we were going to Arawn."

Alek's hands clenched on the steering wheel. "We are."

"But—"

"Just wait. You'll see."

Unease prickled through her. "You know that I *can* still use my magic, right? And that I will if I'm threatened."

Alek snorted. "Please. Like I'd hurt a hair on your head when you're my mate's best friend." A dark glance. "Not to mention I'd rather rip off my arm than harm a pregnant female."

"Well, okay, then." She rubbed her nose. "Just so we're on the same page and all."

"We're simply taking another way to Arawn's." His voice was threaded with a growl.

She raised her brows just as he parked at the side of a road near a towering cliff half-covered by evergreens. "I thought the lake was *the* way to his lair."

"So did I." Alek got out of the truck, his growl becoming more distinct. "Ten years. Ten damn *years* I've been working for the bastard, and he never once deigned to show me this route, much less let me use it." He stalked ahead of her toward the cliff. "I had to go through the fucking lake each and every time he summoned me."

And thus arrive in front Arawn dripping wet, cold, and uncomfortable, which was kind of the whole point with the Demon Lord's insistence that people use the lake to get to him.

"Yeah, me too." She followed Alek up into a cave that hadn't been visible from where they parked, the shimmer in the air betraying the magic most likely used to conceal this entrance from anyone not privy to its location. She was probably only able to see it because she was with Alek. "All these months I've been traveling to his lair to perform magic for him, he made me go through the lake."

"He's a prick," Alek ground out.

Merle frowned as they walked into enveloping darkness, sounds hushed as if wrapped in velvet. "So why did he reveal this to you now? To me?"

"Take my hand," Alek said. "I can see in the dark. You can't."

She grabbed his hand, and he guided her farther down the tunnel, the air increasingly abuzz with power.

"I don't know why he'd give us this easier route now," Alek said after a moment. "Who knows what's going on in that fucked-up head of his? Maybe it's another ploy. Another move on his chess board or whatever."

"Do you know the moment I knew you were an okay guy?"

"When I saved Lily from killing her brother?"

"Well, yes, that too." She waved it away, knowing he could see it in the pitch black. "No, I mean when I realized you resent Arawn even more than I do."

"Bonding over Arawn hate," Alek muttered. "That's one way to become fast friends."

The air changed, a fresh, chilly breeze blowing into the tunnel. Light glowed up ahead.

Merle breathed a sigh of relief, swallowing down the slowly rising fear of being enclosed beneath tons of stone. "I take it this passage is enchanted, similar to the lake?"

"I suppose so. The exit is definitely not from the same cliff where we entered. Miles and miles between."

"Magically linked."

"Yep."

She scoffed. "He really could have let us travel to him without getting soaked all this time."

"Like I said. Rat bastard."

She let go of his hand when it was light enough for her to see the path. Soon after, they stepped out of the cave and onto a trail leading into the forest.

Fairies flitted past, the air glittering in the wake of their flight. Fireflies swirled over the path and illuminated the ground enough for Merle to make out the way. She narrowed her eyes in anger as she remembered how Arawn had once ordered her to change the fireflies' color to red. Just for shits and giggles. *Asshole.*

"I wonder what he wants now," Merle whispered. "He paused the deal, and Maeve's surrendering herself to him fulfilled the initial bargain anyway, which means I'm free of him. So *what* could he *possibly* want from me now?"

Alek grimaced. "You know I can't tell you anything reassuring." He gestured at a cluster of trees up ahead that looked suspiciously like a...cathedral. "This is where he told me to bring you."

Doors of intricately interwoven branches swung open as if pulled by an invisible rope, and Merle and Alek stepped into what indeed looked like a lofty, vaulted hall, the walls and ceiling made of trees that interlocked in complex, beautiful patterns. Gently glowing balls of light floated in the air and bathed the natural cathedral in soft, warm radiance.

Merle's breath stalled in her lungs as she noticed the platform on the other end of the hall, the person sitting on one of the chaise lounges there. The world paused in its turning, just like her heart stopped beating for a moment.

"Maeve," she whispered.

And fell to her knees.

CHAPTER 17

Maeve rose on wobbly legs from the chaise lounge and everything else fell away—the game of mahjong Lucía had suggested playing with her here in the Grove, the presence of the demon-shifter hybrid next to her, the beauty of the floating lights drifting about the room.

Everything but the sight of her sister, on her knees on the moss-covered ground, tears streaking down her face.

Maeve rushed to her. Tackled her with a hug that toppled them both to the floor in a tangled, hugging, sobbing mess. They clung tight to each other for achingly long moments, and Maeve's lungs burned from her happy crying.

Sniffling, Merle drew back, both hands cupping Maeve's face, her sky-blue eyes—reddened now from crying—searching Maeve. "Are you okay? Are you hurt? Did he—"

Her attention snagged on Maeve's forearm. Pushing up the sleeve, Merle scowled, magic crackling in the air around her. "Did he do that?"

"What?" Maeve glanced down at her arm, at the bandage there. "No! That was a bobcat. It was injured, and I tried to help it, and it freaked out and scratched me." She shook her head. "Arawn hasn't laid a hand on me."

Merle's eyes narrowed, her features pinched tight. "Right."

Tension locked Maeve's muscles, and her stomach knotted. "No, seriously. He treats me very well."

The doubt didn't dissipate from Merle's expression. If anything, she seemed even warier than before. And it hit Maeve that not too long ago, she would have been just as unconvinced and mistrustful. Merle still believed Arawn to be the ruthless monster they all made him out to be, as Maeve had done when she walked into his lair. How much her impression of him had changed…it was even more apparent, more striking in its realization, when contrasted with Merle's lingering resentment.

Deciding to leave it be for now, to allow her sister's suspicion to fizzle out over time when faced with the reality she couldn't yet accept, she asked, "So how come you're here? Are you okay? Do you need anything?"

Merle frowned, glanced at Lucía, who had retreated to another corner of the Grove, giving them some privacy. "No, I… Arawn summoned me. Ordered Alek to bring me here."

Surprised, Maeve drew back. "He invited you. To come see me."

Merle's wary expression deepened. "I don't think that's the only reason he—"

"Such doubt," Arawn said, emerging from the shadows between trees.

Maeve's stomach made a cute little flip-flop, and her pulse kicked into high gear. She hadn't even known he was around. And did he own any shirts that did not mold to his muscled frame like a sensual caress?

When she saw Arawn, Merle stiffened, moved in front of Maeve in a not-so-subtle gesture. Maeve's chest drew tight while fine-clawed irritation raked along her nerves at her sister's reaction. She very deliberately stepped out from behind Merle to stand next to her.

Arawn's eyes flicked to her, some dark appreciation flashing through them, before he turned to Merle. "I did indeed invite you to see your sister. You are free to visit her anytime, as are her friends. Just request it, and Aleksandr will bring you here."

A muscled ticked in Merle's jaw. "And is Maeve free to leave and visit us anytime as well?"

"Careful, fire witch." His voice lethally quiet, he tilted his head, regarded Merle with a primal warning lurking behind his focus. "You would do well not to push me. She is mine, and I will keep what is mine close to me."

Maeve should have bristled at his words, his tone, the *insinuation* in his statement. She waited for some form of dread to chill her limbs, or anger to snap at her composure. But all she got was a wayward prickle of excitement that stole her breath for a moment. So *wrong*.

"Now," Arawn said, dismissing Merle's patented death glare as if swatting away a fly, "enjoy your visit. Aleksandr will escort you back out once you are finished."

After signaling Alek, who'd been watching the entire exchange with a rather uneasy look on his face, Arawn strode out of the Grove.

"It's good seeing you," Alek said to Maeve with a small smile before he followed Arawn.

Merle watched Arawn's retreat with narrowed eyes.

Not in the mood to combat Merle's mistrust, Maeve opted for redirection. "How are things at home? Have you heard from Basil and Hazel?"

Merle's features darkened even more. "They're back. In one piece, and they brought Rose with them."

"But?"

"Juneau kidnapped Rhun." Her eyes bore a hard glint. "But we're going to get him back, and when we do, I am going to burn that bitch alive."

⚙️

ARAWN WAITED OUTSIDE THE GROVE FOR ALEKSANDR, TURNED to him as soon as the *pranagraha* exited.

"I have a new assignment for you."

The young demon tried to keep his expression neutral. Failed. Resentment hardened his features, the grudge he bore Arawn too embedded in his mind, his heart. "I'm at your service, my lord."

Ten years now he'd been taking care of Aleksandr, provided him and his family with safety and the means to lead a good life, and it was still not enough to balance out what Arawn had unwittingly taken from him. Might never be enough.

That didn't mean Arawn would stop providing for him the only way he could without breaking the proud demon's spine. Aleksandr had spit on Arawn's offer to pay for his and his brothers' living expenses after their parents' death. He wouldn't accept charity. So Arawn made him work for it instead.

"You will guard Maeve with Lucía from now on," he said. "You will have your usual nights off, but your shifts will be spent at Maeve's side. Close to her if she wishes for company, from a distance if she wants to be alone." A pause, a pointed look. "From a *great* distance whenever I am near her."

Flecks of red glimmered in Aleksandr's eyes, quickly extinguished as the *pranagraha* wrestled his temper under control. "I will not stand by," the demon said quietly, "if you hurt her."

Arawn stared him down until the other male lowered his eyes.

"In the time you have worked for me," Arawn said with the precision of a sharpened blade cutting into flesh, "did I ever force you to act against your conscience?"

Aleksandr's nostrils flared. "No, sire."

"Did you ever hear or see me mistreat a female I courted?"

"No, sire."

"Then you might understand," he said while his powers clawed at him from the inside, "why I might consider snapping your neck for that comment alone."

The muscles in Aleksandr's jaw tensed. "My apologies, my lord."

He glowered at the young demon for another long moment, then added, "Make sure you use that protective streak of yours to guard her well."

"Yes, sire."

"Go back inside."

Aleksandr bowed and stalked back into the Grove.

The night wrapping gently around him, Arawn lingered, his footfalls cushioned by moss and shadows as he walked around the Grove, his attention caught by the gleam of red under the will-o'-the-wisps' lights within. Even though two fire-haired women now sat inside, only one drew his focus like a flame lured a moth. Through the gaps in the latticework of the tree-wrought walls, he watched Maeve while she talked with her sister.

They hugged again, and Maeve's eyes darted down to Merle's belly, her face alight with happiness.

And then she smiled.

His world ground to a halt.

He froze where he stood, everything, *everything* within him grown still, hushed into awe. He'd seen innumerable sunsets over snow-capped mountains and glittering seas, he'd seen civilizations rise and fall, merciful deaths, and the tender beginnings of life. And yet nothing compared to the resplendence of Maeve when she smiled.

The transformation of her features was striking, the way she seemed to glow from within, and that scar she so desperately tried to conceal…it should have been a contradiction to the radiance of her beauty, only it wasn't. Far from a disfigurement to be hidden in shame, it turned into a statement all its own, a fitting piece in the puzzle of her flawed perfection, a stark proclamation of beauty inherent in strength and survival.

His powers whispered out into the night and reached for her, hungry, craving, *seeking*. He yanked them back with a low snarl. *Not yet*. There were steps yet to take in this dance of instinct and reason, before he could glom on what—*who*—kept him awake even in those few hours he liked to devote to sleep.

He'd had thousands of years to learn the virtue of patience. He'd perfected it to an art form. And the anticipation of his reward…it hummed over his nerves, infused his blood with a sweet thrill. He was on the prowl, with slow, measured steps, his leash the ever-present awareness that if he pounced too soon, he'd lose her. But he'd begun his hunt. He would see it to a close. Unhurried, he would coax her until she felt safe enough to tumble into him in spite of the horrors ensnaring her mind.

And then he'd recreate that dream she had of them together. Every. Single. Detail.

He wrenched his gaze away from the allure of her, turned his back on the Grove, and went in search of one of his most trusted enforcers. Finding the shifter in his apartment belowground, he cut to the chase.

"I need you to find something for me," he said to the male who was the most skilled of all Arawn's enforcers at locating or retrieving even the rarest oddities that struck Arawn's fancy.

"My lord." The fox shifter bowed his head, listened to

Arawn's description, and vowed to bring the object to him by tomorrow night.

Knowing the wily male, Arawn would have it by morning.

Leaving the fox's den to ascend to the surface again, Arawn decided to check on another project. He pulled out the cell phone Lucía had pestered him to get, dialed a number.

He didn't like this piece of technology. Far from being averse to some of modernity's more useful inventions, he still didn't see much sense in getting used to a communication device he had to leave lying around more times than not, considering how often he shifted and roamed in his animal forms.

However, Lucía had poked him until he agreed to at least carry—and use—it when he was in human shape and fully dressed.

It did have some perks. Long-range communication far beyond the reach of his magic. Access to the Internet and its wealth of knowledge. The Fruit Ninja game.

The demon on the other end of the line picked up. "Lord Arawn."

"Stasya. What is the status?"

"I was just about to call. She accepted your offer, sire."

"Good. When is she coming?"

"She'll arrive tomorrow."

"Excellent. Make sure she has everything she needs, and let me know when she gets here."

"Of course, my lord."

He disconnected the call, just as another of his enforcers— a storm demon on border patrol—approached him.

"Lord Arawn," he said, bowing deep from the waist. "There is an alp here to beg for a favor."

"Bring it into the lower chamber. I will be down in a minute."

Another creature willing to bind itself to him for assistance with whatever issues plagued it. Another brick in the empire he was building.

Hands in his pockets, he strolled underground, his thoughts on a witch with an ancient beast waking inside her.

CHAPTER 18

I t wasn't until noon the next day that Arawn came to see
Maeve again.

Her heart light in a way it hadn't been for a while,
the warmth of seeing Merle the night before still lingering,
she sat on a moss-covered boulder under the arching canopy
of the forest, the bobcat she met the other day curled up next
to her.

Perplexingly, the feline had sought her out this morning,
followed her on her walk through the woods, first with some
distance, then closer, until it brushed up against her legs
when she paused on the path. She could still make out the
areas on its body that had been burned, the fur there a bit
shorter, if otherwise shiny and healthy.

And she still had no idea what the hell had happened to
cause the cat to heal from such grievous wounds so quickly.

Maybe it had something to do with her blood? Her own
injuries—the cut in her wrist from the first day, the scratches
and bruises from her fall—had healed practically overnight. A
gift from the bond with Arawn, perhaps? If so, maybe some
of her blood had mixed with the bobcat's when the animal
clawed at her, transferring her healing ability to the feline.

It would explain why the animal now seemed bonded to her. As aggressive as the cat was when she found it yesterday, it now purred next to her, even allowing Maeve to pet it. She'd have to ask Arawn.

As if on cue, the dark caress of his energy brushed her strengthening magical senses right before the undergrowth rustled as he stepped out from between the shadows of the forest—in his wolf form.

Twice the size of the standard version of *canis lupus*, his fur an inky black that seemed to swallow the light the same way Arawn's hair did in his human shape, the sight of him robbed her of breath for a good few seconds. He was magnificent. Primal, predatory perfection, wild dominance in his every move, the feral focus of a creature that was as much an expert killer as it was capable of binding loyalty to its own.

The bobcat looked up and merely blinked at the canine, no doubt recognizing the enigmatic being within the animal shape, because it didn't panic and run. Instead it stretched lazily, arching its back and flexing its legs, before it hopped off the boulder, sauntered over to the wolf, and rubbed its cheek against him. With a chirp, the feline strolled away into the forest.

"I figured out what you are," Maeve said.

Arawn's focus grew laser-sharp, his powers vibrating around him.

"You're Tarzan reincarnate."

He huffed, sent her a positively insulted look out of those yellow wolf eyes.

"It would explain your preference for prancing around shirtless."

A *very* wolfish grin.

Amusement curled inside her, buzzed through her veins. When the corners of her mouth twitched, she glanced away, biting her lip.

Velvet stroking over her senses, a touch of his power

against her mind. Her pulse suddenly thumped in the spot between her thighs, her body reacting to this slightest of mental caresses like a dry wood to a spark.

When she turned to him, he stood right in front of her, still in wolf form...close enough to touch.

So she did.

Tentatively, she raised her hand, ran her fingers through the fur at his neck. Silky soft, with a coarse topcoat, it was a sensual pleasure to stroke. He moved closer to her, pressed his flank against her legs, the boulder's height such that her knees were almost level with his back. A rumble came from his massive body, a distinctly contented canine sound.

More dark power poured off him, twined around her hand in prickling shadows as she massaged his head, caressed his wolf ears. That compelling, tenebrous magic of his that coiled around her arm seemed to caress her in turn, and she inhaled sharply at the sensation. Not in fear, but in welcome.

As her body went molten with longing for more of that touch, she withdrew her hand, clenched in her lap.

A *tug* on that bond inside her had her tumbling forward, off the boulder, until she fell on the wolf, had to grab his fur with both hands to steady herself.

"You jerk," she hissed and raised her hand to slap at him.

He danced out of her reach on agile wolf legs, his tail swinging high, his mouth open in a grin, eyes sparkling with challenge. Was he—? Yes, he was *playing* with her. Not as in toying, not the kind of predatory amusement of a cat batting around its prey, but a real, honest enticement to have fun.

The Demon Lord invited her to *play*.

The corners of her mouth wanted to twitch upward again, a fuzzy sort of warmth spreading in her chest. Dropping her raised hand, she feigned sudden interest in retying her shoes, saw him move out of the corner of her eye.

She jumped up just as he lunged with his head aimed to

thump against her back. She was quick—but he was quicker. He still half caught her with a head bump on her side, making her stagger as she darted out of his way.

Not missing a beat, he dashed after her.

With a muffled shriek, she zig-zagged around trees, her heart pounding up into her throat, adrenaline pumping through her veins. The good kind of adrenaline, the one that left you gasping for breath with a wide grin in your heart.

If only she had control of her powers, she'd send a rocket of sparks shooting after him to singe his tail. But as it was, she could only run, had nothing in her arsenal to turn the tables on him—except… The idea was as devious as it was thrilling, making her pulse hammer even faster.

As she darted around yet another tree, Arawn hot on her heels—he was clearly holding back, could have tackled her a thousand times already—she brought up a memory, let the details flood her mind.

And then, with what little skill she'd scrounged together after years of training with her grandmother, she lowered those fragile shields around her thoughts and *sent* the images out.

Skin on skin, coarse hair tickling her face, her lips closing around…

A crash behind her, a growling yelp. She turned, swinging with one arm around a tree, to see the wolf scrambling to his feet after what looked like a nasty tumble.

"Missed a step?" she asked with a grin.

He stilled, his expression sharpening into hunger tempered with…awe? A low tremor took hold of her at the intensity of his attention.

The air shimmered around him, misting in shadows and light. The being prowling over to her the next second might have been human in shape, but every inch the same feral hunter as the wolf she petted minutes ago.

Petted.

Heat shot up into her neck, her face, sweat coating her skin. As her eyes tracked down the expanse of impressive muscles and pure, unfettered strength crammed into the mouthwatering form of a man who could be the dictionary definition of "beefcake," the realization that she'd basically caressed him—albeit in wolf form—dispelled her thoughts for a moment. Fur or not, for him that touch must have been...

"...invigorating," he murmured.

She startled, and wrenched her gaze from the part of his anatomy that clearly had received most of that invigoration.

"I have been called many names," he said, leaning close, "but 'beefcake' is a new one."

She'd left her mind open to him. "Oh, gods."

"Just me," he corrected with a smirk.

He leaned closer still, his heat rolling up and over her like waves to the shore, and she froze, her heart thumping as he... grabbed a pair of pants from somewhere behind her, stepped back and pulled them on.

She whipped her head around, caught a glimpse of a dryad vanishing back into her tree. Facing him again, she asked, "Do all of the tree nymphs just hang around waiting for you with a pair of pants?"

"They are a patient and undemanding lot."

"I feel watched."

"We could always go to your cabin and close the curtains."

The flood of effervescent warmth inside her would surely bubble over at any moment. Clearing her throat, she inched away from him, from the sensual promise in his regard. "So, will you study the spell again?"

"If you let me."

She gave a jerky nod. She *wanted* those powers, not just to chase him with sparks in play, but to—*finally*—be able to defend herself, dammit. All her life she'd been dependent on others for protection. Always the liability, never the asset.

I don't want to be weak anymore.

"The beast inside me," she said softly, "it's strong, right?"

His eyes seemed to bore into her. "Every Old One was as powerful as an entire witch community."

Holy crap. That kind of force… "I want that." A whisper. A pledge.

His eyes gleamed. "As is your birthright."

Swallowing, she took a seat on a fallen log. "Go ahead."

She inhaled a startled breath as his presence entered her mind. Rough silk over her senses, a gentle caress from those powers that were humming with brute strength, yet ever careful not to touch what she didn't offer. Entirely different from the violence of her only other experience of having someone else in her head…

His finger under her chin. "Eyes on me, Wildfire."

With a shuddering breath, she looked up at him, at that face of raw male beauty, held his gaze with a thundering heart. And the horrors wanting to claw at her fell away, eclipsed by her fascination with every harsh line of his features, the depth of swirling shadows in his eyes.

That awareness inside her stretched on a sigh, pressed against her core. Wings flaring in the dark, whispers of smoke, and an age-old ferocity that gentled at Arawn's nearness.

Come get me.

۞

ARAWN COULD ALMOST MAKE OUT WHAT LURKED AT THE BOTTOM of Maeve's soul, that ancient creature so at home in the flicker of flames, the blistering heat of a mighty blaze. And yet its form was hidden in shadows still, the fog of its confinement so thick it wouldn't fully reveal the beast.

Again he examined the intricacies of the spell, probed the layers and the locks with the same kind of cautious consideration a bomb disposal expert might show an armed explosive device. If he could not be sure where to start the dismantling, he'd rather leave it alone for a while longer, lest he trigger a blast that might erase the spirit of the redhead who'd entered his lair a subdued, withdrawn thing, only to blossom into a female who eagerly met the Demon Lord's dare to *play*.

She'd grinned at him.

Grinned.

It had taken every ounce of his finely-honed self-control not to kiss the curve of her lips in that moment, push her up against that tree and *devour* her. Whatever tenuous trust he'd built with her would have crumbled to dust at that move, shattering something between them that no power in the universe would be able to mend.

So, he waited, hungered, contented himself with an ever-growing list of things he wanted to do to her once she was warm and willing in his bed. Or on a boulder. Or the mossy ground. Or... He created a new list just for all the locations where he planned to pleasure her.

This time, he stopped the session before her energy levels were so low she was in danger of toppling over when she stood. Withdrawing from her mind with a subtle sensual caress that made her part her lips on a soft sound—his body hardening in reaction—he grounded her back in the physical world by twirling a lock of her fiery hair around his fingers, tugging gently.

"Hungry?"

Her eyes skittered to his mouth in response, and she clenched her thighs together in a move she probably wasn't even aware of. Her breath a tad faster, she licked her lips— and he remembered with torturous clarity the memory she'd sent him earlier. Yet again, his thoughts stuttered to a halt at the erotic allure of her dream, of sensing her imagined pleasure as her mouth closed around his cock.

"Just tell me when," he murmured, his fingers still tangled in her hair, "you would like to put me on the menu."

Copper lashes fluttered over eyes gone liquid fire kissed with smoke, her cheeks painted with a lovely blush.

A brush across his outer awareness, which was cast wide so he could monitor the area, the mental approach coming from Barnabas, the fox shifter he sent out last night. Equivalent to a polite knock, the male let him know from a distance that he was on his way to Arawn, the shifter's tact one of the reasons Arawn appreciated him so.

"Wait here," he said to the witch who was well and truly enthralling him, and headed out to meet Barnabas.

The log on which he left Maeve now several rows of trees away, he nodded at the fox, his attention darting to the box in the male's hands.

"I assume you found it."

Barnabas bowed. "Of course, my lord."

Arawn accepted a square package the size of a shoe box, thanked the shifter and sent him off again. Opening the lid, he examined the content, ran his finger over the object's edge. Satisfied with the quality of the workmanship, he closed the box, returned to the spot where Maeve waited.

Her delicate ginger brows drew together as she noticed the package. "What's that?"

"A gift."

Frown deepening, she took the box from his hand, opened it. A soft sound of surprise. Carefully, she lifted the bowl from its cushion, turned it to study it from all sides, her features slack with open astonishment. Lacquered in hues of dark red, the ceramic dish was interveined by gold threads.

"*Kintsugi*," he said in answer to the question written on her face. "It is a Japanese craft of mending fractured objects by gluing the broken pieces together using a golden lacquer. In this philosophy, breakage and repair are part of the history of an object, and instead of disguising the fracture points, they are highlighted and embraced as a form of beauty. If something breaks, it does not lose its value or appeal."

Her breath hitched, her lashes fluttering yet again, over eyes shimmering wet.

"When our bodies break," he added gently, "we heal, and we often realize we are stronger at the mended points."

She inhaled on a shudder, the hands holding the bowl trembling. An echo of her emotions pinged along the bond between them, so piercing, so consuming, he couldn't quite name it. The moisture in her eyes spilled over, silent tears tracking down her cheeks.

He shifted his weight, curled his fingers into his palm. Had he miscalculated? Had what was meant as a thoughtful gift hurt her in a way he hadn't intended? Was he beyond arrogance to have relied on thousands of years' experience learning to read people to correctly guess their desires and fears? Perhaps he should have—

"Thank you," she whispered.

He held his breath.

She swallowed, wiped the tears away with the heel of one hand, the other cradling the bowl. "Thank you for this."

"You are not broken," he said, his voice pitched low. "But if you feel you are, if you cannot help seeing yourself that way, then regard yourself as *kintsugi*."

He turned, wanting to leave her to settle her thoughts and feelings.

A touch on his hand. The warmth of her fingers on his.

"Arawn."

CHAPTER 19

Heart aflutter in her throat, Maeve held on to Arawn's hand, watched him slowly turn around to her. The contact of his fingers on hers was a hot brand she felt searing through the fiber of her soul. His shadowed green eyes studied her face, seemed to strip her bare of all the layers she liked to hide behind.

"Tell me," she said, her voice brittle, "something people don't know about you."

The crumbling walls of her composure, eroded by the depth of insight and consideration behind his gift, threatened to collapse, leave her exposed and shaken amid the awareness of just how well he knew her. She needed something in return, a piece of him she could shelter.

He regarded her for a long moment, and whatever he read on her face prompted him to grant her wish. "I do not like to sleep."

He stepped closer, and she clasped his hand more fully.

"I have trained myself," he went on, "to go without sleep for weeks while still being able to function, and when I do take a rest, it is only for a few short hours. I do not allow anyone to sleep next to me. Ever. My bed...the one I use for sleeping"—a smile playing around his mouth—"is in a secret room hidden so far beneath the earth, and behind wards so thick a hundred Elder witches could not breach them. I am the only one who has ever set foot in there."

That…was not simply a dislike of sleeping. Precautions like these spoke of *fear*. If there was one thing Maeve had become an expert in, it was the kind of compulsive behavior dictated by the scars terror would claw into your soul. Her heartbeat drummed in her head at the realization that Arawn…could be afraid.

Of what? What could possibly have been powerful enough to leave such an indelible mark on his soul?

A part of her longed to ask him, and yet it would be foolish to do so. She didn't have the right to request he bare his pain to her, not when it obviously went so deep. She knew all about the intricacies of vulnerability and sore spots in the heart and mind, and she'd be the last person to poke at someone's wounds, would rather wait to be given the gift of his trust in this, when he was ready to share with her of his own accord.

And she wanted that trust.

She marveled at the feeling, at the desire to be the one he entrusted with those aspects of him that were fragile with destructive potential.

Gods knew she was familiar with that combination.

So instead of prodding him for an explanation of his statement, she nodded. "I get that."

Because she truly did. And she didn't need to know the root of his fear to understand the implications, the way it would become second nature.

"I thought you would." One side of his mouth tilted up.

She was transfixed by the sensuality of that half smile. By his lips, which seemed the only soft part in a face that could have been hewn from hard rock. She'd felt the touch of those lips on her *lashes*, the caress of his breath on her nose, her cheeks, a sensory memory she hadn't been able to shake since that moment in her cabin.

Her mouth went dry while the craving she'd failed to stifle over the past days infused her blood with prickling fire, *pushed* at her.

She rose to her feet, tugged at his hand. "Sit down."

A gleam in his eyes. "Giving me orders?"

"I may want," she said, excitement pulsing under her skin, "to put you on the menu."

She didn't even see him sit down. One moment he stood in front of her, the next he lounged on the log, his hands on the moss-covered bark on either side of him, his shoulder muscles flexing. A looming predator, no matter what position he was in, no matter how relaxed and lazy he appeared, his undivided attention and sensual intent merely hidden well behind a veneer of languid idleness.

She didn't fool herself. He was still very much a wolf on the prowl, his sights firmly set on her. It was fascinating to realize she rather enjoyed being stalked by him.

He lounged in that quintessentially male way of taking up the entirety of any available space, his legs spread wide, and heat flushed her at the thought that he might have taken her bold declaration to mean something even bolder.

"Just a kiss," she whispered, clearing her throat.

Not that an insistently hungry part of her didn't yearn to reenact the images she sent him earlier, but tackling that particular fantasy was still a far-off goal.

"We can work our way down the menu." The spark of his sly smile lit his eyes. "In time."

"In time," she agreed on a whisper, and set the box with the bowl down beside the log.

He leaned back a little, the heat of his attention pulling her closer, and she stepped between his legs. Her knees brushed against his thighs, his power curling around her.

"Keep your hands on the log," she murmured, her fingers

itching to stroke his skin once more. All that glorious skin over taut muscles, the breathtaking display laid out for her by his lack of a shirt yet again.

"Pushy." An intimate rumble.

But he complied with perfect, prowling patience, with that unyielding focus that clearly said he was indulging her while he took pleasure in drawing her in even further. She knew his easy agreeability for what it was—simply another measured step in a game he still very much controlled.

She was okay with it, as long as the pretense of control he granted her allowed her to stave off the insidious fear that might yet lunge at her.

She laid both her hands on his shoulders. His muscles tensed under her touch, his heat seeping into her. Breath coming faster, she stroked over those impressive shoulder muscles and up to his neck. Corded strength under silken skin, power humming beneath her palms.

Dark energy twined around her arms...to her waist. A sneaky caress, one she found herself utterly incapable of rebuking. His hands remained on the log beside him, his posture all calm attention, and for the epicenter of her fears, that was what counted.

Up to his face her fingers went, gliding over the stubble on his jaw, the strong lines of his chin...to the sensual feast of his lips. Her pulse ticked low in her body, heat and desire unfolding with each beat of her heart, rolling out into her every nerve.

She let her fingers run over his lips, and she had to clench her thighs tight against the throb of desire at the touch. His power whispered along her hips.

Leaning forward a little, she bent down until only an inch separated their mouths, the air hot from their mingled breaths.

The gentlest of tugs on that bond between them. A dare. A reminder.

Holding his gaze, she touched her lips to his.

Prickling sparks down her spine, pooling heat between her legs.

She cupped his face as she brushed her mouth against his again, the sort of featherlight kiss that would make her knees weak.

And, yes, they wobbled.

She would have swayed were it not for the press of his thighs against her legs.

Flickering memories of darkest horrors in a dank room. *The weight of a heavy body on hers, sweat and wet sounds and pain, roaming touches that turned her stomach—*

Breath too shallow and fast, she whimpered, crushed by the force of a flashback that eclipsed the light of day, plunged her mind into the stifling black of a hole she couldn't crawl out of. Flames itched to shoot out of her and...met the ink-drenched magic of a stronger power.

Fire fizzling out under the wave of that dark energy, she gasped for air, her chest choked tight, her body numb and tingling at the same time. The chilly, rattling blackness engulfing her mind gave way to blinding light, too much, too strong, all colors dissolved into glaring white.

Count your breaths.

She tried, failed. It was all one breath and none at all. Her lungs burned.

Breathe.

The power in that one word. It shook her, made her haul in air past the block of her most basic function, circumventing the icy clutch of fear in her mind.

Several breaths later, pastels emerged from the whiteness all around, shapes took form, sounds returned. The chirp of birds. The scent of wood and earth. Soft moss under her face, her hands.

She came to her senses curled into a ball on the ground, a

yard away from Arawn, who still sat on the log, his expression inscrutable as he looked at her.

The shame of her humiliation burned hotter than the flames he'd soothed back into her core.

⊗⊗⊗

THE SIGHT OF MAEVE CURLED INTO A BALL OF MISERY ON THE ground sharpened Arawn's ever-present hunting instinct into lethal focus. Only there was no one to chase down and tear to bloody shreds, no focal point for the urge to murder with mad methodology.

So he drew it inward, directed that rage at the other impulse beating at his brain, the need to gather the tense form of his witch and stroke her fears away. Doing so wouldn't help her. Not yet, anyway. What she needed, at this point, was support of a different kind.

She sat up, shaking, her shoulders drooping, her hair hiding her face. He didn't need to see her expression to know it was one of abject defeat, her humiliation smothering her like a mantle of failure, fringed by fear. Rising silently to her feet, she turned her back to him, as if wanting to slip away.

He would have none of that.

"One setback," he said, keeping his voice conversational, "and you are ready to throw in the towel?"

She stiffened, anger in the set of her tense shoulders.

Anger was good. Anger was better than defeat.

"You wouldn't understand," she rasped. "It's not that easy."

"Who said it should be?"

She crossed her arms, and a muscle in her jaw twitched.

"Someone once," he said on a silken murmur, bracing his elbows on his knees, "broke every bone in my body. When I tried to walk again after I started to heal, I fell on my face

169

more times than I can count. It hurt. It was humiliating. But it would have been even more so had I given up."

Eyes wide, she faced him, her arms falling to her sides. Surprise flickered over her features, and an echo of a stinging emotion flowed along the bond.

"Who did that to you?" she whispered.

"You would do well," he said softly, "to remember what sort of reactions you dislike in others when they hear of your struggles."

She blinked, those copper lashes lowering and lifting over gray-streaked amber. "I'm not pitying you," she said after a moment. "I want to know who dared lay a hand on you, and whether they're dead, or still mine for the killing."

He barked a laugh, the sound startling him. He hadn't laughed in ages. Not like this. Unrestrained, taken unawares by the sort of rousing amusement that came out of nowhere, yet consumed him.

He was still grinning, his chest feeling wide open, when he said, "I wish I could bring them back to life, then, just to watch you burn them to cinders."

Her features had gentled, her eyes glowing as she beheld him, her lips parted on a sigh. "You're magnificent when you laugh."

Raw. She had to be ripped raw still from her flashback to be saying such things. "Tell me again tomorrow, and I may believe you."

"Show me more of your laughter, and I will tell you every day."

"Careful now," he murmured. "If you stroke my ego any more, I will demand you stroke other parts as well."

The blush on her cheeks was belied by the way her eyes flicked down to his crotch, his cock hardening at the unfettered hunger written on her face.

"First things first," she said, focusing back on his mouth.

He straightened again, one hand braced next to him on the

log, the other crooking a finger at her. She followed his call, her hips swinging in a way she was likely oblivious of, yet managed to rivet his attention, holding him spellbound.

Her curves were made to fit his hands, the impulse to comply with that surely perfect fit and to mold his palms to her flesh a surge in his veins. He had to dig his fingers into the moss and bark to keep from claiming what should be caressed, enjoyed, appreciated, in the most physical of ways.

She stepped back into the space between his legs—which he took the utmost care now to keep from trapping her again —her hands once more stroking feathered caresses over his face. He allowed his powers to twirl around her like before, a tiny taste of *touching* her that must suffice for now.

Her breath went uneven as she bent down again, pressed her lips to his, and he luxuriated in the feel of her heat, the silken curtain of red that fell around their faces, her scent of fire and wind another sort of kiss to a different sense of his.

Every muscle in his body hardened almost painfully as he forced himself to remain still, to let her lead. She needed that leeway, the promise of freedom and choice, the sort of passivity on his part that would allow her to reclaim what she lost in that warehouse.

And when—not *if*—she regained her confidence and kicked the terrors out of her mind, he'd be ready to pounce and play in a wholly different way than they'd done earlier.

All his thoughts scattered like leaves in a wind at the brush of her tongue against his lips.

Claws slid out from his fingertips, embedded in the log with the effort it took him not to reach for her, tug her closer. Instead he opened his mouth to hers, to her sensual invitation, drank in her soft moan when their tongues met. His powers vibrated over his skin...over hers.

She gasped at the touch of his energy, inched closer to him. Deepening the kiss, she leaned nearer still, and his body became, impossibly, more rigid as she slid one knee up his thigh, slowly slung that leg over his. Continuing the sensual exploration of his mouth, she repeated the move with her other leg, until she straddled him, her weight a lush caress in itself.

"You," he muttered against her lips when she broke away for a breath, "are killing me."

"Hm." An unrepentant smile that he felt more than saw. "You look very *invigorated* to me."

That teasing side of her…it slayed him.

Her fingers running through his hair, more touches of her tongue against his. Her teeth on his lower lip, sending a surge of need directly down to his cock. The scent of her arousal thickened the air, a lure to everything male in him.

"I want"—his teeth now nipping at her lip—"to *feast* on you until I drown in your taste."

"You are." A breathless whisper.

"Lower."

A squeaky sort of moan. A roll of her hips against him, and she froze at what she obviously felt between his legs, his desire unmistakable.

"Eyes on me, Wildfire," he repeated the words from earlier in the day, not letting her slip into a different place and time.

Quivering, she kept her focus on him as she deliberately rolled her hips again, rubbed against him in sinuous little moves that threatened his now tenuous control. He'd always prided himself on having a firm handle on the primal wildness of his nature—thousands of years of practice *should* bear fruit, after all.

Maeve grinding on his lap while he wasn't allowed to touch her held the potential to shred the last of his civilized veneer.

Breath coming faster, she kissed him again, her own control in tatters as well, it seemed, for the licks of her tongue were more aggressive, her tiny moans more frequent, her fingers now gripping his hair. His powers snapped their leash, flowed into and through her, pushing all the buttons that needed pressure—and she shattered.

A low, long moan broke from her throat, which he swallowed with a kiss, more demanding than he'd thus far allowed himself to be. She shuddered, her eyes glazing over —not in a good way.

He grabbed her chin, made her look at him. "Here." He tugged on the bond between them. "Now."

Her lips trembled. She swallowed.

"Who am I?"

A soft inhale. "Arawn."

The sound of his name spoken in her husky voice made his cock throb even harder, but he ignored it. There would be time for that. Later. When she was not on the verge of splintering for all the wrong reasons.

"You are in control," he said, rubbing his thumb over her chin. "You decide. When. What. How much."

She gave a shaky nod.

"But for now," he added, pitching his voice to a low caress, "we are finished."

Elegant ginger brows drew together over eyes of molten amber. "I know I am. What about you?"

"Sleep," he replied with a dark smile, "is not the only thing I can forego without dying."

CHAPTER 20

"So," Lucía said to Maeve, popping a grape in her mouth while they lay on a rolling meadow under the canopy of the stars, "you seem different tonight."

Maeve froze. Keeping her eyes studiously on the twinkling lights above her, she cleared her throat. "How so?"

"I don't know." Lucía's probing stare was a physical thing. "More relaxed, I guess?"

"Hm." She pressed her lips together, trying hard not to squirm.

"You're less tense," Lucía went on. "I mean, not that you were super uptight or anything, don't get me wrong, but you know I'm a shifter, and I just can't help noticing people's body language and scents—"

Maeve furtively clenched her thighs together. She'd showered and changed, but still...

"—and there was just this tension in you, like in a shifter who hasn't turned into their animal for a while—we get, like, super intense when we don't go for a run in our fur regularly —but now it's like you've shaken that off somehow—"

More like rubbed it off. Heat flushed her face.

"—and I just thought I'd tell you, because I'm happy you're feeling better. So, you know, whatever you've been doing, it's looking good on you, girl." She rolled onto her side facing Maeve, propped her head on her hand. "What *have* you been doing?"

"Nothing." Why was her voice so dang squeaky?

"Uh-huh." She plucked another grape from the bunch she'd brought, threw it into her mouth. "You do know shifters can smell lies?"

She cleared her throat. Again. *Subtle, much?* "Okay, so I may have...exercised a little."

Lucía's pale green eyes—glowing like her puma's in the dark of the night—narrowed as she studied her. Her nostrils flared as she sniffed—and then her features slackened. Eyes wide, she gaped at Maeve.

"Nooooooo," Lucía drawled in that tone of utmost disbelief paired with surprise, laced with a touch of excitement. "You. Did. Not."

Maeve scratched her nose. "You're right. I didn't."

"You *so* did." Lucía sat up, a grin on her face. "With *who*?"

"I don't know what you're talking about."

"Sure, yeah." She tapped her nose. "Lies. Scent. Remember?" Tilting her head, she frowned. "Speaking of which, I'm not smelling anyone on you..." Her frown deepened, her voice trailing away. "...except..." A gasp, her mouth forming a huge O, her eyes rounded once more. "*Noooooooo.*"

"You've...said that already."

"No *way*." She closed her mouth with an audible click. "You and Arawn." Shaking her head, she held up both hands. "Now, I don't want any details. That'd be weird. Super awkward, seeing as he's like my uncle and all. But...good for you!" Grinning, she bumped her fist against Maeve's shoulder.

Maeve fidgeted with the seam of her sweater. "We didn't...I mean...it was just..."

"No details!" Lucía covered her ears with her hands. "But seriously," she added a moment later, uncovering her ears again, "if you wanna chat—in non-detail form—I'm here. He can be really obstinate, so if you need to unload, I'm your gal."

"It's not...we're not..." Gah, would she be able to put together a whole sentence again anytime soon?

"That's okay." An easy smile. "You'll figure it out. No need to slap a label on it just yet."

She hadn't been aware of holding a breath until it rushed out of her. Opening her mouth, she was about to thank Lucía when the other woman's eyes shifted to her cougar's, her entire body going on tense alert in the way so innate in feline predators.

Lucía flowed into a crouching position, lifted her head and scented the air, her gaze on the night sky. Maeve looked up too, unease curdling her stomach. The forest around the meadow had fallen silent, not a single rustle of nocturnal animals to be heard anymore.

A whisper in the distance...floating near.

"Maeve," Lucía said, her voice quiet but sharp. "Run into the forest. Call Arawn."

"How...?"

Lucía tossed her a cell phone. "First one in the favorites. Go!"

A whistling breeze, followed by a gust of wind that whipped Maeve's hair around her face. She backed away toward the edge of the woods, still searching the starlit sky, her finger pressing the call button on the phone. Heart in her throat, she listened to it ring, roll into voicemail.

Crap. Arawn was miles away for all she knew, tending to his business in some other part of his dominion, and short of a phone call, she had no means of—

An idea flitted through her mind. Maybe...

She reached down into herself, touched mental fingers to the bond—gave it a *tug*.

More whipping, tornado-like wind howling through the trees, flattening the grass on the meadow. Lucía now moved toward Maeve, away from the open field.

A shadow blotted out the stars.

"Run!" Lucía's voice barely rose above the din of the storm.

Her ears buzzing from the roaring wind, Maeve sprinted for the tree line. Something huge slammed down in front of her, and the pressure wave of its impact hurled her back. She crashed down hard, pain shooting through her as she tried to break the fall using her hands and arms.

She lifted her head, fought against the dizziness that attacked her, glanced around. Lucía lay several yards away, unmoving, and there, in front of her…loomed a gargantuan, hulking beast.

Against the backdrop of the night, she couldn't make out its form, the light of the stars not bright enough but to hint at the sheer *size* of the creature. A helicopter? A private jet? Something giant along those lines.

Fingers digging into the earth, she tried to calm her racing heart, to find at least a smidgen of courage to *move*. Her muscles didn't obey.

And then her thoughts simply vanished in instinctive gecko-brain fear as the beast lunged forward. Talons rammed into the ground inches from her hands. Talons as big as *machetes*.

Shivering, she looked up, and up, and up, craning her neck until she could see all the way up to the creature's head. Was that…a beak?

Something enormous stretched on either side of its massive body, rustling like…feathers.

The thing moved, a silken grace to its prowl that spoke of feline elegance despite its unbelievable size. Crawling back wards, Maeve pivoted with the beast, not exposing her back. *Useless.* That monster could crush her with one of its clawed paws.

With a flash of starlight on feathers, the beast lunged at her again. She shrieked, fell back, curled into a ball, her sight blinking out as terror speared her—

Heat and flames and roaring power.

She blinked, her heartbeat like thunder in her ears, her skin burning...quite literally. Unsinged by her own fire, she peeked out from under the arm she'd thrown over her face.

A ring of flames around her, and behind the flickering heat, the beast. The firelight illuminated what darkness had veiled before, and she stared slack-jawed, her mind uncomprehending.

Back half of its body that of a giant feline, feathered wings jutting from its powerful shoulders, the fur giving way to plumage covering its neck, front legs, and head...which was that of a huge bird of prey. And those front legs didn't end in paws, but in taloned bird's feet.

That...wasn't...possible.

That couldn't be a... Her mind drew a blank at the absurdity.

The beast regarded her with eyes that held a far too intelligent glint for a monster. Cocking its head—a move unmistakably bird-like—it took a step forward, beat its mighty wings once...and the powerful blast of air snuffed out the ring of flames.

Just like that.

She scrambled for her magic, tried to grab some of the fire that seemed so ever-present in her core, but she only encountered darkness and despair. She couldn't call upon her powers at will. They were still bound. Erratic, uncontrollable bursts of flames were all she could manage, and only subconsciously.

Breath stuck in her throat, she could only watch with

abject terror while the beast stepped over the line of ash, prowled closer. It stalked over her, a taloned foot on either side of her body, its size dwarfing her to an inconsequential insect to be carelessly squashed. The magic pouring off it raised the hair on her arms and neck.

Slowly, it lowered its head, and she couldn't even see all of it hovering above her. It was just too huge. Its beak—if she wrapped her arms around it, her fingers wouldn't touch, the girth that massive—loomed closer, closer, closer, until…

Sniff.

Her heart stumbled over its rapid rhythm.

Sniff.

She'd die here, wouldn't she? Eaten by a giant monstrosity of a thing that shouldn't exist…

A rumbling vibration, the beast cocking its head to the side, its eye—night-glow like a lion's, and that was *another* absurdity in a string of bizarre impossibilities—now level with her face, so close she could have reached out and poked it.

Maybe…

She raised her hand on a flash of impulse—and found her fingers buried in softest feathers.

The beast had moved its head toward her touch, as if welcoming a caress. But…she'd intended to poke its eye out.

Transfixed, she slid her fingers through the plumage, the filaments tickling her. That rumbling again, vibrating against her palm.

And somewhere, deep inside her, an ancient awareness coiled and uncoiled, stretched in fire-edged darkness.

The words tumbling out of her mouth were foreign and familiar at once, her own…and someone else's.

"Hello, old friend."

An answering rumble, that piercing intelligence in its eye now tempered with a warmth that should be as inconceivable in a beast like this as was its existence.

The stars above winked out on a wave of darkness. The next second, power crashed down with the force of a missile, shaking the earth. Inky blackness over her senses, a blanket of magic so consuming, so *enraged* it stole her breath.

The beast screeched, tensed above her, flaring its wings.

An answering roar that made her quake from the inside out.

Arawn.

⚜

HE SLAMMED ONTO THE GROUND ON A WAVE OF DARKNESS AND rage, and the earth groaned and cracked under his wrath.

The beast hovering over Maeve let loose a screech that shook the world, the span of its wings such it veiled the sky. Even otherworld creatures would run from a primal force like this, demons and shifters and fae alike.

He was none of those. Cut from the cloth that had shaped this world, he was fury made flesh, his singular focus on the beast that *threatened what was his.*

So he roared right back in his most lethal form, a panther as black as the night, his size enhanced by the sheer magnitude of his powers so it nearly matched the beast's. When the Old One jumped in front of Maeve, blocking his view of her body, its talons digging into the ground as it spread its front legs in a defensive stance, the last threads of reason in his mind snapped.

Mine.

A wave of his magic lashed out, and the beast screeched, reared up on its hind legs, wings flaring wide as it took the blow, beat some of it back with a mighty flap of its wings. The muscles in his back and legs flexed in preparation for a lunge—

"Stop!"

Dimly, his mind registered the shout. He glanced to the side, to the flash of red hair in the dark of the night. *Mine.*

"Stop it!"

He narrowed his eyes, sent a tendril of his magic out to push her back, out of the way. The beast let loose an enraged cry as he shoved her—*gently*, with what was left of some heretofore civilized part of him—farther to the side. She landed with an *oof* on her behind, and he faced the beast again just as it launched itself at him.

They collided in the air, the crash of power rending the sky.

Thunder and earthquakes and a crippling tidal wave of magic.

Talons flashed, slashed, teeth snapped at feathers and fur, and they broke apart on another surge of power. Circling each other, a primal rhythm to their dance.

Faint yelling behind him. He ignored it. Prepared to lunge once more—but a *yank* on the bond inside him wrenched him back. He skidded several yards until his claws sank into the ground, found purchase. He glared at the fiery witch who stepped between him and the beast, her hands raised in each of their directions.

"I said, *stop!*" She glanced over her shoulder at the beast hulking behind her, its attention on him a lethal, writhing thing. "You, too," she muttered.

And the beast...obeyed her. Remaining where it was, it did not attack him again. And neither did it pounce on her. It could have easily grabbed her and taken to the skies by now.

Her chest heaving with her fast breaths, she faced him. "Don't hurt it. I think it...recognizes me. As a friend." Her ginger brows drew together, as if she couldn't quite make sense of it herself. "It wasn't going to harm me."

The Old One now paced behind her, wings rustling in the dark, its night-glow glance darting between her and him.

Arawn's heartbeat pounded in his ears while the need to crush his foe waned. Slivers of logic and reason returned, and he *remembered*… This was not how he'd meant to handle an encounter like this. *Bloody brilliant.* He'd nearly ripped to shreds that which he intended to lure and ensnare.

Puzzled at the force with which all rational thought had fled him, he changed back to his human shape. Even though the beast now dwarfed him in size, his power still more than matched the Old One's, and he made sure it felt the pressure of it in the air.

He took a step forward, eyes fixed on the beast, as he wove a whisper of his magic toward the creature.

You know me, that whisper said. *You know what I am.*

The ancient beast cocked its head, rustled its wings.

His powers twined around it, cajoling, soothing. *Remember.*

The Old One stopped its pacing.

Heed my call, as you once did.

Wings quivering, the beast stalked closer, closer…and lowered its head to meet Arawn's outstretched hand. He touched its giant beak, stroked up into the feathers. The Old One closed its eyes on a sigh.

The night stood still for a breathless moment.

"Welcome home."

࿇

MAEVE STARED. AND STARED. HER THOUGHTS A JUMBLED MESS, she gaped at the scene playing out in front of her. At the display of power that was all the more staggering for its quiet. If Arawn had been intimidating in his battle rage, the way he brought a beast like this to heel with nothing but dark magic hushing the night robbed her of breath.

He angled his head, glanced at her over his shoulder. "Check on Lucía."

She started, rushed over to the slumped form of the other female who'd become more her friend than her guard over the past few nights, and touched her fingers to her neck. A steady pulse greeted her, and she breathed a relieved sigh. With no apparent injuries—all limbs accounted for and no blood—she was likely just knocked unconscious by the blast when the beast crashed down. She *had* been closer to the impact than Maeve.

"Still breathing?" Arawn asked.

"Yes."

"Then she will be fine." What could have been a callous remark was tempered by the affectionate confidence in his tone. He wasn't dismissing Lucía—he was simply that sure of her strength.

After checking her friend over once more, Maeve went to his side, and the mighty thing that could have jumped straight out of a fantasy novel inclined its head to her as well. Shrewd, night-glow eyes studied her, seemingly to the bottom of her soul, and the creature who dwelled there stretching its talons toward it. Maeve reached out and caressed its feathers again.

"Tell me," she murmured to Arawn, "that this is not really a griffin I'm petting."

"You have grown up knowing magic and all sorts of creatures that humans would relegate to the realm of myths and tales. This is where you draw the line?"

"I've grown up hearing something like *this* being referred to as myth and legend by witches who fight demons every night. There are *no* accounts of beasts like this having ever been real."

"Because you have been made to forget." A murmur laced with an edge of age-old anger.

She frowned at him. "The Powers That Be?"

He nodded, his attention on the griffin as he stroked its mighty head. "They could not abide the beasts. Wanted them caged, their power leashed. But power such as this" a languid caress, the griffin rumbling in response—"should never be shackled. Directed, perhaps. Guided. By those who know how."

A shiver ran down her spine. "What are you?"

One side of his mouth tipped up. "The male to stoke your fire."

She narrowed her eyes. "You're being evasive."

"And you are being nosy."

She uttered a sound of frustration. "You're not a demon, you're not a shifter, and you're certainly not fae."

"Astute observations."

"What else *is* there?"

"Given that you are still agape at this magnificent creature you did not believe existed before tonight, I would say the possibilities are myriad."

"You truly are insufferable," she muttered, turning back to the griffin.

"And you are sublime in your beauty when you climax," he replied, his voice dark silk and lush seduction. "I want to see you like that again."

Her heart jumped into her throat so fast she saw stars for a few seconds. Heat washed through her, centered throbbing between her legs.

Catching her breath, she asked, "So what other beasts are there?"

"What sort of myths have survived through the ages?"

She swallowed. "The one inside me…is it…?"

"You know its name."

Her arms and legs tingled while an ancient presence breathed in darkness, in flame. "It's a dragon, isn't it?"

The smile he gave her was edged with feral appreciation.

Movement to the side, followed by a feminine groan. Silence, then— "If you guys wanted to adopt a pet, why not start with a damn puppy?"

CHAPTER 21

"Down here," Hazel said, and held open the door to the basement of the Murray mansion.

Merle watched Thorne and Madhuri Gupta drag the unconscious witch through the hall and down the stairs. Blond hair hanging into her face, Lydia Novak didn't look worse for wear except for a few scratches.

"This is even better than I hoped for," Merle said to Thorne as she followed them into the part of the basement fortified to hold prisoners of the otherworldly sort. And now, witches too, in light of the tragically ironic turn of events in their community. "How did you manage to snatch an Elder witch?"

Thorne just smiled, his wintry blue eyes sparkling, but Madhuri—daughter of Shobha, and next in line to inherit the magic of the Gupta family—muttered, "He has quite the creepy talent when it comes to sneaking up on people."

"*Mausi*," Anjali, Madhuri's niece, said, the word an affectionate address meaning "aunt" in Hindi, as Maeve had once explained to Merle.

The young witch had insisted on accompanying her demon mate to the Murray mansion after they decided to lock up the head of the Novak family here instead of at the Gupta residence. Hazel's home did have the most advanced cells for holding prisoners, another legacy of the severe stance her sister Isabel had taken toward demons while she was head of the family.

Madhuri looked at her niece, shrugged with the shoulder not holding up Lydia's body. "There's only so much I can bend for him, Anju."

"It's all right," Thorne muttered.

Anjali's green eyes glistened, her features softening as she looked at him.

Hazel picked up the magically enhanced shackles in the cell, fastening them around Lydia's wrists and ankles before Thorne and Madhuri laid her down on a cot. The manacles would sap her powers, make sure she wouldn't be able to break through the wards enclosing the cell.

"Okay," Merle said when Hazel locked the door after stepping out, "so we'll start interrogating her when she wakes."

"I've been thinking," Madhuri said, retying her mahogany hair, "we might not need to use force on her at all."

Merle frowned. "What do you mean?"

"Why not offer a prisoner exchange? Juneau has one of ours, we have one of hers. Let's propose an exchange, and if she agrees, we won't even have to storm into wherever they keep Rhun. This all could go down without resorting to unnecessary violence."

Merle crossed her arms, chewed on her lip as she considered. "I will still burn her to a crisp at the first chance I get."

"Of course," Anjali chimed in. "She has that one coming. But I think I see what Madhuri is trying to say. If we get Rhun back first, we can attack her at a time of our choosing, with our ranks closed and at full strength, instead of scrambling to free him and maybe having to hold back because we don't want to risk harming him during the attack."

"She's got a point." Hazel nodded, her dark hair sliding over her shoulders.

Merle heaved a deep breath. "All right. Let's send a note to that bitch."

And hope to the gods she'll agree, and soon. Every hour Rhun spent in the woman's clutches cut another slice off Merle's very soul, the faint echoes of his pain along the mating bond —which wasn't enough to trace him with, *dammit*—raking claws over her heart.

CHAPTER 22

A rawn somehow found himself sitting on the couch in Maeve's cabin while she cleaned the few of his injuries from the fight with the griffin that hadn't yet healed. Completely unnecessary, seeing as those wounds —really, they were barely more than scratches; none of his internal organs hung out, and he wouldn't even have to regenerate a limb—would close and disappear within the hour.

But he'd be damned if he told her not to put her hands on him.

Well, more damned than he already was…

So he sat, patiently, choosing wisely not to remind her how fast he healed. Instead he watched her face while she dabbed at the scratches with a cotton ball dunked in hydrogen peroxide. Studied her lips, pressed together in concentration. Counted the freckles sprinkled over her nose and cheeks. And those *lashes*… Unable to resist, he reached up and brushed a finger over them.

She stilled in her ministrations but didn't draw back. "What is it with your fascination with my eyelashes?"

"They are copper-colored."

A twitch of her lips. "I can't be the first redhead you've met." Her voice became deliberately casual. Too deliberately. "I'm sure you must have come close to a lot of gingers' lashes over time."

"None of them were *yours*."

Her cheeks blushed rose. Those mesmerizing coppery lashes lowered, lifted again, revealed eyes of liquid fire woven with tendrils of smoke. "I thought you dangerous before," she murmured, laying her free hand on his shoulder while she disinfected another scratch on his chest, "but for wholly different reasons than I do now."

"Oh?"

Her throat muscles worked as she swallowed, and he had to lock his entire body in order to fight the impulse to lean forward and lick over that creamy skin.

"I had no idea," she continued, "how much of a threat you'd be to a woman's senses."

He allowed himself a self-satisfied smile.

She tilted her head. "You heal fast, don't you?"

"Yes. But this serious wound here needs your attention." He tapped a scrape on his abdomen.

There was that almost-smile again, lighting up her eyes. "Well," she said, her voice a tad huskier than usual, "I certainly don't want to ignore your needs."

And then she knelt in front of him, in between his legs, to dab at that negligible, blessed scratch. Every single muscle in his body tensed to the point of pain, his powers writhing under his skin. Her fiery hair teased him, invited his fingers to tangle in the strands...to tug and hold fast. He curled his hand to a fist instead, added this position and the erotic embellishment of the fantasy that went along with it to the list of things he would do with her. *Later.*

"I think," he said, releasing the stranglehold he had on his powers just enough to twirl a dark vine of his energy around her, "you are as much of a threat as I am."

She looked up at him, and the impact of that eye contact, in that position, nearly made him growl with sensual hunger. Not breaking that searing connection until the last second, she leaned forward…and kissed the scrape.

The touch of her lips on his skin, the heat of her breath, sent a bolt of molten lust straight to his groin. His hardened cock twitched against the fabric of his pants. Breath coming unsteady now, he allowed himself to stroke that hair of silken flames when she drew back—and he made sure she saw his hand before he touched her, knew it was him. Her lids half lowered as he caressed her hair, running his fingers over her scalp in sinuous moves.

Still, her posture held a whisper of tension, of apprehension, as she regarded him from between his knees.

"In time," he murmured.

She nodded at the reminder, her shoulders relaxing.

"I've been meaning to ask," she said after a moment, her voice a little shaky from his caress. "The bobcat…it healed so fast. I do, too—even though not quite as quickly as the cat—and I was wondering if maybe that's because I got some of your healing power when I bound myself to you, and I transferred it to the bobcat? I'm not sure, but I think my blood dropped on its open wounds when it scratched me."

He twirled a lock of her hair around his finger. "My blood needs to be ingested to catalyze any self-healing of the body. Mixing it with someone's blood is not enough."

"But…" She frowned. "I didn't drink your blood."

He inclined his head. "Whatever healing power you have is your own."

"Huh." Her brows shot up. "Fancy that."

"I believe," he said with silken sensuality, "there is another brutal gash on my back." More like a bruise, probably, but who was he to split hairs?

She pursed her lips, humor glinting in her eyes. "Of course there is."

Picking up her cleaning and disinfecting supplies, she stepped onto the couch, kneeling behind him as he scooted forward. Her hands slid over his back, and he closed his eyes for a moment, his magic humming inside him.

"What was the griffin doing here?" she asked after sizzling silence filled the space between them for a few heartbeats, her hands languidly busy with tending to his "wounds."

"I assume it sought you out."

He could *feel* her frown.

"But," she said, "how did it even find me?"

"Power draws power. It must have felt yours awakening."

Her fingers glided over his shoulders. There were *no* scratches on his shoulders. "And where was it before? How come no one has...mentioned a beast like this roaming around? If it was out there already, it must have been seen by at least one person."

"As to where it slept"—he tilted his head to the side when she stroked up his neck, her touch sending fiery pleasure cascading down his spine—"it was likely a natural place of magic. And I think it has not been awake for long, otherwise there would have been more widespread accounts of sightings. As it is, I am not aware of any reports, though it is possible a few humans saw it, but had their stories dismissed as fantastical illusions."

"Like those people claiming to have seen UFOs," she muttered.

"I suppose it probably spent much of its time in the air, and did not venture into or near human settlements, thus avoiding attention."

More silence wove between them while her hands mapped his back, featherlight strokes and tentative caresses, each touch at once soothing and heightening the hunger clawing at him from the inside.

"What will happen now that it's awake and...out there?"

Her fingers curled into the hair at the back of his head. His eyes nearly crossed at the sensation. "Where will it stay?"

The griffin had flown off again soon after Lucía woke up, but he could still sense it nearby. "It will linger close to us, given that is has bonded with me and seems to feel some sort of kinship with you."

"How did you bring it to heel?"

"Power recognizes power."

An irritated tug on his hair. "Stop being cryptic."

Most anyone else would find themselves choking on the floor for that. In Maeve, each moment of familiarity and daring annoyance with him was a step worthy of celebration, of praise.

"It senses that the strength of my magic is a match for its own," he said. "And it will heed my command because part of my power lies in authority over all things wild."

A beat of silence, her fingers stroking down his neck again. "Are you saying you're some sort of horse whisperer for beasts?"

The laugh rising up from his chest surprised him. "That is one way to put it."

The soft pressure of her leaning into him, her front resting against his back.

He held his breath.

Her arms slid around his shoulders from behind, hands gliding down to his chest. Playing with the hair that dusted his front, she kissed his nape. "Laugh again."

He turned his head to the side. "Make me."

The air between them sizzled, charged with the slow build of a force that could consume him.

"When I was drowning in the memory of my dream of you," she said, her breath fanning over his neck, "and didn't want to give in, I tried to fight it by imagining you dancing in a princess dress in the woods."

He choked on another laugh, his shoulders shaking under

the sweet weight of her arms. "It appears it did not work as intended."

"No." A dark grumble. "That dream superimposed itself on everything else."

Chuckling, he reached for her hand, played with her fingers.

"I was wondering," she murmured, responding to his touch with equal play. "What does the griffin eat?"

"In ancient times"—he shrugged—"anything and everything that moved."

She stilled. "Humans, too?"

"I recall they were quite easy for the beasts to catch."

Her breath left her on a whoosh. "That is…horrible."

He frowned. "It could get messy these days, yes. Human casualties are notoriously hard to cover up."

Silence.

"You don't care about humans," she whispered. "Do you?"

He didn't like the chill that pinged along the bond. Half turning his head to her again, he said, "They are not my priority, no."

"So you consider them dispensable." Not a question, but a quiet statement, laced with a hint of bitterness.

She withdrew her hands from around his neck, and her retreat cut into pieces inside him that had been softened by her trust, her affection. When she moved out from behind his back, stepped off the couch, he itched to grab her and pull her to him again. He remained still, knowing the move would shred what was left of her appreciation for him.

He leaned back instead, laid both arms on the backrest of the couch, studying her as she looked out the window. "You care for them?"

"Of course I do." Soft conviction in her tone, a silent backbone of steel underneath her gentle appearance. "I certainly don't want them to be killed and eaten, whether by demons or some mighty beast."

He could have figured as much. After all, she was brought up among witches, in a community long considered the last bulwark between the safety of humanity and the threats of otherworld creatures—not by accident, but by design.

He was about to reply when he received a mental message from Deimos.

Sire.

Speak. His second wouldn't contact him while Arawn was with Maeve unless it was important.

Ms. Morgan is here.

He pursed his lips. *Good. Is she ready to meet?*

Yes, sire.

Bring her here.

Understood.

Deimos closed the mental pathway just as Arawn rose from the couch, stepped closer to Maeve, who was still gazing out the window, her arms crossed.

"I would like to introduce you to someone," he said.

She looked up at him from underneath those glorious lashes. "Who?"

"Someone with the skills to help you." He inclined his head. "If you wish."

Her fine ginger brows drew together, but she followed his lead as he ushered her out the door and over the bridge to the slope beyond it. Deimos approached with his guest at that very moment, the fireflies' glow above the forest path shedding enough light to reveal a petite female wearing business attire.

Arawn nodded at his second, and Deimos left with a murmured word to Ms. Morgan before they reached the slope where Maeve waited, her widened eyes not on the female but on the male accompanying her. As soon as Deimos disappeared down the path again, Maeve's posture relaxed.

"Ms. Morgan," Arawn said. "Welcome to my lands. I assume your journey was uneventful?"

"Smooth sailing, my lord." The female bowed, the light of the will-o'-the-wisps floating over the bridge gleaming on her jet-black hair, which she'd pulled into a tight chignon.

"I would like you to meet Maeve." He nodded at his witch beside him. "Maeve, this is Tashia Morgan. She is a licensed psychotherapist who specializes in counseling survivors of trauma." He made a pause. "Incidentally, she is also a demon."

CHAPTER 23

"Hello, Maeve." The female demon—Tashia—held out her hand, her elegant smile enhancing the beauty of her light brown face. "It's nice to meet you."

Maeve shook the other woman's hand, her mind and heart spinning trying to catch up. Of all the perplexing, poignant things Arawn had done, this ranked among the most astounding. He found an *otherworldly* therapist for her, so she'd have someone to tell her story to. All of it.

Arawn seemed to absorb her tiniest tells, his evergreen eyes piercing in their perceptiveness. "Ms. Morgan will be around for you, should you choose to talk to her. It is entirely up to you. You do not need to see her if you prefer not to." He nodded at Tashia. "One of my enforcers will be waiting for you at the fork in the path when you are ready to return to your quarters."

Facing Maeve, he gave her a look that could very well have singed the clothes off her and burned deeper, to the bottom of her heart. Shadows swirled in the depths of his eyes, like dark mist spreading in the woods. "I will see you tomorrow."

She didn't reply, simply watched him turn and walk down the path, the fireflies' soft light caressing the taut muscles in his broad back...the way she had just minutes earlier. Before the flame he kindled chilled at the reminder of the sort of callousness she should not have forgotten to expect from the Demon Lord.

Tashia cleared her throat. "I'd like to reiterate that there's no obligation to see me. I want you to know that you shouldn't feel pressured to talk to me. I'm here if you want to try a session, or we could always have a casual chat over coffee first, so you can get to know me. Or"—a shrug of her graceful shoulders under her black blazer—"we needn't meet at all. It's entirely your choice, and if you decline the offer, I won't take it any way other than you choosing what's right for you, and what you feel comfortable with."

Maeve's hand itched to pull her hair in front of her face. She crossed her arms instead. "What do you know about me?"

"Just that you had a traumatic experience you're struggling with. Nothing more than that. Whether or not you want me to know more, and how much, is totally up to you."

Maeve nodded absent-mindedly, pressing her lips together.

"You can sleep on it," Tashia said, her voice gentle. "If you want to see me, simply send word. I'll be ar—"

"Would you like coffee?"

The female demon didn't miss a beat, simply gave her a graceful smile. "Yes, thank you."

ॐ

IN THE CABIN, MAEVE PREPARED THE COFFEE IN THE SMALL machine stocked in her kitchenette, set sugar and cream—from her mini-fridge—on the table in the corner, where Tashia had taken a seat. While the aroma of the brew wafted through the room, Maeve turned to study the female demon.

"Where are you from?"

"Los Angeles," Tashia replied. "Although I lived in Atlanta for a while. Originally from Boston, though."

"And you came here…just like that?"

"Well." A small smile played around Tashia's mouth. "Lord Arawn made me a *very* generous offer for relocating here. To be honest, I wouldn't even have to work anymore thanks to his generosity." She shrugged. "But I want to. And I like the area. I used to come up to the Pacific Northwest to hike."

When the coffee was ready, Maeve poured two cups and carried them over to the table. "What about your clients back in LA?"

Tashia nodded. "Perceptive question. It's always a bit tricky to move when you're a therapist and have clients who trust you—sometimes even depend on you for their mental health. None of my cases are truly critical in that sense, which made the move easier, but I made sure to recommend my human clients to trusted colleagues who match the client's individual profile. As for my otherworldly clients, I'll still be seeing them until their therapy needs are fulfilled, because finding another non-human therapist for them is so difficult. We are few and far between."

Maeve frowned. "So you'll fly down there regularly to see those clients?"

"Yes. I don't mind traveling." Another elegant smile, the female's brown eyes glowing warmly.

Taking a sip from her mug, Maeve pondered for a moment. She didn't know what to make of the feeling spreading in her chest at the sheer thoughtfulness and effort Arawn had put into making this possible for her.

We are few and far between. She didn't know hard numbers, but chances were good that otherworldly therapists were indeed a rare breed, probably only a handful of them in the entire United States. And Arawn managed not just to find any one of them, but a *female* who specialized in dealing with trauma, plus he had succeeded in recruiting her for permanent relocation—so there'd be no deadline for Maeve to decide if she wanted to see her. If the therapist lived and worked in this area from now on, Maeve would be free to go to her at any time, even if it was months down the line.

Shaking off that train of thought and the unsettling—for it was far too warm—feeling that went along with it, she returned her attention to Tashia. "What kind of demon are you?"

"A reflector." The other woman sipped from her mug. "My power is mirroring. I can sense people's feelings and reflect them back to them, which enhances that particular emotion at the expense of others."

Maeve gasped softly as a full understanding of that kind of power sank in. "You could drive someone mad."

"I choose to do the opposite." A small smile. "A lot of my kind deliberately mirror negative emotions to feed on them. There is a certain rush when absorbing feelings on the darker side of the emotional spectrum, but feeding on positive emotions is just as nourishing for us. Many *reflectors* simply go for the high of negative feelings. I refuse to do it."

"So you...use your powers during therapy sessions? How does that work?"

Tashia shook her head. "I only mirror with my otherworldly clients, because I can ask their permission beforehand. With humans that's not possible, for obvious reasons, and I'd never just reflect without the client's consent. That would be inappropriate. There has to be a foundation of trust between the client and me, so they'll feel safe allowing me to decide which emotions to reflect."

The petite woman took another sip of her coffee. "With those who give me permission, I mostly mirror the feelings they need to nurture in themselves with regard to whatever issues they have. Someone who is struggling with a negative self-image from years of verbal abuse, for example, would need to feel good about themselves and nurture self-love. So I'll mirror those feelings when they arise while we talk."

Maeve stared at the demon, her coffee nearly forgotten on the table. "That is incredibly fascinating. I've never heard of *reflectors*, much less how their powers work."

A sparkle in Tashia's smile. "Would you like a demonstration?"

Maeve considered it for a second, nodded, her heart aflutter in her chest.

Tashia's eyes shifted from warm brown to quicksilver. The air hummed with power, a gentle buzz, and then… Excitement pounded through Maeve's veins in prickling, sparkling waves chased by the astounded awe of fascination on steroids. Her heart jumped into her throat, her pulse a drumbeat in her ears. Skin flushing hot, she nearly wanted to leap to her feet and dance for the sheer force of her overjoyed agitation.

Tashia regarded her out of eyes that were back to their usual brown, then winked at her. "I overdid it a bit for the sake of example. It can be much subtler."

Maeve cleared her throat. "I'm ashamed to admit that if I had that power, I might use it for baser motives. Making the guy who looks at you all creepy on the way to school suddenly cry for no apparent reason sounds way too tempting."

Tashia smirked, rubbed her nose. "*Well*, I never said I've always been a saint."

Maeve grinned. "I think we'll get along well."

They drank coffee in companionable silence for a moment, before Maeve ventured, "How…how would it go, if I did want to talk about…"

Tashia set down her mug. "First of all, you need to know

that you can tell me as little or as much as you want. Actually, I don't even need to know details of what happened—unless you *want* to share them. Sometimes, it's important to unload, to get it out there, especially with someone neutral, someone you don't have to worry about hurting with your pain."

Maeve lowered her eyes. Damn, Tashia was good.

"Second," the other female continued, "apart from talking about it if you need to, therapy is mainly about helping you deal with whatever PTSD symptoms may be impairing your life and comfort. That's really the big deal for most of my clients. They have open wounds impacting how they go about their daily lives, and sometimes those wounds make it difficult to have any sort of normal life at all. So my questions would really be about what negative effects your trauma has had on your life, and then we'll figure out how to deal with that."

She didn't realize she was crying until a tear plopped onto her hand. Sniffing, she wiped at her cheeks, her face heating. "I'm sorry."

"It's all right." Tashia pulled out a tissue, handed it over. "I want you to know that this—talking to me—is a safe place for you, okay? There'll be no judgment from me, and my oath as a healer stands that I will not pass on anything you tell me here—to anyone. Not even Lord Arawn."

Maeve sniffed again, nodded. "Okay."

"Whenever you'd like to start," Tashia said, leaning back in her chair, "some things I would ask you about are how you're sleeping and whether you have intrusive thoughts or flashbacks. I would try to gauge how severe the PTSD symptoms are for you, so we can work on reducing them." A pause. "Take your time to answer—if at all—and just know that I'm here for you. You're safe."

Those last two words sent more silent tears rolling down her cheeks, her chest both filled and hollowed out by the promise of a catharsis she hadn't seen coming.

CHAPTER 24

Arawn found her and Kelior in a clearing bordering a stream—with the griffin languidly sunning its wings between them.

The fae male lingered a healthy distance from the beast, kept glancing at it with unabated shock written all over his face, whereas Maeve sat between its feathered front legs, a book on her lap, and she seemed thoroughly unconcerned by the nearness of claws the size of sabers. The griffin inclined its head as Arawn approached, a glint of welcome in its primeval gaze.

Guard her, his powers whispered to the Old One. *Protect her when I am not near.*

The griffin gave him a look that clearly said it didn't need to be told that.

Some invisible weight lifted off his shoulders at knowing he could rely on one of the most formidable forces in the world to keep her safe, and he nodded at Kelior, sending him away.

Maeve glanced up as he walked closer, her expression shuttered. Exhaustion lined her face, as if she hadn't slept. He hadn't sensed an outbreak from her during the night, so whatever kept her awake wasn't enough to ignite her innate fire at least. Yet it was enough to rake claws over his nerves, knowing she was struggling.

"Are you here for more spellwork study?" she asked, reservations in her tone. Gone was the easy familiarity, the budding affection in the way she looked at him.

He wanted it back.

"That," he said, "and more."

She closed her book but didn't rise to her feet, remained sitting with the griffin at her back as if lounging on a throne of primal power. It made her look like a queen of fire and fury, and he liked the sight of it so much he wanted to have it immortalized on canvas.

Memorizing every detail of the scene so he could later mentally send the image to the artist he'd commission for the painting, he put his hands in the pockets of his dress pants. "I have been pondering parts of our conversation last night."

Something shifted in those eyes of smoke-kissed flames. "Me too."

"Since we were interrupted, I want to get a few things straight."

She pressed her lips together.

"I do not care for humans," he went on. "And you cannot hope to awaken in me an appreciation for something I have dismissed for all of my long-lived life. I come from a different time, a different…place, and I will not be able to break with a way of thinking I have cultivated over the course of millennia."

৩৯৩

MAEVE WINCED AT THE LAST WORD, AT THE HINT OF JUST *HOW* long Arawn had been around already. But it drove home a point she'd come to on her own since last night.

"I know," she said to him. "And I understand."

203

Despite her knowledge of how he'd been shaped by an existence on the upper end of the food chain, looking down at a race that had to be as inconsequential to him as ants were to her, she was…disappointed, above all else. And it was silly. She should have known better.

She'd simply seen so many other surprisingly different sides of him since she arrived here that she forgot just what—who—he was, always had been, the gentleness and playful sensuality he'd shown her notwithstanding. In this, in the way he regarded humans as dispensable, he was every bit the ruthless, callous Demon Lord his reputation made him out to be.

And she didn't know if she could see past that.

Her heart ached at the thought of pulling back from him, had pained her all through the night, keeping her awake for most of it, alternating with slivers of memories that haunted her. Though thankfully not strong enough to shove her into fiery panic, those blinks of images and sensations of her time in the warehouse had robbed her of sleep for long hours.

The talk with Tashia was transformative, had started to lift a weight on her chest she hadn't realized dragged her down until it began to vanish, but the conversation with the female demon also pulled up more memories, yet again opening wounds that had barely scabbed over.

It was necessary, she knew, because those wounds would not have healed properly—not when they were still infected. She hadn't drawn out the poison during those months she'd attempted to self-heal, had pretended it would simply…go away. Instead, her mental injuries had festered.

"I will likely never care for humans," Arawn said, pulling her out of her thoughts.

She was about to say, *I know, and I can't expect you to,* when he spoke again.

"However"—his eyes held her spellbound—"I respect the fact that you do."

Her breath stalled.

"And I will make sure the griffin preys only on animals from here on out."

Heart thudding fast after it skipped a beat, she stared at him. "You can do that?"

"It listens to me." A look out of darkly glinting eyes. "Seeing as I am the horse whisperer of beasts."

Her world brightened in a storm of emotions, and she knew, right then and there, that she *would* have seen past it if it meant she got to keep seeing this side of him, as well as the teasing lightness and deadpan banter he was capable of. If she got to be the one he joked with this way.

"I'm glad," she said, clearing her throat. "And I admit to being a tad hypocritical."

He raised a brow.

"I like Griffin." She petted the feathers on the beast's front legs. "And knowing he might snack on people didn't make me push him away." Lowering her eyes, she added, "So why should I do that to you, when I like you a lot more than him?"

Arawn's power thrummed in the air, a physical thing, an energetic caress for her senses. When tendrils of his magic touched her, the touch felt proprietary, staking a claim she had neither the strength nor the skill to refute. Nor the desire.

Welcoming his touch—and craving the physical one as well—she stood up, started toward him but stopped short with a frown. "Wait. Just to get this clear—you *don't* snack on people, do you?"

Molten desire in his eyes. "There is one I plan to make an exception."

She shouldn't still flush with heat at his teasing, yet here she was, getting all hot and bothered by a few targeted words...which resurrected a number of blushworthy sequences from her dream. Unable to withstand the unadulterated force of his gaze, she glanced down as she walked up to him, grazing her fingers over the buttons on his dark purple shirt.

"Last night," he murmured, running his thumb over her cheek, "you asked me what I am."

She went motionless, her breath trapped in her throat. Daring a look up, she drew out the one syllable in a cautious tone. "Yes."

"Remember when," he went on while he drew a finger around her ear, making her shiver just right, "I told you that I was around when the Powers That Be forced the beasts to sleep?"

She nodded, her pulse ticking fast.

"There were those among the gods"—his fingers glided down her neck, sending prickling waves of pleasure down her spine—"who were not in favor of it. Some were in opposition because they despised humans, some because they cared more for the beasts, and wanted them to remain free."

Dizziness grasped her mind with chilled, tingling fingers, her knees going weak. She held herself upright by clutching at his shirt.

"There was a coup," he continued, and laid his hands on her upper arms—lightly. Preparing to steady her should her knees give in after all? "A sneak assault by those who favored humankind. They smote the ones in opposition, made them fall. When they crashed onto mortal lands, their powers scattered, leaving them human in strength but for their immortality."

She wasn't sure she was breathing anymore. *Where did the air go?*

"It took centuries"—his thumbs stroked over her shoulders—"to reclaim the first pieces of scattered magic. Many hundred more to gather enough to become a power once again." His eyes harbored age-old knowledge and unrelenting *patience*, and now she knew exactly why. "I have almost regained full strength."

206

"Oh, my gods," she whispered. "You're a *god*."

CHAPTER 25

"Fallen," Arawn said, watching her reaction closely, his magic on a tight leash. "But yes, cut from the same cloth as those whom witchkind calls the Powers That Be."

Her breathing flattened out, and her eyes glazed over. Not a full-on panic attack from what he could tell—at least not like those brought on by her trauma—but enough of a visible rush of uncontrollable emotions, among them likely shock, that she swayed in his hold.

"I kissed a god," she rasped.

"And you ground on his lap as well." He gave her a smile intended to distract her with sensual promise. "That was...*divine*."

She blinked, shook her head as if coming to, her eyes turning sharp again, flicking to his face.

"Having you warm and loose and willing on top of me," he said with calculated precision underneath his intimate murmur, "felt *heavenly*."

She closed her eyes, the corners of her mouth twitching up. "Stop it."

"Tasting you," he continued, a wicked sense of play

infusing his blood, "was like *paradise*."

Her shoulders shook as she buried her face in her hands. "Oh, gods."

"Just one. Me."

Her laughter, when it broke from her, stole his breath. Light and lovely and daringly infectious in its mirth, it dispelled all his thoughts save one—

"I did not know," he said quietly, his heart gone still, "how much I needed your laughter until I heard it."

On a gasp, she met his eyes, hers grown wide, liquid amber striated by gray.

He traced her lips with his thumb. "I would rend the world to keep your laughter in my life." Dark, dark conviction behind every word. "To keep you safe enough to laugh."

"I'd rather," she whispered, "you keep the world to keep me."

He studied her face for a moment, the solemn fire in her eyes, the determined set of her brows. Nodding once, he said, "As you wish."

She swallowed, and he allowed himself the luxury of tracing the movement of her muscles with his fingers.

"I want to lick you here," he muttered, his attention on the creamy skin of her neck. Catching her gaze, he clarified, "For starters."

She inhaled sharply, but her scent stayed free of fear—instead it was drenched in the musk of her arousal. "So do it."

Body tightening, he bent down—the difference in their heights making this an interesting exercise—and kept his senses aware of her tells as he kissed the curve of the neck she bared to him, her head tilted to the side. Her breathing sped up, but he didn't sense her mind slipping into her past. He licked a slow path up her throat, and she shivered, her lips parting on a soft sound of pleasure.

Lips he was going to taste again. Power curling underneath his skin, he kissed his way to her chin, paused briefly to let her catch her breath, gather her senses, and then indicate she was ready to take more.

"Stay here," he murmured before he gently cupped the back of her head with one hand and took her mouth in a kiss that was but a sample of the wildness lurking behind his calm.

She grabbed his shirt again, melted against him—and stayed, indeed, in the here and now, with him. He rewarded her with a curling caress of his powers…over her breasts.

Gasping, she broke the kiss, only to look at him out of heavy-lidded eyes, her cheeks dusted rose. "Do that again."

So he did…with his hand.

ELECTRIC SHOCKS OF PLEASURE ARCED THROUGH HER BODY AT HIS touch, her nipples tightening under her sweater and bra. His eyes riveted on her face, he ran the back of his hand over her other breast too, the intensity of his attention nearly as intoxicating as his caress.

The desire to feel his hand on her bare skin instead of through layers of clothes was a full-body ache, yet she had to pace herself. The specter of her nightmares loomed just behind a thin barrier of sheer will and grit, its strength still untested. Every second she remained in control of her body and her mind was a hard-won victory over the terror meant to break her.

Closing her eyes, she curled her hands, still holding his shirt. She wanted to enjoy this with him, wanted to relish his touch and trust him with her body without always waiting for the other shoe to drop, without having to keep one eye open and her senses alert so as not trip and tumble into the pitfalls of her mind. Dammit, she wanted her untroubled sex life back!

He clucked his tongue. "While I do want you to tremble at

my touch, I was hoping you would do so for a reason other than anger."

She focused back on him. "Not at you. I'm not angry at you."

"I know." He stroked a finger along the neckline of her sweater. "In general, anger is good, but not when you direct it at yourself." Eyes that were far too perceptive studied her face. "Not in this."

Grinding her teeth, she looked away, blew out a breath, and nodded. "I just want myself back."

"It will happen—in time."

Amusement bubbled in her chest at his play on their shared promise. "I feel like we should start a list."

"I already have one."

She raised her brows.

An insouciant shrug. "Or two."

Her quiet amusement broke free when she gave him a wink. "Then I guess I better catch up."

"We should compare notes when you are done."

Such dry humor in his tone, and yet...something dark lurked behind his voice, his eyes, and without knowing how, she *sensed* it had nothing to do with her. This was something else, well hidden except for that knowing inside her...as if their bond, maybe, clued her in to another layer of his emotions.

"What's troubling you?" she asked.

Surprise flashed over his face for a millisecond, before he was in full control again.

When he opened his mouth to give her an undoubtedly evasive answer, she grabbed his shirt tighter, pulled herself up on her toes and said, "Tell me."

He looked down at her hands, then met her eyes again, a smirk playing about his mouth. "Do I have to worry about scorch marks on my favorite shirt, Wildfire?"

"Only if you keep being evasive."

Pure appreciation glinted in his eyes before his expression sobered. "There have been a series of attacks on my territory."

She blinked, smoothed her hands out over his shirt, over the taut muscles beneath. "And it's serious." It wouldn't upset him like this if it was a run-of-the-mill border issue.

"It is also curious."

She gave him a look.

"In a deranged sort of way," he amended.

"How so?"

What he told her next, of piles of butchered humans with a strange pattern of displaced organs—the latest of which he'd apparently found just this morning—turned her stomach, but she held it in. He trusted her with this information, even the gruesome details, displaying a belief in her strength to take it in, and she wouldn't dishonor that belief by puking on his shoes.

"I suspect," he said, "this is the work of one of us who fell."

Her heart stumbled. "Another god?"

He nodded, old memories shifting in the shadowed green of his eyes. "In all the millennia since the fall, I have never encountered one of the others. We were likely spread too far, the world hard to travel until more recent times. It is possible, however, that they have been gathering their powers back as I have, and one of them managed to find me."

"And you think they're a threat?"

"We did not all see eye to eye." He shrugged. "Some of us disliked each other as much as the Powers That Be. And if the one here was friendly toward me, they could have simply come to see me."

She frowned, tapped her fingers on his chest. "But you said it was weird they would kill humans to threaten you."

He inclined his head, conceding her point.

"What if those kills aren't meant as a threat?"

His look sharpened. "Elaborate."

"Well," she said, feeling a bit silly to bring it up, "this morning when I opened the door, there was a dead rabbit on the veranda."

Narrowing his eyes, he grew preternaturally still.

"Relax." She stroked down his sides. "It turned out the bobcat put it there—it caught and killed it for me."

"As a gift," he murmured.

"Yeah. Cats pull that sort of thing all the time. A gruesome way to show appreciation, I guess, but it makes sense for predators. And you guys…you're like…"

"…the apex predators of the world."

She nodded. "I'd say there's a good chance someone is trying to say hello in a super-creepy godlike way."

CHAPTER 26

Having left Maeve with the griffin after another round of spellwork study—he'd carefully taken down the first layer of the spell now he was certain it wouldn't cause immediate decay of the entire structure—and a lingering kiss that rendered her breathless for all the right reasons, Arawn took to the skies in the form of a huge eagle. He had some pondering to do.

Maeve's theory was like the missing puzzle piece that had kept him from seeing the big picture, and he brooded over the fact he hadn't come to that realization himself. He should have. There was no excuse for his lack of focus here, except, perhaps, that he'd been distracted by his consuming fascination with a certain witch with copper-colored lashes.

Now, though, with all the hints gathered and laid out on the table, he saw it clearly, knew there was only one of the other fallen who would play this sort of game. And that elusive scent, the faint trace of age-old magic he'd picked up and couldn't quite place, made sense now. Put together—finally—with the correct memory of the one they belonged to, they pointed him to the most probable location of his long-lost peer.

Leaving the airspace over his dominion, he made for Mt. Hood.

The snow-covered peak of the dormant volcano rose above the surrounding lush green of the Oregon wilderness like a lone guardian of old. Circling over the mountain on air currents for a few moments, he banked, followed the pull of the magic he could trace now he knew on whom to focus. He spotted the figure on one of the upper slopes of the volcano.

He touched down in a measured landing yards away from his target, pulled on the pants and boots he'd easily carried in his eagle's claws. The cold wouldn't bite at him, his body generating enough heat he could take a stroll through wintry Alaska and not even shiver, but the boots in particular were handy on uneven terrain.

Gaze fixed on the figure standing on the snowy blanket over a jagged edge of the slope, he approached. "You always did like mountains."

Eyes of thunder and lightning met his own as the male turned, a slow smile spreading on a face many would describe as hauntingly beautiful, in a broken way. "Hello, brother."

"Velez." He inclined his head.

"It is good to see you again." Piercing intelligence in his regard, edged with a feral playfulness. "Though I must admit I had hoped you would decipher my gifts of greeting much sooner."

Arawn put his hands in his pockets, sauntered around him, not acknowledging the taunt. "You still have a certain sense of…theatrics, it seems."

A smirk on that face capable of mesmerizing mortals. "Staging is so much fun. You should try it."

He didn't ask why Velez hadn't simply come to meet him, why he'd chosen to play and poke in a most gruesome, bloody way. They'd been close companions once, brothers born of the folding of time and space before the earth took shape, bonded as family…as much as gods could be. And long ago, before the fall, Arawn had shared in Velez's antics, his own detached ruthlessness a barely sheathed blade.

A part of him still was, still understood the dynamics of games played by those with nearly unlimited power.

"I see," Velez said, black hair lifting in the breeze, "you have done well for yourself. Quite the dominion you have built."

Arawn acknowledged it with a nod. "What about you? Where have you been?"

"Here and there." Flurries of snow swirled around him in a gust of wind. "Mainly what they call the Old World now. Russia for a long time. Europe. That is where I found most of my power." Storm gray eyes met his. "The beasts are waking."

"I know."

A flash of excitement on his face. "Just think what the world will look like when they roam free again. When the ones who drove them into oblivion lose the last shreds of their power, and those they sought to protect will know the terror they have been shielded from."

Arawn's muscles locked even as a tingle of the same wild excitement ran through him. Yes, the beasts would be magnificent in their restored power, would be met with the awe they deserved. And he was looking forward to the moment the failing force of the Powers That Be would cripple completely, leaving the field wide open…

"You have felt it, too, have you not?" Velez's expression was tight, his form vibrating with his magic. "The Powers That Be will not *be* much longer."

"I suspect," Arawn said, "their decline is directly proportional to our renewed rise and the waking of the beasts."

"Yes," Velez hissed. "Their reign is coming to an end. Our time is near."

"Do you know of the others?"

Velez shook his head. "You are the only one I could find."

Likely because they had been so close, brothers in magic at a time when the world was newly minted.

"I have often wondered," Arawn said, "whether some of us did not survive the fall after all."

Velez shrugged, a swift motion reminiscent of the lightning he could conjure. "There are those I would not mourn."

Arawn smirked. "I know the feeling."

"Brother," Velez said after a moment, turning to him with a storm brewing in his eyes, "let us join forces. The time is ripe to wield our power, to reclaim what is our due. We have lived among the vermin for too long, hiding what we are. Now the beasts are waking, we can rule the world."

If there was one thing that had carried Arawn through the ages, through centuries spent learning how to live without his magic, human and weak except for his inability to die, would regenerate even when they hacked off his limbs, it was the anticipation, the sheer *determination*, to reclaim the power he'd lost. He'd lusted for it until it became the obsession that drove him in times of darkest need, when he lay broken and bleeding from wounds no being should recover from.

Now it was a steady, thunderous beat of longing underneath his skin, the sense that he could reach out and grasp it fully. Joining in power with Velez would catalyze the last stages of reacquiring his magic. But—

"Vermin," Arawn said with silken softness.

Velez made a dismissive hand gesture. "They truly are the worst infestation this world has ever seen. I thought them laughable before, when they were little more than a pet project of a deluded handful of us, but now they have swarmed over this place like a plague, I must say I will cheer when the beasts prey on them again."

Arawn's hands slowly curled to fists in the pockets of his pants. With deliberate nonchalance, he said, "You would allow the humans to be hunted."

"Of course." A disbelieving snort. "Do not tell me you have come to like them?"

"No. I have not." He looked out over the expanse of wilderness, to the edges of his lands where a witch waited for him, an immortal beast inside her, and a gentle, mortal's heart. "But I will not allow them to be dispensed with." He met Velez's eyes again. "Not in my dominion. Not on my orders."

His erstwhile brother angled his head in a quintessential non-human way. "You have changed."

"As much as I appreciate your offer," Arawn said, "I will have to decline. My territory is my own. I will not share my power."

"Maybe you should take some time to think about it."

"No need. My decision stands."

The air crackled around Velez. "You would push me away for the sake of humans?"

"No." He held that storm-whipped gaze. "Not for humans." For someone else who *cared* for them, her affection a flame in his heart. "I will not abide any cruelty dealt to them, and you will not be able to restrain your powers. Which is why I need you to leave, and stake your claim elsewhere."

Cold winds gusted over the slope, rustling Velez's dark hair. "I expected more of you."

"And I do not live by your expectations." He shrugged. "I bear you no ill will, as long as you respect my borders."

Since Velez spelled trouble for humankind wherever he went, eliminating him to keep his promise to his witch even beyond the perimeter of his lands would be the wise choice. But...they *were* brothers, and for the sake of old times, he found himself incapable of striking him down.

Not to mention it wouldn't be easy, would be a fight with the potential to devastate this corner of the world—and they were much too close to his territory to chance those consequences. Better to send Velez off and fortify his borders instead.

Velez narrowed his eyes, stared at him for a long moment before he shrugged again, inclined his head. "Let us part on good terms, then."

He held out his arm, and Arawn grasped it in the greeting and farewell of warriors, his hand clasping Velez's forearm while the other male did the same with him.

"Goodbye, brother." Velez let go, and vanished with a roll of thunder, lightning splitting the sky.

Arawn stared at the spot where his erstwhile brother stood for a long time afterward, the mountain wind whipping around him.

CHAPTER 27

The humidity from the hot bath filled the room to the point the mirror above the sink fogged over. Maeve took a deep breath and wiped at the surface with a towel so she could see her reflection.

A chill spreading through her despite the warmth in the air, she forced herself not to reach for a towel or her clothes to cover her body. Forced herself to look at the reflection she'd shunned for far too long.

Take a bath, Tashia had said. Maeve laughed at that at first, but the petite demon insisted, gave her the task as "homework."

Your body was turned into a battlefield, she explained, *and it's hard to live inside the relic of a war that devastated you. It's understandable if you disconnected yourself from your body, ignored it for all this time. But you mentioned that you want to reclaim your sexuality, and the first step to that is to learn to love yourself again. If you want to be comfortable while being naked with someone—* and, boy, did she ever—*then you need to feel comfortable being naked when you're alone.*

So she was to look at herself, really *look*, without judgment, pushing back against negative thoughts, and then enjoy a nice, hot bath. To notice all the little details of how her body reacted to the water, to simply *feel*. Easier said than done, it turned out.

Ever since she'd come back from that warehouse, she took care of her personal hygiene with the utmost speed and efficiency, lest she spend more time than necessary dealing with this body that had failed her so. She hadn't been able to bear the sight of it—naked—after the initial shock when she was well enough to take care of herself again.

And now she trembled in front of the mirror, trembled at seeing the proof of how she'd been broken, used, degraded. Even though the healer witches who came to see her did their best to mend her injuries and remove her scars, they weren't able to erase all of them. A pattern of white markings and raised flesh still criss-crossed her skin in far too many places, among them her breasts—a particularly obnoxious cruelty, marring the very area that should appeal to a lover.

Disfigured, that hated voice inside her whispered. *Ugly*.

Her hands clenched to fists against the urge to cover herself.

Once he sees your scars, he won't desire you anymore. He won't even want to touch you.

She hauled in air with burning lungs and shuddered. It took her a moment, but then she shook her head in quiet defiance and said, "Not ugly." An unsteady breath. "*Kintsugi*."

Her eyes flicked to the bowl she'd brought into the bathroom with her, set on the shelf above the tub as a reminder, as a focal point.

"Beauty in repair," she whispered, and looked back at her reflection, imagined each scar filled with golden lacquer, each fracture point lovingly decorated, its mending celebrated, kissed with light. Imagined it so vividly, so intensely, finally the mental picture of herself superimposed itself on reality, and her mirrored self shone with a filigree pattern of golden lines.

In the end, she smiled.

When she slipped into the hot water, steam curling around her, she watched, and felt, and relished each slosh and wave lapping at her skin. How the water flowed over her, trickled from her arms, her breasts, closed around her knees.

And she looked, did not avert her eyes, and mapped the landscape of horrors on her body. Only now those horrors had lost some of their hold on how she saw herself—for the image of golden lines seemed to flicker where before she only saw the hateful reminders of how she'd been made a victim.

Not a victim. Tashia's voice echoed in her thoughts.

"Survivor," Maeve muttered.

That was another of her lessons, another impression Tashia had offered her. A shift in perspective, a seemingly simple change of vocabulary, yet it turned the tables in her head. That word gave her courage, strength, and a budding sense of pride.

She'd made it. She'd gotten out, alive. He meant to kill her —he'd failed. He thought he'd broken her beyond repair—yet here she was, taking steps…admittedly shaky so far…to reactivate what he hadn't been able to destroy.

Slowly, gently, she stroked over her arms, her shoulders, her legs. Massaged her skin, her muscles, not shying away— for once, for the first time—from the areas that were difficult to think about, much less touch. And with each languid, careful, loving stroke over her body, a twisted part inside her unraveled, another crinkle smoothed out, until she felt it, truly *felt* it—how her self, the core of her, so inextricably entwined with her physical form, breathed free for the first time in months.

And like a mistreated dog that finally, finally found the affection it yearned for, her body seemed to whisper, *Thank you. Thank you for wanting to see me again.*

The tears were silent at first. Then her chest heaved with

powerful sobs, but it was a good sort of crying. A cleansing one.

She hugged herself, golden scars and broken pieces and all, and remained that way until the water cooled around her and the steam on the mirror cleared.

☙❧

WHEN MAEVE OPENED THE DOOR TO ARAWN'S KNOCK, HER natural scent of fire and wind was caressed by the heavy sweetness of bath oils, her hair curling wet down to her shoulders. An image of another time she'd stood before him with dripping hair—when she walked into his lair that day—flashed through his mind, and the difference between the two, the change in her, struck him hard.

The Maeve who faced him now glowed from within with a new kind of quiet confidence, her poise infused with soft assurance, as if she'd settled a bit more into her own skin. The effect on his senses was irresistibly alluring.

"I have always thought you beautiful," he murmured, "but tonight you are breathtaking."

Her cheeks blushed, but she didn't lower her eyes, simply smiled and said, "Thank you."

He followed her invitation to step inside, sat with her on the couch. She pulled up her legs, clad in soft, flowing pants, and draped them over his lap. Raising a brow at her, he laid his hand atop her shin, watched her reaction as he pushed the fabric up until he touched skin.

That quiet assurance of hers didn't waver.

He stroked small circles over her calf. "I found him."

She didn't miss a beat, her eyes becoming sharp. "The other god."

"Velez." He nodded, his thumb still tracing idly over her skin, soothing the touch-hungry wildness in him. "We agreed to disagree."

She frowned, so he told her of the encounter, ending with how he'd let him leave.

"I get that," she said to the sliver of doubt in his voice, the unspoken question behind his words. "If he's like family, it's not as easy as black and white, even if he's difficult."

So discerning. He cocked his head, regarded her for a minute while he caressed her lower legs, dared to stroke up to her knees. "Do you hold it against your grandmother that she bound your powers inside you?"

"No." A shake of her head. "I mean, I understand now why she did it. That kind of power inside me…it could have seriously hurt someone, maybe even me, if it broke out. It's just…weird that she wouldn't simply say so. Why make up a story about how I was born without powers?"

He stilled, his focus zeroing in on her. "Probably to keep you safe," he said, playing along, his casualness belying the suspicion prickling in his nape. Careful, he had to be careful here.

She shrugged, lowered her eyes. "Yeah, seeing as I was kidnapped to be harvested when the knowledge about my powers got out." She sighed, rubbed her shoulder. "I miss her, though. After Mom died, and Dad was…lost, she was my rock."

Clearing her throat, she added, "Speaking of my father…I would like to see him sometime."

"Of course." Another lazy stroke up to her knees.

"I would have to go visit him, though." A probing look from underneath her lashes. "He can't come here."

"I know." Frank MacKenna was bound to a nursing home in Portland, his mind too addled for him to live without constant supervision. "I will arrange for you to see him." He massaged her feet, watched with satisfaction how her features slackened in pleasure.

"The healer witches," he said after a moment, carefully

laying the path, "have not been able to reverse your father's mental impairment?"

"No." She pressed her lips together. "They tried, but the damage is just too deep. You know, sometimes he has these lucid moments when I visit him, but only ever with me. He looks at me, and suddenly his eyes are clear like they used to be, and he recognizes me…even talks to me. Just a few words, but outside of those moments, he doesn't speak at all. He doesn't recognize Merle, ever. It hurts her so much to see him react to me but not her that she only goes to visit him alone now."

"How close was he to the blast?"

"I'm not sure." She frowned. "Not as close as my mom or Moira, obviously, but somewhere in the outer radius of Moira's spell, and still it hit him hard enough to cause some sort of damage to his mind."

His heart thumped faster with the dizzying confirmation he'd been waiting for. He dared probe her more directly now, at the risk of sounding moronic if he was wrong in his suspicion after all. "Where were you?"

"In the house, with my grandma. I didn't even see it happen. I just remember my grandma screaming, running outside, and…" She shook her head, dark shadows swirling in her eyes. "It was like a bomb had gone off."

"Do you resent Moira," he gently asked, "for what she did?"

A deep breath. "No. It wasn't her fault, not really. She just…lost control."

He stroked up her legs again, soothing her as much as himself, for underneath his outward calm roiled a storm of rage.

She didn't know. Maeve didn't know it wasn't Moira's spell that was responsible for the blast.

And that acidic taste of the slivers of thought she unknowingly projected at him, her shields lowered in familiarity with his presence, it was enough to tip him off. Her gap in knowledge about this crucial part of her past wasn't natural—she'd known it once.

Someone had messed with her memories—and recently so —had made her forget it was her magic breaking through at the age of eight that killed her mother, her sister, and mentally maimed her father.

CHAPTER 28

That silent rage continued to twist and turn inside him when he went in search of the one responsible for Maeve's lapse in memory. Well, not just lapse. Her memories were *altered*, an alternative, fake reality planted in her mind. The thought made him snarl.

He was still growling under his breath when he stepped onto the property to which he'd tracked his quarry, having followed her scent from the Murray mansion to the simple family home protected by his very own wards, as part of the extended security he gifted those who were his. Dimitri Kuznetsov didn't belong to him, but his brother Aleksandr did, and Arawn granted him a measure of protection by proxy.

Because the magic guarding the house was his, it didn't alert the people assembled here to Arawn's presence, and he silently stepped out of the shadows of the night, into the spacious backyard.

Aleksandr, his mate Lily Murray, Basil Murray and his new mate, Merle, and the rest of the Kuznetsov family sat or stood on the patio, some moving in and out of the house with food and drinks. Balloons fastened to the chairs and railings swayed in the night breeze, and a garland spelling *Happy Birthday, Lucas*, decorated with fire trucks, hung over the table.

Two demon younglings ran around—Aleksandr's nephews, Lucas and Jordan, aged five and ten. Aleksandr currently chased them around the patio with a toy that looked like a sword made of light, and their screams and giggles filled the air, the eyes of the adults riveted to their play.

Arawn was about to make his presence known when something tugged at his pants leg.

Some*one*.

He looked down at the tiny *pranagraha* girl. Dimitri's toddler daughter, Chloe, gazed up at him with her silken blond hair fastened into a wobbly pony tail, her small frame clad in a pale rose miniature dress of tulle and sparkles.

"Pick up," she said in her tiny voice.

He raised a brow.

"Pick *up*." With an expression of utmost concentration edged with budding frustration at his obvious slowness, she stretched her arm higher.

Demon Lord and god he might be, but he took the only course of action when faced with a toddler holding out a toy phone to him demanding he accept the call.

He picked up.

"Hello," he said, putting the plastic thing to his ear. "Who is this?"

She held the twin of the phone she'd handed him to her own ear. "Me. More cookies!"

"You want more cookies?"

An earnest nod. "Yes. Need more."

"Is that so?"

More nodding, her ponytail swinging. "We're all out!"

"And why is that?"

"Daddy ate them all," Chloe said, lowering her voice to a dramatically loud whisper. "But Mommy needs them. She had a baby, and she's hungry. She needs alllllll the cookies. So." She took a breath. "Bring more cookies."

Arawn nodded in understanding, amusement a prickle in his veins. "That sounds like an emergency. I will bring you more right away."

That's when he noticed the silence. Looking up, he took stock. Every single person in the backyard stood or sat frozen, gaping at him with varying degrees of shock written on their faces. Before anyone could move, the door to the house burst open, and Dimitri's mate, Tori, stormed out.

She ran over to Arawn and Chloe, grabbed her daughter, and screamed, "She's not yours! You won't take her from me!"

His powers hushed in darkness.

Dimitri dashed up to Tori as she hauled the toddler away from Arawn, the male *pranagraha*'s despair over his irate mate yelling at the Demon Lord a pulse in the night.

Tori, all protective mother demon, shook her head wildly, her eyes a feral, swirling red-and-black. Baring her teeth, she shouted, "I won't let him steal her away!"

Dimitri managed to herd her back into the house along with his two sons, shutting the door behind them.

Arawn's control over his breathing was an iron shackle, his magic threatening to pool darkness around him like a cloak of death. He clenched his jaw, the only outward sign of the corrosive anger inside him...and the barbed-wire edges of a hurt that pierced too deep. He dropped the toy phone on the grass.

Turning to the others on the patio, he caught Merle's wide-eyed stare. "A word, fire witch."

She blinked, shook herself, and came over to where he stood. Rings of exhaustion lined her eyes, her face a mask of worry and painful determination. He did not give a shit about it. Not tonight, not when his mood was dark enough to blacken the world.

"Did you tamper with your sister's mind?" he asked without preamble, lethally soft.

Merle reared back, her mouth falling open. "What?"

His voice turned to a whip. "Did you?"

"I don't know what business of yours that—"

"Do not," he snarled through gritted teeth, "try my patience tonight. You will find it stretched precariously thin." He stalked closer, his force pushing against her. "Did you alter Maeve's memories of how your family was killed?"

"Yes," Merle gasped, crumpling under his pressure. "Yes, okay? I did."

"Why?" His powers coiled around him.

"It was too much for her." Merle's eyes glittered hard. "She was falling apart. When we got her out, that demon had just told her what happened back then. She never knew it was her magic—our grandmother had changed her memories, too, told her the same story I believed, but that fucker of a demon made sure she learned the truth, to break her even more. I *had* to delete that knowledge again."

"Did you ask her permission?"

Her brows drew together. "What? No, I…" She narrowed her eyes, her hands clenching to fists. "What's it to you?"

"You messed with her mind when she already suffered manipulation worse than you can possibly imagine. You took away her choice."

She scoffed, her face a study in outrage. "That's rich coming from the guy who *bought her with a bargain!*"

His power exploded.

Black velvet energy suffused everything, filled the air with crackling magic, snuffing out all light. The earth rumbled, rippled, quaked, broke apart on a crack just as he yanked himself back under control again, called his powers back into his pores, under his skin.

Light returned to the world, the moon's glow illuminating the ashen face of Maeve's sister—whom his magic hadn't touched. In all his cold rage, he hadn't harmed a hair on her head. Obviously intimidated, she glanced around at the flattened grass, the leveled trees, the hairline fissure in the earth that stopped just before her feet.

At the reminder of just how much power he kept on a tight leash most of the time.

"She has a right to know," he said, and stopped the approach of her friends with a flick of his hand.

They froze, stumbling against an invisible wall.

Merle's face became impossibly whiter. All confrontational attitude and biting defensiveness apparently sucked out of her, she stared up at him. "Please, don't tell her. Please. It will break her."

He curled his lip at her.

"You don't know what she was like when she came back." She shook her head, her voice breaking. "I was losing her. I wasn't sure I could hold her here, she was so distraught… It was the only way. I *had* to make her forget."

"And you would keep her oblivious still," he growled.

"She won't survive it!"

Stepping closer until she started to inch back, he softly said, "Such little faith you have in her. She deserves more credit than that."

Utterly disgusted, he turned his back on her and stalked out of the yard, over the leveled fence, and through traces of glittering dark power hanging in the air, ignoring the sobs following him into the night.

CHAPTER 29

By the time Arawn found Maeve in her cabin again, he'd ruthlessly beat back the cold fury biting at his nerves because he didn't want her to see it. She'd have enough of her own emotions to battle if she accepted his offer.

He'd perfected his facade of bored indifference or cold cunning over lifetimes, fooling even those who knew him best about his feelings and thoughts, but Maeve...when she opened the door to him for the second time this evening, she took one look at his face and asked, "What's wrong?"

Deciding to take that as his lead-in, he indicated her to sit down, and said without further ado, "Your memories have been tampered with."

Her mouth flattened into a thin line. "The demon."

She never called him by name, the vile piece of shit who'd scarred her in the most vicious of ways, and Arawn understood the—probably subconscious—psychology behind it. To name him was to acknowledge him in a certain form, whereas to keep referring to him by pronouns and generic terms relegated him to insignificance.

He didn't deserve to be named, his personhood acknowledged. Who he was should sink into oblivion, his name forgotten in history.

"No," he corrected Maeve's assumption. "By someone else."

"Who?"

No matter how little he cared for Merle, he didn't want to drive a wedge between the two sisters—for Maeve's sake—so his first impulse was to give an answer for which Maeve would undoubtedly call him out as evasive again. But as he told Merle, Maeve had a right to know, not just that her memories had been changed, but also who did it.

"Your sister," he said, adding gently, "She meant well. It does not excuse the fact she did it without your consent, and without ever letting you know afterward, but her intention was to protect you."

She swallowed, glanced to the side, and though her eyes were soft, her jawline hardened, her hands curling to fists. "It's all she's ever done." She rubbed her upper arms. "I know she loves me, but sometimes…"

"Love can be suffocating."

The look she sent him said he'd guessed right. "She came for me," she whispered, deep emotion in the shimmering amber-gray of her eyes. "When I was dragged into darkness and pain, and he told me everybody had given up looking for me"—a hard swallow—"she came."

That barely leashed anger snapped at him again, though this time for the cruelty of an experience her description only hinted at. Her lived reality was a thousand times worse, could never be expressed in simple sentences.

"I love her so much it hurts sometimes," Maeve went on, "and I'll *always* be grateful for how she relentlessly searched, and found, and came for me. But I think the…protectiveness in her, it's almost too strong." Shaking her head, she brushed a lock of her hair off her face—and didn't push it right back. "It blinds her sometimes."

"I can restore those memories for you," he said into the heavy silence that followed. "If you wish."

Her copper lashes trembled as she looked at him. "You know what she made me forget?"

He heard the question behind her question, nodded. "And it would hurt you more than anything you lived through in that warehouse."

Her breath left her on a rush.

"Your sister thinks it would break you."

"And you don't?"

He touched her cheek, ran his fingers down to her lips, deliberately over part of her scar, but only as in passing any other part of her face, because that mark wasn't what defined her. Her mouth opened on a soft gasp, as if she read his gesture correctly.

"I happen to believe," he said in an intimate murmur, "you are made of fire and darkness and the strength to harbor a force inside you that even gods fear. The beast in you"—he laid his hand on her chest, over her heartbeat—"would never have chosen to be reborn in a body and soul too weak to house it."

He stroked up to her throat, all the while watching her face and the tiny tells of her body with utmost alertness, and curled his hand around her nape. She didn't flinch, didn't shrink back, her eyes glowing and focused as she held his gaze.

"I think," he continued, "your flame is so strong it will not be snuffed out by this."

He squeezed her nape, caressed her with tiny movements of his fingers. "It is your choice," he said after a moment. "You can decide to keep that particular box closed and the demons in it forever confined. Knowing of a sore spot and choosing to leave it alone can be as wise a choice as facing your darkness."

She laid her hand on his arm, close to the hand grasping

her nape, but not to push him away—she stroked her thumb over his skin, *held onto* him.

"However," he continued softly, "if you choose to open that box, I will be here, facing that darkness and its demons with you." Another squeezing caress of her neck. "It does not have to be tonight or tomorrow. Take the time you need to think about it."

She closed her eyes, her facial muscles tightening. "You'll be here?" she whispered.

"Every step of the way."

When she looked at him again, her eyes were ash-kissed flames. "Then let's take the lid off that box."

☙❧

MAYBE, MAEVE THOUGHT, SHE WAS A CERTAIN KIND OF INSANE to willingly tap into memories that could likely destroy her. Maybe the demon had given her a taste for pain, to the point she now sought it out. Because this *was* masochistic.

Or maybe she was simply tired of hiding, of cowering, of shying away from a challenge at the slightest flicker of fear. She'd indulged in that kind of evasive, escapist behavior all summer, spent months holed up in her room, in the safety of the Murray mansion, not daring to fight back against her anxiety. She'd let her fear control her, but she was *done* with that.

She started spitting in the face of her demons the moment she decided to walk into Arawn's lair, and she wasn't backing down now. Not confronting those memories was the same as locking herself in her room. Even with the demons confined to a box, they still controlled her. Because if she was afraid to open it, it was just another way of caving in to their power.

Aside from this deep determination to never run from her fears again, the other reason that made her decide to poke that hornets' nest was a simmering, inappropriate curiosity about what could possibly be worse than her memories from the warehouse. She'd already scraped the bottom of hell.

"Just tell me when," Arawn said, his voice of rough silk a sensual caress.

She still held on to his arm, to the strength in those corded muscles, the power vibrating beneath his skin. She wanted to sink into that power, wrap it around her, until every breath she took was of him.

With a nod, she said, "Now."

He entered her mind on a whisper of darkness, and just like the times before, when he'd looked at the spell inside her, his presence was a consuming kiss of unadulterated energy to her mental senses—even though she suspected it was only a fraction of his full power.

That ancient otherness inside her stretched toward him, fiery filaments licking out from a yet-locked vault in her core. But this time his awareness didn't veer in that direction, instead heading for another corner, the one holding memories of the second most painful time in her life.

The day her mother and sister burned to ash, her father turned into a living corpse.

She jolted under a dizzying suspicion. Why would he go for that time, those memories? What could—?

You are strong enough. A stark reminder, unwavering faith in his mental voice.

His power touched upon her recollection of that day…and what she'd believed for the past sixteen years melted away, dissolved to reveal the harrowing truth.

The backyard behind the old Victorian. Moira, smiling at something their father said from his chair on the back porch. Her mom, tending to the herbs close to the cherry tree, glancing up to wave Maeve over.

"Look at how the sage is growing," her mom said, stroking the big leaves. "Want to help me dry these when I harvest them?"

Maeve nodded, giggled when her mom tickled her with the rose-

mary she'd just cut. Moira, caught in that time between childhood and adolescence, joined them and sorted the harvested herbs neatly into little bags, rolled her eyes when their mom tried to tickle her as well.

"Mooo-oooommm," she said in that drawn-out tone her teenage friends used perfectly at any and all occasions.

"Come on, Monchichi." Maeve grinned, knowing she'd get a rise out of her sister with that hated nickname. "Don't be a spoilsport."

Moira shot her a look, opened her mouth to give her some no doubt snarky comeback—she never got the chance.

A feral force of primeval fire hurtled out of Maeve on a wave of pure destruction. Screams rent the air—her own, and two others that shattered her flame-encased heart. A storm of red and orange and heat that caressed her, and then—a blast of witch magic, shaking the ground, compressing the air, pushing back against the blaze.

The flames let up enough for Maeve to see...two charred lumps where her mom and Moira crouched before—and the firestorm died down in a keening wail that tore from her throat.

The next second her grandmother ran through the swirl of smoke and ash, stumbled at the sight. With a choked sob, she fell to her knees, reached with trembling arms for Maeve.

Her grandmother's face fell when she met her eyes. Cupping her cheeks, using pulses of magic to feel deep inside her, she whispered, "Your powers...they shouldn't be this strong." A shake of her head. "It's not possible. You—" She swallowed, stroked Maeve's face, her voice breaking. "You need to sleep, child. Sleep, and I'll...take care of everything."

"Mom," Maeve sobbed. "M-moira. They're—I—"

"Hush now." Tears thickened her grandma's voice. "I'll take care of you, darling."

Blessed darkness like a velvet embrace, the mercy of oblivion.

Gasping, Maeve tried to haul in air—her lungs seized, her throat burned.

Burned, like the bodies of her mom and sister when she turned them to ash.

"No," she rasped. "*No.*"

The light of the cabin filtered back into her eyes, Arawn's hand on her nape a brand, a promise kept, and yet it wasn't enough to stave off the roiling horror of the truth.

"No," she cried again, her voice breaking, a thousand serrated knives slicing through her heart, her soul, the very fiber of her being. "I killed them."

"Maeve."

"I killed them."

"Look at me."

"*I killed them!*"

The scream that ripped her apart was nothing human, nothing mortal, echoing with the screech of a beast from the dawn of time. And, rolling out like flaming thunder, that same primeval power that had torn a charred hole in her family blazed its way out from the confines of its prison to consume the world.

⚝

THE FIRE EXPLODED OUT OF MAEVE WITH HER SCREAM OF AGONY, threatening to tear Arawn to shreds. Not because of its power —because of the pain that razed her.

A shock wave of heat and flames hit him straight on, scorched the clothes off his skin and filled the cabin. He threw himself over her, wrapped his power tight around her small frame, a kiss of darkness to her blaze.

Delving deep into her mind, her core, he found the disintegrating spell, its layers giving way to the force of her pain, found the beast clawing out of the darkness.

He shoved out his power toward it.

Not yet, his magic whispered. *Not like this.*

Over and over he let his power sing a song of cajoling

persuasion laced with the force of his command, his authority. The beast, yet hidden in the black of its confinement but for its talons scratching at the edges, writhed and rumbled, bucked against his voice.

Not yet, he repeated. *Wait until she calls you.*

Because she wasn't consciously doing so at this moment. This staggering blast and her surrender to the power that lived inside her were nothing but side effects of the battle she was waging with herself, with the horrors of her past. It was not her choice to loose the beast from its leash.

But it should be.

And so he worked and wove and twined his magic around her core, whispering the beast to sleep once more. All the while, his wards limited the firestorm to the cabin, his innate power making him immune to her scorching heat.

When, finally, the blaze died down, he held her amid whorls of ash and smoke, her body a light weight in his arms. Cradling her to his chest, her head tucked against his shoulder, he stood, stepped over soot and charred wood, and wrapped his magic around her like a cloak of black mist as he walked.

No one would see her like this. No one but him.

Through the shadows of the night he carried her, under the earth and past the main hub of his dominion, down to the most private center of his lair. Through wards so heavy they chafed at his own skin, to the safest place in the entire world.

He laid her down in the heart of his home, laying both of them at her feet.

CHAPTER 30

M aeve woke to dark, dark energy enveloping her senses, stroking sinuously around her mind, over her skin. She opened heavy lids to a gloom of a different sort. A warm semi-darkness.

A windowless room?

Just as that thought beat along her nerves with panic building in its wake, she made out the twinkling lights above her. Stars were scattered amid swirls of indigo on a sea of black und midnight blue. Shooting stars went swishing across the vast space, and the full moon hung overhead, bathing everything in its soft glow.

Staring up at this incredible canopy of the night sky, she frowned at the lack of a chill on her skin, no breeze tickling her hair. If she was under the open sky, why was she not feeling the cold?

"Because you are, indeed, inside."

She jerked at Arawn's voice, rolled over to see him lying next to her—on a bed?

"Yes. My bed." Moonlight kissed his bronze skin with strokes of silver, dark sheets covering the lower half of him. He was lying on his side, head propped on his hand, his weight braced on his elbow. "The one I use for sleeping," he added with a smirk. "Although I would gladly make an exception and give it another use with you."

"Are you just plucking my thoughts out of my brain?" A defiantly flippant question, ignoring the pulse of some harrowing truth lurking just outside her awareness.

"No. You are throwing them at me."

She threw another, less well-mannered thought at him, and he chuckled.

"Is this your private lair, then?" she asked, her eyes flicking back to the tempting sight of his mostly naked body right next to her, eclipsing even the allure of the spectacle above her.

"Yes."

"The one no one but you has ever set foot in?"

He inclined his head, and a warm tingle spread in her chest, made her stomach do a flip. He'd brought her here, to this secret place, revealed to her the part he kept hidden from everyone else.

"Why?" she whispered, her eyes prickling hot. She couldn't be that important to him...

"It is fitting." Those eyes of shadowed forests, the wild evergreen of the lands he made his home, glowed with an intensity that branded every cell of her being. "This is the safest place I know, and how better to protect my heart than to bring it here?"

She blinked, uncomprehending.

"You heard right," he said, amusement deepening the lines around his eyes.

Something inside her stretched and spread, reaching with tendrils out to every aspect of her, and it had nothing to do with the ancient presence in her core. It was a hurt so refined, so raw, it veered right into pleasure sublime enough to steal her breath.

"Say it again," she whispered.

"You are my heart."

On a choked sigh, she touched her hand to his face, stroked down to those lips that were such an impossibly soft part in a face of harsh angles and hard planes. And knowing she had the right to touch those lips, to feel their kiss was a thrill in her veins.

Leaning forward, she claimed that right to kiss, tugged him to her with her hand curved around his nape—

A flash of memory. *Arawn's hand on the back of her neck. Thoughts and impressions and images flickering by, centering on a storm of fire and the scorched remains of the people she loved.*

She jerked when it rushed back in full. Sobbed when it broke over her yet again, that knowledge of how this lethal thing within her had tainted her childhood with the ashes of her mom and sister, had taken them from her—along with her dad. She was responsible for his state as well.

She was responsible for all of it.

My fault, my fault, my fault…

"No." Arawn's voice cut through the sickening haze in her thoughts, his hands a hot brand on her as he pulled her on top of him. "That is not true."

"I killed them." A broken whisper, barbed wire raking across her heart.

He cupped her face with both hands, forced her to meet and hold his gaze when her eyes wanted to skitter away, to stare unfocused at nothing while the guilt and horror consumed her. "It was an accident."

"They're dead because of me. Because of that beast in me."

"Which you had no chance of controlling back then"—he tightened his grip—"*when you were a child.*"

Hiccuping on a building sob, she shook her head—or rather, wanted to, but found his grasp kept her still. Kept her focused. On him, on the heat between them. All the minute details of how it felt to lie on top of him, on *Arawn*. The tickle of his chest hair against her breasts. His power seeping into her cells. His slow, steady breaths under her arms. His heart-beat under her hands.

You are my heart.

This thought, the knowledge helped push back against the despair threatening to pull her under. She dug her fingertips into his chest and... Everything ground to a halt as realization swept through her.

She was naked on top of him, skin to skin but for the sheet covering his lower half, the only barrier between their bodies.

She waited for the panic to set in, for one of the land mines in her mind to explode and shred her. Nothing happened. Nothing but sinuous heat sinking into her very bones, melting the jagged edges of pain from her recently recovered memory.

"This will not break you," Arawn said, unwavering faith in his voice. "It did not break you when I unlocked your memories, and it will not do so now...or ever."

"But—" Flashes of flames in her mind. "I exploded. In the cabin. When I found out. I *exploded.*"

"You feel very much in one piece to me." He slid one hand from her head down over her back, to the curve of her waist...lower.

With a gasp, she stiffened—and relaxed when the touch of his fingers on her butt didn't cause an avalanche of fear to bury her. Because this was Arawn under her, caressing her. The male who'd allowed her, with endless patience, to famil-iarize herself with his body, his touch, who'd been so incred-ibly gentle with her through it all, yet pushed her at all the right moments and in ways she hadn't known she needed.

But he'd known.

He'd seen her pain, her fear, her scars—especially the ones in her mind—and he'd known just how to navigate them all. She wanted to laugh at how she once believed him to be entirely and utterly wrong for her, hadn't believed him to be the right man to help her rediscover her sexuality.

Turned out he was exactly *right*.

The smile playing about his mouth said he knew it too. And his hand caressed her butt, squeezed…his fingers sliding lower.

She had to catch her breath when he brushed *so close* to the pulsing heat between her legs. Her heart jumped into her throat, her fingers digging harder into his chest.

And the icy grip of the harrowing truth she'd learned loosened a little more around her soul.

"You're doing that on purpose," she whispered. "To distract me." From the stain in her past, to keep its oily sickness from spreading into her present, her future.

"That," he said on a silken murmur that had her curling her toes, his hand stroking with languid intent down her thigh, up again, "is not the only reason."

She trembled in just the right way, and in all the right places.

"In fact," he went on, using his hand on her hip to shift her position on him, "I am far more selfish in this than you might believe."

Her new position on top of him let her *feel* the evidence of that selfish interest caressing her mindless. The hard length of him was unmistakable through the thin sheet…and it cranked her simmering arousal into a blaze.

She knew there was still a reckoning to come, that she'd have to face the newly opened wound of her childhood, would have to fight to come to terms with what she'd learned, but right now, every single part of her wanted nothing more than to follow the pulsing pull of her desire for Arawn, and let it drown out everything else.

Later. She'd deal with her pain and guilt later.

This, here, was the pleasure she'd been waiting to reclaim for herself, and having Arawn hard and naked under her was too much of a temptation to ignore.

So she wiggled a bit, and watched with rapt fascination—

and not a little feminine pride—how his eyes became sharper with sensual intent while his lips parted in reaction to her rubbing over him.

She did that. To him. It kicked her pulse up a notch.

"Tell me," he said, one finger under her chin, "what you like."

A throb of lust between her thighs at the sheer *purpose* in his attention, at the hint of steely authority beneath the deceptively soft velvet of his voice. Oh, sure, one might think his question and his restraint so far indicated he'd let her take the wheel, but her instincts told her the thought was dangerously misleading. He was still fully in control, simply giving her the opportunity to set certain boundaries…within which he would *play*.

His next comment was proof of the strategy behind his asking. "I also need you to tell me what may be an issue for you."

Her breath caught on the bolt of visceral fear at the flash of memory, though it didn't pull her under. "You can't be on top of me." She swallowed. "Not yet." *Maybe not ever.*

He smiled, stroked both hands back down to the curve of her butt, pressed her to him, causing a shiver of finest pleasure to arc through her. "I rather like having you hot and shivering on top of *me*."

Easy. He made it so easy for her. And she loved him all the more for it.

Arawn stilled beneath her. He didn't even breathe anymore, gone preternaturally quiet, his focus on her searing in its intensity. And she realized…

Her heart thumping madly in her chest, she deliberately thought, *You heard right.*

A glint of amusement in his eyes, though his expression remained all harsh concentration and predatory hunger. "Say it. Out loud."

Her voice soft but steady, she said, "I love you."

She felt the ping of the wild response in his emotions along the bond inside her, the echoes of it flickering across his face, as he pulled her head down for a bruising kiss of feral passion. A claiming. *Mine*, it said. *You are mine.*

Breathless, she broke the kiss with a gentle bite on his lower lip—making his cock twitch against her thigh—and murmured, "I'm claiming you, too, just so you know. You're mine. My Arawn."

His eyes flashed. "I have no issue with that," he purred. "As long as you do not expect me to walk on a leash."

"Likewise."

One side of his mouth tilted up, his hand tangling in her hair. "Deal."

She itched to kiss that arrogant half-smile—so she did, tracing the curved line of his smile with her tongue, until he snapped at her with a playful growl. She snarled right back, and slid down to kiss a trail over his chest, luxuriating in the feel of his coarse hair against her cheeks, her chin, her nose.

His hand remained on her head with just enough of a tug on her hair to deliciously remind her of how he still held the reins. She explored the expanse of muscles and strokable skin beneath her, kissing, rubbing her cheeks over his skin, bathing in the scent of him.

Because smelling him, being wrapped in the aroma that was Arawn, was another way to root her in the present, to make sure she knew, down to her bones and the instinctive parts of her, who this was she was touching, and allowing to touch *her*. Another defense against the insidious conflation of male touch and sexual intimacy with the one who'd tried to break her.

A tug on her hair. She looked up, met eyes of dark green gleaming with anticipation.

"Any time," he murmured, "you need a break, you tell me. Keep telling me what you need. Out loud or in thought."

She buried her face against his hard stomach, and his

muscles flexed in response. *Thank you,* she thought. Her chest would shatter under the pressure of what she felt for him.

The caress of his fingers over her scalp. "I had the distinct impression," he said with silken precision, "you were going somewhere just now."

Her eyes shot wide, and she jerked up her head to stare at him. His grin and the directive tug on her hair—*down*—might have irritated her were this any other man, but with Arawn, the sneaky move only fueled her desire.

And, yes, she *had* been going in that direction. With that intent.

Her thighs clenched at the mere thought of taking him in her mouth, tasting him. Hell, she'd been salivating for it ever since her naughty dream. Beyond that, though, she wanted to, *needed* to, feel him like this, on her own terms, before she could open to him another way.

His smile deepened.

Tug.

Narrowing her eyes at him, she moved down, vowing sensual retribution for his cockiness. Plenty of ways to take him to the edge without giving him exactly what he wanted.

Because he damn sure needed to be brought down a peg, or he'd start thinking he was some sort of god.

CHAPTER 31

Arawn had experienced various forms of pleasure over his long life, from light and fleeting to razor-edged and mixed with pain, but the way Maeve made him feel was *new*. It was a feat bordering on the impossible, but he'd resigned himself to the fact that she defied expectations.

And he'd never known pleasure to be infused with as much *amusement* as it was with her. The thoughts she continued to toss at him...they made him want to laugh in a way that seemed almost foreign to him, loosened parts in him that had become too rigid, too jagged.

So when she drew the sheet down off his hips with narrowed eyes and dared to teach a god a lesson—because she was fearless when it came to him, and he wouldn't want to have it any other way, would *hurt* if she ever treated him with cowering awe—he grinned, free and open, with a kind of fun he hadn't experienced in far too long.

White-hot lust washed over that sizzling amusement the instant she closed her hand around his cock. He nearly bucked in her grip, the need to feel her creating friction around his most sensitive body part a driving, maddening force.

Her eyes flicked to his face, burning amber and swirling smoke, holding him mesmerized as she lowered her head... and licked at the tip.

His power blotted out the magic-made night sky above.

At her soft gasp, he brought it right back, and stroked tendrils of his energy around her in apology. In addition to not wanting to frighten her, he made sure the pitch black didn't return, because he wanted enough light on her while she sucked him. He could see in the unrelenting darkness, but to have her creamy skin caressed by the glow of the moon and stars while she gave him such pleasure was a beauty in and of itself.

"So," she asked in her sensually husky voice, her breath cooling the wetness that had gathered at the head of his cock, "is this like a light switch, then?"

His laugh broke from him on a flash of surprise and delight only she brought out in him. Her features softened in that way they did when she saw him laugh, her eyes glinting with sexual intent the next instant.

She licked him again, and this time he directed the excess push of his power in response to her touch to enhance the magic of the star-studded midnight above. Wide-eyed, she stared at the pulse of lights, looked back at him.

"It *is* a light switch," she whispered, her expression a perfect pretense of serious awe.

He knew, at that moment, that he would fight a sky full of gods to keep Maeve *his*, to keep her wanting to tease him like this, unguarded and lovely and disarming with her charm.

"Keep flipping it, then," he said, all sensual dare and unvarnished demand.

Her answering grin was a fleeting thing, giving way to renewed sexual focus as she gripped him harder, brushed her lips over the head, her tongue along the especially sensitive underside. She sucked at the vein there, and he felt that suction throughout his entire body, groaned low at the hint of teeth when she closed her mouth completely over his cock.

Bursts of starlight above them.

Down she went, and up again, keeping her eyes on his face, equal parts to remind her of his identity and to watch his pleasure—which he knew from the thoughts she didn't quite throw at him, but nevertheless let him see.

And he didn't hide his pleasure, allowed her to see what she did to him, and was rewarded with a lush boost of the most exquisite fragrance he'd ever smelled. He inhaled the heavy scent of her arousal, vowed to taste the source of it *soon*.

He tightened his grip on her hair, incrementally, carefully, a question in the tug he gave her.

Hair-pulling, she thought at him, *is safe. He never did that.* Heavy-lidded amber eyes held his. *Don't stop. I like it.*

And that was all the answer he needed. He grasped the strands more firmly, began to direct her movements—having picked from her thoughts, from the way she *chose* this type of intimacy first, that it was another thing untainted by her experience. With all the acts of violence that demon had committed against her, forcing her to take him in her mouth hadn't been among them.

The part of him that hungered for control less vicious now he could guide her, he drank in the erotic sight of her lips around his cock, her head bobbing as she sucked him. Pressure building in his balls, he directed her to go faster, and she complied with a spark in her eye that did him in.

Lightning bolts of pleasure shot down his spine, through his groin, made him buck against her. His head fell back on the mattress as he came, the night sky above a tapestry of silver bursts and shooting stars, his power rolling out to fill every corner of the room.

Maeve kept sucking him until he was spent, and let go of

his cock with a wet kiss and a lingering caress. He watched, riveted, as she crawled up his body, her breasts swinging with the movement.

His fingers closed around one of her nipples before she stopped above him, and he circled the tight nub, tweaked it just a little. She inhaled sharply, and he paused to check her expression.

"It's all right," she whispered. "I'm okay."

"Good." Even to his own ears, his voice was drenched in pleasure, a sated rumble. "Because I have plans for these." He cupped both of her breasts, an erotic weight in his palms.

She arched into his touch, no sign of shyness or shame about the scars visible on her skin—which were symbols of strength, of survival—and a deep sense of pride flowed through him. She was conquering her demons, one by one.

With one of her nipples lightly pinched between his fingers, he tugged at her to move forward, until her chest was level with his face. She braced her arms on either side of his head, her breath coming fast as he ran his hands over her breasts, massaged and caressed in alternating strokes of feather lightness and increasing, targeted pressure.

"No biting." Her voice was but a rasp, echoes of pain behind her words.

And his mind short-circuited at the thought of how much she had been mistreated to fear something that should be an exquisite pleasure between lovers.

"In that case," he said on an intimate murmur, "I will have to lick you twice as thoroughly to feast on you."

She shuddered in his hold, the amber of her eyes molten with lust. That was when he rose up, sucked a nipple into his mouth and swirled his tongue around it.

Her hips rocked against his abdomen, a choked sound of pleasure tumbling from her throat. He worked her left breast with his lips and tongue while flicking the hardened nipple of the other one with his thumb. She undulated above him, her breathing turning ragged.

"Still with me, Wildfire?"

Her response was to tunnel her fingers through his hair, caress him with light, affectionate strokes.

He played his fill with the supple curves of her breasts, making sure she was writhing with excitement, her scent a consuming perfume in the air, before he moved his hands down her sides, to her waist.

"Come here." He applied enough pressure on her hips to make her scoot forward. "I want to taste you." He ran a careful finger over her thigh toward the red triangle that glistened wet with her desire. Watched her expression with utmost attention as he grazed that finger over her curls, over skin swollen with need. "Here."

She jolted, her breath unsteady, her muscles visibly tightening.

"Safe or not?" His finger lingered.

Voice shaky, she said, "He...did that."

He waited, taking his cue from the fact she hadn't pulled away.

"But," she went on, "I want to overwrite that memory. With you."

Nodding, he slid his finger in lazy circles around the center of her pleasure. "Courage should be rewarded."

Her skin was slick with her arousal, and he used her wetness to glide over her intimate flesh, make her quiver with need. Her thigh muscles trembled with the effort it obviously took for her to keep hovering over him, too much tension in her small, lithe body.

That wouldn't do.

"Place your hands behind you, on my chest," he ordered.

She complied without hesitation, and he grabbed her tight with both hands on her ass, brought her directly over his face. He held most of her weight like this, his strength such that he didn't even feel strained. Her hands on his chest merely served for extra balance—and the angle of this position meant she was opened even more for his pleasure.

"Relax your thighs."

After a moment she did, and most of the tension drained out of her body with that small surrender. *Better.* Though not enough to satisfy his own need to see her drown in sexual bliss. He would make her go boneless yet.

She jerked at the first touch of his mouth to her slick folds, and he deliberately tugged at the bond, to remind her, to ground her.

I'm okay, she thought at him.

He rewarded her with a leisurely lick up to her clit, though not touching it directly. Instead, he used his lips and the flat of his tongue to apply wide pressure to the mound above it in a slow rhythm designed to make desire fire up her nerves and pool in her intimate flesh.

Her fingers digging into his chest and her breathing turning choppy were the sweetest praise of his effort.

When she was shaking with *lust*, he finally licked down, gave her deep, thorough kisses on her wet folds, teasing her entrance with touches of his tongue, though careful not to push in.

"You taste like fire," he murmured against her hot, wet skin. "Power wrapped in flames."

Her response was a strangled moan.

"I want to see you come apart again." He touched his mouth to her clit. "Burn for me."

He sucked, and her back bowed, her hips jerking against him as she shattered with a husky moan. Her scent, her taste, her power, filled his senses, the ghost of flames bursting forth from her, caressing him in turn.

He wasn't done yet.

Relentlessly, he kept going, drove her over the edge again and again. She gasped for air, her arms shaking as she tried to keep herself propped up, her head thrown back in ecstasy. He dared lightly licking into her slick opening, a teasing hint of erotic intrusion—and it pushed her to another shuddering climax.

She collapsed completely, her arms giving in, and he let go of her with a kiss to her swollen folds, watched her virtually flow off him to lie in a molten tangle on the mattress beside him.

"Now this," he said, stroking her with his power, "is how I want to render you limp."

CHAPTER 32

When Maeve finally recovered her ability to speak, her muscles still loose, her bones fluid, she rasped, "I didn't know how much I needed this."

Dark power caressed her senses, the heat of Arawn's hand like a brand as it rested on her thigh. It was a familiar touch by now, her nerves no longer alarmed by it. *Arawn*, a knowing assurance whispered inside her. *Safe*.

For the first time since her rescue, she felt completely at ease, all tension drained out of her. Relaxed and satisfied, floating on the high of sexual bliss.

"I've missed this," she whispered.

"You got it back."

Always distilled things to their most salient point, didn't he? Helping her move forward instead of getting stuck looking back.

"Speaking of moving forward," he said, his hand stroking with lazy intent up her thigh.

"Plucking thoughts again?"

"Catching them," he corrected, a sly smile in his voice.

She might have tossed him a thought that started with

Catch this, and his laughter rippled through her like a kiss to her senses.

"Come back here." A rumbling murmur of silken seduction she was powerless to resist.

She let him pull her on top of him again, shivered with delight as he wrapped his arms around her. The steady thump of his heart a beacon to her soul, she buried her face in his neck, breathed him in.

"You didn't even break a sweat." A grumbling complaint, her own skin slicked with the evidence of her exertion.

"Is that your way of asking for more?" His hand gliding over her butt, *squeezing* the curves in sinuous moves, clearly said he was up for it.

Was she?

She pondered that for a minute, her lips pressed to his neck. As sated as she was, as mind-blowing as her orgasms had been, a sense of…emptiness pulsed within her. When she'd come, her inner muscles had clenched around *nothing,* and—another first since her rescue—she'd craved to be filled.

Still craved it, judging by that steady throb of longing between her legs.

And yet, the thought of penetration sent fear slithering down her spine.

Which was exactly the reason she should do it. No more running from her fears. She'd keep spitting in the face of her demons, would spit on *that* demon's non-existent grave and rob him of his legacy.

"I have no idea," Arawn said in a near whisper, "why anyone would think you fragile. You are far stronger than they all give you credit for." Such pride in his voice, deep appreciation in the caress of his dark power.

"You see me." A tender kiss to his jaw. "You've always seen me."

"That is"—his hand slid over her back with loving possessiveness—"because you are a sight to behold."

He made her heart *ache* with love. She sought his mouth, kissed him long and deep, framing his face with her hands. It stirred the simmering need inside her to a boil again, until it was her core that ached—for him.

His one hand shaping her butt, his other cradling the back of her head, he sat up…and the change in position placed her directly on his hard cock. Not sliding down it, the angle not quite right, but the length of it pressed against her sensitized skin sent a shock wave through her body.

She stiffened, her heart stumbling. Fear clawed at her.

Arawn broke the kiss, but held her face close to his. "Just breathe."

She waited, went through the exercises Tashia had taught her to calm her nerves, to root herself in the present. Breathing in a pattern, she noted the details of her surroundings, reminded herself that this was her choice. And held on to Arawn for dear life, her hands gripping his nape.

The drumbeat of panic subsided, giving way again to the desire curling in her core. She moved, tentatively, and rubbed along his hard length with tiny thrusts, getting used to feeling him like this before she took him in.

A thought flitted into her mind, and she paused. "Um. I'm not on birth control."

"And you do not have to be." Some dark echo in his voice. "I cannot procreate."

"You can't have children?"

"No." That twist behind his words intensified. "Few gods have the gift of fertility. Creating life is not one of my powers."

She blinked, drew back enough so she could look at his face. And what she saw in those harsh lines pierced her heart. "You want that, though," she whispered. "Children. A family."

The fact he allowed her even a glimpse of what had to be a deeply hidden hurt touched on tender parts of her soul. This, right here, letting her see this vulnerability of his, this sadness…it was the utmost trust.

"Even I," he said without concealing the raw pain behind his statement, "do not get everything I want."

Remembering how much he disliked being pitied—and understanding that particular feeling thanks to her own twisted experience—she gave him the hint of a smile. "Well, there's this one thing you want that you're about to get."

And she underscored her teasing words by rocking her hips against him. She was so wet, from her arousal, from the way he'd pleasured her with his mouth, that she slid along his erection with erotic smoothness.

His expression tightened with lust, and the hand he still had on her butt flexed, grabbed her harder. "Whenever you are ready."

His chest hair rasped over her hardened, sensitive nipples, and her core clenched in response. She was as ready as she could be.

"I *want* this." A whisper, a reminder, a pledge.

"Then take it."

She rose a bit, took one hand off his neck to grab his cock, position it right. The tip nudged her entrance, and she paused, breathed past the flicker of instinctive fear. Knowing he wasn't pushing, wouldn't move before she told him to, and would stop if she asked him—or even just *thought* about it—helped ease the budding panic.

Safe, she repeated to herself. *I am safe.*

With that reminder, that assurance, she began lowering herself onto him. Inch by inch, her breath fast and shallow, her pulse racing. He held her gaze, kept her bound to him, to his presence, to the feel of *him* so it would drown out the whisper of her nightmares, keep their shadows from reaching for her.

"Take your time." For all the gentleness of his words, his voice was edged with searing hunger.

"You're stretching me…" She gasped, but it came out as half a moan. "Oh, gods. "

His smile was wicked and incredibly arrogant. "*Arawn* will do from now on."

She laughed, short and quick, but it was enough to relax the tight curl in her belly, to let her breathe more freely. After a moment of getting used to the size of him, she moved farther down, until he was sheathed in her up to the hilt. She paused, relished the pleasure laced with pain of the erotic intrusion.

A brush of his energy over her clit, sparking more lust in her core. She clenched around him, and—oh, damn, it felt incredible.

"*Arawn.*" A whispered prayer.

That glint in his eyes was positively roguish. Kissing her, he stroked the back of his hand over her breast—and pinched her nipple between his fingers.

Her inner muscles tightened again, and she could move, gave in to the need to feel the friction of him sliding in and out. Holding on to his shoulders, she rocked up and down, slow at first, building momentum and pleasure.

Prickles of anticipation burst along her nerves, and she rode him faster, harder. His hands came to rest on her hips, squeezed…with the hint of a question.

"Yes," she whispered against his lips. "Move. I want to feel you."

He kissed her with a touch of teeth, raw and hungry, and she *felt* the moment he loosened one of the shackles he'd been keeping on his consuming power, the wildness of his nature. It shuddered through her via the bond, a full-body earthquake that left her breathless for a few seconds.

And then he moved.

Gripping her hips, he thrust up while his magic twined around her, licked over her skin with pulsing zings of finest pleasure. Her breath caught, her heart skipped a beat, but she held on to the pure joy of feeling him this way, and left no room for horror to invade where it should never be endured.

She met his thrusts, let her body take over, gave herself fully to those instincts that were honed before the attempt to break her. Hot, ravenous kisses, her fingers digging into his shoulders, his hands grasping her hips tight, making her ride him in a primal rhythm that shattered and dissolved some of the ugliness that had taken root in her mind.

A pinch of his power on her clit—and she flew apart.

He swallowed her moan with a devouring kiss, followed her over the edge a moment later. Rocking out both of their orgasms together, they clung to each other.

And the night sky rained stars above them.

CHAPTER 33

Merle stared at the note in her hands, reading it for the second time and not comprehending it any better than the first.

"She *what*?" Lily snapped.

"She rejected the prisoner exchange," Hazel said, her voice calm, though her brown eyes glittered hard.

Crumpling the note up into a ball, Merle ground her teeth. "That fucking bitch."

Two days. Juneau sat on the offer for an exchange of Lydia Novak for Rhun for two whole days, only to send a curtly worded rejection now. What the fuck was she thinking?

"She's batshit insane." Lily crossed her arms. "Seriously, there's no reason left in that woman."

"Or in the rest of the Draconians." Merle threw the note in the trash. "I mean, how can the others not even step up and talk some sense into her? This was a *good* proposal. It made sense. It would have saved lives."

"Well," Hazel said, "now we know that's not what any of them care about anymore."

Anger a sizzle in her veins, Merle turned to the hall. "I'm going to pay a little visit to our guest." Time to start interrogating Lydia for real. So far the captured Elder witch had refused to discuss anything.

"I'll join you." Hazel started toward the door as well but stopped, turned to the open French doors leading from the kitchen into the dark backyard.

Merle followed her glance. Rose stood on the back porch, Isa near her, and cleared her throat.

"Talk?" Rose asked Hazel, her Fae accent still strong. She was picking up English words here and there, making an effort to learn the language of her birth family.

And she slowly, hesitatingly, made moves to get to know Hazel, her real mother, whom she only met recently. Hazel, who'd been restraining her instincts to pounce on her lost-and-found child and hug her breathless in favor of giving Rose time, and allowing to her seek contact on her own terms.

So of course when Rose now wanted to talk to her—with the help of Isa as Fae interpreter—Hazel threw Merle an apologetic glance.

"Go," Merle said with a smile. "I'll handle Lydia."

Hazel nodded and joined her daughter, who looked at her twin sister Lily with wide indigo eyes and waved her over as well. Merle's best friend, so assured in most everything else and always taking life in stride, still battled speechlessness when it came to her newly returned real twin, and walked to the back porch in uncharacteristic silence.

Merle made her way down to the basement and opened Lydia's cell, but didn't step inside. Leaning against the door-jamb, arms crossed, she glared at the Elder.

"So," Merle said, "Juneau doesn't want you back. Fancy that."

Lydia raised her head from her knees. She was sitting on the cot, legs drawn up to her chest, wrists and ankles still magically shackled to subdue her powers. Dark rings under her eyes spoke of how little sleep she'd managed.

Merle should have no sympathy for her. She made her bed

with Juneau, had refused to help the Aequitas in any way. But knowing of the staggering loss the other woman had suffered recently, Merle's heart still ached for her.

Didn't mean she'd be going easy on Lydia, not when the other witch could tell them where Rhun was held.

"Are you going to torture me now?" A flat question, Lydia's expression impassive.

"I'm going to ask you one last time—nicely—where Juneau is keeping Rhun. If you still refuse to talk, we will have to resort to other methods to get the information."

Lydia snorted. "You can hurt me all you want. I'm not telling you anything." Her facial muscles tensed. "No matter what you do, I'm not helping you demon-loving blood traitors."

"I find it remarkable that you still spew this kind of hatred after what happened with Aveline."

The youngest witch of the Novak line—Lydia's grand-daughter—was kidnapped and turned into a *pranagraha* demon, like Lily and Sarai Roth. Unlike those two, however, Aveline did not make it out of her captivity alive. She slit her own throat—and both arteries in her thighs, according to Lily, who had to witness the whole bloody scene—in order to kill her mate, the leader of the *pranagraha* group, and thus give Lily a fighting chance to escape. *Pranagraha* mates were bound together in life and death—if one of them died, so did the other.

Aveline sacrificed her life to help Lily flee.

"She would still be alive," Lydia hissed, "if it weren't for demons. My entire family is gone because of these abomina-tions, and our line will end with me. Hatred is all I have left." She spat on the floor.

Goosebumps prickled over Merle's skin. Marissa, Lydia's daughter and mother of Aveline, had been so consumed by grief over her only child's death that she took her own life as well. Which indeed left Lydia as the only living witch of the

Novak family, and she wouldn't have any more children, not at her age.

So, yes, the Novak bloodline would fade with Lydia's passing.

"I'm sorry about Aveline's death," Merle said. "I truly am. And about Marissa's. But to go from valid hate of deranged individuals to hating the entire race?" She shook her head. "There has to be some middle ground. We're trying to find it."

"And I'll have no part of it." Hard eyes in a face etched with unforgiving grief. "So go ahead, start the torture. You'll get nothing from me."

Merle pursed her lips. "Well, I don't think we'll have to go that far." She shrugged. "We could always hit you with a truth spell. I hear Hazel has a knack for them."

Lydia blanched.

"I'll let you stew on that for a bit," Merle said. "And when I come back down here with Hazel, it's either you telling us voluntarily what you know, or Hazel will rip it out of you with the spell."

Leaving a decidedly uncomfortable-looking Lydia in her locked cell, Merle went back upstairs and asked Hazel to tell her when she had finished talking with Rose. The Elder witch did so about twenty minutes later, and Merle filled her in on her unsuccessful talk with Lydia.

"You can do the truth spell again, right?" Merle asked as they took the stairs down to the basement. "The one you used on Tallak."

Hazel nodded, her expression thoughtful. "It'll cost me, but yes."

"You have to draw on a lot of outside power for that one?"

"Yes." Hazel grimaced. "I haven't had to pay back for it yet, but I can feel it looming. It'll *hurt*."

Merle pressed her lips together, wincing in sympathy at the thought of upholding the balance, let alone giving back for tapping into great power. She did it recently, and it almost cost her the life of her unborn baby.

"I'm sorry for asking you to do this," Merle said softly. "If there was another way…"

"No." Hazel shook her head. "It's all right. Everything else would take too much time."

Time they might not have. With every passing day, Juneau might yet decide to try to kill Rhun. Not that it would be easy, since his demon species was particularly resilient, but the risk was still too high. Not to mention that he was suffering every minute he spent in the Draconians' clutches, the faint echoes of his agony along the mating bond a constant reminder of his ordeal.

Merle had to numb herself to most of those echoes in order to even function at all. She poured her worry and pain into various fantasies of how to take revenge on Juneau once she finally had Rhun back.

At the cell, Merle opened the door…and her heart stumbled, her bones icing over.

"No."

She rushed into the cell, grabbed the slumped form of Lydia—whose wrists were bleeding from raw, shredded wounds. How the fuck—?

Her eyes flicked to a jagged chip of brick on the bloodied cot, the edge just sharp enough to have torn through skin to open veins.

"Fuck!" Merle pressed down on both wrists, tried to staunch the flow. "Hazel, come in here. You have to heal her!"

A thump outside in the basement hall. Merle jerked her head around. Hazel lay on the floor, convulsing in obvious pain, her jaw clenched and hands balled to fists.

No. Not now.

Hazel screamed in agony as gashes opened up on the skin exposed by her clothes, red lines seeping into the fabric of her sweater, her pants. Blood welled up, pouring off her body, carrying her magic. It dissolved in the air, fed the power she'd tapped for her spells back to the layers of the world in the exchange necessary to uphold the balance of magic.

Lydia slumped even more in Merle's arms, her wrist wounds still bleeding.

Footsteps thundering on the stairs, and the next instant Basil and Lily came running down the hall, followed by Tallak, who was visiting Basil for some father-son bonding.

"Mom!" The cry came from both Baz and Lily, and they rushed to Hazel's side, supported her through her pain.

Isa and Rose descended into the basement moments later.

Hazel screamed again, her back bowing.

Tallak's blond brows drew together, his eyes glued to Hazel. "What's wrong with her?"

"Balance," Basil threw over his shoulder, crouching next to his mom. "As the head of our family, she's required to pay back the magic she's drawn from the world to supplement her witch powers. She'll bleed until the Powers That Be are sated."

Tallak tilted his head. "That's fucking barbaric."

"Seems about right," Baz muttered, while he stroked Hazel's hair off her pale, sweat-slicked face.

Merle's focus zeroed in on the *hæmingr* demon, a desperate idea forming in her mind. "You," she shouted. "Tallak."

Basil's father looked into the cell, raised a brow.

"I need your help."

He appeared slightly bored as he studied the bleeding witch in her arms. "I can't help her. I'm not a healer."

"I don't want you to heal her," Merle pressed out. "I want you to kill her."

Every single head in the basement—except for Hazel's and Lydia's, of course—whipped around toward her. Slack-jawed, all assembled and in their right minds stared at Merle as if she had grown horns.

But this was the only way. Lydia had been bleeding too long already—an ambulance wouldn't get here in time to save her. And with Hazel out of commission while she was upholding the balance—which could take a while—and Merle unable to use her magic without risking the life of her baby, there was no way to keep Lydia alive.

"The what now?" Lily asked, her face a mask of shock.

"I need you to kill her," Merle said to Tallak, "and take her powers and memories." As a *hæmingr* demon, that was his special gift—when he killed an otherworld creature, or witch, he could absorb their magic as well as their memories.

Tallak raised another brow. "And why should I do that?"

"Because that way at least we'll learn what she knows. Kill her before she dies!"

Tallak picked some dirt from underneath his fingernails. "I'm not particularly in a killing mood tonight."

"Baz," Lily said. "Can't you…?" Being half *hæmingr* demon himself, he shared his father's powers.

But Basil shook his head, swallowed. "I don't have the hang of it yet. Can't guarantee it'll work."

"Tallak," Merle choked out, her heart hammering in her throat. "If you don't kill her and take her memories, I swear to the gods I will make your life a living hell."

"Fine, I'll do it." With a long-suffering sigh and a roll of his shoulders, Tallak walked into the cell.

ॐ

THE SCENT OF FRESH BLOOD HUNG HEAVY IN THE AIR AS TALLAK entered the cell. Lots of it had spilled on the floor already, and he had to step one foot into a pool to reach the dying woman. *Eh.* He'd waded through much more, though he did prefer to dirty himself like this when he was the one who'd spilled the blood.

With a glance at the ginger-haired witch—Merle was her

name, wasn't it? She could be *scary*—who held the other woman, he placed a hand on the dying witch's chin, the other on the back of her head, and snapped her neck with an effortless move. At the same moment he made the kill, he reached out with his demon powers to grasp at the witch's magic.

It flowed into him with the stopping of the woman's heart, while her memories, thoughts, feelings, hit him like a mace to his mind. He gritted his teeth, tried to brace himself for the impact...and still couldn't help staggering back.

Always, always, *always*, it hurt like acid poured into his head. He could stave off the effect for a while if he was jacked up on adrenaline, like when he butchered the rotten royal court of the fae, or took out the guards when they freed Basil's sister Rose, but at some point it would catch up with him.

And tonight, when he made a kill out of the blue, absorbed power and memories without having fought, the pain slammed into him right away.

The entirety of the witch's life, her experiences, the wealth of her emotions and the tangle of her thoughts, all washed over his own thoughts and feelings until he couldn't quite tell anymore where he ended and her stolen life began.

A life built to lead her family, her pride diminished over time as the Novak line thinned...broke. The wrenching agony at losing her granddaughter, her young life ruined at the hands of soulless demons, the hope and future of the family destroyed. The helplessness at witnessing the bottomless despair of her daughter, wasting away day by day, unable to move on from Aveline's death. The shattering pain, heartrending grief when Marissa took her own life. *Dead, they're all dead. My family is gone.*

Oh, he knew *that* feeling quite intimately himself, didn't he?

He breathed past the pain, swallowed it all down and waited for his senses to clear so he'd be in control again.

When the fog did lift enough for him to see once more, he blinked at the expectant face of the scary witch who seemed to be one of his son's best friends.

"So?" she asked. "Where is he?"

Rhun, Tallak thought. *She means Rhun, her husband, her mate*, the knowledge supplied by the newly acquired memories of the dead witch. *Right, then.* How to break it to her?

"She didn't know." He stood, dusted himself off.

"What?"

His head still throbbing from taking in the memories, he snapped at her. "She didn't know! She had no idea where they keep your precious demon."

Merle jerked back, her face losing color. "No," she whispered.

Tallak was already stalking out of the cell again. "Yes," he hissed back over his shoulder. "I can't believe I slurped down those memories for nothing."

"Not for nothing."

He froze at the voice, coming from the witch he'd been trying hard to ignore all night. And every other time he saw her. He attempted to glance at Hazel without actually having to turn his head. Didn't quite work. Dammit.

So he looked. And gritted his teeth at the sight of her all bloodied and broken by whatever fucked-up games the witches' gods liked to play with them. Hazel was many things—annoying, overbearing, prickly, and way too Goody Two-shoes—but weak and bruised on the floor shouldn't be one of them.

"What?" he barked at her, his nerves frayed.

She heaved herself into a sitting position, helped by Basil —Tallak still had to restrain himself from rolling his eyes at the ridiculous name Hazel had given his son—and her daughter Lily.

"You have Lydia's powers and memories now," Hazel said. "So use them."

Newly absorbed witch magic crackled between his fingers, and courtesy of the dead witch's memories, he knew just how to wield it.

Still, he narrowed his eyes, asked, "What—shall I make a few fireworks tricks for your amusement?"

"Your parlor tricks wouldn't impress me." Cold, cold words, those brown eyes glinting. "I mean that since you can shapeshift as a *hæmingr* demon, you could waltz right into Juneau's house wearing Lydia's form and dig around until you find out where they keep Rhun. Since you took Lydia's powers, you can fake her witch energy and get through the wards, and with her memories you'll be able to act and talk like her, so no one will suspect you're not her."

Merle walked out of the cell, uncaring of the blood staining her clothes. "That is brilliant."

"And not going to happen." He resumed walking, headed for the stairs.

"Wait!" Merle shouted. "This is our best chance at getting Rhun out."

He shrugged. "Fuck if I care."

"You can't just walk away and not help us."

He stopped, turned on his heel. "I think I need to get something straight. I am here for my *son*"—he gestured at Basil—"and only for him, because I missed his entire bloody childhood due to rotting away in a fucking dungeon. I am not your lackey, and I don't give a rat's ass about anything other than catching up with my kid. Got that?"

"If you don't help us, we need to start back in square one!"

He grimaced, clucked his tongue and snapped his fingers. "Ah, damn. I used to have a bucket of fucks to give, but somehow it got emptied into the rusty drain of a moldy dungeon cell."

He was heading for the stairs again when Basil said, "Dad."

The word stopped him cold. He rarely called him that. Slowly turning around, Tallak met Basil's gaze.

"Please," was all his son said.

Tallak clenched his jaw. Breathed through his nose. Looked at the ceiling, and cracked a kink in his neck when he glanced back at Basil again. "Your witch friends will owe me for this."

CHAPTER 34

When Maeve woke again, she was wrapped in the heat of Arawn's arms, his energy a blanket of power over her naked skin. The magical night sky was still blinking with stars, and she was about to stretch and say something teasing when she noticed his slow, deep breathing. Eyes closed, Arawn lay…sleeping.

A sense of wonder tingled in her chest, touched on the tender part of her that had attached itself inextricably to this powerful, complex male. He'd not only brought her to his private refuge, he trusted her enough—trusted her more than he did anyone else—to fall asleep in her presence.

His harsh features softened a bit in sleep, and that ever-present predatory alertness gave way to real, quiet peace. He didn't look vulnerable, but this was Arawn at his most relaxed, his guard entirely down.

Her heart expanded just seeing him like this, knowing it was another precious gift he gave her, this trust.

With her hand resting on his chest, she watched him sleep, until, after a long while, he opened his eyes with a deep breath. His power rose as if it, too, woke from slumber, and he twined it around her in a full-body caress.

"Hey," Maeve said, the smile on her face an echo of the one in her heart.

His answer was a deep rumbling sound that made shivers race down her spine in sensual appreciation.

She drew circles on his chest. "Did you sleep well?"

"Hm." The hint of a smile played with the corners of his mouth. "Never slept better."

Sobering a little, she asked the question that had been on her mind for a while now. "When the Powers That Be made you fall...did they ambush you in your sleep?"

Eyes turning hard, he nodded.

"Which is why you don't like it." She swallowed. "Why you built this place here to protect yourself while you rest."

"That," he said, "and the many times I woke to pain after the fall, because I was not used to having a human body without powers and did not sense threats coming when I was asleep. I had to learn how to stay alert with dull senses, to use the diminished strength of a far more fragile body to fight off aggressors I could have crushed with a thought before."

"Yeah." Maeve bit her lip. "I see how that would leave a mark."

They lay in silence for a while, his heartbeat a reassuring rhythm under her hand.

"I've been wondering..." She shifted in his arms, rubbed her leg over his. "When you told me about your meeting with Velez, you mentioned that the Powers That Be are...losing power? Is that why they haven't interfered? I mean, given that they were the ones who forced the beasts to sleep and kicked you guys out, you'd think they'd be up in arms now you're all coming back."

He twirled a lock of her hair around his finger. "They are fading into insignificance, yes."

"Okay." She cleared her throat. "Just to put this all in perspective: Ancient beasts who like to eat humans for snacks are waking up all over the world, and a bunch of gods who fell to earth because they didn't mind—or worse, *liked*—the idea of humans as food are coming into power again, and the one group of higher beings who have been protecting mankind all this time is getting too weak to stop it."

"That sums it up nicely."

Lightheadedness seized her, white spots dancing before her eyes. "I think I'm going to be sick."

"Not in this bed." He tugged on her hair.

She glared at him, then rubbed a hand over her face. "Holy hell. What—what is there—is there any way to…"

"Stop it? No."

"Please, *please*." She massaged her temples. "I can't take that much optimism."

The corners of his mouth kicked up. "There is one thing that needs to be done if mankind is to stand any kind of a chance in the future."

"What's that?"

"Well," he said with a shrug, "maybe two things. The first being that your witch friends need to stop killing each other."

"You mean the conflict with Juneau?"

He nodded. "The witches cannot afford to be divided, not in the face of what is coming. Especially since their powers will grow weaker, too."

She frowned. "Why?"

"Witches draw on the magic which has been worked into the layers of this world to add to their innate power."

"So?"

His dark green eyes glittered. "Who gives them the access to tap into those layers?"

She gasped. "*No.*"

"Yes." His smirk really shouldn't have been that sexy, not with the seriousness of this topic. "The Powers That Be granted witches the ability to supplement their magic so they could protect humans. Unlike the beasts, the otherworld creatures populating the world could not be forced into sleep.

They were too many, so the Powers That Be had to find another way to keep humans from being overrun by stronger species. They chose witches, and imbued them with the ability to draw magic from the world so they'd be able to keep the otherworld creatures in check."

Her stomach was filled with dread. "And now the witches will lose that extra power and won't be able to protect humans anymore—let alone fight off ancient beasts and gods."

"There is…a way to prevent that."

She stared at him. "Spill."

"The access to the layers of the world is a god-granted power. The witches received it in return for a pledge of allegiance to the Powers That Be, a promise to do their bidding, to protect the humans." His shrug was all fluid strength and sinuous power. "They could change their allegiance."

Again, she could do little more than stare in bafflement. "You. You're saying the witches could pledge allegiance to you, and you could give them those extra powers."

"Simply put, yes."

Her laugh was dry and humorless. "They'll never agree to that."

"They may change their minds when they find their powers waning."

※

AFTER AN ENTIRE NIGHT AND THE FOLLOWING DAY SPENT cocooned in his private lair, where he and Maeve had tangled over and over in sexual bliss and soul-crushing intimacy, Arawn finally admitted it might be time to return to the surface. For now.

They stopped in his non-secret quarters in the underground lair to shower and grab some clothes, since both of theirs were incinerated in the blast in the cabin when he restored her memories. He'd kept Maeve clad in shadows on the way up, going in his wolf form himself, and she now donned a pair of his flowing shifter pants and a casual shirt of his, while he dressed in his usual attire of formal pants and shirt.

As Maeve pulled the drawstring on the pants extra tight to fit her small waist—the legs already stuffed into her socks— he told her the part he'd neglected to mention.

"The spell binding your beast has disintegrated."

She jerked her head up, amber-gray eyes wide. "What?"

"It broke down during the explosion in your cabin."

Frowning, she rubbed at her breastbone. "Why…hasn't the beast come out yet?"

He walked over to her, traced her lips with his thumb, every male instinct of his preening at the fact she was wearing his clothes…covered with his scent. "Because I told it not to."

"You horse-whispered my beast?"

He chuckled, nipped at her ear. "I convinced it to heed your call alone. It will only come forth if you wish it."

She opened her mouth, closed it again. Her copper brows drew together, and she bit her lip. "What would happen if I called it?"

"From what I could tell, its essence is completely fused with yours, which means you are one and the same. When you are *you*"—he stroked a finger down the neckline of the shirt, to the dip between her breasts, and smiled at her shiver —"the beast is dormant in your core. When the beast takes over, you will be hidden inside its form."

"I'll…shapeshift?"

He inclined his head. "Would you like to try?"

She froze, her face blanching. "Now?"

"I will be here to keep it contained should you lose control."

A moment ticked by as she held his gaze, her still-wet hair dripping water on the stone floor. "Okay."

He nodded. "Go inside you and call it forth."

She closed her eyes, her attention turning inward. Her face scrunched up in concentration.

Nothing happened.

"Is there something special I should say?"

He crossed his arms. "Not that I am aware of."

"So why is it not working?" She opened her eyes, smoke-licked fire with a hint of age.

"That," he said, studying her closely, "is a good question."

"Can you...check?"

Nodding, he dove into her mind, and deeper, into her core. Flames in velvet darkness, and the shadow of a mighty beast lurking in stygian mist—and it didn't move when he called it.

Leaving her mind again, he shook his head. "It is there, though it does not appear inclined to come out."

She narrowed her eyes. "Oh, so now it's suddenly sulking?" A soft noise of frustration. "I swear, if I didn't know it was a dragon, I'd say it has to be some sort of cat."

With a chuckle, he kissed her, and nodded toward the door. "You can try again later. Right now, there are some things I need take care of."

Being close to twenty-four hours incommunicado when one had a dominion to run did cause some tasks to pile up. Not that he regretted even a second of his time spent alone with Maeve.

"Of course." She nodded—and took his hand as they walked out of his quarters.

He paused, looked down at their linked fingers, then at her face aglow with an emotion so deep, it was purest plea-sure-pain in his heart.

She laughed. "You look like no one's ever held hands with you before."

He just stared.

"Oh." Her face fell. "I'm the first woman to ever hold hands with you?"

Frowning at her, he pondered the strange feeling in his chest.

With a soft gasp, she let go of his hand. "I'm sorry. That's probably totally inappropriate for the Demon Lord to walk around like—"

He snatched her hand back and grabbed it tight as he drew her forward into a walk again. She stumbled to keep up.

"Let them see your claim," was all he said.

She squeezed his hand, her eyes shimmering wet while her mouth curved up in a trembling smile.

Wherever they passed, his people would stare, wide-eyed, some even open-mouthed, some forgetting to bow and greet him. It didn't faze him. On the contrary, he walked taller knowing they saw the female he'd chosen to be at his side. After all, it was time they knew their queen.

He contacted Lucía and Kelior on the way, ordered them to come and be with Maeve for the night. The griffin was apparently out hunting, which meant Arawn insisted on two guards for her.

When they met near the scorched remains of the cabin, Lucía's eyes nearly bulged out of their sockets at the sight of them holding hands. Kelior appeared close to fainting.

Arawn sent both of them a dark look. "Is there something you would like to say?"

Lucía pressed her lips into a tight line that looked suspiciously like a suppressed grin, shook her head frantically and made a sound—half hum, half squeak—that was likely intended to mean no.

"No, my lord," Kelior said, and bowed at the waist.

"Good," Arawn purred. He bent down to place an openly possessive kiss on Maeve's mouth, and murmured, "I will find you later."

Swaying a bit from the force of his kiss, Maeve squeezed his hand before letting it go. "See you."

With a nod at the other two, he turned and strolled into the night, grinning at Lucía's choked-off squeal.

He'd barely walked five minutes when a boom shook the earth, like a distant explosion of epic proportions. Shedding his clothes, he swung himself into the air in his eagle form, shot up above the treetops to scan the horizon. His focus snagged on the faraway silhouette of Mount Hood—which was lit with glowing red, a plume of smoke rising up from the peak.

That same instant, a shock wave of magic slammed into him, hurled him back a mile before he could catch himself. That power...age-old and feral and hot.

Not even hesitating a second, he raced toward the erupting volcano on wings of otherworldly speed.

Toward the beast that just awakened.

CHAPTER 35

Tallak resisted the urge to crack a kink in his neck as he made his way to the imposing gate of the Laroche residence. Witches truly lived in exaggerated style, didn't they? He'd thought the Murray mansion an example of pomposity, but Juneau's house trumped even that.

A high-curving gate of black wrought iron in a fence of the same material barricaded a property that had to be several acres. The long driveway meandered toward a villa of castle-like grandeur, lined by expertly trimmed bushes in geometrical shapes.

He curled his lip before he remembered Lydia wouldn't show such disdain. She'd always admired the Laroche property, secretly longed for the power and wealth of the larger family.

He pressed the bell button and waited. When a buzz came over the speaker and a female voice demanded to know who he was, he rasped, "It's me…Lydia. Let me in."

"L-Lydia? Novak?"

"Yes. Please let me in."

"Hold on."

He waited some more, and a few seconds later a woman

came running toward the gate. Lydia's memories identified her as Carissa Hart, so he smiled and tried to look like someone who'd just escaped a prison cell.

Oh, wait—he didn't even have to act for that one.

"Hi, Carissa."

The Elder witch's face was a study in shock. "Oh, my gods, Lydia. It's really you. How…?"

"I'll explain inside. Please, just let me in."

Carissa nodded. "Of course."

She opened the gate, and stepped back, waiting for Lydia/Tallak to walk over the line of the wards. A smart test to see if he was even able to cross the magical protection.

He stepped over the perimeter without batting an eye, the wards recognizing his aura as Lydia's.

Carissa let out a breath and threw her arms around him. "I'm so glad you're back. When Juneau said Merle rejected her offer of a prisoner exchange, we all feared the worst."

Tallak raised a brow, the move invisible to Carissa, who was still hugging him. *Merle* rejected the prisoner exchange? Nice way to spin it.

"Well," Tallak said, "I managed to get out just after that." He pulled back, and they walked toward the house. "I still don't quite believe it myself, but…Hanna Roth helped me."

Carissa gasped at the mention of the other Elder witch. "Why?"

"She said she's indebted to Aveline for making it possible for Sarai to escape. If Aveline hadn't"—he added a pause and a hitch in his breath to satisfyingly convey Lydia's grief—"made the sacrifice, Sarai would not have gotten out…and she'd never have been able to take that cure."

He balled his hands to fists and gritted his teeth. "*Aveline* should have gotten that potion to turn her back." Staying in character was so important for a convincing performance…

"I know." A sympathetic glance from Carissa.

Sniffling delicately, he continued, "Hanna said that by

helping me escape, she'd paid her family's debt to me. I'm glad I'm out, but I know she didn't do it for me. She only did it to soothe her own sick conscience."

Carissa scoffed. "Of course." Opening the front door for him, she waved him inside. "Well, no matter, the important thing is you're back with us."

Once inside, he was swarmed by several other witches, some of them Laroches, some from other families who apparently were camped out here. He repeated the same story to them, and they all gobbled it up like the finest dessert.

"Where's Juneau?" he finally asked, after stuffing his face with food and enduring endless questions.

"She's out." Estelle, Juneau's eldest daughter, leaned against the doorjamb to the royally overdecorated sitting room in which he currently held court. Her green eyes, same color as her mother's, tracked his every move.

He would have to watch out for that one.

"Oh," he said, and he didn't even have to feign disappointment. If the head bitch was here, he could have simply killed her on the spot and taken her memories, and the whole thing could be wrapped up in a snap.

He could also have easily taken out the entire group of witches assembled here to absorb their memories and powers, but he had to swear—on the life of Basil, dammit—that he wouldn't kill witches unless he was forced to protect himself.

Inwardly, he sneered at Merle and Hazel's restraint. When you were at war, you took out as many of your enemies as possible. You didn't try to dance around the inevitable by pretending to *care*. Kill or be killed.

Since he couldn't outright ask where they kept Rhun— that would be idiotically suspicious—and his roundabout, careful digging hadn't brought any results, he snuck away at the first opportunity and descended into the basement. He could at least check the cells here to make sure they could rule out this location.

The musty smell that clogged his nostrils the farther down he got nearly made him gag. Too many shitty memories associated with that odor, a quarter of a century spent shackled to a moldy stone floor. He breathed through his mouth as much as possible and silently walked from cell to cell, peering through the slits in the doors.

Plenty of creatures languishing away here. *Sorry bastards.*

But no sign of Rhun, the *bluotezzer* demon he'd seen the night he arrived on Hazel's doorstep to claim Basil.

"Looking for someone?" Estelle's voice, floating down the corridor.

He heard the threat behind her tone, and knew, within a split second, that she was onto him. Which was why he didn't hesitate.

He whirled around and hit her with a combination of witch magic and fae powers, the latter a lingering gift from when he recently butchered Rose's captors. The mix of it threw Estelle off, and she choked as water filled her throat, unable to block his fae magic—which she hadn't seen coming.

She drowned in under a minute.

Her body slumped to the floor with a wet thud while he absorbed her memories, her magic. As high as his adrenaline was, he didn't feel the impact of the taking right away, was able to drag her body into an open cell and lay a glamour on her to make her look like Lydia.

He closed the cell door, locked it, and with his heart still pumping fast, he texted the location of Rhun, which he'd gleaned from Estelle's memories, to Merle. Next he took on Estelle's shape—including her clothes—and faked her aura. He ran up the stairs to keep his blood rushing fast, slowed down only when he opened the door to the main floor.

With a soft click, he closed it behind him. Walked toward the garage.

"Hey."

He froze. Turned slowly.

Thea, head of the Callahan family, stood in the doorway to the sitting room. "Where's Lydia?"

He gave her Estelle's patented *don't you worry* smile. "She's gone to lie down in the guest suite downstairs."

Lucky to know, courtesy of Estelle's memories, that there wasn't just an extensive dungeon in the basement, but also a finished lower level living area complete with spare rooms.

"She's so tired, the poor dear," he added with an appropriately sympathetic grimace.

Thea nodded. "I bet. Well, I'll check on her in a bit." And with that, she turned and walked back into the sitting room.

Tallak didn't dare breathe a sigh of relief, not when it might lower his adrenaline level enough that the pain of the memories might hit him.

Instead he thought back to the moment he slaughtered the haughty royal fae in their throne room of gilded cruelty. The remembered sensations of their blood spraying around him, their screams and their pleas ringing in his ears as he took sweet, sweet revenge were enough to keep his heart pumping wildly while he walked to the garage.

A twist of power, and he unlocked one of the cars, slid in, opened the garage door with another well-aimed flick of magic—the power of *two* witches, one of them an Elder, was currently at his beck-and-call, in addition the lingering magic of the fae he'd killed—and ten seconds later, he steered the car out into the driveway.

His hands and arms began to shake as he turned onto the street, the adrenaline fading, and he made it one more minute at full speed, putting several blocks between the Laroche house and himself, before the pain slammed into him. Tires screeching, he managed to stop at the side of the road without crashing the car.

While he endured the agony pouring through him like corrosive acid, a boom rocked the earth, the car, and a wave of teeth-rattling magic crashed over and through him. Pain clawing at his brain, he turned to look out over the twinkling sea of nightly Portland stretching out below the hills of the neighborhood, to the usually dark shape of Mount Hood in the distance—

—now lit up in a blazing explosion.

☯

"I'm sorry, Merle," Hazel said, her features gentle, "but this is in your own best interest."

Merle glared at her from inside the bedroom—which Hazel had magically sealed to keep Merle from leaving. "I can't believe you're doing this."

Elaine, who stood next to Hazel in the hall, sighed. "We wouldn't have to if you were reasonable enough to just stay home."

"I'm not going to twiddle my thumbs while you free Rhun!"

"You can't use your magic." Elaine's eyes were hard. "We've been over this. If you come with us, you'll be a liability, since you can't actually fight at our side and we'll have to protect you."

Gods. She'd heard those words before, or at least similar enough. Rhun once said much the same to her when he was about to rescue Maeve while Merle was without her powers. And the command, the fucking *reasonability* of it chafed at her now as it had then.

Of course she understood the risk of going along, and the logic of staying out of the way when she was at human strength—or rather, weakness—and she could see where they were coming from. The problem was, the knowledge didn't soothe the burning need to be there when the person who held her heart was freed.

What if something went wrong, and her presence could

make a difference after all? What if, by staying behind, she would never see Rhun again?

Her breath got stuck in her lungs, and she choked, couldn't breathe. "Please," she whispered.

"Merle." Hazel's eyes shimmered. "Just…trust us. We'll bring him home for you."

"But only if we move now," Elaine said. "If it's true the *hæmingr* killed Estelle, then Juneau will have felt the link to her sever, and she'll be alarmed something's happening. She may move Rhun to another location."

Lily and Alek, who'd been out for a feeding, were already on their way to join the other Elders, having been called by Hazel. Basil had gone with Tallak when the demon went his on mission earlier, to linger in the area and provide backup— and pickup—after Tallak was done. Isa, who was currently taking a shower in her and Basil's room, was to remain here with Rose…and Merle, according to the stupidly overprotective plan of Elaine and Hazel.

The head of the Murray family sent one last sympathetic look at Merle and followed Elaine down the hall, while Merle grabbed the doorjamb and stared after them.

The wards singed her skin, and she let go, jumped back with a curse. *Dammit.* She kicked at the doorjamb and yelled her anger out into the quiet house, stalked over to the window—sealed with wards just like the door—and looked out. The horizon toward the east seemed…lit up somehow. An unusual orange glow. Weird, like that booming sound followed by a strange magic wave just minutes earlier. Her stomach curled with an uneasy lurch of foreboding.

The sound of a door opening. Merle turned, saw Rose peeking out of the room opposite Merle's.

"Oh, hey," Merle said. "Sorry if my yelling scared you. I'm having kind of a bad night…"

Rose opened the door wider, her dark brows drawing together over eyes identical to Lily's—something that still baffled Merle for a second every time she saw them—as she studied the entrance to the bedroom where Merle was trapped.

She asked something in Fae, but Merle shook her head.

"I don't know what you're saying, sorry."

Rose stepped out into the hall, crossed the space and raised a hand to the invisible wall of the wards. She gasped when she apparently felt the magic.

Forehead scrunched in lines, she enunciated the word carefully. "Locked?"

Merle nodded. "Yes. I can't get out." She heaved a sigh. "I know it's for the best to stay here, but—*dammit*—I need to go and find Rhun."

Rose hadn't withdrawn her hand from the wards, her eyes darkening. White lines formed around her mouth, and her aura pulsed. Her hand began to glow.

"Whoa." Merle backed up several steps. "Are you—"

The entire wall exploded. Merle jumped behind the bed for cover just as splintered wood flew toward her and embedded in the opposite wall. Coughing from the dust, Merle lowered her arms from over her head and peered out from behind the bed.

Rose stood in the hall, eyes wide, mouth open and half covered by her hand. The wards were gone.

"Well," Merle said, scrambling to her feet and walking over to her. "You didn't know you could do that either, huh?"

"Did I just hear an explosion?" Basil came running down the hall.

Apparently he and Tallak had just made it back home. His father trailed behind him.

Tallak didn't look any the worse for wear, and Merle exhaled a sigh of relief.

At least Basil's dad made it out okay. If something had happened to him because she asked him to walk into the lion's den—or snake pit, more like—she would have never forgiven herself. Yes, in that moment in the basement she basically demanded he help them, but in the time he was gone, nausea boiled in her gut every time she worried he might not come back.

Basil had only just found him. To lose him now…

"I'm glad you're okay," she said to Tallak.

He gave her a hard look. "You owe me."

"I know." She nodded, swallowed.

At that moment, the door to Basil and Isa's room farther down the hall opened, and the female fae darted out, fully dressed, knives strapped to her body, her dark hair wet from her shower. She brandished a dagger in one hand, a short sword in another. Scanning the hall with her slate-gray eyes, she relaxed when she assessed the scene.

"What was that noise?" she demanded. "Is everyone all right?"

"Yes," both Basil and Merle replied at the same time

Baz walked over to his mate and drew her close for a quick kiss.

"Then why," Isa said with raised brows, leaning around Baz, "is that wall gone?"

Merle rubbed a hand over her face and filled them in. When she finished, Basil's mouth was a flat line, his expression grim.

He, too, knew what it was like to be excluded from action because he wasn't strong enough, knew how much it chafed to be regarded as a liability. Before he found out he was half fae, half demon and claimed his powers, he had to fight not to be coddled. When Lily was kidnapped, and Merle, Hazel, and Rhun went to get her back, Hazel only allowed Basil to come along after Merle put her foot down and vouched for him.

"So your sister took down the wards," Merle said with a nod of thanks to Rose, who was glancing back and forth among them.

Isa said several sentences in Fae, apparently explaining

the situation, and Rose raised her brows, her mouth forming an O.

"Right. Okay." Merle blew out a breath, put her hands on her hips. "I'll make a call and then I'll go over there. You in, Baz?"

"Sure." He flexed his fingers with a grin. "I've been meaning to get out my bow and do some shooting again." Turning to Isa, he raised his brows in question.

"I promised Hazel I'd stay and look after Rose," Isa said grudgingly. "I don't like the idea of not going with you, but—"

"I'll have his back."

They all turned to Tallak, who stood with his arms crossed, leaning against the wall.

"Dad, you don't have to. You've already risked enough."

"You're going," Tallak said.

"Yeah."

"So I'm coming, too." His tone brooked no argument.

Basil nodded, his throat muscles working as he swallowed. "Thanks."

"I'll be right back," Merle said and walked into one of the other bedrooms, pulling her cell phone out and dialing.

"Hello, gorgeous." Bahram's voice, rich and seductive as dark chocolate, stroked her senses over the phone line. It wasn't even anything he *did*—just the general effect of his incubus nature.

"Hey," Merle said. "Remember when I recently told you I might ask you for help in getting Rhun out?"

"That was yesterday, darling. Of course I remember."

"Right. Anyway. It's time. Can you bring your irresistible incubusness over to the Baldwins' house? That's where they're keeping him."

"And you would like me to…charm them, is that right?"

"Well, yeah." She waved her free hand, even though he couldn't see it. "You know, just target Juneau's witches with your powers and make them all hot'n'bothered for you until they forget their own names."

"Hm," he purred. "You're giving me free rein to seduce some witches? It will be my *pleasure*."

"Hey—knock them *out*, not *up*. Got it?"

His laugh was like an acoustic manifestation of bliss between the sheets. "I'll do my very best."

CHAPTER 36

The glow of fire in the night, the thick smoke suffusing the air, the taste of ash on his tongue. The sight that greeted Arawn when he banked over Mount Hood was one of a natural disaster of primeval magnitude.

The top of the mountain was blown off, collapsed much like the peak of Mount St. Helens decades earlier. Lava had shot up in the explosion and now rained down the slopes, still glowing orange-red and working its way toward the base of the mountain. A massive plume of dark smoke rose up from a gaping hole revealing the fiery depths of the volcano.

And out of those fiery depths...crawled a beast of such ferocity and sheer destructiveness, the magic of the world hushed at its approach. It had been eons since Arawn last saw one of its kind, and now even his power stilled in admiration when he beheld the dragon.

Dark red scales covered its giant body as it crept over the ash-covered mountainside, its folded wings attached to the front legs, which ended in mighty talons. A long tail whipped behind it, and along its back rose a row of spikes. Smaller spikes studded its head above its yellow-glowing eyes and massive jaw, and two large horns protruded from the top of its head.

It was magnificent.

And it would be *his*.

He veered toward the beast, landed on the mountain slope between the lava flows in a safe distance from the dragon, and changed to his human form. The beast's attention snagged on him, and it let out a mighty roar that shook the ground.

Arawn sent out his power, to whisper and to snare. The dragon flared its wings, bared its huge teeth.

Obey my command, his magic sang, twining around the beast. *Follow my lead.*

The beast roared again, clawed at the ground with sharp-gleaming talons.

His power cajoled and seduced—and bounced off a barrier of age-old magic. Another god's claim, blocking Arawn's attempts to snare the dragon. Someone had beaten him to it.

"Velez," Arawn ground out, balling his hands to fists.

"The very one."

Whirling around, Arawn met the storm-gray eyes of his brother. Standing on the other side of a river of lava, Velez took a bow and made a courtly gesture.

"Quite curious," Velez said, "that you did not sense the dragon rousing in the mountain when we spoke here." He shrugged and clucked his tongue. "Of course, that might have been because I concealed it." A cold smile.

"You roused it?"

Velez tilted his head. "I helped its awakening along just a tad."

Arawn's mind whirred in high gear, going through the catastrophic implications of this new development. Velez in control of a dragon...would cause death and destruction of genocidal dimensions.

"You should have taken me up on my offer," Velez said, his eyes flashing. "Now I am afraid I need to take what is yours."

His smile razor-sharp, Velez vanished on a bolt of lightning.

Arawn's heart stopped cold. The slithering suspicion of what—*who*—Velez was talking about froze his soul. *No.*

He turned into his eagle again, shot up and headed for his dominion.

Or rather, that was what he wanted to do—before the giant dragon slammed into him, clawed him from the sky.

☙❧

Lucía lasted all of one minute after Arawn strolled into the woods before she pounced on Maeve.

"Ohmygods," the demon-shifter breathed, her pale green eyes sparkling. "Are you really *with* him now? How did that happen—no details, please! Did he actually take you to his super-secret hidey-hole? Are you aware that by putting you in his clothes he's basically tacked a giant 'property of Arawn' sign on you? And that I've never seen the look on his face I saw just now when he looked at *you*?"

"Um." Which was about all Maeve could say in response. Her face burned up to her ears, and she resisted the urge to hide behind her hair again. "I'm really hungry," she said after a moment, rubbing her nose. "Let's go eat."

Lucía's chuckle was downright dirty. "Burned a lot of calories, hm?"

Maeve pressed her lips together to keep from grinning. "Quit it."

"All that bed sport...gotta keep up your strength." She waggled her brows.

"*Lucía.*"

"Did you catch any sleep at all?"

Maeve made as if to give her a smack on the back of her head, but Lucía flowed out of the way with feline grace.

Laughing, she bumped Maeve's shoulder. "Messing with you is *so* much fun. But seriously, I'm happy for you. Both of you."

"Kelior," Maeve said after accepting Lucía's hug, "would you like something to eat, too?"

The fae shifted his weight, his face pale and glistening with perspiration. "No thank you."

Maeve frowned. "Are you all right? You look a little sick."

Kelior opened his mouth, but before he could reply, a boom shook the earth.

"Get down!" Lucía shouted.

Maeve went into a crouch, Lucía at her side, sniffing the air. Kelior was on his knees, too, glancing around.

A surge of ancient magic hit them like the shock wave of a bomb, and Maeve stumbled over, into Lucía. The woods hushed, the night eerily quiet.

"What was that?" Maeve whispered—though a niggling feeling deep inside her *knew*.

Lucía scanned the sky with narrowed eyes, scented the air. "I have no idea. Gut feeling? This is something super nasty. It feels a bit like…"

"When the griffin found me," Maeve concluded.

Lucía whipped her head to her. "Don't tell me there's another one coming."

Maeve bit her lip. "Well…"

"*Shit.*" She exhaled through her nose. "Okay. Let's get you underground. It'll be safer." Snapping her fingers at Kelior, she added, "You, too."

Kelior threw a nervous glance at the sky again, a bead of sweat now trickling down his right temple. "Sure."

They ran through the woods toward the nearest entrance to the subterranean lair, the entire forest around them unnaturally silent. No fireflies left, as if they all fled, not even will-o'-

the-wisps floating between the trees. Only looming shadows...and the distant roll of thunder.

Up ahead, an old oak tree with access to the underground system beckoned. *Almost...there.*

The sky lit up, lightning striking down, splitting the tree. Part of the charge hit Lucía, who ran in front of Maeve. The demon-shifter flew back against a tree, and the sickening sound of snapped bones turned Maeve's stomach.

"Lucía!"

She wanted to make a dash for her friend when someone grabbed her from behind. Her mind blanked, horror icing her muscles.

His hands on her body, holding her down, squeezing so hard it hurt...

"I'm sorry," Kelior rasped in her ear.

She barely registered those sensations, her thoughts hijacked by the terror of her memories.

Another strike of lightning jolted her halfway back into the present, and she blinked at the silhouette of a man emerging from the shadows. Tall, dark-haired, elegantly dressed despite the distinct vibe of a being from the time before fashion was even a thought, he looked nothing like Arawn...and yet she knew.

"Velez," she whispered. The sheer volume of power pouring off him with an electric buzz was unmistakable.

His smile chilled her blood. Angling his head at Kelior, he said, "Thank you for holding her for me. I will take her now."

Power grabbed her, immobilizing her limbs and pressing down on her lungs. With a flick of his hand, Velez pulled her to him as easily as a magnet attracts a piece of scrap metal.

Or a prized coin, judging by the gleam in his eyes.

"W-what about me?" Kelior asked. "You promised you'd break the deal for me and send me back to Faerie."

"Oh." A sigh. "You must have heard wrong. I said I was going to send you back *home*."

Velez winked, and a lightning bolt shot down on Kelior, incinerating him on the spot. Maeve jerked—or would have, had her limbs not been paralyzed.

"And now," Velez purred, "let's play."

He grasped her arm, and she was sucked into whipping wind and lightning as the world around her vanished.

CHAPTER 37

When Merle arrived at the Baldwins' house with Tallak and Basil, Bahram was already waiting in the driveway, leaning against a car. Clad in casually formal clothes probably costing thousands of dollars, he could have easily jumped out of an ad for a high-class Italian fashion label.

Bahram was all but oozing sensuality, his body a woman's wet dream, from tanned skin and dark hair to eyes of crushed gold and features hinting at Persian royalty.

Merle could appreciate his appearance and recognize the effect he had on the female population, but unless Bahram directed his incubus powers at her, he didn't do anything for her—unlike a certain *bluotezzer* demon, who was the reason she was here.

Writhing and moaning at the feet of the incubus were about half a dozen witches in various stages of undress. The heavy pulse of Bahram's demon power filled the air, and Merle had to stop and catch her breath for a moment when they came closer. And to think, Bahram wasn't even targeting her directly.

"Great job," she told the incubus.

He smiled and shrugged with sinuous grace, and the witches on the ground swooned in unison.

"Impressive," Tallak said, raising a brow.

Bahram gave him a slow grin. "It does come in handy."

"Okay," Merle said to the incubus. "You hold the position out here and charm any other of Juneau's witches who come outside."

"My pleasure."

"Don't touch them, though."

"What if they touch *me*?" He waggled his brows.

"No."

"Not even a little rubbing?"

"*Bahram.*"

He heaved a sigh. "All right."

Satisfied the incubus had the situation under control, Merle turned to Tallak and Basil. "Let's go."

Tallak took point, Merle ran in the middle, and Basil brought up the rear. They entered the house unimpeded, the wards already taken down by Hazel and the others. Inside, they were greeted by chaos.

The fight raged in all rooms, spells flying everywhere, singeing furniture and walls, blasting apart lamps and picture frames. It was hard to figure out what was happening where and who was doing what, so much smoke and magic clouded the air. Merle thought she saw Lily and Alek in the salon to the left, fighting in a whirl of otherworldly-quick martial arts moves and slashing blades, and maybe Madhuri Gupta and Kristen Frost facing off with three Draconians in the room to her right.

Basil fired off arrows and used his shapeshifting ability to temporarily confuse some of Juneau's witches by turning into one of theirs while he moved up the staircase. Unfazed by the chaos, Tallak ran after Basil, and hurled some charms of his own, apparently completely familiar with witch power due to his stolen memories.

And Merle ran like hell, dodging spells and throwing some prepared magical grenades while trying to make her way to the door of the basement at the back of the hall.

The sounds of witches—Draconians—coming directly toward her made her leap behind a large armchair. She was out of grenades, and had nothing else to throw.

The two witches dashed past, and she wanted to move out from behind the chair as the door to the basement flew open, and Hazel ran out, followed by Hanna and Elaine—who steadied Rhun between them.

Merle's heart seized. He looked dreadful, beaten up and bloodied and too sluggish for his lean, powerful body.

Rage a storm in her veins, she vowed to make Juneau pay for every minute he suffered at the Draconians' hands.

She was about to run to his side, help carry him out, when a flash of white caught her eye. Unnoticed by Hazel, who gave Hanna, Elaine, and Rhun cover from the witches coming at them from the front, the head of the Laroche family had appeared in the doorway just behind them.

Juneau hissed a word and flicked her hand, and Hazel cried out and collapsed. While Hanna blocked a spell from the two other Draconians, Juneau struck again, her face twisted into an expression of horrifying madness. Rhun screamed and convulsed so hard he pulled Elaine down with him as he crashed to the floor.

Hanna barely disentangled herself from Rhun's grasp in time to avoid going down as well, but the moment of inattention cost her. A spell by one of the approaching Draconians hit her just as she sent out a wave that made the other two witches stumble and fall. Hanna made a muffled sound of anguish, and crumpled to the floor.

Another spell of Juneau's slammed into Elaine just as she crawled out from under Rhun, and the head of the Donovan family slumped down again.

Holy hell, no.

While Hazel rose on shaky legs, the other three were out of commission, but breathing. At least the two Draconians lay motionless a few feet away…but right now, it was only Hazel facing off with Juneau.

And the blood trickling down from Hazel's nose didn't bode well.

Juneau raised her hands, which glowed with gathering magic the taste of which hinted at death, and smiled grimly at the group.

And Merle made a split-second decision. If she didn't step in they would all die. Hazel, Elaine, Hanna…*Rhun*. Chaos still reigned in the rest of the house, and no one would come in time to stop Juneau.

"Into hunger, pain, and darkness, hidden from the light," Merle whispered, calling up her magic, her focus on Juneau, who stood only feet away from her but hadn't noticed Merle's presence, "I bind thee in the Shadows, in never-ending night."

Juneau gasped, jerked, her eyes bulging. The first line of the spell was already enough to paralyze her, giving Merle time to finish the verse.

"Leashed and helpless, thou shalt pine," she continued in a whisper. "Held ever after by the magic of my line."

Swirling, writhing darkness rose up from the floor, snapping at Juneau's feet, twining around her legs. The stygian mist covered her body as if intending to devour her. The last image Merle saw of the witch before the Shadows took her was her face frozen in horror and pain.

And then nothing in the place where Juneau stood just seconds ago.

A moment, a heartbeat of shock at what she'd just done, and then Merle dashed over to her friends, to Rhun.

"Merle!" Hazel whirled toward her as she spotted her running over. The Elder witch had to steady herself on the wall, her breath uneven. "What are you doing here?"

"Settling a score," Merle replied grimly, glancing at the spot where the Shadows had taken Juneau.

Rhun groaned in that moment, and everything fell away, dissolved into insignificance as Merle crouched by his side.

"Rhun," she whispered, stroking his blood-matted hair. "I'm here. We're getting you out. It's all over."

"I was just," he rasped, "getting cozy down there."

"Hush." She kissed him, not caring a bit about the blood on his face, her cheeks and mouth wet with tears.

Elaine stirred and grimaced. Hazel helped her to her feet, assessed the scene quickly, and knelt next to Hanna, holding her shaky hands over the other witch's body.

A moment passed, then Hazel balled her hands to fists. "She's gone."

Merle clenched her jaw, her throat burning. *Godsdammit.*

With a shuddering breath, Hazel closed Hanna's eyes, whispered, "Travel well."

"Downstairs all clear," Lily yelled from the living room.

Basil came thundering down the stairs, followed by his father. "Upstairs is clear too."

Elaine, who had gone to check the kitchen and the back rooms, nodded, her face not as pale anymore as a few minutes ago. "All Draconians present here are either dead or incapacitated." With a disdainful look at the witches lying on the floor, she added, "With Juneau gone, they might come around. Some of us should stay and make sure they get a good talking-to."

Hazel glanced at Elaine. "Can you do that? I'd like to go with Merle and Rhun, make sure he'll be all right."

The head of the Donovan family nodded. "I think I'll rather enjoy cleaning up this mess."

"Let's go," Merle said. "Thank you, Elaine—let's talk later."

Together with Hazel, Merle helped Rhun stumble outside, Tallak and Basil in their wake, Alek and Lily joining them too.

NADINE MUTAS

Bahram straightened from his lazy slouch against the car when he saw Rhun.

"Damn, man," he said, "you look almost as bad as that one time you asked a puma shifter if he uses a litter box or a toilet."

Rhun's mouth twitched up. "It was a legit question."

Bahram came over, indicating to Merle and Hazel that he'd take him from here. Putting one shoulder under Rhun's arm, he clapped him on the other shoulder. "I'm glad you made it out."

Bahram hauled Rhun to Basil's car parked a few blocks away, put him in the back seat, and walked toward his own car to follow them. Merle slipped in next to Rhun, Basil sitting down behind the wheel. With Tallak in the front passenger seat, Hazel opted to drive her own car back to the mansion, Alek and Lily taking Alek's truck.

Rhun leaned his blood-streaked head back on the seat. "Did you really send Juneau into the *Shadows*?"

"Death would have been too nice for her."

"I always knew you were a feisty witch." Dark appreciation in his tone, affection pulsing through their mating bond.

She took his hand, her heart heavy despite the joy of having him back. *I drew on outside magic to weave that spell*, she said mind-to-mind to Rhun.

He met her gaze, the knowledge in his eyes stark. *How much?*

She swallowed. *I don't know if it'll be enough to warrant a payback.*

He twined his fingers with hers, silent, because there were no other words to be said. They both knew the stakes, knew the impossible choice she had to make, and its probable consequences.

If the magic she tapped caused the Powers That Be to demand payback, she'd lose the baby.

302

CHAPTER 38

Magic clashed in the sky as Arawn collided with the dragon again and again. Smaller his eagle form might be, but his power still matched that of the beast, and the essence of their battle was of the non-physical kind.

Time and again, he tried to take off and head toward his territory, toward that spot where he saw lightning strike down out of the corner of his eye, but the dragon thwarted every attempt to break away. Roaring, it launched itself at him, a wave of primeval magic making the air wobble, the world groaning on its hinges.

He narrowly escaped the giant claws, executed a deft move to turn in mid-air when a huge shadow slammed into the dragon, took it down toward the mountain. A flash of golden feathers and fur, followed by a feral screech.

The griffin.

Breathing hard, Arawn whirled around, wanting to make for his territory now the dragon was distracted.

Lightning on the slope of the mountain.

His heart stopped as his senses picked up her presence, the bond between them pulsing with her nearness. Again, he whirled around in the air, only this time, he shot toward the volcano. Toward Maeve.

He could make out Velez, who was holding her pressed tight to his body. Red tinged Arawn's sight, primal instincts swamping him, demanding he tear the other male to pieces.

He slammed down on the ground in an explosion of power that rocked the mountain, disturbing the ash around him until it created a whirlwind storm of white and gray and black. His magic writhed and clawed, ready to snap and rip.

"Ah," Velez said genially. "There you are. So glad you can join our party. I brought a guest."

He squeezed Maeve's waist, making her whimper. Her amber-gray eyes wide, she stared at Arawn, and the sight of her in Velez's grasp was enough to want to make him raze the world. His power built to a crescendo of brute force.

Velez clucked his tongue. "Come now. You know as well as I do that you cannot use your magic against me. Not with her so near. Not when she is still in such a lovely mortal form." He pressed her closer again and gave her a smack on her cheek.

Arawn snarled, fury raking across his nerves—because Velez was right.

"Anything less than an attack at full force will have no effect on me, brother. Going full tilt, however, would kill her human form at this proximity." He pursed his lips. "Such a dilemma."

"Let her go, and I will let you leave."

Velez laughed. "And why would I do that when she is my best bargaining chip? Really, the nerve of you." He shook his head. "See, I was wondering how I could gain your coopera-tion. Was thinking I would threaten to turn your entire dominion and all its inhabitants to ash. I do have a dragon now, after all." He winked.

Said dragon still battled it out with the griffin in the skies above, causing tremors to shake the air and the ground, sending waves of buzzing, jolting magic over the mountain.

"But then," Velez went on, "a little birdie told me there is something you value even more than your territory, some*one* you care for more than for your power." He stroked over Maeve's hair, and Arawn wanted to stick that hand in a shredder and turn it into mincemeat. "She really is special. Seems like she has been through a lot." He grimaced. "It would be so unfortunate if I ripped out the beast inside her and killed her in the process."

"Do that, and I will hunt you to the ends of the earth, and hack you into little pieces while you are conscious, then let you heal to do it all over again. For eternity."

"Hm." A cold, cold smile. "You do care a lot about her. So you might actually consider my second offer. See, the first one was better, but—alas—you refused, and now it is off the table." He shrugged. "If you want her to live, all I need in return is a binding pledge of servitude—in blood."

Arawn barked a harsh laugh. "You want me to bend the knee to you?"

"Since that would make sure you do not stand in my way, and has the lovely side effect of me gaining control over your dominion and the impressive network of favor-bound creatures you built, yes, I want you to bow to my will."

Maeve stirred in Velez's grasp, struggling against his magic. "No," she choked out. "Don't."

Arawn met her shimmering eyes, fire and smoke and a passion burning so deep, so true, it was the purest thing he'd ever touched in his life. If her flame were to be snuffed…no other light should be permitted to shine. And while he would have fought a sky full of gods to keep her—if he had to shred his honor, his pride, his soul to make sure she survived, he would do so.

He would even do what he had never, in all the millennia he had lived, dreamed of doing.

"All right," Arawn said to Velez—and went down on one knee.

૭%૭

MAEVE FOUGHT AGAINST THE INSIDIOUS POWER HOLDING HER immobile. To no avail. She wasn't strong enough. How could she be, when she didn't even have access to her magic, or the beast lurking inside her?

Again, she turned inside, tried to reach the ancient force in her core. If only she could call it forth, then Velez would lose his leverage—when *she* was the one who commanded the beast out, she'd survive.

It should be so easy. The spell was dissolved, nothing should keep that beast in there anymore. Why wasn't it coming out? *Why isn't this easy?*

She gritted her teeth and called on the beast again. *Come out. I want you out.*

Darkness and silence and the weight of her failure. She was too weak, wasn't she? The one thing she should be able to do, the one power she had—and she couldn't manage it.

The impact of her abject incompetence was like a blow to her guts.

This was her reality, though, wasn't it? Always too weak, always dependent on others to protect her. The one time she dared move out of her family's home and take charge of her life, she was kidnapped and tortured and raped. Because she wasn't strong enough to fend for herself.

Filled to the brim with ancient power, and yet unable to use it to protect herself. She didn't know whether to cry or to laugh. Both?

And even now she couldn't call that beast forward, even now it failed her—but it was active enough to kill her family, wasn't it? Important enough that she was abducted and tortured because others wanted to harness the immense power waiting quietly in her core.

Those damn powers, that damn beast... How could she ever truly embrace them when they brought her nothing but pain and loss and scars?

She couldn't. A simple and shattering truth.

Slumping in Velez's grip—which didn't change her position at all, since he'd paralyzed her—she choked back a sob, crushed by the weight of her despair, and listened with rising horror while Velez laid out his nefarious plan.

He wanted Arawn to submit to him, wanted him to make a binding pledge of allegiance to Velez, and thereby hand him the power over Arawn and his dominion. *Holy hell.* If Arawn surrendered, if Velez was given that sort of power...

The world would drown in blood.

But Arawn would never agree to it. It went against his very nature to submit to anyone, to give up the power he'd been gathering back over *thousands* of years, to hand over the dominion he built with painstaking effort. He wouldn't throw all of that away just for her.

As well he shouldn't, not for someone who was so *fucking weak.*

"I want you to bow to my will," Velez said.

Her heart stumbled when she saw the shift in Arawn's expression, as if he was...actually considering it.

"No," she choked out past the magic holding her in place. "Don't."

Arawn met her pleading look, the forest green of his eyes in stark contrast to the glowing red of the lava flowing down the mountainside—and the love shining in those green depths pierced her heart, her soul.

"All right," he said to Velez, and went on his knee.

"No!" Maeve struggled again, threw herself against the power encasing her.

Velez clutched her even more tightly. "You will bind yourself to me in blood and submit?"

"Yes."

Her pulse raced, stampeded through her like a maddening drumbeat that stole her breath. She couldn't let this happen. She couldn't let him submit. Not Arawn. He was *hers*.

Something roared inside her, and it *wasn't* the beast.

Closing her eyes, she dove deep, deep, deep, and driven by the explosive mix of fear, love, protectiveness, and sheer teeth-gritting *will*, she rushed past the shards of the broken spell, past the pain and the shame and the resentment, the agony of accepting the fact she killed and maimed her family, past the fear of a power she had no idea how to handle, to the beast…

…trapped in a cage of her own making.

She'd kept it in there. By not fully embracing it, by resenting it for the bloody trail of pain it had left in her life. It hurt to acknowledge it. It ripped her raw to reach out and touch the force that was responsible for the death of her mom and Moira, for mentally crippling her dad. For causing her to be kidnapped and tortured.

It fucking hurt, but she reached out through that pain, reached out to the beast, for the first time in her life.

Come forth, she whispered, her heart gentle and open. *I want you with me.*

The ancient presence uncoiled and stretched in the darkness. *I have been waiting for you,* it whispered back.

And then it lunged at her, in a flash of fire and ash, and the world lit up in an atomic blaze.

"You will bind yourself to me in blood and submit?"

Arawn glared at Velez. "Yes."

His erstwhile brother smiled and held out his hand. "Do it, then."

Arawn's attention flicked back to Maeve, who was shuddering in Velez's grasp—more than before. Something was wrong. Pulses of deep emotions reached him across the bond, a maelstrom of feelings he couldn't figure out.

Her skin began to glow, the light growing brighter and brighter...and she exploded in a firestorm. Flames surged out in a blinding supernova of ancient power, the force knocking him back. Velez crashed down in the periphery of his vision, several yards away, and didn't move.

The griffin screeched above, followed by the roar of the dragon.

His entire body hurt, as if his bones had been smashed—and he remembered well how it felt—but Arawn managed to get swaying to his feet.

"Maeve!" he roared.

She didn't answer. He stumbled forward, his muscles sluggish, and scanned the area, his stomach in knots. Nothing but ashes where the firestorm rolled out.

His blood iced over. *No.* It wasn't possible. She couldn't be—

Lightning struck him, and he jerked, every cell in his body electrocuted. He toppled over, crashed down on the ash-strewn ground. In the periphery of his vision, a shape moved...Velez.

With a groan, Arawn rolled over, out of the way of the next lightning strike. The bolt of unadulterated god power slammed into the spot where he lay just seconds ago, cracking the earth and rattling the sky.

Maeve. He couldn't focus on anything else, his thoughts consumed by the drive to find her.

Sending out a wave of dark power toward Velez—taking care to keep it leashed so it wouldn't spread to where Maeve had been standing before—he turned, searched the slope of the mountain for her...or the beast. If it came out of her, where was it? Maeve was supposed to be a dragon. *Dragons don't die in fire.*

"Pity." Velez's voice carried over the wind, Arawn's traitorous brother coming to his feet again after his blow took him down. "She had such potential."

In the sky above them, the dragon and griffin still battled, the air sharp and biting with the force of their ancient magic. Arawn barely noticed. He had difficulty blocking Velez's next lightning strike, and some of the electric force hit him, nearly fried his right leg. He half-heartedly threw out a tendril of his own power to break his brother's spine.

Velez cried out, fell, and coughed. It didn't last long. While Arawn staggered—every step hurting—over to the field of ashes where Maeve had been, Velez heaved himself up again, his eyes a storm of wrath and lightning.

Arawn reached out...and he felt it. The silence. The emptiness.

A severed link where the bond should be.

She's dead. Nothing else would cut that connection.

The world clouded over in bloody darkness. Out of the corner of his eye, he saw Velez crawl closer.

And Arawn's powers snapped their leash.

He let go, broke each of the seals that kept his dark, writhing, ravenous magic in check, and released it to hurl toward the being responsible for Maeve's death. There was no reason anymore for him to restrain his devastating power. Maeve was gone. He could wipe Velez off the face of the earth.

For the first time since his fall, he let his true nature show, born of the clash of beginnings at the dawn of time, its force so potent it could break through the layers of the world itself.

With a roar of primeval fury, he struck out with a blast of dark energy. It shot out to all sides, much like the magical shock wave of the awakening dragon—only a thousand times more destructive. Its impact rocked the still-fuming volcano, cracking the earth, so powerful it would level what was left of the woods surrounding the mountain.

The blow blocked Velez's strike, made his lightning fizzle out, and Arawn whirled, hit Velez with every last bit of his magic—and smote the other god.

Velez shattered like glass under Arawn's power—his essence, his form, his very being erased from this world. The earth quaked, the mountain spewing more ash, the air crackling and groaning. The magic of this plane shifted in response to the elimination of a power of Velez's caliber, the precarious balance of magical energy thrown off kilter for a moment.

Breath heavy, Arawn stared at the spot Velez had occupied. The shifting of magic continued, slithered over his skin, through his bones, the fabric of his soul. Groaning and whining, the layers of the world adjusted to the hole ripped in their midst, trying to knit it closed.

Arawn should help. Should use his power to speed the mending, ensure this world would survive the annihilation of a force as old as Velez.

He couldn't make himself move. His foe vanquished, his revenge taken, he was left with the unrelenting silence of destruction, and immeasurable grief building in his soul.

He sank to his knees at the place where Maeve died, dug his fingers into the ashes, and hung his head, his soul splintered into a million pieces, each one stinging him with every breath.

Something warm and wet dripped down his face, onto the backs of his hands. *Tears.* He hadn't shed any in centuries, maybe even millennia. He couldn't remember the last time he cried.

It didn't matter. Nothing mattered.

She was gone.

A gust of wind whirled up the ashes, and a second later, the griffin landed at the edge of the field. Wings flared, it bowed, bent down on its front legs and lowered its head. Grieving for its friend.

Overhead, the dragon roared, now free of Velez's influence. Arawn should snare it. He didn't. What was the use?

She was gone.

More wind whirled up the ashes, and Arawn blinked—not in surprise; he didn't feel surprise anymore—as the dragon landed close to the field as well. The mighty beast of old crawled closer, rumbling in its throat. It halted, like the griffin, and bowed its head.

So they were all mourning.

Fitting.

The ashes moved—without a gust of wind. His heart, that useless, dead organ, thumped against his ribs, his power vibrating. More movement in the field, particles floating up in a spiral, swirling in a circle like a building tornado in slow motion. Sparks lit inside the whirling cloud of ash. Flames licked over the smoke.

The tornado built and built, a fire crackling within—and with a burst of sparks and a surge of ancient magic that laid him flat on his back, a beast rose from the ashes.

Feathers of flame, a soul of fire, red-licked orange and talon-tipped feet, the phoenix robbed him of breath with its glory. It flared its wings and let loose a screech that echoed over the wilderness—and both the griffin and the dragon answered in kind.

The firebird stalked forward, its size that of the griffin, and touched its beak to the other beast's. The griffin rumbled deep in its throat, rustled its feathers. The dragon kept its distance, but spread its wings while bowing its head as if in deference.

Awestruck, Arawn could only stare.

With a flash of fiery feathers, the phoenix turned to him, piercing intelligence in its age-old eyes. Once more flames licked over its form, smoke whispered over its massive body, and it morphed, grew smaller, smaller...until it slumped to the ground in the shape of a tiny, red-haired female.

Arawn's breath caught, his world grinding to a halt, centering on the hopeless hope burning in his heart.

He was at her side in an instant, gathered her naked body in his arms, felt for her pulse. Slow but steady, the tick that greeted his fingertips was like a beacon to his soul. He crushed her to him, buried his face in her neck.

She stirred with a moan. He still held her tight. Probably too tight. But he couldn't convince his muscles to ease up, his need to feel her too consuming.

"Arawn." A choked whisper. "I need to breathe."

With a sound of half-anguish, half-relief, he gave her enough room to suck in a deep gulp of air. Though the fact he covered her mouth with his in a kiss of desperate joy might have made it harder for her.

She gasped against his lips, laughed into his kiss. "I love you, too," she rasped.

He cupped her face, drank in the sight of her, tiny pieces of his broken heart mending with every breath she took in his arms.

"I thought I lost you." His hands shook. "I was ready to raze the world."

She smiled, her eyes of fire and smoke glistening. "You've got me back."

Such simple, simple words, and yet they held his salvation. And with his soul mending, he helped the world mend as well. Sending out tendrils of his power, he reinforced the knitting effort of the layers around the hole Velez's destruction had ripped into the fabric of magic, ensured the damage could be repaired.

Maeve needed a world to live in.

Frowning, she stroked his lips, this woman who held his heart in her delicate hands. "My beast is a phoenix. I thought it was a dragon."

"It had both of us fooled."

"Sneaky." Her expression darkened. "Velez?"

"I smote him."

She blinked, raised a brow. "How godlike."

His eyes flicked to the pattern of scars on her body—and the golden shine to them. As if she was lit from within, and the scars the seams through which her light shone.

She followed the direction of his gaze, gasped as she beheld the change in her appearance. "W-what is that?"

"I would say"—he grazed the glowing lines with a finger, delighting in her shiver—"that your phoenix made you into *kintsugi*."

Her eyes widened. "That is…"

"…beyond beautiful."

She swallowed, her smile wobbly but radiant. "Yes."

"I want another bond," he said, the horror of losing her having eroded all finesse in his speech.

"Oh." Her focus turned inward. "It's gone."

"Not for long." He bit into his wrist, nodded at her. "Open your mouth."

She complied, probably sensing how raw he was, how much he needed this. He placed his bleeding wrist to her lips, and she drank without him asking her. The first suck sent fire down his spine, and the next one sent the rest of his blood flowing south.

"Do you bind yourself to me," he asked, "in magic and blood?"

Maeve let go of his wrist, her lips stained red, her pupils dilated. "I do."

His magic lunged for and fused with hers, darkness to flame, power to power.

He took her arm, licked over her wrist—and looked at her with a question in his eyes. Her lips parted on a gasp as she understood. Swallowing, she nodded.

Another loving lick over her wrist…and then he bit. His

shapeshifted fangs sliced into her skin, opened her vein. He drank, the flavor of her blood a heady rush. Ancient power, a touch of fire, and a sweetness that was all Maeve.

Her fingers stroked through his hair. "Do you bind yourself to me in magic and blood?"

He licked over the puncture marks, met her eyes of phoenix flames. "I do."

The bond that snapped taut between them this time ran equally strong in both directions—and glowed like a rope of embers in velvet darkness with their love.

CHAPTER 39

When Maeve climbed up the steps to the old Victorian, ash from the volcanic eruption still coated the veranda—like it did most other surfaces in the greater Portland area, as well as large parts of north Oregon and south Washington. It would take weeks, if not months to clean up the mess, the devastation horrifyingly similar to the eruption of Mount St. Helens in 1980.

And yet the human population was still blissfully oblivious to the far-reaching consequences of that blast. Arawn had snared the dragon while they were all huddled on the mountain slope of fire and ash, and he made sure to impress upon the beast to stay hidden from human eyes for now. Arawn's territory offered more than enough room for the dragon to roam without being seen by humans, and, as with the griffin, he'd also cast a glamour on the ancient beast to further conceal it from non-otherworld creatures, should it venture past his borders.

How long that secrecy would last was anyone's guess. The eventual discovery by humans of the awakening of the Old Ones loomed as a certainty on the horizon—it was only a matter of when, not if.

For the time being, however, Arawn agreed it would cause catastrophic panics and unpredictable defensive maneuvers among human authorities, as well as the general population, should the knowledge of what was going on spread beyond the otherworld communities. And even in the circles of supernatural beings, word of what exactly was happening had yet to pass through the grapevine.

Had Merle heard news about it? Making sure her sister was up-to-date with developments that would shake up the world was one of the reasons Maeve now stood on the doorstep to their shared childhood home the day after the dragon awoke. She could have simply called, sure, or she could have invited Merle to travel to Arawn's lair as she recently did.

Some revelations, though, were better delivered in person, and with the added gesture of paying a visit instead of asking someone to come to you.

She told Merle in a quick phone call that she was coming, thanks to Lucía, who'd survived the Velez attack with a few broken bones and scratches that healed quickly due to her demon and shifter natures. She made sure Maeve got a new cell this morning.

After ringing the doorbell, Maeve now threw a glance at the silent shadow of unadulterated power at her back.

Arawn inclined his head, his eyes of evergreen depths searing with an intensity that made her knees wobble. "I will wait outside."

"Thank you." She grasped his hand before he turned, gave it a quick squeeze.

A ping of white-hot love along the newly forged bond between them, and then he strolled down the steps to loom in the front yard like darkness given form. And, oh, how she adored that form.

The door opened at that moment, and Maeve's attention flicked back to—the male demon holding the door for her.

She inhaled sharply. "Rhun. Hi. I'm so glad and relieved you're back." Merle had told her on the phone, very briefly, that they'd managed to free Rhun from Juneau's clutches.

"Maeve. I'm glad you're still in one piece." He glanced at the dark presence that was a caress against her back...even though Arawn stood about a yard away.

She sighed inwardly, yet she couldn't fault Rhun—and the others—for thinking just like she once did...for expecting the worst of Arawn, when the reality of him was a surprise she would never have been able to predict in a million years.

Rhun stepped aside and gestured her in, eyeing the Demon Lord as she walked by. Raising a brow, he asked, "Should I get him some water? In a bowl? He's not in the habit of digging up stuff, is he?" He closed the door, tilted his head with a long-suffering sigh. "Please tell me he's at least yard-broken. I *just* redid the landscaping out front—I'm really not in the mood for more replanting."

A grin threatened to take over her face. "I get how you make Merle laugh all the time."

He winked at her just as Merle emerged from the downstairs bathroom.

"Sorry," her sister said, her face a bit pale. "Morning sickness taking its toll..." She stopped short for a second when she saw Maeve, then pulled her into a crushing hug that lasted several heartbeats.

"It's so good to see you," Merle whispered when they finally broke apart.

"You too." Maeve blinked away her tears while following her sister into the living room where they sat on the couch.

Rhun had apparently disappeared somewhere in the house while they were hugging, leaving them to talk in private.

Merle told her about Rhun's rescue, how she'd bound Juneau in the Shadows—a fitting punishment, if there ever was one—and how the witch community now scrambled to find its footing in the aftermath. And how—because she didn't have a choice—Merle had used her magic to tip the scales of the fight, incurring the risk of having to pay back to the Powers That Be soon…and thus jeopardizing her baby.

Maeve swallowed hard, her chest pinching tight. *Arawn,* she reached out mentally along a pathway he always kept open for her. *If a witch pledged allegiance to you, and you granted her access to the layers of the world, you'd be in charge of demanding payback, wouldn't you?*

Yes, came the answer without hesitation.

Would you be able to postpone that payback for a while?

He took a moment to reply this time. *That is possible, yes.* She was about to turn her attention back to her conversation with Merle when he added, *It could be more painful if delayed, but pushing it back by, say, eight to nine months should not be a problem.*

She almost smiled at his instant offer, but that would not have been the right reaction to what Merle just said, so she bit it back. She'd have to tell Merle…in a moment. First, there was something else she had to get out in the open. Something that might—or might *not*—smooth the way to enticing Merle to switch her allegiance.

As it turned out, Merle gave her the perfect opening when she composed herself after revealing the new risk to her pregnancy, and said, with a shaky smile, "Tell me how you're doing."

Maeve cleared her throat. *Where to start, where to start…?* She'd been racking her brain for the best way to break any one of the overwhelming news items to Merle, the most benign of which—her relationship with Arawn—might already be enough to give her sister a heart attack. She had to be smart about phrasing it and—

"I'm in love with Arawn, and we're bonded. Like mates."

Or she could simply blurt it out. *Awesome.*

Merle blinked, her body gone motionless. "Come again?"

Anxiety fired along Maeve's nerves, made her fidget and shift her weight. "We're together. In a relationship. He loves me, I love him, and we share a...mating bond. Kind of."

A hollow sadness filled her chest in anticipation of Merle's reaction. Oh, Maeve's unparalleled ability to overthink everything and anything had made sure a merry variety of possible scenarios buzzed in her brain, and she'd already pulled up defensive walls around her heart for the worst one imaginable.

If Merle now accused Arawn of manipulating Maeve into falling in love with him, or worse, *compelling* her to be with him through the magical custody bond he used to have over her, Maeve wouldn't even flinch. *Much.* She braced herself for the impact, reminding herself that however hurtful that kind of reaction might be, it came from a place of love and protectiveness from her sister.

A sister who currently stared at her out of sky-blue eyes gone wide, her mouth hanging open. Maeve tried to think of a moment when she'd seen Merle as blankly shocked as she seemed now. Failed. Nope, this was the most gobsmacked Merle had ever been in Maeve's presence.

Maeve was beginning to think she'd broken something essential in her sister's mind with her revelation when Merle blinked again, closed her mouth, shook her head as if to clear it and whispered, "You're happy."

Maeve's breath hitched, her eyes prickling hot. "Yes. I am."

Tears shimmered in Merle's eyes as she reached out and touched Maeve's face with a trembling hand. "Is he... He's..." She frowned, shook her head again. "He's good for you."

It wasn't phrased as a question, but even so, it sounded more like an astonished realization that perfectly mirrored the confusion in Merle's expression.

"You're glowing," Merle added in a whisper.

Maeve raised a hand to her own face, to that scar that was still so prominent—now maybe even more so because of the way it shone as if lit from within. "Oh. Yes. That. Um, I'll explain it in a bit."

Merle shook her head again. "No. I mean, yes, I do need you to...explain that. But I meant that—you're radiant. As in, you're happy like you haven't been since..." Her brows drew together. "No, scratch that. I have *never* seen you this happy."

Maeve gave in to the smile that wanted to steal across her face, and lowered her eyes. "He really is good to me, you know. I understand it might be hard for you to imagine, because you haven't seen that side of him. But he's...the best thing that could have happened to me."

Merle's jaw slowly dropped again as she regarded her for a moment. "I may not know that side of him," she said carefully, "but I know to trust my senses. And everything I see and sense in you tells me you're thriving. There's just no way to fake that kind of thing. Which means it's true." She blinked, sat back against the couch. "You're truly happily mated to Arawn."

"Yes." She couldn't resist grinning.

Merle's forehead wrinkled. "Does he still own you?"

"No." Maeve stopped short, considered. "Actually, yes, but...not in the same way as before. Or rather, I belong to him like he now belongs to me. We're bound to each other mutually."

"Like a true mating bond," Merle muttered, and Maeve nodded. Merle turned her head and stared at the wall. "My baby sister is mated to the Demon Lord."

Maeve wanted to say something when Merle flinched and sat up straight. "Wait. Oh, my gods. That makes me... That means he's my..."

"Brother-by-mating?" Maeve supplied helpfully.

With a high-pitched groan that sounded suspiciously like a wail, Merle covered her face with both hands.

Maeve bit her lip. If this was Merle's reaction to learning she was now related by mating to the Demon Lord, she didn't want to imagine her response to that tiny tidbit of extra knowledge that Arawn was actually a god.

"Everything okay in here?" Rhun poked his head into the room. "No one getting skewered, I hope? Are you in need of my manly protection?"

"Rhun!" Merle whined. "You won't believe this."

"You threw something and actually hit the mark?"

Merle narrowed her eyes and threw a pillow at him—which missed him by three feet.

"Apparently not," Rhun said with a smirk.

Merle's expression turned wicked. Mischief glinted in her eyes, and she gave him a small, gloating smile. "Guess what, *honey*."

At that endearment, Rhun stiffened, and his expression grew wary.

"You just got a new brother-by-mating," Merle said, her tone ominous.

Rhun crossed his arms and frowned. "By mating? But who —" His attention flicked to Maeve, and his face lit up. "For real? You got hitched? To who?"

Merle's grin was all sorts of evil. "I believe he's standing outside looking menacing and scaring our neighbors."

Rhun snorted. "Yeah, right. Like he'd get past Ar—" He broke off, glancing from Merle to Maeve and back again a few times. "No."

"Yes." Merle sent him a sweetly acidic smile.

Rhun turned incredulous eyes to Maeve. "Tell me my lovely mate's pulling my leg."

Maeve grimaced and shrugged apologetically.

Rhun whipped his head around to stare out the window into the front yard, then whirled back to stare at Maeve, repeated the moves a couple of times until he clutched his chest and sank into the nearest chair.

"Um," Maeve started, but Rhun held up a hand.

His eyes closed, he pinched the bridge of his nose and whispered, "Shh. I'm processing."

"This might take a while," Merle murmured, and patted Maeve's knee.

Maeve cleared her throat. "Right. Okay."

"While we're letting that sink in," Merle said, "why don't you do that explaining thing you promised." She waved at Maeve's face—at the glowing scar.

"Oh." Maeve rubbed her nose. "Yeah. So." *How do I even...?* Maybe bluntness served best here, too. "I've got an ancient phoenix in my core, and when she came out and shapeshifted back into me, she thought it was a nice idea to turn my scars into *kintsugi*."

Silence.

Maeve dared a look at Merle. Her sister eyed her with the same expression one might see on the faces of people confronted with adults who still wrote letters to Santa.

"You lost me at *phoenix*," Merle said. "I need you to elaborate on that."

So she did. Told Merle—and a quietly horrified Rhun—all about the ancient beasts, how they'd been forced to sleep, how one had fused its essence with the MacKenna magic and reincarnated in Maeve, how the beasts were now waking up...and how there were, on top of that, a bunch of fallen, misanthropic gods who were also regaining their power, while the protectors of humankind—the Powers That Be— were gradually losing theirs.

And she delivered the cherry on top of the heap of bizarre and overwhelming news when she finished with, "And Arawn is one of the fallen."

Merle just stared at her. Rhun looked like he might have been shocked out of his body. A minute ticked by. Maeve fidgeted, curling the seam of her cardigan.

"I can't have alcohol anymore, can I?" Merle finally asked weakly.

Maeve shook her head.

"Damn. I really need a drink right now."

Maeve glanced at Rhun. "Still processing?"

He shuddered. "Yes."

Maeve pressed her lips together and nodded.

"If Arawn is one of those who opposed keeping humans safe," Merle said after another moment, "what is his attitude regarding humans now?"

"While he doesn't much care about them," Maeve said quietly, "he promised to keep them from being eaten or overrun within his territory and beyond, as much as he's able."

Merle studied her with the kind of discernment Maeve had always admired in her. "For you."

Maeve swallowed. "For me."

Taking a deep breath, Merle rubbed her face with both hands.

"There's more," Maeve ventured.

Merle groaned behind her hands. "Oh, gods."

"Yeah. About that."

Peering at her from between her fingers, Merle raised a brow.

"Since the Powers That Be are getting weaker, witches will lose some of their power, too. Soon you won't be able to tap into the magic that is worked into the world anymore. That ability is tied to the Powers That Be, and with their authority fading…"

Merle closed her eyes, massaged her temples. "We're fucked."

Maeve cleared her throat yet again, shifted on the couch. "Well…not if you switch your allegiance to Arawn."

Merle let her hands fall into her lap, tilted her head forward and stared at Maeve. "I beg your pardon?"

"You could pledge your allegiance to him, and he could grant you access to the layers of the world and its magic. He's a god, and he's *gaining* power."

Merle huffed out a dry laugh. "This really takes the cake. I can't believe you're suggesting I—"

"He'd be able to postpone the payback until after your baby is born."

Growing utterly still, Merle stared at her. "I'll do it."

Her eyes slid to Rhun, and Maeve glanced at him as well.

Rhun's expression was a mask of vicious determination. "Yes," was all he said.

Arawn, Maeve said mentally, *if Merle were to pledge her allegiance to you—*

I would not ask her to do my bidding, came his response before she even finished her question. *She is your family.*

A smile bloomed in her heart. *Yours too, now.*

A considering silence. *And how does she feel about that?*

Let's...give it some time.

His chuckle echoed in her mind.

Focusing back on Merle, she said, "There are no strings attached. You'll be as free as you are now."

Merle regarded her silently for a long while. "He really loves you, doesn't he?"

Maeve just nodded with a smile, her eyes lowered to her hands in her lap.

"I can't promise I'll ever grow to like him," Merle said softly. "But I'll make an effort to...accept him. For you."

Maeve swallowed past the lump in her throat. "I appreciate it."

Rhun cleared his throat.

Maeve looked at him. "Done processing?"

He waved that away. "Sure, sure. I'm just...going through the implications of having a god in our family. I mean, that's even better than marrying into royalty, right?"

"Rhun." Merle rubbed her forehead with one hand.

"No, no. Think about it. All that power by proxy. The glory rubbing off on us."

"*Rhun.*"

"We're like…the divine family."

Merle sent him her patented glare. "You can*not* say that sort of BS in front of him."

Rhun looked offended. "Of course not. Just in front of all our friends." He shrugged, his smirk making his eyes flash. "And everybody else who needs to have the fear of that particular god put into them."

Maeve couldn't help it. She giggled. Merle glanced at her, surprise written in every line of her face, before she joined Maeve in her laughter, her expression so full of love and light in spite of everything looming on the horizon, and in that moment, Maeve knew.

Whatever challenges the future would throw at her, she'd be okay. Because she'd face it all with her family—*including* Arawn—by her side.

EPILOGUE

"**D**o you really think it'll work?" Maeve bit her lip, and Arawn resisted the urge to suck that lip and lick over it. *Later.*

"It is worth a try," he answered and nudged her forward with a hand on her lower back.

She dug in her heels right outside the door to her father's room at the nursing home. Merle's voice drifted out, her sister already inside telling Frank MacKenna the latest of what had happened in their lives.

Anxiety zinged along the twofold bond. Maeve's hand tightened around the cup of tea she'd brought for her father.

You have nothing to lose, Arawn said in her mind, *and everything to gain.*

Her throat muscles worked as she swallowed. *I just...don't know if I can do this.*

There is a good chance it will work.

She was silent, then— *That's exactly what I'm afraid of.* Barely more than a whisper in his thoughts.

After a moment of consideration, he replied, *No matter the personal outcome for you, do you not think he deserves this chance?*

Her breath hitched. *Of course. You're right.*

It was the mental nudge she apparently needed, for she opened the door, walked into the room, and crouched next to her father. Frank was sitting in an armchair in front of the panoramic window displaying the nursing home's backyard rose garden, his expression blank, his eyes unseeing. His ash-gray hair framed a face carved with years of wasted living, his skin pale.

Merle stopped speaking when Maeve entered, and for a second hurt flashed over her features, before she caught herself and sent Maeve a friendly smile, oblivious to her sister's plan.

"Here," Maeve said to her father, holding the cup to his lips. "Drink this. It's Earl Grey, your favorite."

Frank didn't move his hands, but he was responsive enough that Maeve could pour the tea into his mouth, making sure he swallowed. She set the cup on the small side table, her hands shaky.

Turning back to her father, she touched his cheek lightly. "I love you, Dad."

She got up just as he drew in a rattling breath. Maeve froze, glancing at Frank again, and what she must have seen on his face had her inching away, toward the door. While Merle rose from her seat and went to his side to check on him, Maeve quietly snuck out and plastered herself to the wall outside the room.

From his vantage point in the shadows of the hall, Arawn had a good view through the open doorway, watching as Frank's expression sharpened, his eyes cleared. Maeve's father raised his head, looked around.

"Dad?" Merle asked, leaning forward and grasping his hands.

Frank's eyes fell on his oldest living daughter, the one he hadn't *seen* in close to seventeen years. The one he never recognized, even in his rare moments of clarity, unaware of the hurt he caused her.

He frowned, opened his mouth. According to what Maeve had told Arawn, this was always the moment he would ask for her instead of Merle—breaking her heart without even meaning to.

"Merle?" It was but a rasp, Frank's voice rusty from years of neglect.

Merle uttered a sound close to a sob. "Dad? You can... You see me?"

Frank raised a shaky hand to Merle's face, stroked her cheek. "I see you, pumpkin."

At that moment, Maeve turned carefully to peek around the doorjamb, her pulse loud enough for Arawn to hear. He reached out with his energy, caressed her with a tendril of his power.

Shivering, she closed her eyes for a second. *Is this really happening?*

Courtesy of your phoenix magic.

She released a shuddering breath, grabbed the doorjamb tight with one hand.

"You look so much like your mom," Frank whispered, still touching Merle's face. "Among the three of you, you've always resembled her most. She called you her Mini Me. Mini Me Merle."

Merle hiccuped, smiling through her tears. "I remember." Hugging her father, she added in a thick voice, "I've missed you, Dad. So much."

"Me, too, pumpkin." He squeezed her back, his arms shaking from the effort.

After a long moment of tearful embrace, Merle withdrew, her face creased with worry. "Do you know...that Mom and Moira..."

"I know." A pained rasp. "I remember."

A beat of silence.

"Where is she?" Frank asked.

Merle looked toward the open door, met Arawn's eyes for a second before glancing to the side—to Maeve's face still peeking around the doorjamb. Maeve startled and jerked back to plaster herself against the wall again, her chest heaving.

Arawn leaned close to her, his mouth at her ear. "He is coming."

Maeve let out a choked squeak and made as if to skip away, but Arawn caught her with a tug on their bond. Laying his hands on her shoulders, he turned her around to face him.

"You are meeting him. Now. It is time."

He squeezed her shoulders once, kissed her hard with a hint of teeth, and retreated to a position farther down the hall, leaving her to face her father.

⚬❦⚬

ARAWN'S PRESENCE WAS A DARK REASSURANCE AT HER BACK, even though he stood far enough away to give her some privacy with her dad. Who, at this moment, stepped out of the room, grabbing the doorjamb for purchase, his legs a little shaky. His eyes landed on her—and widened.

Maeve flinched. Of course...her scar. Her dad probably reacted not only to the fact it was glowing, but to the scar itself. In all the months since her rescue, she only made it out here to the nursing home once, and her dad didn't have a moment of clarity that day. This was the first time he saw it.

"Merle told me..." He swallowed hard, took a deep breath. "I know he's dead, but I sure wish he wasn't. So I could have him tied up tight in a room, alone with me and a knife."

She barely kept herself from crumpling. "Rhun made him suffer," was all she could choke out.

330

"Not enough." He shook his head. "It would never be enough."

Tears spilled over as she pressed her lips together. Arawn's power wrapped around her, a loving stroke of darkness.

"I'm so sorry, Dad." A broken whisper, her heart splitting open.

His brows drew together. "What for? It wasn't your fault. That rotten bastard—"

"Not that." She fought for air. "What I did... Mom—Moira. Y-you. I'm so, so sorry."

Unable to face him any longer, she turned away, shoulders hunched and chest too tight to breathe. A thousand things to say to him, and not enough air to speak. *I wish I could make it okay. I wish I could bring them back. I love you. I understand if you'd rather not see me again.*

And she wouldn't even blame him. When every time he looked at her face, he'd be reminded of how she took everything from him. Even if he loved her still, how could he stand having her around? After what she did?

Arawn waited in the shadows like the dark specter he was, arms crossed over his massive chest, his forest-green eyes glinting.

You must think me pathetic, she whispered in his mind.

I might just spank you for that thought, was his silken reply.

Heat shot up to her face—not least because she found that suggestion inappropriately appealing.

"Maeve."

Her father's rough voice made her straighten her spine.

"Look at me."

Hauling in air with a shudder, she turned, met his eyes... which shimmered with unshed tears.

"I've spent the last seventeen years locked in the past, mourning those I have lost." He stepped closer, steadying himself on the wall with one hand. "I want to spend what time I have left with those who are still here."

"Dad, I'm sorr—"

"And I don't ever want to hear my daughter apologize again for something that was beyond her control. Stop it. No one blames you but yourself."

A sob broke from her throat.

"Now," her dad said gruffly, "are you going to make me stagger across the hall, or will you come here to give me a hug, sweetheart?"

Succumbing to the sobs racking her chest, she dashed over to him, flung herself in his arms. He held her close, rocked her, petted her hair, and murmured soothing words, each one a balm to her bleeding soul. When Merle joined them, they pulled her in as well, until they were huddled together in one big knot of sobbing joy.

The last three living MacKennas, reunited in spite of loss and pain.

Merle's reddened eyes found Maeve's when they pulled apart eventually. "How?" she whispered. "I know it was you. How did you bring him back?"

Maeve wiped the tears off her cheeks and turned her fingers so Merle and her dad could see. "My tears. They heal. It's one of my phoenix powers."

Merle's brows rose as she understood. "The tea."

Maeve nodded. "I didn't know if it would work."

Arawn had suggested she try, having connected the dots of her true nature and potential powers with the miraculous healing of the bobcat. When she thought back to it, she remembered some of her tears dropping on the cat, on its open wounds. And seconds later it was healed.

It wasn't her blood that did it.

"You're a what?" asked her dad, his forehead creasing.

Apparently Merle hadn't gotten to that part yet when she

talked to him earlier. "I'll tell you all about it. But let's get you out of here first."

Because, with his mind healed, Frank MacKenna would never have to spend another day at the nursing home.

They dove into the process of checking him out and tackling the amount of paperwork that went along with it, but by late afternoon, he had the okay to leave with them, and they went straight to the old Victorian.

Where, after a long evening spent talking, reminiscing, catching up, their dad retired to the room he once shared with their mother—still furnished and kept clean through all these years—while Rhun, who'd joined them at some point to meet his father-in-law properly for the first time, carried Merle to bed muttering something about being "hungry."

Maeve strolled out to the backyard, lacing fingers with the man who held her heart, who stood waiting for her in front of the charred stump of the old cherry tree.

The one she burned to the ground when her phoenix exploded seventeen years ago.

It still hurt, would probably always pain her to look at this symbol of their loss, but...the wound was healing. Slowly, gradually, like the progress she was making in reclaiming her life, her body, her mind. She still had spells of panic and slithering, paralyzing fear, moments when she was with Arawn and they'd have to stop so she could root herself in the present, fight back the lingering shadows of her nightmares.

But they were getting rarer.

Talking to Tashia helped. Having Arawn supporting her with *endless* patience helped. And in response to every inch of reclaimed dominion over herself, her phoenix preened and rustled her feathers, stroking along her senses and underneath her skin.

She squeezed Arawn's hand. "I'd like to introduce you to my father tomorrow."

They hadn't taken that step yet, having decided to not overwhelm her dad with too many revelations all at once.

Arawn peered down at her. "Think he can handle it?"

"Well..." She shrugged sheepishly. "I figure once he's gotten used to the idea of Rhun as Merle's mate and husband, we can try to give him a heart attack with you."

One side of his mouth lifted in a sensual half grin. "I want to show you something."

"Oh?"

He curved one arm around her waist, pressed her close. "Hold on."

Whipping wind and lightning whirled her into shadows and mist, and the next second she was standing on the lava-crusted slopes of a mountain. Her hands still gripping Arawn's shirt hard, his arm a reassuring heat around her waist, she glanced around, the cold night breeze barely affecting her, courtesy of Arawn's warmth.

"Mount Hood," she whispered as she recognized her surroundings. She stared at Arawn. "How?"

"It seems," he said, sliding his energy around and over her like a blanket of tingling heat, "that I gained some of Velez's powers when I destroyed him."

"And now you can teleport." She exhaled on an incredulous laugh. "If I weren't so breathlessly in love with you, I'd find that scary as hell."

He made a disbelieving sound. "You were never scared of me."

"No." She gave him a lopsided smile.

"And I might take offense at that"—he cupped her face, stroked over her lips with his thumb—"if I did not consider it such a precious gift."

She rose on tiptoes, tugged him down to her and kissed him, long and slow and soul-crushingly thoroughly.

When they broke apart, he murmured, "Where would you

like to go? I can take you anywhere in the world in the blink of an eye."

Her heart flipped at the look on his face, and her chest ached with love so deep it almost hurt. "Take me home."

He paused just long enough that she had to make sure he knew what she meant by sending him the image—and he smiled and flashed her into the heart of his dominion, into the room where he'd given her *his* heart.

Home, she whispered in his mind as he laid her out on their bed.

Books in the *Love and Magic* series by Nadine Mutas:

Novels:

To Seduce a Witch's Heart (Love and Magic, #1)

To Win a Demon's Love (Love and Magic, #2)

To Stir a Fae's Passion (Love and Magic, #3)

To Enthrall the Demon Lord (Love and Magic, #4)

To Tempt a Witch to Sin (Love and Magic, #5), coming in 2018

Novellas:

To Caress a Demon's Soul (Love and Magic, #1.5) **Sign up for my newsletter to receive this novella as a free read!**

ABOUT THE AUTHOR

Polyglot Nadine Mutas has always loved tangling with words, whether in her native tongue German or in any of the other languages she's acquired over the years. The more challenging, the better, she thought, and thus she studied the languages of South Asia and Japan. She worked at a translation agency for a short while, putting to use her knowledge of English, French, Spanish, Japanese, and Hindi.

Before long, though, her lifelong passion for books and words eventually drove her to give voice to those story ideas floating around in her brain (which have kept her up at night and absent-minded at inopportune times). She now writes paranormal romances with wickedly sensual heroes and the fiery heroines who tame them. Her debut novel, *To Seduce a Witch's Heart* (first published as *Blood, Pain, and Pleasure*), won the Golden Quill Award 2016 for Paranormal Romance, the Published Maggie Award 2016 for Fantasy / Paranormal Romance, and was a finalist in the PRISM contest for Dark Paranormal and Best First Book, as well as nominated for the Passionate Plume award 2016 for Paranormal Romance Novels & Novellas. It also won several awards for excellence in unpublished romance.

She currently resides in California with her college sweetheart, beloved little demon spawn, and two black cats hellbent on cuddling her to death (Clarification: Both her husband and kid prefer her alive. The cats, she's not so sure about.)

Nadine Mutas is a proud member of the Romance Writers of America (RWA) and the Silicon Valley Romance Writers of America (SVRWA), the Rose City Romance Writers (RCRW), as well as the Fantasy, Futuristic & Paranormal chapter of the RWA (FF&PRW).

Connect with Nadine:

www.nadinemutas.com
nadine@nadinemutas.com

Printed in Great Britain
by Amazon